Oddfellows

Born and raised in Glasgow, J
product of his home town
degree in English from Glasgow univ......
several trial runs at a variety of careers including fashion
designer, model, roadie and bouncer. His short fiction has
been published widely in the USA, mainly through Circlet
Press (Boston) and Masquerade Books (New York). His
second novel – *Freeform* – will be published by GMP in
November 1997.

Oddfellows

Jack Dickson

Millivres Books
Brighton

First published in 1997 by Millivres Books (Publishers)
33 Bristol Gardens, Brighton BN2 5JR, East Sussex, England

A CIP catalogue record for this book is available from the British Library

ISBN 1 873741 29 4

Typeset by Hailsham Typesetting Services, 2 Marine Road, Eastbourne,
East Sussex BN22 7AU

Printed and bound by Biddles Ltd., Walnut Tree House, Woodbridge
Park, Guildford, Surrey GU1 1DA

Distributed in the United Kingdom and Western Europe by Turnaround
Distribution Co-Op Ltd., Unit 3, Olympia Trading Estate, Coburg Road,
Wood Green, London N22 6TZ

Distributed in the United States of America by LPC Group, 1436 West
Randolph Street, Chicago, Illinois 60607, USA

Distributed in Australia by Stilone Pty Ltd, PO Box 155, Broadway, NSW
2007, Australia.

for

David and Brian

CHAPTER ONE

"6543897, Macdonald, sir. Nine months. Week five of sentence, sir." Joe stared straight ahead, rigid. Hands stiff at sides, thumbs aligned with seams. Eyes on the wall.

Hot breath on his face, then a voice. Soft, cold: "You need a shave, soldier. See to it."

"Sir."

Silence. Then the sound of creaking leather. "There's mud on those boots, soldier. Get them cleaned."

"Sir."

More silence, then tutting. "Messy, soldier . . . very messy."

Sweat beaded on Joe's forehead.

Then: "A six year man: is that right, soldier?"

"Sir."

More tutting. "You should know better than this."

"Yes, sir. Sorry, sir."

Fingers plucked at wool fibres. "Oil, soldier. Take it off."

"Sir." Joe struggled out of the khaki sweater. Eyes brushed a blond outline.

"Eyes front, soldier!" Voice from behind now.

Face impassive, Joe refocused on the wall. A trickle of perspiration dribbled from under one arm.

"This hair's too long . . . get it cut."

A hand on the back of his neck.

Joe groaned.

The hand removed. "Shut up, soldier."

"Sir."

"Not good enough, Macdonald . . . just not good enough."

"Sir."

"Discipline, soldier . . . self-discipline: that's what The Glasshouse is all about. You struck an officer, Macdonald – am I correct?"

"Sir."

"You struck an officer . . . " Voice moving round, circling. " . . . Answer me, Macdonald!"

"I struck an officer, sir."

1

"That's better."

A hard finger poked his chest. Joe shivered.

"You also disobeyed a direct order – correct?"

"Sir." Joe frowned.

Sigh. "You need keeping in line, Macdonald . . . "

"Sir."

The finger poked again. "Well, that's what I'm here for, Macdonald. To keep you in line."

"Sir."

The fingers moved away, then resettled on his belt. More tutting. "What's this, soldier?" A thumb and forefinger rubbed heavy webbing.

A shudder racked Joe's body.

"We can't have any of this, soldier. You know that . . . "

Joe clenched his fists.

"Get those thumbs aligned!"

"Sir." Joe closed his eyes.

Fingers toyed with belt buckle. Sneer. "You're a cocky little bastard, Macdonald. What are you?"

"A cocky little bastard, sir." Voice low, breathy.

"I didn't quite hear that, soldier . . . "

"A cocky little bastard, sir!" His voice filled the room.

Pleased. "Better . . . not great, but better."

"Sir." His prick was about to explode.

The toying stopped. Voice in his ear: "I'm going to break you, Macdonald . . . if it's the last thing I do, I'm going to break you."

"Sir." Joe closed his eyes.

"Good . . . I'm glad we understand each other . . . "

Joe opened his eyes.

Pulsating thumps shivered up his spine.

He levered himself from the wall, stubbed out a cigarette and walked to the side door.

The thumps followed, muffled but still there.

He unlocked the door, pulled, and stared out at the snake of silent figures. The queue stretched down Mitchel Street, curving round into Argyle Street. Joe watched.

The queue moved forward, then stopped.

Joe scanned.

The queue moved again. Then stopped.

Billy's words: 'Another bust and they'll revoke the licence. Over-eighteens only, no weapons . . . an' no dealers!'

Joe continued to scan. From this distance, in this light, they all looked the same. Identikit. An army of innocent young faces. He waited for the queue to move again.

It didn't.

Joe glanced at his watch – almost eleven.

He looked back at the queue.

Still no movement. Murmurs of discontent.

Joe looked over at the main entrance. A flabby form was stemming the flow. Joe scowled, closed and relocked the door. The thumps were back: same volume, different rhythm. He strode past the body-scanner and metal detectors towards the cashdesk. The girl behind the grill grinned.

Joe frowned. "Whit's the hold up, this time?"

She nodded towards the head of the queue.

Flanked by two bulky figures in Matrix tee-shirts, a small, stocky figure in a white DP jacket was shaking his head.

Joe walked over. Snatches of speech broke over distant thumps:

Calm, but only just: "Come oan, son . . . ."

Squeaky. Pointing: "Ye didney stoap them. Why . . . ?"

"You ken why. Nae . . . "

"Whit's the problem?" Joe came to a halt behind one of the bouncers.

Red sweaty face turning. Malkie. Resigned half-smile. "This wan's nae ID."

Joe stared at the orange DP logo. Another identikit figure. "Over eighteen?" He looked at the face.

Vociferous nod.

Joe smiled. "Aye, sure."

Insistent squeak: "Ah um, man."

Impatient voices from the queue behind, supporting the claim.

More insistent: "Ah've bin here afore, man." Pointing to door. "He kens me." Shouting: "Georgie? Tell this guy how

3

old ah um?"

Joe looked to the door.

Georgie Paxton's large form turned. Glassy eyes focused.

Joe raised an eyebrow.

Georgie nodded.

Joe looked at the boy, then nodded to the bouncer-flank.

It parted.

Joe smiled at Malkie. "An' try an' speed things up a bit okay? We waant them in afore closin' time . . . "

The boy scurried through the metal detector up to the cash-desk. Grateful over shoulder: "Thanks man."

The queue moved forward.

Joe turned and walked back towards the thumps.

Above the dance-floor, silver slivers of sweat slid down silver walls in strobelit stripes. Joe blinked and continued to patrol the perimeter. He watched the mass of twitching bodies, then peered at his watch – nearly one. Break soon. He walked on.

A swaying girl drifted across his path.

Joe swerved to avoid her.

She smiled, mouthing to the music.

He smiled back and continued to walk, scanning the dancing sea. Then stopped.

Down near the stage, an undancing huddle of figures.

Joe moved swiftly towards it.

In the middle of the huddle, a fluorescent orange logo balancing on one leg, hunched over.

Joe approached, paused, tapped a white, nylon-clad shoulder.

Three boys looked up, then scattered into the crowd. The fourth wobbled. One hand held a trainer. The other flailed for balance.

Joe seized an elbow, jerking the head up.

The mouth was open and moving. Nothing audible.

Joe propelled him towards an exit.

In the corridor, mouthing became shouting. "Whit's a' this, man?" Recognition. "Ah'm nineteen, oanest! Georgie'll tell ye . . . "

"Shut up!" Joe released the shoulder. "Geeze it!"

4

Feigned innocence. "Whit, man? Ah wisney . . . "

"Waant me tae find it masel'?"

Blasé eyes. "Okay, okay . . . " The trainer dropped. Hand to bare foot. Sound of Sellotape ripping.

Joe watched as the kid unpeeled a two-inch square plastic package from the instep of his right foot.

"Here." Sulky.

Joe took the package, looked at it, then the boy.

Shrug. "Jist a wee bitta sulph, man . . . fur ma ain yiss."

Joe slipped the packet into a pocket. He bent down, picked up the trainer and held it out.

The boy took it, mumbling.

Joe waited while it was replaced on a foot, then grabbed an arm and led the kid towards the fire-exit.

Protesting: "Ah wisney dealin', man – honest! Ask . . . "

"If ah see ye here again, ah'm haundin' ye ower tae the polis – okay?" Joe opened the fire-door and thrust the kid out into the night. He closed the door and walked back towards the foyer.

Leaning against the counter, Joe watched the cloakroom girl apply another layer of red lipstick. Gina . . . thirty-five, going on seventeen.

"Ach, they're guid kids, really." Mouth contorted to outline corners.

Joe smiled. "Ah've jist flushed aboot two hunnerd quid's wortha speed doon the toilet!"

She replaced lipstick in pocket. Shrug. "Ye canny search them aw'."

Joe scowled. Body-searches: Georgie's job. He'd been on the door.

"So . . . how's life, Joe?" Cigarettes produced, one taken then packet extended.

Joe took one, lit both. He exhaled. "Life's good, Gina." He grinned.

"The boss keepin' well?"

Joe laughed. "Billy's okay. How 'bout you?"

Grin. Elbow on counter. "Aye . . . no' bad."

Comfortable silence.

5

Joe drew on the cigarette. "Angie wis askin' efter ye."

Smile. "Yeah? Ah huvney seen hur fur a while . . . how's she daein'?"

Joe frowned. "Same as eye-ways. Three joabs, noo. Goat anither cleaning wan last week – the soap factory, up Queenslie? Ah waant tae help oot mair, but she'll no' let me."

Gina rubbed at scarlet cigarette-filter. "Canny be easy, her oan her own. Sean still giein' her a hard time?"

Joe sighed. "It's a nose ring, noo."

Behind, thumping bass increased as a door opened, then closed. Laughing. Two voices. One male, one female. Singing. One out of tune. A damp hand thrust past him, holding two pink tickets. Gina took them.

Joe turned.

Girl with long hair, centre-parted. Twitching to the thumps. At her side, a boy, sweat-soaked tee-shirt, still singing.

Joe grinned: "Cuttin' oot early the night?"

Gina passed two jackets – one leather, one white canvas – across the counter.

The girl grabbed them, laughed. "Better things tae dae, eh Stevie?"

The boy's arm circled her thin waist. "Aye man, that's right . . . " Giggles. Then a chorus: "Seeya, Gina . . . Joe." Waves. The main door was opened for them. More waves.

Behind, a chuckle. Then Gina: "Changed days, eh Joe? Nae fights, nae drunks . . . Christ! Maist o' them don't even smoke." The rasp of phosphorous on sandpaper. Then: "Best thing that ever happened tae this place, raves . . . " Exhale.

Joe stared into the foyer. "Ah'm no' so sure."

Quizzical. "Whit, E?"

"That, an aw' the rest." A door opened and closed. The sound of happy, female voices. Joe's eyes followed the group.

Low laugh. "At best, they huv a guid time, an' the eccy makes them too happy tae cause ony hairm . . . "

Joe turned. "An' at worst?"

Gina sobered. "At worst, they ainly hurt themsels . . . "

"An' risk oor licence." Joe scowled.

Shrug. "Well, personally ah'd raither deal wi' a hundred kids oan eccy than a hundred drunks onyday."

Joe laughed. "Ye're probably right." He lit another cigarette, looked at his watch, then Gina: she was applying more lipstick. "Ah'll get back in, then."

Red smearing twisted mouth. "Easy money fur ye – eh Joe? Efter the Bogside, a hall fulla dancin' kids must be a dawdle!"

He laughed, and walked towards a fire exit.

Corridors . . .

Patrolling the corridors.

Part of the job.

Joe patrolled.

Thumping bass echoed in his ears, sound bounced back from odd directions.

Tonight the basement was deserted.

Joe turned towards the back stairs.

Voices.

Joe paused, listened.

Two . . . no, three voices. One loud, angry, the others muffled.

Joe began to climb, listening. The loud voice: Georgie Paxton. The other two? Indistinct . . . laughing? Joe walked towards the sound.

Ahead, on a landing, he could see a bulky figure blotting out a corner. The other voices were louder now. As he approached, Joe could make out a smaller, red-haired figure to one side. Bare back, baggy jeans, shirt tailing from belt:

"C'moan, man – he didney mean it!" Two pale hands pulled at a well-muscled arm.

Behind Georgie's unflinching form, a baseball-cap bobbed. The heavy bouncer growled: "Ye cheeky wee bastard." Arm raised.

Joe caught the wrist, lowered it. "Whit's goin' on?"

Georgie turned, red-faced, scowling. "This wee . . . "

7

Lazy vowels: "Hey! Joe!" The greeting slid into another laugh.

"Sean?" Joe pushed Georgie aside. In the corner, a tall boy lounged against the wall. Grinning. Baseball-cap the wrong way round. Wiping face on hem of soaking tee-shirt. Tapping one trainered foot to distant, echoing thumps. Gold nose-stud. Mouth moving, like chewing. Lazy smile:

"Tell this gorilla tae chill-oot, Joe – eh?"

Georgie moved forward, quick for his size. Mitt of a hand whipped across pink, glowing face. "Shut it, cunt!"

A yelp.

Joe seized a well-padded shoulder. "Let me haundle this, okay?" He stared past the heavy form at the grinning figure.

Georgie didn't move.

Joe turned. "Okay?"

Red face. Shrug. "Makes nae diff'rence tae me."

Joe watched massive thighs climb metal stairs, then turned back to the corner. To the red-head: "You: oot!"

Hands up, palms facing. "Ah wis jist goin'." To Sean. "Catch ye upstairs, man."

Chewing again. "Sure."

Joe watched a soaking shirt trail the stairs, listened for a door closing then turned back. He looked at the pale face, flushed where Georgie's slap had impacted. "Whit you oan?"

Eyes wide. "Me? Nothin', Joe." The chewing again.

Joe grabbed skinny shoulders.

Sean laughed. "It's the natural high, man." He began to sing.

Joe shook boney shoulders. "Wis it E? C'moan Sean, tell me!"

"There's a rainbow inside yer mind. There's a rainbow inside . . . "

E. Joe shook the form again.

The singing continued.

Joe sighed. "Wait here!" He lowered the boy into a sitting position, turned and jogged up the stairs.

8

In the foyer, Georgie was slouching at the cigarette machine.

Joe walked up to him. "Whit wis that aw' aboot?"

Heavy breathing. Head down. "Trouble-makers . . . " Pant, pant. " . . . Ah wis askin' them tae leave." Turning away.

"Whit wis the slap fur?" Joe pulled him back.

Head rising. Eyes narrowed. Large shoulders tried to shake off restraining hands.

Joe moved closer. "Ye ken the rules, Georgie. Ye don't hit them . . . " Singing at his side:

"There's a rainbow inside yer mind. There's a . . . "

Joe recognised the voice. "Ah telt you tae stay put, Sean." He stared at Georgie. "There wis nae need fur . . . " An arm pushed him aside. Joe seized it. "Ah'm no' finished, Georgie . . . "

"Ah don't answer tae you! Git yer hauns aff me, ye . . . " Words dangling.

Joe twisted the arm. "Ye . . . what, Georgie?"

"There's a rainbow inside yer mind. There's a rainbow inside . . . "

Joe turned. "Gonny shut it, Sean?"

Georgie's arm pulled free.

A dull ache spread over Joe's cheek. Then stinging.

Then laughing.

Other voices now. Gina, Davie the manager. Malkie. Sean . . .

Joe looked at Georgie, who was shaking fingers.

Hard, scowling face. "Ye fuckin' . . . "

Red billowed in his brain. Joe raised forearm and pinned a fat flabby throat against the wall. He pressed forward. Cartilage dug into flesh.

The voices closed in on him. Gina, in his ear: "He's no' worth it, Joe. Come on, calm doon . . . " Arms seized him. Not Gina's. Pulling.

Georgie gurgling.

Sean singing.

Joe shook his head. Turning, he met three sets of warning eyes. Two sets of broad arms held him. Something wet trickled down his cheek. He lowered his forearm.

Georgie coughed, spat. "Away back tae yer bum-boy, Macdonald!" Hoarse. Clearing throat.

Joe strained forward. Arms held him fast. He clenched his fists. "Ah'll git ye, Paxton . . . "

The laughing again. Joe watched as the bulky form grabbed a jacket and staggered to the door. Voices in his ear:

- Take it easy, Joe . . .
- Let's get you into the office . . .
- There's a rainbow inside yer mind . . .

He stopped straining, blinked and looked around.

A crowd of anxious faces, mostly kids. Then arms pushing him towards the door marked Manager.

– Come on, Joe. Have a drink, calm doon . . .

He shook himself free and walked. Behind, someone sang something about rainbows and minds . . .

Two whiskies later, Joe lit a cigarette. The office was empty. On the desk beside the Glenlivit, a cotton-wool pad and bottle of TCP. His cheek stung. Joe picked up the bloody pad and pressed it to the stinging. He inhaled, then looked at his watch: nearly two.

A knock at the door.

Joe glanced up.

The door opened a crack. Baseball-capped head appeared. Smiling face. "Kin ah come in?"

Joe stubbed out the cigarette and nodded.

The door opened wider.

Joe scowled. "Didn't think rave wis your kinda thing."

Sean jiggled. "There's a rainbow inside yer mind . . . " Head moving to the words.

Joe groaned.

Sean strolled into the room and perched on Davie's desk. Mouth chewing, long limbs twitching. The singing stopped. Wide eyes stared. Then: "You okay?" Peering at the cotton-wool.

Joe smiled. "Ah'll live." He removed the pad from his cheek, tossing it into a bin.

10

Sean stared, silent. "He's cut ye, man . . . that big, flashy ring he wears."

Joe looked at the floor. Hitting the punters: not part of the job. He looked up at Sean.

More chewing. No sign of the slap. No saliva. Dehydration.

Joe frowned. "How many tabs ye take: wan . . . two?"

Sean wiped his face with a hand, feet drumming against the desk.

Joe waited for an answer, staring into the pink, sweating face which kept moving.

A voice behind. Joe raised his eyes.

In the doorway, the red-haired boy, still bare-chested, now wearing leather bikers' jacket. A thin, black nylon jerkin extended. To Sean: "Ready?" Eyes past Sean, to Joe: "Hey! Totally brand new, man!" Admiring.

Sean grinned. "Yeah, total!" Fist punching the air in time to words. He leapt off the desk. "Ewan!" Surprised. Palm into air. Met by corresponding palm. "Aw'-right, man!"

Sean spun round and draped an arm around Joe's shoulder. To the red-haired boy: "Ewan? This is Joe . . . ma uncle Joe." Slurring.

Disbelieving: "The wan that wis in the airmy? Naw!"

Sean draped another arm around a leathered shoulder: "Joe? This is Ewan . . . ma best mate!" Mouth moving sloppily.

Joe extracted himself from the sweaty arm. "Hi, Ewan." He stared at Sean.

Two voices: "There's a rainbow inside yer mind. There's a rainbow . . . " Singing again. Turning towards the door.

Joe frowned.

Capped-head over shoulder. "Catch ye later, Joe . . . "

Joe stood up. Angie had enough problems. "Sean? Haud oan." He walked to the door.

Sean turned, smiled.

Joe sighed. Angie had enough problems. "Comin' back tae the flat?"

The singing stopped. Grin. "Ewan tae?"

Joe laughed. "Ah suppose so . . . "

"Total!"

Joe picked up his jacket. "Come on, then . . . the fresh

11

air'll dae ye guid." He closed the office door, locked it and followed two dancing figures out of The Matrix.

CHAPTER TWO

Joe inhaled.

Frosty December air rushed into his lungs.

He exhaled and walked on. In front, Sean and the red-haired kid had stopped. Joe quickened his pace to catch up.

A shoe-shop, displaying every type of footwear imaginable. Joe stared.

Sean was pointing, nylon jerkin tied round skinny waist. A bare arm flailed, white, shining. "They wans . . . see? The wans that go a' the way up tae yer knees . . . fourteen holes . . . "

"Whit, the Cats?"

Baseball-cap shaking. "Naw, the Docs . . . " Scathing. " . . . Cats ur fur posers! Ah waant the wans like Joe's."

Joe grinned.

Insulted. "Ah've goat Cats . . . "

Laughing. "An' you're a poser, Ewan, so that's a' right . . ."

Deeper laughing. Grabbing the nylon jerkin. "Check the Daniel Poole copy . . . "

"S'no' a copy . . . " Shouting.

"Aye it is! Ye kin tell by the stitching. Real wans huv a line o' double stitchin' aroon' the DP. That wan o' yours disney . . . "

Joe moved away. Behind, the argument continued. He scowled. "C'moan, you two. Ah'm freezin'!"

Two sets of footsteps jogging behind.

Joe walked. Argyle Street was deserted – the council's midnight curfew saw to that: no admittance to any club after twelve. He looked at his watch: another half an hour or so until two dozen discos tipped their contents out into the night. At three am on a Sunday morning Glasgow city centre was busier than a Saturday afternoon. He thrust hands into pockets.

Fifteen minute walk home . . .

Behind, the footsteps had stopped.

. . . Usually. Joe turned.

Another shop window.

He pulled jacket collar up. "Move it, wull ye?" He walked on.

The footsteps fell in behind.

Joe smiled. At least the singing had stopped.

Fragments of conversation drifted past him as he turned up Glassford Street:

"He really yer uncle?"

"Sure . . . ma dad's wee brother."

"An' he lives . . . ?"

"Ye should see it, man . . . ye wull see it, it's jist roon' here . . . totally brand new . . . "

Sniff. "Where'd he git the money?"

"Aw', it's no' Joe's place. He shares it wi' . . . "

"Christ, man! Check this!"

Joe yawned, turned.

Another shop window. Two noses pressed against grilled glass.

Sean. Proud: "Boabby Gillespie shoaps in there, when he's in Glesga. Ah seen him!"

"Naw!"

"Aye!"

"When?"

Shrug. "Coupla weeks ago. When ah wis comin' hame fae Joe's."

"Total!"

Joe walked back to where the two boys stood. He followed their gaze through meshed, reinforced steel. Two sets of eyes transfixed by a pink, Versace jacket. "Dream oan, boys! Noo, move it." Joe caught wistful blue eyes in the misty glass and frowned. "It's late."

Sean grinned. "Sure, Joe." To the red-head. "C'moan, you . . . " Pulling a leathered arm.

Freckled face tilted upwards: "He really buy his stuff fae there?"

Joe studied the freckled face. "Who?"

"Boabby Gillespie."

Joe looked at Sean, who looked at the red-head, then back at Joe.

Laughing. "He kens nothin' – eh?" Mock-patient.

14

"Boabby Gillespie sings wi' Primal Scream. 'Member ah played ye the live tape fae . . . "

"Skip the lecture, eh man?" Ewan batted the baseball-cap's skip. "Ye're makin' it aw' up, onyway!"

Daniel Poole jacket removed from waist and used as towel. Sean flicked a red head. "Naw ah'm no' – he really dis . . . noo c'moan!" Padded trainers catching on paved tile. He tripped, laughed louder, clutching at Ewan. Both boys staggered, then righted themselves.

Joe fumbled in pocket for keys. He strode ahead to the wrought-iron gate, inserted a Yale, then looked up.

Three floors above, a single green light burned in the darkness.

Behind, whispering. Then: "Yer uncle lives . . . here?"

Nonchalant. "Sure . . . " Voice lowered. "It's totally brand new inside, so don't you touch onythin'!"

Huffy. "As if ah wid!"

Sound of hand hitting leather. "As if ye widney!"

Joe turned the key and opened the security gate. "Keep yer voices doon."

Sean at his side. "Sure, Joe." Whispering. To Ewan: "Yeah . . . nae problem . . . " To Joe: "Ma mooth's a' dry. Ye goat ony o' that . . . ?"

"Ah suppose so . . . " Joe smiled. " . . . If ye didney finish it last time." He held the gate open.

Sean and Ewan trotted in, then waited.

Joe closed the gate, and moved past them across the courtyard to open the controlled-entry door. Muffled exclamations from Ewan followed him up three flights of carpeted stairs. At the top landing, Joe checked the alarm – off – then inserted three keys into three locks, turning twice each time.

Whisperings behind, then another laugh, then: "Shhh . . . "

Joe pushed open the door and walked into the flat.

A hallway. Four doors leading off. At the end of the corridor, the kitchen. Joe turned, closing the front door.

Sean and Ewan shuffled forward.

Joe pointed. "Through there . . . until ah see Billy."

Two figures, one tall, one shorter, padded forward.

15

Ahead, the lounge door opened. Light leaked out. Soft voice from doorway: "You're early . . . " Tailing off.

"Hi, Mr King!" Sean nudged his companion. "This is Ewan."

Mumbled response from the red-head.

Joe pushed one bare and one leathered shoulder in the direction of the kitchen. "Ah'll huv a coffee, Sean . . . " He turned towards the soft voice. "Did we disturb ye?"

Ahead, various oohs and ahhs were curtailed by the closing of a door.

Billy moved back into the lounge without answering.

Joe followed, shrugging off his jacket.

On the far side of the room a PC screen glowed. Billy pulled out a chair and resumed. Tapping.

Joe walked over and stood behind him. Billy's blond hair was tinged with reflected green. Joe peered over a slim shoulder. The on-screen numbers meant nothing to him. He straightened up. "They'll no' be here long, Billy. Ah jist waanted a word wi' Sean afore he went hame."

Billy removed a diskette from the PC, inserted another, and tapped the key-board.

Joe looked around the green-lit room. "Thought ye'd still be oot . . . "

"Not gone yet . . . " Eyes on the screen. " . . . As you can see."

Joe flinched. "Ah'm sorry we . . . "

Soft laugh. "I've told you before, Joe – I don't mind him hanging around. He's family, you worry about him. I can understand that."

Joe rubbed the back of Billy's chair with index finger. "Kin ah git ye onythin'?"

Head shake. Then: "Where did you find him and his pal, anyway?" More tapping.

Joe sighed. "It's a lang story, Billy." He fingered his cheek. The cut was still wet.

One tap. Then silence. Billy removed the diskette and pressed a button. The room darkened as the screen died. He leant back in the chair. "Well? I'm listening . . . "

Joe could feel Billy's low, even breathing in the silence.

16

Then the thumping of his own heart.

Abruptly, a triangle of light illuminated the room as the door swung open.

Joe turned.

Two silhouettes.

Joe peered.

Ewan holding two bottles of Caledonian Clear, drinking from one. Sean clutched a mug, extending it to Joe. "It's affy dark in here . . . "

Joe stepped forward and took the mug.

Behind, Billy stood up and flicked a switch. A row of shell lights leapt into life on the far wall.

Joe blinked.

Sean strolled over to the beige leather sofa and threw himself onto it.

More restrained, Ewan walked slowly, gazing around himself. "Awesome!"

Billy looked at Joe. Eyes met.

Joe smiled, looked away.

"What happened to your face?"

"An accident . . . " Joe shrugged. He watched Sean grab a handful of CDs from the rack and begin to flick. Ewan continued to gaze.

Billy at his side. "Let me see."

A hand beneath his chin, tilting face upwards.

Joe tried to move away.

Fingers held tight.

He could smell Billy now. Joe closed his eyes and inhaled: Oddfellows. He knew the cologne's name but the odour always reminded him of the chalky, scented sweets.

"Trouble at the club?"

Joe could feel Billy's fingers on his cheek now, gently probing. Suddenly he was hard. "It's nothin'. Somewan goat a wee bit carried away." The fingers removed.

Ewan's voice. Low, growling. "That Georgie's a mad bastard."

Sean. "Shut up!"

Joe blinked.

Billy was staring at the beige sofa. "What's Paxton got to

17

do with this?"

Joe sighed. The licensing board. He looked at Sean: under-age and on E. In the wrong.

Georgie Paxton had only been doing his job, throwing out drug-users.

Joe was in the wrong. He'd over-reacted, lost it. "It's nothin', Billy. There wis a misunderstanding. Ah goat in the way o' Georgie's signet ring . . . "

A hand on his shoulder, fingers kneading. "Come on, let's get it washed." To Sean: "If you're gonna play CDs, keep the volume down – okay?"

A chorus: "Sure, Mr King!"

Joe walked ahead of Billy from the lounge into the bathroom.

In the mirror, Joe watched as Billy carefully poured antiseptic onto a pad and began to dab. The muted twang of Oasis drifted through from the other room.

"You lose your temper?" Dab, dab.

Joe nodded. Billy's hand slipped.

"Keep still!" Stern, then softening. "Did you start it?" Dab, dab.

Sean's frightened face. Paxton's huge hand across a pale cheek. Joe sighed. "Aye . . . Georgie wis . . . " Too complicated to explain. " . . . ah suppose ah coulda haundled it better." He watched the reflection of Billy's fingers dab one last time.

"Paxton okay, though?" Antiseptic replaced in First-Aid box.

Joe smiled. "Ah think so."

Soft hands clasped face, lowering head.

Joe draped arms around Billy's shoulders, pulling the man to him. A mouth sought his, found it. He could taste grapefruit juice. Joe pressed Billy's face harder against his, tongue probing. He hoped Billy couldn't taste the whisky.

Sometime later, they pulled apart.

Billy sat on the side of the bath and looked at Joe. "The Matrix is becoming more trouble than it's worth." Eyes scanning face. "You never did tell me where Beavis and Butthead fit into all this."

18

Joe frowned. He couldn't lie to Billy. "They were there."

"Where?"

"The Matrix . . . "

"What?"

"Ah don't ken how they goat in: Malkie an' the boays ken better. Ah caught Georgie giein' Sean a hard time. Ah wis tryin' tae fun' oot whit it wis aw' aboot when . . . " Joe stared at the tiled floor. " . . . must've rubbed Georgie up the wrang way."

Sigh. Then gently admonishing: "Joe . . . Joe . . . " A hand on his shoulder, then: "Talk of the devil!"

Joe glanced up. In the doorway, tall boy holding baseball cap, twisting it between nervous fingers. Fair, curling hair falling over pink face. Nose-stud twinkling. Adam's Apple bobbing. A rush of words. To Joe: "Look, man . . . ah wisney listening in – oanest! Ah jist came tae tell ye Ewan hud tae go home . . . "

"Wait in the other room, Sean." Joe turned on the tap, splashed water over a hot face then lifted a towel.

Head shake. Garbling: "It wisney Joe's fault, Mr King. Georgie wis way oota line. Ah wis jist askin' fur ma money back . . . "

Billy stared at the nervous boy.

Sean chewed on a nail. Mumbling: "Ewan bought four tabs o' eccy aff Georgie an' . . . "

Joe seized a bony arm. "Ye didney tell me a' this!" The flesh was clammy beneath his fingers.

Huge eyes. Shouting: "It wisney eccy, though . . . didney dae nothin' fur me – asp'rin, mair like . . . " He looked at Joe. "Ah wis gonny tell ye, Joe – oanest! It jist . . . " Voice lowering. A shiver shook the skinny body. " . . . Slipped ma mind. Ah . . . " Pink face paling. " . . . Ah wisney feelin' well . . . " Already pale skin blanching. Hand to mouth. "Oh, Christ! Ah think . . . " Sean threw-up silently over Joe's arm.

Billy stared.

Joe sighed, reached over and pushed damp, vomit-streaked hair back from a deathly face.

A groan, then more retching.

Billy snorted, looked at Joe, then his watch. Faint smile.

"Get him cleaned up. I've got to go now . . . " Laugh. "On top of all this, I can't risk the night's takings lying around longer than necessary." He ruffled Joe's hair. Voice in his ear. "Make sure he's not here when I get back . . . " Fingers brushing face. " . . . okay?"

Sean had stopped vomiting, and was resting his face against Joe's shoulder. Joe grinned. "Sure, Billy. Seeya later." He stroked Sean's hair.

Seconds later a door slammed.

Sean moaned.

Joe grabbed limp arms and propped the boy against the sink. Turning on a tap, he soaked a sponge and began to wipe the lolling face.

An hour later, Sean was sleeping peacefully on the beige leather sofa. Joe lifted the mobile and punched in the number of a local taxi firm.

Angie would be home about five.

Sean needed to be home before that.

Having arranged a cab for ten minutes' time, Joe replaced the phone on the desk and walked over to the inert form. He shook it gently.

"Wha . . . ? Go 'way . . . " Snuffling. Hair in mouth.

Joe shook harder. "C'moan, Sean . . . time to go hame."

Eyelids fluttering, then open. Staring, unfocused, then closed again. A groan. "Ah feel ill, man. Let me stay here."

Joe seized an arm.

It snaked away from him.

Joe frowned. "C'moan."

Reluctant stirring. Sean peered out from beneath Joe's jacket, then sat up. "Whit happened?"

"Ye threw up, then passed oot!"

Horror. "Did ah make a mess o' yer bog?" Standing up, swaying.

Joe steadied him. "That disney matter." He stared into the wan face. "Listen tae me, Sean: nae mair eccy – okay?"

Long fingers through matted hair. "Don't worry, man. Christ! Ah'm wrecked!"

Joe laughed. "Ye're okay, noo', but stay away fae The

20

Matrix. Ye're too . . . "

Sniff. "Aw' ma pals go, Joe . . . there's nothin' else tae dae . . . "

"Ye kid stay in, watch TV."

Snort. "No' oan a Setturday night, Joe . . . "

The door-bell buzzed.

Sean jumped.

Joe smiled, hand into pocket. "Here . . . " He thrust a fiver at the boy. " . . . An' don't think aboot walkin' hame an' keepin' the money. Ah've telt the driver tae see an' take ye a' the way – okay?"

Head lowered. "Sure, Joe." Mumbling. "Thanks fur . . . thanks." He walked towards the door, then turned. "Seeya soon?"

"Aye . . . ah'll come up wan night next week."

Grin. "Total!"

Joe opened the door. "Guidnight, Sean."

Long, easy strides. "Seeya Joe – tell Mr King ah'm sorry aboot his bog!"

Joe laughed and closed the door.

By the time he heard Billy's key in the lock, Joe had cleaned the toilet, the kitchen, and tidied the CDs away. In the bedroom, everything was ready. Silk sheets, bed turned down. In combat trousers and boots, Joe stood to attention by the door, waiting. Hard.

An eternity later, Billy walked past him and stopped at the small safe near the bed.

Joe stared straight ahead. He heard a jacket removed and tossed onto a chair. Then more keys. Then a beep. He knew the ritual.

King Billy trusted no-one to take charge of the night's takings. Billy didn't trust night-safes either. During the week, takings were left on the premises, to be banked next morning with any money from the chain of betting-shops taken after 4.30pm. But at weekends, everything came back here. Safer, Billy said. It probably was. Any would-be thief had to get past two security doors and up three flights of stairs, then an alarm, and three double locks.

21

Then past Joe.

Rattling behind, then the sound of carefully-counted notes slipping between four-inch reinforced steel walls. Then the beep again.

No locks, no combination number. Only an electronic code punched into a remotely-controlled handset then aimed at the safe.

Only Billy knew the code.

Only Billy kept the handset.

King Billy didn't take any chances . . .

. . . as far as security was concerned.

Other sounds now. Sitting-on-bed sounds. Then a sigh. "Joe."

"Yes, Billy?"

"Over here."

Joe turned and walked towards the bed.

Billy was leaning against the metal headboard loosening his tie. Green myopic eyes glinted behind steel-rimmed glasses.

Joe stopped a few inches away, focusing on the far wall.

Again. "Joe."

"Yes, Billy?" He looked down.

Billy was taking off shoes now, rubbing feet. Socks thrown on the floor. He caught Joe's eye, smiled faintly, then stood up.

A hand brushed his groin. Joe shivered, grabbed the hand and held it there.

Billy laughed. "What's this: insubordination?"

"No, sir. Sorry, sir."

"Stand to attention, soldier!"

"Sir." Arms rigid at side, thumbs aligned with seams. Joe stared at the wall.

Billy began to circle.

Breath on his neck, a hand on his arse, stroking, teasing through olive canvas. Blood pounded in Joe's head.

Two hands now, gripping buttocks, thumbs probing arse-crack.

Prick throbbed.

Voice in his ear. "Soldier?"

Grinding against his arse. "Sir." His voice was hoarse.

"Get undressed."

"Sir." Joe bent down and began to undo laces. He removed the Docs and placed them beside the bed. Then webbing belt folded and lain on a chair. Turning, he caught sight of Billy's face. Joe's mouth twitched.

"Don't smile at me, soldier!"

"Sir." Joe unzipped combat trousers and stepped out of them. Sweat dribbled from an arm-pit.

A sigh, then: "On the bed, soldier!"

Prick straining to navel, Joe turned and stretched out on the red silk sheet. It was cold and slightly moist-feeling. Slidy.

"Spread those legs, soldier!"

Silk wriggled beneath his arse. Joe moaned.

"Now!"

Joe raised knees and stared at ceiling. Waiting.

Movement in front of him, the mattress dipping. Sounds of unzipping. Then two cool hands under burning thighs, lifting.

Spine dragged red silk into folds. Heels touched at the back of a cool neck. Joe gazed up at a parallel body. Billy's eyes were closed.

Soft fingers traced the line of his arse-crack.

Joe's balls contracted. Hands scrabbled for skin, finding the rough linen of a shirt-collar.

Closed-eyed smile. Then two hands on two hard mounds of muscle, stroking, spreading.

Joe stared at Billy's smooth face.

One hand removed. The sound of paper tearing. Then a smoothing sound.

Joe clenched fingers, still waiting.

Soft voice. "I'm going to break you, soldier – what am I going to do?" Myopic green eyes appeared from under eyelids.

Joe stared. "You're gonna break me, Billy . . . "

One soft finger stroked cold moisture into his anus.

Joe sighed, moving hips against thighs.

Returned thrusts.

The hairy squashiness of Billy's balls at the base of his spine. Then hands on waist, gripping hard, pulling. A linen-clad chest against thighs. Blood flooded to face. Joe closed his eyes.

Pause. Cold. Stretching. Then Billy's prick was in him.

Joe moaned and arched his back.

A wet mouth on his neck.

Joe unclenched fingers. Billy's shirt collar slipped away. Then red silk slithered beneath his spine.

One hand clasped his wrist, then the other, pressing his arms against the mattress.

Joe clenched buttocks, holding Billy in place as his heels slid down onto linen-clad shoulders. Knees bent, legs relocking either side of the slim waist. Red filled his vision, his brain.

Billy was thrusting harder now, breathing more quickly, panting.

Joe inhaled the exhaled breath: grapefruit. Linen dragged along the length of his prick and back again. A sea of red silk ebbed and flowed beneath. Pressure in his balls. Joe tried to think of something else . . .

– Georgie Paxton's ugly face.

– The Matrix

– There's a rainbow inside yer mind. There's a . . .

Billy exhaled sharply in his ear, mumbling. Metal-rimmed lenses dug into Joe's neck. Warmth filled his body, travelling up into his brain. A low moan echoed somewhere in the distance.

Then a scream.

Joes' body rippled with contractions as shining droplets of milky spunk spread from stomach onto a red silk sheet.

CHAPTER THREE

Soft buzzing in his brain.

Joe opened eyes, blinked.

Darkness.

The buzzing continued.

Joe closed eyes, reached one arm across to the bedside table and hit the digital alarm's reset button.

The buzzing continued.

Joe hit it again.

Movement above him, a noise, then pressure on his feet.

Joe opened his eyes. Less darkness. He blinked. At the bottom of the bed, Billy. Streaks of watery sunlight from the slatted blinds zebra-striped his outline. White shirt, blue tie, blond hair combed back and gelled. Joe watched as Billy moved the electric shaver over his chin one last time then switched it off.

Billy smiled. "Sleep well?"

Joe yawned and stretched. "Aye . . . whit time is it?"

"Almost three."

Joe sat up. "Christ! Ah . . . "

"What's the hurry?" A hand snaked under the red duvet.

Joe's prick twitched as cool fingers toyed.

Billy laughed.

The hand moving upwards, edging duvet aside.

"Stay in bed for a while – you've earned it!"

Joe watched as fingers played amidst his chest hair, rubbing one nipple. He seized narrow shoulders and pulled Billy to him, mouth on the smooth neck.

Soft laugh, then tutting.

Joe buried his face in gelled hair. A voice in his ear:

"Later. I want to talk to you."

Joe pulled away, coughed, and reached for a cigarette. The smell of petrol flared in his nostrils as Billy flicked the Zippo. Joe leant forward, inhaled, then propped himself up on the bedhead, waiting. His prick twitched again.

Billy stared, eyes narrowed, then spoke. "Tell me what

happened last night . . . the whole thing."

Joe rested cigarette in ashtray and began . . .

. . . lifting the cigarette Joe could smell burning filter. He stubbed it out.

Billy stood up and walked to the window. Low voice: "Underage kids and drugs . . . I don't see what more I can do. Installing the metal detectors seems to have solved the weapons problem, but as far as the drugs go . . . we can't do anything if they're taken outside the club." Sigh. "The age-thing we'll just have to live with." Laugh. "Reading through their birth-certificates would take all night, and it's far from fool-proof, anyway."

Joe lit another cigarette.

Fingers drumming on window-sill. "But I won't stand for dealing."

Joe inhaled.

Silence, then more drumming. "No-one pushes in my club." The drumming quickened. "You think any of the other bouncers are at it?"

Joe shook his head. "Malkie and the boays ur straight-up. They're no intae nothin' like that."

Sigh, almost drowned by staccato fingertips.

"What ye gonny dae 'boot Georgie?" Joe blew a smoke ring.

The drumming stopped. Billy turned. "Paxton?" Scowl. Slow head shake. "He's gone."

Joe smiled. Georgie didn't deserve the job anyway: even before the dealing, he'd been a bad bouncer.

Billy picked up a jacket and brief-case from a chair.

Joe watched as he opened it and checked the contents. "Another meetin' wi' the cooncellors?"

Silent nod.

Joe sighed. "Even God rested oan a Sunday, man!"

A smiled twitched the thin lips. "God's licence wasn't on the line . . . and he didn't have an obstreperous bastard like Frank Connolly to deal with!" Billy walked over to the bed and traced the cut on Joe's cheek. "Nasty. Bathe it again when you get up."

26

Then the smell of Oddfellows and a wet mouth on his, hot tongue forcing lips apart.

Billy pulled away. "Has the Datsun been valeted?"

Joe nodded. "Did it yesterday." He grinned. "Slummin', ur we?"

"Doesn't do to look too prosperous sometimes, Joe – you know that." He turned, fiddling with the brief-case catch. "Over-Twenty-Fives tonight, isn't it?"

Joe groaned. "Aye . . . early finish, at least."

"I'll see you 'bout three then – okay?"

"Sure, Billy . . . guid luck with yer business-meetin'. "

Billy walked towards the door. "Luck has nothing to do with business. I'll see you later." He left the room.

Minutes later the door slammed. Joe snuggled back down and pulled the duvet over his head. The bed stank of sweat, spunk and Oddfellows. Joe sniffed.

A warm smell.

A safe smell.

Their smell.

He smiled and rolled onto his stomach. Prick brushed warm silk.

Joe shivered and closed his eyes. Beneath, stiffening. He wriggled, taking the scent of Billy's fading cologne into lungs. Images danced on his eyelids . . .

Naked.

On his knees.

Billy in front of him, fully-clothed.

Orders . . . obeying orders . . . Billy's orders.

Joe flipped onto his back and seized seven hard inches . . .

Just before 8pm he was locking the flat's solid-core door. Joe frowned.

Over-Twenty-Fives night at The Matrix.

A club full of forty-year-old men looking for sixteen-year-old girls, and deciding to drink themselves into a stupor – at happy-hour prices – when they couldn't find any.

He set the alarm, pocketed the keys and turned.

Three other solid-core doors loomed in subdued lighting.

27

He'd not seen, never mind met, any of the neighbours in the ten months he'd been here. Joe smiled: if he'd paid £140,000 for a penthouse flat in the prestigious Italina Centre he'd make sure he showed his face.

Still smiling, Joe jogged down three flights of stairs, across the courtyard, past the fountain and out onto Ingram Street. Frost glistened around mock-Georgian street-lamps.

He scowled. Over-Twenty-Fives: fuckin' idiots.

But at least he didn't need to ask for ID or search the punters tonight. Cold air stung his cheek.

Georgie.

He didn't want any more trouble. Joe thrust hands into pockets and walked briskly towards Mitchel Street . . .

. . . which was surprisingly busy for early Sunday evening. As he turned down past Oddbins, Joe could see the pink stripe of police-cars, plus another vehicle he didn't recognise. He looked round for the inevitable leather-clad traffic-cop.

Parking was out anywhere in the city centre over Christmas. A tow-truck would be here any minute to impound the offending vehicle.

He walked past a gaggle of uniformed cops and pushed open the club's side door.

Inside, Davie the manager was talking to a silver-haired man in a sheepskin coat, who was nodding. Joe caught Davie's eye, raised an eyebrow.

Davie frowned and stopped talking.

The sheepskin turned, looked at Joe then turned back to Davie.

Joe spotted Gina leaning against the cigarette machine. He walked past a huddle of bouncers, recognising Malkie in their midst. He was talking to two uniformed cops. A joke was exchanged. Everyone laughed. Joe smiled beyond them, to Gina.

She frowned.

He stopped at the other side of the cigarette machine and fumbled for change. "Whit's aw' this?" Joe looked up.

Sombre face, no lipstick. Whisper: "It's Georgie."

Joe stared. "Whit aboot him?"

Gina produced cigarettes, extending the packet.

Joe continued to stare, then shook his head.

She took one, replacing the packet on top of the machine. "He's deid."

Joe blinked. "Whit?"

"He wis shot." Cigarette tapped on formica casing.

"Whit dae ye mean, he wis shot?"

Slow, even words: "Wi' a gun, Joe. Somewan shot him last night." The flare of a match.

"Where?"

"At hame . . . his wife fun him when she came aff the nightshift." Drawing on cigarette.

Joe sighed and fed three pound coins and a fifty pence piece into the machine.

It rattled, then spat a gold package out at him.

He unwrapped cellophane. "Dae ye ken whit happened?"

Head-shake. "Nae idea." Low voice, nod towards a hatless police-officer. "Ah've already gied ma' statement tae the guid-lookin' wan, but they'll waant tae talk tae you, Joe."

He lit a cigarette. "Whit fur?"

Laugh. "They're talkin' tae everyone – it's jist routine . . . so that wan says." Pointing.

Joe inhaled. "Ur we openin' the night?" Eyes on the bouncer / police huddle.

"Davie says aye . . . " Stubbing out cigarette. " . . . But this'll take fur ever – ye ken whit the polis ur like."

Joe frowned. Military polis, yes. Civilian polis were an unknown quantity.

A hand on his arm. "C'moan through tae the bar. It'll be ages afore they git tae you." Gina pulling.

A voice at his side:

"Mr Macdonald?"

Joe turned. The smile froze.

The sheepskin coat. Hard face. Harder voice. "DI Monroe, Stewart Street, Mr Macdonald. You wur working here last night?"

"Aye."

29

"Ye knew Mr . . . er, Paxton."

"Aye, ah worked wi' him."

"Ye saw him leave last night?"

"Aye." Joe blinked.

"Well, gie yer statement to PC Hunter when . . . "

Gina's voice: "Okay if we wait in the bar 'til yer ready fur him, Inspector?" Respectful.

Joe glanced at her, then sheepskin-coat.

Frown. "Ah think the oaffice wid be more suitable, Miss MacKay."

Gina acquiesced, smiled briefly and walked away.

Joe stared at the sheepskin-coat.

It stared back, then: "Whit happened tae yer face, son?"

Joe shrugged, ran a hand over crew-cut bristles. "Ah walked intae a . . . "

"Sir?"

New voice. Deep, resonant. English accent. Joe turned. The hatless uniform.

To Sheepskin: "That's everyone done, sir, except . . . " Eyes to Joe.

"Take Mr Macdonald intae the office, Hunter."

"Sir." To Joe. "This way, Mr Macdonald." A serge-clad arm extended.

Joe stubbed out the cigarette and walked towards the door marked Manager.

Instinctively, he remained standing.

So did the hatless uniform. Then it smiled, pulled out a chair and beckoned.

Joe perched on the desk.

The officer sat down and began to flick through a small note-book. "Now, Mr . . . ?"

"Macdonald . . . Joe Macdonald . . . " He stood up. The urge to salute was overwhelming.

Laugh. "Relax, Mr Macdonald." He pulled out cigarettes and extended the packet.

Joe took one and stood as Andy Hunter rose to light the cigarette. Tall . . . nearly as tall as Joe. Fresh-faced, young . . . but the voice said older. Good build. Short, fashionably-cut

30

brown hair. Pretty, almost feminine face apart from massive eyebrows framing the large brown eyes. Long lashes . . . Joe inhaled and reperched on Davie's desk.

PC Hunter replaced cigarettes and lighter in pocket and returned to the note-book. "Right, Mr Macdonald." He sat down. "Let me get a few details before we start – this is just routine, you understand?"

Joe understood. He nodded.

A pen was produced. "Right: it's Joe – Joseph? Macdonald."

Joe nodded.

"And you live . . . ?"

"Three-wan, the Italina Centre, Glesga."

Bushy brows rising while writing. "That the new development, down from the City Chambers?"

"Aye."

"Nice . . . used to pass it when I was on the city centre beat." Pause. "How old are you, Mr Macdonald?"

"Thirty-one."

"Date of birth?"

"Six-seven-sixty-six."

Laugh. "You've done this before!"

Joe inhaled.

PC Hunter cleared his throat and looked up from the notebook. "You work here as . . . ?"

Joe smiled. Billy's phrase: Head Security Consultant. "Ah'm wan o' the bouncers."

Writing. "And you've worked here . . . ?"

"Eight months."

"And before?"

Joe closed his eyes. Colchester. Military prison. "Royal Engineers."

Smile, then more writing. "Good training for what you're doing these days, I expect."

Joe smoked.

Then: "Now . . . you were working here last night?"

"Aye . . . ah telt him oot there . . . " Joe looked towards the door, then back at PC Hunter.

Apologetic smile. "Sorry – we've got to go through it all

31

again." Sigh, then: "I don't know if you've heard: one of your colleagues – a Mr George Paxton – was found dead early this morning. We're trying to establish his movements between leaving work here at . . . " Flicking of pages. " . . . Approximately 1.30am and 4.30am this morning . . . "

"That when he wis shot?" Joe frowned. "Gina telt me – the cloakroom girl."

Nod. "Between half three and half four. Seems . . . " Abrupt stop. Self-conscious smile. "Inspector Monroe knows all the details. I just take statements."

Joe shrugged.

PC Hunter sucked on the end of his pen. "Right. How well did you know Mr Paxton?"

"Ah worked wi' him." Joe stubbed out his cigarette in a large glass ashtray.

"Did you know him well – I mean, did you socialise with him outside, Mr Macdonald?"

"Ah worked wi' him – that's aw'." Joe fumbled in pockets then lit another cigarette.

"I see." More sucking of pen. Pause, then: "What time does The Matrix close, Saturday nights?"

"Three-ish, but it's closer tae four by the time we git them aw' oot."

Pause. "That's what I thought." PC Hunter leant back in his chair. "Any idea why Mr Paxton left early? I mean, did he usually knock-off before closing time?"

Joe tensed.

The door opened.

Joe glanced up. Sheepskin-coat now coatless. Sports jacket, shirt and tie. PC Hunter stood up:

"Sir."

Sheepskin-coat ignored him. He walked across the room and stopped at the desk. Hard eyes. "Whit happened tae yer face, Mr Macdonald?"

Joe stared. "It wis an accident."

"Paxton hit ye, didn't he?"

Joe stared.

"There wis an argument last night – quite a fight in fact, accordin' tae eye-witnesses – between George Paxton and

32

yourself, Mr Macdonald . . . "

Joe stood up. "A misunderstaundin', that's aw'."

Hard smile. "A misunderstaundin' during which you
hud tae be dragged aff Paxton."

Joe stared.

"A misunderstaundin', efter which you were heard tae
threaten Paxton – by at least four witnesses."

Joe clenched his fists. "He wis . . . "

"Ye admit tae threatenin' Mr Paxton, dae ye?"

Joe sat down and rubbed his face. "Ah loast ma temper –
ah didney mean it." He looked at the hard face, then the
pretty one.

PC Hunter's expression was oblique.

"Ye luck handy wi' yer fists, Mr Macdonald. No' yissed
tae somewan gettin' the better o' ye – eh?"

Joe blinked.

"We know ye left shoartly efter Mr Paxton: where did ye
go?"

"Hame . . . ah went hame."

Unconvinced snort. "An' where's hame?"

Resonant voice. "The Italina Centre, sir. You know, the . . . "

Snap. "I ken where it is, Hunter!" To Joe: "Didney happen
tae take a wee detour via Provan did ye, Mr Macdonald?
Didney decide tae . . . whit wis yer phrase? . . . 'get' Mr
Paxton, sooner rather than later?"

An explosion in his head. Joe lurched towards the hard
face. "Ah didney touch him – ah widney dirty ma . . . "

Strong hands on his arms, restraining. "Easy, easy."

Red flashed on his eye-lids. Joe wrestled one arm free
and spun round.

Hard voice behind. "Another example of yer temper, Mr
Macdonald?"

Joe stared into huge brown eyes, then sat down. The
hands released him. Resonant tones in his ear:

"Calm down – you're not doing yourself any favours."

The smell of wet sheepskin at his side:

"Where wur ye between three-thirty an' four-thirty this
mornin', Mr Macdonald?"

"At hame." Joe stared at the floor.

"Can onywan corroborate this?"

Joe sighed, mind racing. "Ma brither's boay an' his mate wur wi' me." He looked up.

Sceptical. "Names?"

"Sean . . . Sean Macdonald – the other wan wis Ewan somethin'. Look: ah don't waant them involved wi' . . . "

"Yer brither lives . . . ?"

"Ma brither's deid!"

"Ah . . . er, where dis his boay live?"

"Thirty one-three, Red Road Court, Barnhill." Joe glanced up at PC Hunter. "His mither'll be worried, if she thinks Sean's involved in onythin' . . . "

Sympathetic smile. "How old is he?"

"Fifteen."

Nod. "I'll make sure . . . "

Impatient. "Git a squad car up there, Hunter. Ah waant this soarted oot."

"Sir."

Joe watched Andy Hunter stride from the room. He looked at Sheepskin coat.

Who scowled. "You cool yer jets in here, Macdonald." He left the room.

Joe frowned and lit another cigarette.

Sometime later the door opened.

Joe looked up.

Sean. No baseball cap. Pushing hair from ashen face. Thin black jerkin zipped up to chin. Nose-stud quivering. "Hi, Joe!" Empty bravado.

Joe smiled.

Sheepskin-coat appeared behind the thin figure, closing the door.

Joe stared past, then back at, Sean. "Where's yer mither?"

Shrug. "Workin' – ah left her a note sayin' ah wis wi' you, Joe, okay?"

He nodded. At his side, the smell of wet-sheepskin. Low voice, kinder, but still unconvinced:

"Sean here his confirmed yer whereaboots between the oors concerned last night, Mr Macdonald."

Joe looked at Sean, who looked away.

Sigh. "However, as he seems tae huv bin somewhat involved in the . . . fracas himself, ah really need an independent . . . "

Cool voice: "What's going on here?"

Joe stood up, arms at sides.

Billy's green eyes surveyed the scene, flicking from Joe to Sean to Sheepskin-coat, focusing there. Joe watched the expression on his lover's face change, brighten:

"Inspector Monroe . . . " Hand outstretched. " . . . Good to see you again." Eyes to Joe and Sean, then back to Sheepskin. "I think we can clear this up quickly."

Hand taken, shaken. "Ah hope so, Mr King."

Billy moved past Joe to the far side of the desk, and sat down. "Now . . . " Smearless glasses removed, rubbed then replaced. " . . . What seems to be the problem?"

Sheepskin-coat explained.

Joe watched as the two men chatted amiably, then looked over at Sean.

Grin. Mouthing soundless words.

Joe moved towards him.

Whisper: "Ah didney tell them much, Joe – ainly that Georgie hit ye, then we went back tae the flat an' played CDs. Ah didney mention the . . . you-ken-whit." Puzzled. "Whit's happened?"

Joe shook his head.

Behind, the sound of chuckles and exchanged words. Billy's clear voice:

"By the time we'd cleaned up the mess, it was nearly five. Kids, eh?"

Chuckle, not hard-laugh. "At least it wis ainly whisky, Mr King, no' yer usual proablem."

Cool laugh. "I think you'll find The Matrix is clean, these days, Inspector. Drugs-wise, we run a tight ship here. My bouncers see to that – eh Joe?"

Joe turned, smiled, then looked at the floor.

Low, hard voice: "Ah'd watch that wan, Mr King."

Laugh. Standing. "Oh, I will, inspector . . . I will!"

A strained laugh.

Joe sighed.

Billy again: "Now, if you don't mind, Inspector . . . I've a living to make and . . . "

"Ah understaun', Mr King. We'll be in touch, if we need ony mair information." Turning. To Joe: "Don't let yer boss doon, Macdonald."

Joe scowled.

As Sheepskin-coat reached the door, Billy's voice: "Please give Paxton's widow our sympathies, Inspector. I will, of course, be calling on her myself, in the next few days."

"Ah wull, Mr King. Guid night." He closed the door.

Billy's voice: "Patronising bastard!"

Sean looked at Joe: "Georgie's deid?"

Cool laugh from behind.

Joe turned.

Billy smoothed back his hair and shrugged. "Saves me the trouble of sacking him!"

CHAPTER FOUR

Later, as Joe patrolled the dance-floor, three ill-matched couples shuffled to vintage Diana Ross.

The police had left.

Billy was giving Sean a lift home.

Georgie Paxton was dead . . .

Joe walked on.

. . . Shot, sometime between three and four-thirty this morning.

Between three and four-thirty this morning: Sean asleep in the lounge. Billy doing the rounds of the clubs. Joe alone.

He frowned. Sheepskin-coat.

The alibi was welcome. Billy was there for him.

Like he had been ten months ago . . .

Like Michael had been there for him . . . years ago.

Shouting.

Joe paused.

Diana's chain reaction had erupted into an old rave track, from back when they still had tunes.

The Over-Twenty-Fives had stopped dancing. Six sets of angry eyes directed towards the console.

Joe recognised the track.

More raised voices from the undancers.

Joe watched as a head-phoned figure in the DJ's booth raised two fingers towards the dance floor and turned up the volume . . .

'Do you want . . . to be free . . . live your life . . . the way it's gonna be . . . '

Memory invaded his mind.

Joe closed his eyes: Belfast 1990. Michael.

' . . . Will we live, or will we die . . . '

Joe clenched his fists: Hamburg, 1992. Michael.

' . . . Solitary brother . . . '

Heat spread over Joe's chest: Colchester, 1994.

' . . . Is there still a part of you that wants to live . . . wants to give . . . '

Sweat gathered in the hollow between pecs and began to

trickle onto stomach: Glasgow, 1996.

Billy.

More shouting.

He opened his eyes as husky vocals faded into the Birdie Song: the DJ's idea of a joke. Joe looked at dance floor.

Three couples cheered and began to flap.

Joe frowned and looked at his watch: almost two. Slow-record time still half an hour away. He turned and walked towards an exit.

In the foyer, Gina was handing sports-jackets and mangy non-fake furs to an assortment of punters. She caught his eye, smiled.

Joe nodded and walked towards the stairs which led to the upstairs bar. As he turned the corner, shrieks threatened to obliterate the Birdie Song's dying squawks. He jogged up ten carpeted steps, pushed open the door and scanned: at a far table, Malkie and two other bouncers struggling with a fat man and a very drunk brunette. Joe walked over.

Voices:

Malkie. Patient: "C'moan, pal. She's hud enough. Gitter hame . . . "

Adamant shrieking: "Ah'm waitin' fur the smoochy records!"

Joe smiled. "Need a haun, boays?"

The woman turned. Glassy unfocused eyes focusing. Grin. "You're a big wan, son . . . whit dae they ca' you?"

Joe looked at the jet bob surrounding a sunbed-tanned face. Early forties. Pink smeary lipstick, molten eye-liner streaking cheeks. "Joe." He smiled. "Noo . . . whit aboot some fresh air?"

Lolling head. "Ye're gorgeous, Joe . . . shame aboot that wee scar." Bare, flabby arm reaching up. Ring-encrusted fingers stroking Georgie's handiwork. She swayed to her feet, wobbled.

Joe caught her, an arm around spreading waist.

Laughter. "Ah'm away wi' Joe here, Harry . . . "

"Whit aboot the last dance, Rose?" Whine from the fat man.

Sloppy kiss planted on Joe's cheek. "Fuck the last dance!"

Hands running over his chest. "Joe an' me are away tae dae some dancin' o' oor ain – eh son?" More slevvery kisses.

Joe caught Malkie's eye. "Phone a taxi. Ah'll meet ye doonstairs." He gently took hold of a knobbly elbow and began to steer Rose towards the door. Slurring words in his ear:

"So . . . whit's a nice boay like you dain' in a dive like this?"

He smiled: The Matrix was Billy's flagship. "Ah work here." He moved his head, avoiding yet another attempt at a kiss.

"Well-built boay like you . . . "

He pushed open the door with a foot and began to guide the woman downstairs.

" . . . Loatsa easier wise o' makin' money." Fingernails tracing a nipple.

Joe smiled. Another 'proposition'. There were at least three a week. He'd tell Billy: it would amuse him.

They hit the bottom step.

"Ye ever considered . . . hen nights, Joe? Well-built boay like . . . "

"Dae ye huv a jaicket?" He propped the wilting Rose against the cigarette machine.

She slumped. "Whit . . . ?"

"Did ye put onythin' intae the cloakroom?"

Mumbling. One hand down vast cleavage. Bejewelled fingers emerging with damp pink ticket. "Leather coat . . . an' ma bag."

He looked over at Gina, who was grinning, red-mouthed. Then back at the ticket. "Six-three-nine."

Gina saluted and turned.

Joe manipulated his charge across six yards of blue carpeting. By the time they reached the counter he saw Gina was holding a long black coat and matching shoulder bag. "Thanks." He took them, gave Gina the ticket.

She laughed. "That you goat a lumber fur the night, then?"

Sharp sound of keys on glass.

Joe looked towards the main door, then Rose. "Okay,

here's yer taxi."

Malkie appeared from the bar half-carrying the fat man.

Voice in his ear: "C'moan back tae ma place fur a drink, Joe – ah'll square it wi' yer boss." Arms around his waist.

Joe laughed. "No' the night, Rose." He draped the coat around her shoulders, then the bag over one. Then followed Malkie and the fat man to the door.

Disappointed: "Maybe ah'll see ye again, Joe. Think aboot whit ah've said . . . " One hand removed. Bag opening.

"Aye, Rose, ah'll dae that." He watched as Malkie levered the fat man into the taxi. His own bundle seemed to be more mobile now. Pulling away, Joe helped her towards the cab. Fingers into his hand:

"Thanks, son."

Something crinkly, then a final kiss.

Malkie slammed the taxi door.

Joe opened his hand. Crumpled greenness.

Malkie at his shoulder. "Yer aw' lipstick, man!"

Joe stared into his palm, then rubbed his face.

"Did ramblin' Rosie gie yer hur number?" Laughing.

Joe unfolded a fifty-pound note and stared.

Billy was asleep when he entered the flat.

In the bedroom, Joe switched on a corner light and undressed quickly. He replaced trousers and jacket on a hanger and slipped them into the wardrobe. Naked, he switched off the light, seized Matrix tee-shirt, socks and Ys and walked through to the bathroom.

Brushing teeth, he spat a mouthful of blue foam into the marbled sink, raised his head and stared.

A pink, angular face stared back. On the right cheek, left in the mirror, yellowing skin billowed around the three-inch cut. Joe turned on the tap, filled the sink and submerged his head.

Silence echoed in his ears.

Joe broke the surface. A different silence. He shook his head, straightened up and grabbed a towel, rubbing vigorously. Then he stopped, stared again.

Blue eyes stared back.

The Macdonald eyes.

Joe smiled. Sean had his mother's colouring, but Michael's eyes.

He frowned. Angie. He'd ring her tomorrow, explain.

Joe threw Matrix tee-shirt, underwear and the wet towel into the laundry-basket, replaced it with a dry one from the cupboard and walked back through to the bedroom.

Through semi-closed blinds, a thin horizontal beam bisected Billy's sleeping face.

Joe pulled back the duvet and slid into bed. Other fabric brushed bare skin.

Billy was wearing heavy cotton pyjamas, white with a blue stripe.

Joe smiled, turning the inert form towards him. He began to undo small, white buttons.

Without his glasses, Billy looked younger, more vulnerable. The hard eyes, hidden beneath almost translucent eye-lids, were at rest.

Joe moved his hand to stroke the unlined forehead.

Billy mumbled.

Joe continued to stroke. At times like this it was hard to believe Billy was almost forty. Pale skins seemed to age better . . . or maybe it was attitude of mind: stress-management, Billy called it.

Joe sighed. Billy seemed to manage his stress very well.

There was business . . . and there was pleasure.

In business, Joe knew Billy had to lick a lot of boots.

In pleasure, the boots were licked for him.

Joe stopped stroking. Tingling in his groin. He traced Billy's small nose and thin lips.

Billy had it all worked-out.

Joe leant over and brushed Billy's mouth with his own.

Eyelids sprang open, myopic pupils focusing. "What is it?" Wary.

Joe kissed an ear-lobe. "Nothin' . . . sorry ah woke ye." An arm encircled his waist. Joe nestled down. Billy's fingers in his hair:

"I wasn't really asleep. Just thinking."

Arm around waist removed, lowered, stroking buttocks.

41

Joe rubbed his prick against Billy's cotton-covered thigh.

Hoarse laugh: "But I do want to sleep, now that I know you're home."

Joe licked a pale collarbone and exhaled.

Home.

Where the heart was.

Voice in his ear, sensing disappointment: "Want to go out, tomorrow night? Somewhere . . . special?"

Joe pressed his face to the hairless chest. "Aye, that'd be nice."

"Where do you fancy – Rogano's, The Cul-de-sac?"

Joe frowned.

"Well?"

A finger tracing his arse-crack.

"I want to show my favourite security-consultant how much I appreciated him."

Joe pulled away. "Ah didney dae ye ony favours when ah hid the run-in wi' Georgie." He reached for cigarettes.

Cold voice. "That was unfortunate. You made a mistake, Joe. You shouldn't have let yourself get out of control . . . "

Joe flicked the Zippo. Flaring light illuminated shaking hands.

" . . . But it's all over now."

The hand was back, fingers tugging a nipple.

Joe flinched, bit down on the cigarette-filter as his body began to respond.

Billy's fingers continued to tug, then: "Sean's friend, what was his name? Quite a looker, didn't you think?"

Joe moved away and fumbled for an ashtray. "Who, Ewan?" He propped himself up on one elbow.

"Yes, Ewan."

Freckles and helmet-cut hair. "Ah didney really notice." He sat the ashtray on his side of the bed.

"Think they're a couple?"

"Whit?"

"Sean . . . think he's gay?"

Joe laughed. "Ah don't think Sean kens whit he is. Aw' he's interested in is music an' expensive claes, fae whit Angie sez."

42

"Hmm". Billy coughed and waved smoke away. "Still, he and the red-head seemed very . . . close. It was Ewan this, Ewan that when I was running him home."

Joe smiled. The joking, the mock-fighting . . . "Ye ken whit boays ur like at that age."

"I know what I was like at fifteen." Soft smile.

A hand rubbing his stomach.

Sigh. "Wish I'd known you at fifteen, Joe."

Joe laughed and ground the cigarette into the ashtray. "Ah wis fuckin' useless at that age. A mess . . . "

Soft voice, nearly tender. "You were still a mess when I met you in January."

Joe closed his eyes. Almost a year had passed. He lay down and buried his face in Billy's neck.

A hand stroked his head. "We got you sorted out though – didn't we?"

"Aye, Billy." Oddfellows drifted into his nostrils, lulling, reassuring.

"You understand things better now – don't you?"

"Aye, Billy." Joe shivered. His prick sprang to attention. Then hands gripped his face, pulling him up.

Joe looked at Billy.

"Are you happy, Joe?"

Myopic green eyes, huge pupils seared into his soul. "Ye ken ah am, Billy." Joe seized a soft warm hand and pressed it to his groin.

Smile. "Ah, well . . . we've got to make sure you stay that way."

The hand squeezed gently then withdrew. Joe sighed.

"I suppose sleep can wait."

Pyjama-clad arms pushed him down onto his back.

When Joe woke up Billy's side of the bed was still warm, but empty. He ran a dry hand over the slight indentation, sighed, then swung leaden legs out from under the duvet. He stood up, arched his back and stretched.

Something crinkled on his stomach.

Joe looked down.

Frosted crystals of spunk clung to bristling hair.

His spunk.

Billy's spunk.

Joe smiled and walked through to the kitchen.

On the table, a newspaper and a note. He picked up the latter.

Billy's neat script:

'Book a table at The Buttery for eight. Meet you there. Be good.'

Joe fingered the paper, then turned to fill the kettle.

One hour, four coffees, a shower and a phone-call later he closed *The Record* and stared again at the front page:

'Bouncer Found Dead!' Then a grainy photograph of Georgie and a smiling woman – presumably Mrs Georgie.

Joe scanned the copy.

A bit about Georgie.

A bit about Mrs Georgie.

A bit about the growing number of shootings in Glasgow's club-land.

Then a bit about The Matrix.

Joe frowned. Billy wouldn't be pleased. More ammunition for the licensing board. He glanced at his watch: nearly twelve.

Angie: was Monday her day off?

He walked back to the lounge, picked up the mobile-phone and punched in seven digits. After four rings, it was answered:

Lazy vowels: "Ewan, ma man! Ah've bin . . . "

"Sean?" Joe narrowed his eyes.

Coughing, then: "Hi, Joe! How's it goin'?"

"Why you no' at school?"

Chirpy. "Free period. Nipped hame tae dae some shoapin' fur ma maw. Mondays is hur busy day."

Joe frowned. An answer for everything. "Ah thought Mondays wis . . . "

Voice faint in the background: "Who's that, Sean?"

Swallow. "Yer in luck, Joe – ma maw's jist come in the door." Muffled voice: "It's jist Joe, ma." Unmuffled voice, but lower, less chirpy: "Ye're no gonny tell her aboot . . . ?"

Joe ran a hand through hair. "Don't worry . . . pit yer

mither oan, Sean."

Relief. "Sure, Joe . . . mebbe catch ye later?"

"No' the day. Mebbe the morra . . . "

Clunk, rustlings, then breathless, husky voice: "Joe." Tension lengthened the word.

He frowned. "Hi, Angie. How's things?"

Sigh. "Don't ask, Joe." Stifled yawn. "Ah'm beat."

"Go on back tae yer bed, Angie. Ah kin talk tae ye later . . . "

"Naw, Joe . . . ah'm up noo." Tired laugh. "Ma wee alarm-cloak seen tae that, wi' aw' his racket!"

He sighed. "Sean huvin' a day aff the school?" Lying little . . .

Worried. "He's no' lookin' too well, Joe – ah'm sure that stupit nose-ring thing's goin' septic." Annoyed. "He goat Ewan tae dae it wi' a darnin' needle. Paira idgits!"

Joe smiled. "It lucked okay tae me . . . "

"Aye, well . . . ah said he kid stay aff school the day, onyway." Sigh. "Think he mebbe coat some sorta bug . . . he's affy thirsty – drank gallonsa water. Wis he aw' right last night, wi' you?"

Joe frowned. "Aye . . . he wis a bit late goin' hame, but that wis ma fault." He blinked. She had enough to worry about. "He's on his ain an affy loat, Angie."

Edge on voice. "Ye ken ah canny help that, Joe. Ah've goat tae work tae . . . "

"Ah wisney meanin' onythin'. Ah ken ye dae whit ye huv tae. But ah wish ye'd let me help oot . . . "

Angry. "We've bin through aw' this, Joe! Sean an' me kin manage fine. Ah don't need chairity . . . "

Joe tensed. "Ah wisney offerin' ony! Look: ah've goat a loata free time these days. Send him doon tae me if ye don't want tae lea' him oan his ain – or ah kid come up tae you."

Uneven breathing. "Soarry ah bit yer heid aff, Joe." Pause. "Sure ye don't mind luckin' efter him? Ah mean, he kin be a bit o' a . . . "

Joe smiled. "Nae problem, Angie – he's a guid boay."

Snort. "You dinny huftae live wi' him . . . " Burst of loud music in the background. "Sean!" Voice like rusty piano-wire. "Turn that fu . . . racket doon before ah . . . "

45

"Chill-oot Angie, eh?" Joe frowned.

Silence, then laughing. In the background, the racket dipped to a low rumble. "Christ gie me strength!"

Joe smiled. "Jist try tae keep yer hauns aff his throat!"

More laughing. "Ah think the school might be the safest place fur him, the way ah feel at the moment."

They both laughed.

Joe ran a finger over the telephone's handset, wiping away a speck of dust. Angie sounded better, more like her old self. More like the bubbly blonde Michael had married fifteen years ago.

The sound of a lighter sparking at the other end of the telephone. "So, Joe – whit can ah dae fur ye?" Exhaling.

"Jist waanted tae see hoo ye were gettin' oan, Angie. The soap factory workin' oot?"

"Aye, Joe. Ah'm packin' the night-shift in, next week though, an' I shidd huv Christmas aff."

"That's guid. You an' Sean goin' tae yer mither's again this year?"

"Probably . . . dae us guid tae git away fur a wee while." Pause. "Want tae come, Joe? Ye ken ye're welcome."

Joe scratched his head. "Thanks, but ah'll probably be workin' – if the All-Dayer at The Matrix gets the go-ahead, Christmas Eve . . . "

"You an' Mr King goat onythin' planned fur New Year? We'll be back by . . . "

"Ah think we're goin' tae some party, Angie, but thanks onyway." Joe smiled. He could see Billy's face at the idea of a New Year in Springburn.

"Ah, well – if ye change yer mind . . . "

"Sure, Angie . . . "

Sean in the background: "Onythin' tae eat, ma?"

Angie laughed. "Ah think he's feelin' better!"

"Ah'll let ye go then – think aboot whit ah've said. It's nae trouble fur me tae keep an eye oan . . . "

"Ah wull, Joe. Come up durin' the week sometime an' we'll talk aboot it – if ah'm no' in, Sean'll be here . . . "

In the background, insistent: "Ma!"

Muffled: "In a minute, Sean!" To Joe: "He eats like a

46

fuckin' hoarse, an' there's still no' a pick oan him!"

Joe smiled. The Macdonald metabolism. Or hormones.

Sean in background: "Kin ah huv some o' this bacon, ma?"

"Lea' that alain, Sean! That's fur the tea. Sorry, Joe speak tae ye later. Bye."

In the background: "Seeya, Joe! Ma, kin ah no' . . . ?"

"Seeya . . . " The line buzzed.

Joe continued to hold the mobile. After a few minutes he switched it off and walked back to the kitchen. In a cupboard, overalls. Joe struggled into them, put the mobile in a pocket and picked up a set of keys from the table.

Monday: Billy would have the Merc.

He left the flat, jogged down four flights of stairs to the basement car park.

In the far corner, a red Datsun and a Cherokee Jeep.

Joe walked towards the former, opened the boot and removed a bundle of rags and a tin of Turtle wax.

He began to polish.

At eight on the dot he walked through The Buttery's discreet doorway. Joe straightened tie and ran a hand through wet hair.

Almost immediately a suited figure approached. Eyes on the leather jacket.

Joe smiled. "Ah'll keep it oan, pal."

Flicker of disapproval then jacketless, the suited figure walked away. Seconds later another suit appeared. Professional smile scanning his face, then stopping.

Joe fingered the scar. "Mr King's table."

The suit smiled again, then led him across the foyer through a stained glass door and into the restaurant.

Joe stared straight ahead as he walked, hands jammed into pockets. The stiff linen collar rubbed at his neck.

The figure in front stopped, pulled out a chair then turned. Smiling: "Still raining, is it?"

"Aye." Joe remained standing and looked beyond the maitre'd.

At the table, Billy was punching numbers into a small

calculator.

Joe cleared his throat.

Billy looked up frowning, then smiled: "Sit down, Joe." To the suit: "Thanks, André. Give us ten minutes."

The suit nodded, smiled again, then departed.

Joe unzipped jacket and sat down.

Billy returned to the calculator. Silence, then: "Want a drink?"

"No' yet." Joe lifted a small fork from the white-clothed table and turned it over in his hands.

"I'll be with you in a minute."

Joe shrugged and examined each of the fork's prongs. Behind, muted conversation from other tables. He continued to scrutinise the fork.

"Have a good day?"

Joe looked up.

The calculator had gone. Billy was leaning back in his chair.

Joe replaced the fork beside two others. "Aye . . . did you?"

Billy nodded. "A very good day, in fact." Smiling. "Signed the papers for Summers' café-chain." Myopic eyes gleamed.

"That's great, Billy . . . ye must be pleased." Joe wondered if he had seen *The Record*.

Laugh. "I'm very pleased." A hand into pocket. Suddenly shy: "This is for you, Joe."

Long, rectangular box pushed across starched tablecloth.

Joe looked at the box. Gold writing on black leather: Baume . . . something.

"Go on, open it." Box pushed further forward.

Joe lifted, opened. A lining of white satin. Secured by two small bands, a wrist-watch. Joe stared.

"Do you like it?"

Joe removed the watch and fingered the heavy gold strap. He peered at the wide, plain face, at the delicate, black hands sprouting from a gold crown motif. In the centre of the crown, a tiny purple glint. His throat was dry. "Aye, Billy, it's . . . it's brand new!" He smiled across the table.

Frown. "Of course it's new . . . I wouldn't . . . "

48

Joe laughed. Sean-speak. "Ah didney mean that! It's great, Billy . . . really great." He frowned. "But ah've goat a watch." He pulled up a sleeve. The stainless steel Tag Heur shone dully.

Billy smiled. "Keep the Baume Mercier for special occasions . . . like tonight."

"Okay, Billy." He unclipped the aviator's watch, shoved it into his pocket and began to fasten the new, intricate gold strap. He stared. Against matted black hair the watch looked . . . smaller. He held up a forearm for inspection.

Billy nodded with approval. "It suits you."

Voice from behind: "Ready to order, Mr King?"

Joe stared at the watch.

"Yes, Robert. We'll have the Sole Morney then . . . Steak Tartar, I think."

The fish-thing, then the meat-thing. Joe stared at the watch.

"And from the wine-list, Mr King?"

Laugh. "I think André knows my usual . . . and bring Joe a bottle of that mineral water he likes . . ." Pause for clarification.

Joe looked up. "Caledonian Clear . . . the wild black-berry, if ye've goat it."

Smile, then deferential nod from an olive-skinned man. "Certainly sir." He walked away.

Joe looked back at Billy, then the watch.

"Sure you like it?"

Under the table Joe rubbed Billy's ankle with a Doc. He gazed into clear green eyes.

Billy smiled. "Good. Now, let's enjoy the meal. I've a little proposition to put to you . . ."

Joe held the filter tight between rough fingers. "No way, Billy – thanks, but no thanks." He raised the cigarette to his lips.

Sigh. "Come on, Joe – why not? It makes sense . . ."

"Ah like workin' – ah ken ah moan aboot it sometimes, but ah'm yissed tae a routine." He exhaled. "Ah widney ken whit tae dae wi' masel' . . ."

49

Chuckle. "Oh, I can think of a few things."

Joe looked across the table.

Billy was drinking brandy from a balloon-glass.

The gold strap on his wrist suddenly felt very tight.

"Seriously, Joe: I've got enough money for both of us." A finger stroking the slim neck of the glass.

Joe frowned. "Ah like tae pay ma way, Billy." He looked down at the remains of raw meat. "Ah owe ye as it is."

Fingers drumming on the table-top. Sigh. "Well, at least think about it."

Joe looked up. "Ah don't need tae, Billy. Noo, kin we talk aboot somethin' else?"

A hard, green glint behind metal-rimmed glasses. "Fine."

Silence.

Fifteen minutes later Billy placed a gold Amex card on a china plate. When it came back, with an Armani jacket, Joe stood up and followed Billy out to the car.

CHAPTER FIVE

Joe glanced at his new watch: almost midnight. He took another sip of mineral water and sighed. DiMaggio's Diner was closed. Waiters scurried around, clearing tables. In the distance a hoover hummed over low thumps emanating from beneath. . .

"Get you another?"

Joe turned.

The barman smiled, bottle poised.

"Aye . . . why no'." Joe extended his glass.

The barman poured.

"Thanks." He looked at the unfamiliar face. "You new here?"

Nod. "Holiday relief." Eyes lowered. "You wi' wan o' them?"

Joe followed the eyes to a table where Billy and two men he didn't recognise were deep in conversation. "Aye." He lit a cigarette.

Business, Billy had said.

Only be a minute, Billy had said.

Then we'll go home, Billy had said . . . two hours ago.

Joe watched as a second bottle of whisky was opened.

"'Scuse me."

He lifted an elbow.

The barman wiped.

Joe glanced at his new watch again: just after midnight. He sighed, got up from the bar-stool and walked over to Billy's table.

Hushed conversation ceased.

He stopped behind Billy's chair, looked down at the Armani-clad back.

Two pairs of curious, unfamiliar eyes studied him.

Joe cleared his throat.

"What is it?" Said without turning.

"Ye waant me tae haud oan? Ah mean, ah kid come back an' get ye if . . . "

"Wait at the bar, Joe."

51

"But . . ."

"I said wait at the bar." Impatient.

Joe walked back to wait at the bar.

Behind, conversation recommenced.

The barman smiled, sympathetic. "They'll be at it aw' night." Pouring more water. Then: "Ah'm Chris, by the way."

"Joe." He ground out cigarette in a freshly-wiped ashtray and glanced up.

Mid-twenties, blond flat-top topping pink face. One gold hoop earring in each ear. White, cap-sleeved tee-shirt emblazoned DiMaggios. Small, bluebird tattoo twitching on left bicep. Low voice: "Look: ah'm aboot finished here. Fancy goin' doonstairs?"

Joe raised an eyebrow.

Laugh. "Tae the club." Drying hands on a bar-towel. "It's no' bad oan a Monday – happy oor aw' night!"

Joe smiled. "No thanks, pal."

Feigned pleading: "Aw' . . . come oan -- jist fur half an oor?" Eyes to Billy's table. "Ye'll no' be missed."

"Ah'm no' really intae clubs."

Eyes narrowed, still on the table. Thoughtful. "Naw, ah thought ah hudney seen ye aroon'." Shrug. "He must keep ye busy."

Joe laughed. "Ah work in a club – ah don't need mair noise oan ma night aff!"

"Whit wan?"

"The Matrix – Mitchel Lane?"

"Aye, ah ken it – mainly rave, is it no'?"

Joe nodded.

Expansive gesture. "Ye'll no' git ony o' that doonstairs . . . ah'm talkin' real music . . . Country 'n' Western!"

Joe groaned.

Laugh. "C'moan – ye've no' lived 'til ye've danced tae 'Staun by yer Man' wi' a room fulla drunken queens!"

Joe smiled, looked over at the 'business-meeting'.

At the table, Billy was leaning forward, prodding the checked table-cloth with a well-manicured finger. Joe watched smooth blond hair move along the nape of a pink neck. His prick twitched.

Voice from behind the bar. "Aye, it'll be wall-tae-wall Dolly Parton. Sure ah canny tempt ye? The beer's cheap."

Joe stared at the back of Billy's head, then turned. The mineral water tasted sour in his mouth. "Aw' right then – ye've twisted ma airm!"

"Great! Just let me git ma jaicket."

Joe watched as Chris disappeared though a door at the end of the bar, returning seconds later with a Levi cut-off over one shoulder. Conspiratorial eyes. Whisper:

"Doon the back stairs – we'll no' huv tae pay."

He got up from the bar-stool and glanced over at Billy's table, then at his watch. He wouldn't be missed . . .

Joe sighed and followed Chris to a door marked Staff Only.

He lit another cigarette, replacing the gold packet in his pocket. Joe fiddled with the chrome Zippo. Sweaty hand on his shoulder, mouth to ear:

"So . . . " Out of breath. " . . . Ye don't dance, then?"

Joe sat the lighter on the bar, turned.

Chris grinned at him, grabbing a Michelob. He drank. Behind, the small dance-floor was a sea of denim and gingham.

Joe shook his head.

Another grin, then wiping mouth. Shouting: "Ye don't say a lot either!"

Joe glanced at his new watch: nearly one. He looked up.

Feigned hurt: "Ah'm no' borin' ye, um ah?"

Joe smiled, mouth to a pink ear. "Ah better go. Thanks fur the drink." He stood up. A restraining hand on his shoulder:

"Goat ye oan a shoart leash, huz he?"

Joe laughed. "Who?"

"The big chief upstairs." Eyes narrowing.

Joe shrugged off the hand. "Mebbe see ye again, pal." He pushed into the crowd, heading for the back stairs.

Ten minutes later Joe was still pushing. Leather-clad arms waved in his face. The sounds of some woman wanting to put a blanket on the ground filled his ears. Joe frowned, tried to look at the new watch. Bodies trapped his arms by sides. He elbowed his way to the edge of the dance-floor and leant against a clammy wall.

This was fuckin' impossible.

He reached into jacket pocket for cigarettes. Found them. A body brushed against him, apologised and moved away. Joe dropped the cigarettes, swore then bent down. Eventually finding the packet, he stuck cigarette in mouth and fumbled for lighter.

Nothing.

Joe tensed.

The bar?

He looked back to where Chris had been.

Over the seething dance-floor one hairy arm was raised. Fingers waving a small chrome rectangle.

He relaxed, then smiled.

Then frowned . . .

Through a heat-haze Joe watched as another hand seized the hairy wrist, pulling it out of sight.

Keeping to the perimeter Joe made his way back to the bar.

When he reached it, Chris was talking to someone.

Joe peered.

Someone . . . in a blue Armani jacket.

Joe elbowed two dancing figures out of the way and walked towards Billy. As he neared, he watched Chris's smile fade to a frown, then a scowl.

Billy was holding the Zippo.

Joe draped an arm around thin shoulders and plucked the lighter from between elegant fingers. Mouth to ear: "Thanks!"

Billy spun round, face a mask. Lips moving.

Joe leant forward to hear.

Behind, Chris shrugged and began to walk away.

Billy's words became audible: "You! Out!"

Joe raised an eyebrow and stepped back.

Billy's mouth was an angry line.

"Whit? Whit d'ye . . . "

Strong fingers gripped his arm.

Joe shrugged them off.

The fingers regripped.

Joe stared into steely eyes. Billy's lips were moving again. The woman on the record was now getting a blanket from the bedroom. Joe shook his head. "Ah canny hear whit . . ."

Abruptly, the fingers uncurled. Billy turned and walked into the crowd.

Joe followed. As they reached the main entrance, another voice in his ear:

"Ye're in fur it the night, Joe."

He grinned, turned.

Chris wasn't smiling.

Joe slapped a sweaty shoulder, winked and followed Billy out into the night.

" You . . . "

Joe closed his eyes, palms slippery on polished wood. His prick brushed stomach as body absorbed impact.

" . . . disobeyed . . . "

Joe sighed, bracing arms.

" . . . an order . . . "

Stinging. Joe clenched his teeth. Prick slapped stomach.

" . . . soldier!"

"Sir." His mouth was dry. Knee-cap skin dragged on the floor. Billy's thighs were warm and slippery against his arse.

Arms moved from shoulders. Fingers seized the white ribbon.

Nylon dug into the flesh of his throat. Joe's head jerked back. His balls spasmed.

Fingers twisting the white ribbon. Hips thrusting.

Stars . . .

Another thrust, deeper now . . . different angle.

Stars twinkled on eye-lids.

Fingers tightening.

Joe opened his eyes. More stars, flashing on peripheral vision. Humming in his ears . . .

Billy withdrew. The pain lessened.

Joe moaned. The humming became singing. Somewhere

in the distance, a squidging sound.

The ribbon jerked.

Then a cold, sloppy finger inside him . . . then two, then . . .
The pain increased.

His prick was iron. Through the singing:

"I told you to wait at the bar, soldier . . . "

Four fingertips . . . four knuckles . . . The white ribbon
sank deeper into his throat.

The singing became a chorus. Blackness filled his eyes.
The pressure in his balls was unbearable. Deep inside,
muscle spasmed as something unbelievably large stroked
and rubbed. In the distance:

"You disobeyed me, soldier . . . "

A slow explosion rippled up his prick. Arms buckled.
The white ribbon tightened. A scream echoed through the
singing as he came.

Then blackness . . .

. . . huge, empty blackness deep inside.

Openness . . .

. . . like part of him was missing.

Joe teetered on the edge of consciousness, felt cool,
still-damp fingers on his face. Warm thighs beneath his
head. He opened his eyes.

Billy's face wobbled.

Joe blinked.

Billy's face stabilised.

Joe groaned, coughed. Winced.

Cool fingers on his throat. Billy smiled down. "Like that,
did you?"

Joe tried to sit up. Pain exploded in his arse. His arms
were . . . not his arms, his body . . . somewhere else. He
slumped back down into Billy's lap. "Whit . . . ?"

Laugh. Fingers stroking. "It's what happens when you
cut off blood-supply to the brain."

Cotton wool for arms. Cotton wool for legs. Something
wet beneath . . .

Lips brushed forehead. "You bled a little . . . "

Joe tensed.

"It's okay – nothing serious." Concerned smile. "Finger-nail, I think . . . "

Joe sat up, teeth clenched against the discomfort. Sweat beaded on his forehead. "How lang wis ah oot?"

Billy produced cigarettes, placed one between Joe's lips. "About five minutes . . . "

Pounding in his chest.

"Hey! Don't worry – it's not dangerous . . . " He flicked the Zippo.

Joe lowered his head to the flame. "Ye've done this wi' . . . before?" He drew on the cigarette, coughed.

Smile. "Fisting?"

"Naw, the other . . . thing."

Nod. "I take it you haven't?"

Joe inhaled. "Fuck! It wis so . . . "

Laugh. "Intense?"

Joe nodded. Cigarette smoke singed his throat. He coughed again. A finger traced one nipple.

"So I've heard."

"Ye've never . . . ?" His throat was coated with some-thing thick.

Head-shake. "It's more . . . fun to do."

Joe smiled. "Ah don't ken if ah'd ca' it fun."

"But you enjoyed it?"

Joe looked at Billy.

Behind metal frames the myopic eyes shone.

"Ah . . . ah think so." Fingers dug into the cigarette's filter.

Smile. "I know so."

Gentle lips on his. Then not so gentle. Then Billy's tongue filled his mouth. Joe sighed, crushed the cigarette with numb fingers then wrapped a rubbery arm around the slender waist as Billy's body covered his own.

Later, in the bath, he watched over one shoulder as Billy lathered carbolic soap between palms. Warm water lapped at his knees. "Did ye get that bitta business soarted oot?" Soft hands soaped his arse.

"Mmm . . . ?"

Joe flinched.

"Sorry!" Buttocks patted. Then soaping continued.

"Whit wis it aw' aboot?" Joe pressed a hot face against cool tiles.

Tutting. "Something and nothing." Fingers rubbing back.

"Proablems?"

Laugh. "Nothing I can't handle – and nothing for you to concern yourself with!" Fingers on neck, untying the white ribbon. "You never did tell me why they made you wear this." Damp fabric twisting between well-manicured thumb and index.

Joe sighed. Colchester . . . a lifetime away. "Ah never asked. They give it tae ye when ye come in, pin it tae ye an' tell ye tae wear at aw' times."

White ribbon laid on white enamel. "Like the scarlet letter?"

"Whit?"

Soft laugh. More soaping. "A book I read, once. Hawthorne, I think. In certain rural, turn-of-the-century American communities, adultresses were made to wear a red 'A', so that everyone would know what they'd done." Soft hand moving round onto stomach.

Joe sighed. "Ah don't ken whit yer oan aboot, Billy."

Soapy fingers between hairy thighs. "No . . . I don't suppose you do." Cupping balls. "You never ask questions, do you, Joe?"

He tensed. "Naw, Billy."

"And you always do as you're told, Joe, don't you?"

Tingling in his balls. "Aye, Billy." He turned.

The mask was back. "Always?" Wet fingers unzipping.

Joe nodded. "Yes, Billy." He stepped out of the bath and knelt before Armani-clad legs . . .

Joe looked at his new watch: 10am. He switched off the bedside lamp and tried to get out of bed. Then scowled.

Something hurt . . . not exactly hurt, but . . .

Joe eased onto his side, fingers tentatively prodding the area around his arse-hole. Then inhaled.

Sore . . . not exactly sore, but . . .

Different. He prodded some more, pressing a fingertip against swollen tissue. He risked a nail's length inside.

The same. A little tender, that was all.

Joe withdrew the finger . . .

A ring of muscle snapped shut.

. . . and stared at it.

No blood: a little shit and lots of gooey stuff – presumably the KY – but no blood.

Joe lay still until his breathing returned to normal then turned onto his back and did a few leg-lifts.

After about ten the stiffness, soreness, differentness lessened. Joe eased his body from the mattress, swung his legs gently over the side of the bed and walked slowly to the window. He pulled a cord.

Grey light filtered in.

He sighed, walked to the wardrobe and opened it.

Tuesday.

He looked at the row of jackets and trousers.

Most he had never worn.

A few he had worn once.

Joe grabbed a pair of black 501s from a hanger and struggled into them. He closed the wardrobe and turned to the bleached pine bureau. He opened a drawer and removed a white tee-shirt, white Ys and a pair of grey socks. He closed the drawer and walked through to the kitchen.

Today's orders were propped against the espresso machine:

'The jeep needs cleaning. Peggy's expecting you at the Duke Street shop. Back about six. Kit inspection tonight.'

Joe switched on the kettle and sat down. He rubbed his face, then blinked.

The jeep was due a service, too.

He lit a cigarette. Peggy?

Joe exhaled, remembering. The last race at Ayr yesterday: the favourite falling yards from the finishing-line.

A lot of people had lost a lot of money.

As a bookie, Billy wouldn't have been one of them.

Joe pulled on tee-shirt, Ys and socks, then went to find boots.

Rain was still dripping from a spongy sky as he approached 598 Duke Street. Corner premises. William King: Turf Accountant emblazoned on four smoked-glass windows. Joe pushed open the door and went in.

A couple of soggy punters stood gazing at a wall-mounted TV monitor.

Could be the Australian tennis, or cricket. Some people would bet on the sun not rising.

He looked up, smiled: Richard and Judy simpered soundlessly down at him. Joe looked away and walked towards the counter.

On the other side, behind reinforced, shatter-proof glass, Peggy. Late fifties. Grey hair tied back in a tight bun, white blouse, black tie. Lined, smiling face. "Mornin', son – wet enough fur ye?"

Buzzing sound, then a click. The side door swung open.

Joe grinned and walked through.

The door clicked behind him. Peggy nodded to two bored tellers then beckoned to Joe.

They walked through to the office.

Closing the door he watched as she crouched before a large old-fashioned safe. "So . . . how's life treatin' ye, Peggy?"

"No' so bad . . . no' so bad." Handle seized, twisted.

The safe door swung open.

Peggy bent forward, reached in, then stood up and turned, kicking the safe shut with a three-inch heel. She held out a plastic wallet.

Joe took it. "Ye done the pay-in slip?"

Peggy walked to the desk and lifted an orange, rectangular booklet. She opened it, thumbed, then handed it to him.

Joe took it, unzipped the leather jacket and thrust both inside. He rezipped the jacket and turned to go.

"Time fur a coffee?"

He looked at his watch. "No' really . . . "

The door opened. One of the bored tellers. Young, sulky face. A new face here.

But a Matrix face.

Joe smiled. Billy paid the wages this girl spent in his

60

club: like the acquisition of the Summers' café-chain, another clever investment.

To Peggy. Worried: "That guy's back in, Mrs O'Neil."

Pressed lips. "Okay, Cheryl . . . ah'll deal with it." To Joe: "Could ye hang oan a minute?"

He raised an eyebrow. "Trouble?"

Laugh. "Nothin' ah canny haundle! Naw – ah jist waant a wee word."

Joe shrugged. "Sure."

Peggy moved past him, smoothing down a tight black skirt. She paused in the doorway. "Git the boay a coffee, hen." The door closed.

Joe looked at the pouting girl.

She was peering at him. Thoughtful. "Joe . . . Joe . . . " Narrow-eyed scrutiny. " . . . Ah ken you . . . "

Joe smiled. "Black, no sugar."

She continued to peer.

Joe sighed. "Am ah gettin' that coffee, then?"

Startled. "Oh . . . aye, man . . . jist gie's a minute 'til ah place that face."

Joe produced cigarettes and prompted. "Huv ah no' seen ye at The Matrix?"

Brightening. "Aye, that's it. Didney ken you worked here too." She walked to the percolator. Lowered voice. "D'ye hear whit happened tae . . . " Coffee pouring.

Joe scowled. Fuckin' Georgie was following him.

" . . . Big Pete?" She sipped from a mug, extending another.

Joe took it. "Who?"

Cheryl perched on the desk. "Big Pete Burns – ah worked in the Shawlands shoap wi' him."

Joe lit a cigarette. "Ah dinney . . . "

Confiding. "Ye musta heard – goat caught wi' his haun in the till coupla weeks back." Shaking head. "Mr King wis affy annoayed."

Joe inhaled and grinned. He could imagine.

Cheryl produced cigarettes of her own and lit one. "Well, Pete wis jumped Friday night oan his way hame fae the fitba'." Eyes flashing. "Four broken ribs an' a fractured skull . . . "

Joe took a gulp of coffee.

" . . . He's ower in the Victoria Infirmary." Gossip bulletin ended. She waited for a response.

Joe looked round for an ashtray. "The 'gers?" Out of politeness.

Cheryl supplied one, held it out. "Naw . . . Celtic."

"Thanks." He used it. "So . . . Cheryl – worked here lang?"

Head-shake. "Ma first week – you eye-ways dae the pickups?"

Joe exhaled. "Naw – jist sometimes."

Another peer. "You work behind the bar at The Matrix, dain't ye?"

Joe ground out the cigarette. "Bouncer."

Excited. Leaning forward: "Did ye ken that big guy that goat shoat on . . . ?"

Door opening. "Ah telt ye tae gie the boay a coffee, hen – no' yer life history!" Glacial voice from doorway.

Cheryl leapt off the desk. "Yes, Mrs O'Neil – ah wis jist keepin' Joe company 'til . . . "

"Ye're no' paid tae keep folk company, hen! Noo, back oot front."

"Yes, Mrs O'Neil."

Over Peggy's shoulder Joe watched the girl shuffle from the room. She grinned at him. He smiled back.

"Sorry aboot that – she's a bloody nuisance, that wan!" Peggy poured herself a coffee. "Of aw' the shoaps, we hud tae get her."

He shrugged. "Nae problem . . . she wis tellin' me aboot some guy – Pete, wis it?" He extended cigarettes.

Peggy took one. Scowl. "That big . . . ? Stupid bastard . . . ainly goat whit wis comin' tae him."

Joe picked up the lighter. "Aye . . . the fitba's no' whit it wis." He lit the cigarette for her, then looked at his new watch. "Ye said ye waanted a word?"

Sigh. "Aye . . . " She pulled out a chair and sat down. "You heard onythin' aboot redundancies?"

Joe stared. Billy didn't tell him everything. He shook his head. "Naw."

Peggy removed a shred of wet filter from her bottom lip. "That's whit ah hoped . . . ah've bin wi' Billy fae the beginnin', almost – nearly fifteen years. Ah kent his faither. Danny wid be affy proud o' whit Billy's made o' the business. That's a yooniversity education fur ye, ah suppose."

Joe looked at his new watch.

Peggy didn't notice. "He's bin guid tae me, Billy huz . . . "

Joe blinked. You an' me both.

" . . . An' ah thought he'd tell me hissel', if there wur . . . "

"Where did ye hear this stuff aboot redundancies?"

Peggy looked at the ashtray. "Aroon' . . . ye ken hoo folk talk . . . there's no smoke withoot fire, but." She met his eyes. "You're . . . close tae him, son, huz he said onythin'?"

Joe stood up. "No' a word, Peggy, but ah'll ask if . . . "

Panic. "No – dinney dae that!" Embarrassed laugh. "Ah widney waant Billy tae think ah listened tae gossip." Calmer. "Jist keep yer ears open – if ye dinney mind."

Joe laughed. "Ah'm sure ye've nothin' tae worry aboot, Peggy . . . " He looked at his new watch. " . . . Ah better be goin'."

She stood up. "Sure, sure . . . gie Billy ma regards."

He walked towards the door.

Behind. "By the way – whit happened tae yer cheek?"

He frowned. "Ah walked intae a door." It was easier than explaining.

Snort. "Ah've goat a daughter yissed tae dae that a loat."

Joe seized the handle and turned. Peggy's voice behind him:

"Walkin' intae doors aw' the time, she wis . . . 'til she left that man o' hers." Harsh laugh. "Ye'd almost think she liked it."

Joe paused, smiled. "Ah goat intae a fight at work, Peggy – okay? Happy noo?"

Another laugh. "Ah'll see ye, son."

Behind the security-door Joe waited while Cheryl fumbled beneath the counter.

Another buzz.

He pushed the door and strolled into the front shop.

On the monitor Richard and Judy were attracting a bigger crowd.

From behind: "Seeya, Joe."

He raised a hand to Cheryl and walked back out into the rain. The bank was a few doors down.

CHAPTER SIX

The Jeep took a while to clean.

Joe lifted a rag from the over-sized chrome bull-bars and stared.

A couple of streaks refused to budge.

He bent down and rubbed again, harder.

The streaks smeared, then dissolved.

Joe straightened up and stepped back.

Better.

The sound of wheels behind, echoing in the vaulted concrete carpark.

Joe turned.

A red Mercedes curved around the corner and drew up parallel with the Jeep and the Datsun.

Joe wiped his face on the boilersuit's sleeve.

An electric window slid down. "You've done a good job."

Joe walked round to the driver's side.

Billy was gathering documents from the passenger-seat. He turned. The window slid up. Billy switched off the engine.

Joe opened the car door. "Ye're early."

Billy got out.

Joe slammed the door behind him.

Billy turned. "I'm not staying . . . " He placed the sheaf of documents on the Merc's roof, then looked at his watch. " . . . Meeting Andrew at six for drinks . . . " Green eyes to Joe. " . . . That gives us about an hour – long enough, I think . . . soldier!"

Joe balled the rag in his hand and slipped it into pocket. Billy stepped forward and pushed him back against the car. Joe braced fingers against the waxed metal surface. Another groin against his, a hard prick grinding into the boilersuit's oily fabric. He groaned, nails scraping on metal.

Billy pulled away.

Joe blinked.

"Ready for kit inspection, soldier?"

Hands by sides. "Haven't had time, sir – sorry sir."
Michael's service-revolver: where was it?

Billy sighed, turned and walked towards the stairs.

Already hard, Joe lifted the documents from the car's
roof and followed . . .

In the kitchen, he peeled-off the boilersuit. Underneath, the
Tangas were twisted and slightly damp. He could feel
Billy's eyes on his back.

"Punishment-duty, soldier – you know what to do."

"Yes, sir." Joe walked through to the bedroom. He could
hear Billy's soft footsteps behind. Near the bed, his kit:

Belt: buckle cleaned and polished.

Boots: shining.

Parade gloves: washed and pressed.

White ribbon: still a little damp.

The service revolver: missing.

Joe stared.

From behind: "On the floor, soldier!"

The head of his prick pushed at the Tangas' broad
waistband as he knelt on the polished maple, arms at sides.
Behind, a drawer opening. Then closing. Then more footsteps. Circling. Joe stared at the mirrored wall.

A pair of grey-flannel clad legs strolled into his line of
vision, paused, then strolled out.

Sweat was dripping from one armpit.

"Are you sorry, soldier?"

"Yes, sir." Joe lowered his head.

"How sorry, soldier?"

A spasm in his balls. "Very sorry, sir!"

Sigh. "I left strict orders for full kit inspection, soldier."

The toe of a brogue prodded his arse. Joe closed his eyes.
Where the fuck was the revolver?

"I expect my orders to be obeyed, soldier – that's not too
much to ask, is it?"

Joe's throat burned. "No, sir – sorry sir." Words hardly
audible.

"What was that?"

"No, sir – sorry sir."

66

"That's better."

Voice behind again. "You know what to do, soldier."

"Sir." Joe raised his head, moving arms behind back, right wrist on top of left. Biceps trembled.

"That's it."

Voice in his ear. Then nylon cord bit into hard flesh. Joe's prick twitched.

Billy bound tighter, securing with a double knot.

Pounding in his ears. Then Billy's voice:

"Ready, soldier?"

Joe nodded and focused on the wall. In the distance, a muffled burr.

"Fuck!"

Joe moaned. "Lea' it, Billy!"

Sigh. "I can't . . . it might be Andrew."

A hand on his head, stroking hair.

"Hold on, Joe."

Footsteps on wooden floor.

Joe lowered his head. His balls contracted again.

The burring continued.

Joe clenched his teeth, tried to think of something else. The unwanted image of Georgie Paxton's leering face slipped into his brain. Sean . . . the red-haired kid – what was his name?

Joe concentrated.

. . . Ewan . . . Michael's service revolver . . .

Impatient voice: "Where's the mobile ended up?"

Joe blinked. "In the pocket o' ma boilersuit." He closed his eyes.

The burring stopped.

. . . Ewan . . . a stocky figure pulling at Georgie's huge arm. Angry face . . . 'that Georgie's a bad bastard' . . . two nights ago . . . Sean and Ewan alone in the lounge . . . Ewan left before Sean. When, exactly? About three . . . And Georgie died just after . . . ?

Billy's voice in distance, then nearing: "I'm sorry." Footsteps behind. Soft laugh. "Joe's . . . tied up at the moment. Who's speaking, please?"

Joe turned his head.

Billy was sitting on the bed. "Oh . . . I see . . . " He beckoned.

Joe stood up and walked over.

Billy smiled.

Joe paused inches away, knelt. Panting.

Billy's free hand grabbed the Tangas, and pulled. "No, not to my knowledge . . . "

Tight jersey wedged over hard thighs. Joe groaned as warm fingers wrapped themselves around his prick. Then began to move.

Cool voice: "I think you should have a word with Steven . . . er, Inspector Monroe, officer. I was under the impression Joe's whereabouts on the night in question had been established."

The fingers moved faster. Joe pressed head to Billy's shirt and panted harder. One side of a conversation vibrated in his ear:

"Yes . . . I see. I've really no idea . . . "

Joe nuzzled through cotton at a nipple. The fingers paused, then stroked his balls. Joe gasped:

" . . . And I suggest you talk to your senior officer before bothering me again."

The fingers stopped, tightened.

Breath caught in throat. Red flashed in his brain. Joe flinched, then fell forward against the warm body. Warm spunk splattered his stomach and Billy's fingers.

Fingers removed, then an arm around his waist, steadying. In the distance:

"Goodbye, officer."

Then both arms around him, mouth on his, warm, eager. Joe ran tongue over even teeth. Breath slowing.

Billy's hands on his chest, moving to behind back. Lowering.

The double knot checked.

Joe looked up at Billy.

He smiled.

Joe looked down at a bulging, grey-flannel covered crotch, then began to unfasten Billy's belt with his teeth . . .

Enjoying the feel of spunk-slicked hands on his shoulders, Joe stared at Billy's prick. Six inches . . . six long, slightly brownish inches. Long, like Billy's fingers . . . strong, like Billy's hands . . . demanding, like Billy . . .

The erection was curving outwards, away from the white, hairless stomach, arching towards Joe's face. He sighed, lowering mouth, and began to nuzzle Billy's balls, which were already hard and tight. Joe inhaled the smell of the man, felt the texture of the soft, silky skin against his nose and lips, felt the soft sandpaper rasp of his chin against the delicate flesh.

Above, Billy sighed.

Joe continued to nuzzle, aware of a response deep in his own body. He opened his mouth, taking first the right then the left ball, nudging them with his tongue, playing with each in turn, rolling each of Billy's testicles around his mouth. Then he began to suck.

Hands tightened on the naked skin of his shoulders.

Joe ignored the pressure of Billy's fingers, ignored the tightening in his own groin, lost himself in the task. He sucked contentedly on one ball, teasing, flicking, tasting the dimpled flesh on his tongue. Then he gently spat the saliva soaked testicle from his mouth, turned head slightly and began to service the other.

The sound of Billy's shallow breath filled the room . . . and Joe's head.

He licked the root of Billy's prick.

A gasp, then hoarse words above his head: "You know what it wants, soldier?"

Joe leant back and licked a wormy blue vein. "Yes, sir!" Billy's prick twitched against his tongue. Then a hand on the back of his head.

"It wants you, soldier . . . it wants to be in your mouth, all the way down your throat . . . "

The hand pushed gently but firmly, guiding . . . leading. Joe felt the polished wooden floor beneath his knees as he lowered his mouth onto Billy's prick.

As the fingers of one hand dug into the hard muscles of his shoulder, Joe suppressed the gag-reflex, feeling Billy's prick swim past lip-covered teeth and brush soft palate. Joe swallowed, taking Billy deeper into his mouth, wanting to please, to give pleasure . . . to consume all of the man.

Billy's hands were on the side of his face now, manoeuvring Joe's head, setting the pace, the rhythm, monitoring his pleasure.

Joe relaxed in the grip, moving when Billy moved, pausing when Billy paused. His tongue danced around the swollen organ, darting under the foreskin, dipping up and down the length. Wiry hair tickled his nose as Billy's hands moved more urgently. Breathing became difficult, Billy was all around him: sound in his ears, pressure on his head . . . prick in his mouth.

Joe began to gag. The movement drew Billy's prick further into his mouth. Balls slapped off lip-covered teeth.

Dragging the prick almost completely free of the warm, wet cavern, Billy paused . . .

Joe's body trembled.

. . . then thrust a final time, discharging spunk onto the back of Joe's throat in spasmodic, juddering movements.

Shaking hands were rigid on the side of Joe's head, pressing his face deep into damp pubic hair, obliterating everything. Joe swallowed convulsively, feeding on the warm spunk as it trickled down his throat.

His last thought as soft hands dragged him upwards for a kiss was one word . . . of five letters.

"So . . . who wis that oan the phone?" An hour later, Joe sat on the edge of the bath.

Billy rubbed shampoo into hair, then rinsed. "Some cop . . . " More rinsing. " . . . Said he took your statement, Saturday night . . . " Pale body submerged.

Joe drew on a cigarette. Handsome face, bushy eyebrows. "Hunter?"

Billy surfaced with a splash. "What?"

"Hunter . . . wis that the name?"

"I think so." Billy lifted a bottle of conditioner.

Joe smiled. "He seemed okay – wis guid wi' Sean."

Scowl. Wiping conditioner from eyes.

70

Joe held out a towel.

"Thanks . . . " Dabbing. Then: "It's a pity you had that run-in with Paxton. You know what the police are like – one and one usually make three." Soft voice. "All they need to do is type your name into the PNC – which they've probably done by this time – and they'll know it all." Submerging again.

Joe sighed, rubbed his face and scowled.

Billy resurfaced. He looked at Joe. Concern. "Hey . . . "

Joe looked at Billy. "Think they'll waant tae talk tae me again?"

Billy stood up, towel around waist. A hand on Joe's shoulder. "Don't worry . . . " Wet feet on floor. " . . . Leave the police to me. Remember, I was here with you and Sean when Paxton got what was no doubt coming to him." Rubbing hair. "The police'll not give you any trouble, Joe – I'll see to that . . . "

Billy walked to the door.

Joe pinched the cigarette out and watched him go.

Thursday night, Sean appeared.

Joe unlocked, then opened the door. Stared.

"Hi, man!" Baseball-cap the wrong way round, cheap jeans and tee-shirt, no jacket. Grin. Then: "Well, ye did volunteer . . . " Loping past him into the flat.

Joe sighed. Angie: a vague, baby-sitting arrangement. He closed and relocked the door then followed long strides into the lounge.

Sean was peering at the PC. "Did ye ask Mr King if ah kid huv a shoat on the Apple-Mac?"

Joe smiled. Another vague arrangement. "Lea' it fur now . . . "

Tapping keyboard like playing piano.

" . . . Ah'll ask when he gits back."

One last flouncing tap, then Sean turned. "Where is he the night?"

Joe walked to the sofa and sat down. "Finalisin' somethin' wi' his lawyer, ah think."

Grin. "Real high-finance stuff, eh?" Striding towards CD

71

stack.

Joe laughed. "Lucks like it." Then sobered. "It's no' aw' fun, though – Billy works hard." He watched as Sean rifled through neatly-piled CDs, then turned.

Holding out a fan of discs. "Pick wan . . . ony wan as hang as it's . . . " Mississippi card-sharp accent.

"We've no' goat ony Primal Scream!" Joe grinned.

Whoop. "Aye, you've goat Oasis, but!" Disc whisked from sheath, thrust into player.

A sub-Beatles twang filled the room.

Joe reached over, grabbed remote and lowered volume.

Sean sat cross-legged on the floor, swaying.

"So . . . " Joe lit a cigarette and leant back on the sofa.

" . . . You bin behavin' yersel'?"

Wide, innocent eyes. "Me?" Laugh.

Joe grinned. "Aye, you!"

Sean leapt up and began to wander around the room.

Joe followed with his eyes. "Ah've no' telt yer mither aboot the drugs 'cause ah don't want her tae worry – no' 'cause ah think it's okay."

Sean stopped at the PC, tapped the keyboard a couple of times, then wandered on. Grinning.

"It's no' a joke – ah seen guys in the airmy oan drugs, Sean . . . fucked-up guys . . . "

Humming now.

Joe ignored it. " . . . Guys wi' thur brains fried."

Humming louder. Sean paused at the side of the sofa.

Joe stared. "Mebbe it ainly starts wi' eccy, but . . . "

Laughing. "Ah telt ye Setterday, Joe: ah'm no' intae drugs." Sobering. "That stuff Georgie sold us wis shite!" Perching on sofa arm.

Joe smiled. "They're aw' shite – yer better aff withoot drugs, Sean."

A strand of blond hair sucked thoughtfully. "Whit dae ye think happened, Joe?"

"Whit?"

"Georgie: who dae ye think shoat him?" Trainered heels drummed against beige leather.

"Stoap that!"

The drumming stopped. Strand of hair removed from mouth. "Well?"

Joe sighed. The change of subject wasn't welcome. "Ah've no' idea . . . "

"They thoaght it wis you, Joe, the polis – didn't they?"

Joe stood up. "Well, you ken where ah wis when it happened." He paused. "Ewan go straight home efter he left here?"

Shrug. "Suppose so . . . " Eyes widening. "Ye don't think . . . ?"

Joe stared at the slim boy. "He's your mate, wid he dae onythin' like . . . ?"

Snort. "No goat the bottle, man – oar a gun." Pause. "Ah ken he wis annoyed wi' Georgie an' aw' but he widney . . ." Words fading out.

Joe walked towards an ashtray, ground out cigarette. "Ah dinny want tae talk aboot aw' that onyway, Sean. Jist lissen: keep away fae The Matrix, eh? Billy could lose his licence if the polis catch ye there."

Nodding. "Sure Joe, sure." Grin, then backwards flip onto sofa. "Can ah no' huv a wee go oan the Apple-Mac? Ah ken whit ah'm daein' – the school's goat wan. Ah'll no' break it, honest!" Bouncing upright from sofa.

Joe laughed. "Kin ye no' sit still?"

Grin. "Naw . . . ah like tae keep movin'." Sean seized Joe's arm. "Tell me aboot the airmy – ye said ye'd tell me mair."

Smiling, Joe pushed Sean away and walked through to the kitchen.

Three hours later they were still talking. On the table, five empty Caledonian Clear bottles. And Sean's elbows.

Pink face clasped between two large palms. "Whit's it called?"

Joe drained a sixth bottle and leant back in the chair. "Beasting. Everywan gits it." He sat the empty bottle with the other five.

"How?" Curious. Finally still.

Joe smiled. "'San airmy thing. Toughens ye up."

Eyes widening. "Did they dae it tae you, Joe?"

He nodded. Seven years ago and he still remembered.

"Whit did they dae?" Entranced.

Joe closed his eyes. The last day of two weeks basic training. Body too tired to go out drinking. Early night. Brain too wound-up to sleep: too tense to wank. Dozing in and out of dreams. Then the sound of a door opening, heavy boots and drunken voices. Three sets of strong arms pulling him from bed into shower-block, turning on faucet, holding him there, soaping his body. When he was fully awake, soaking and lathered, a razor produced.

Three sets of arms held him down on a tiled floor while a none-too skilled hand got to know his body in a way no other man had . . .

. . . since Michael.

The process took two hours.

Joe smiled at the memory, opened his eyes.

Sean raised eyebrows. "Well?"

Joe laughed. "A boady-joab!"

Confused. "Whit?"

"They shaved me!" Joe rubbed a hairy forearm at the memory.

The hair had taken six months to grow back.

A year later he'd done it himself: body-hair only.

Snort. "That disney sound too bad – ah thoaght ye wur gonny say they beat ye up oar somethin'".

Joe grinned. "Yer missin' the point, Sean. They did it to me, an' ah let them – it's the airmy's way." He stared into blue pools of confusion and disappointment.

"An' did it . . . toughen ye up?"

Joe fingered cigarette packet. "Aye . . . in a way it did."

In a way, they'd done him a favour.

Joe stood up and walked to the fridge. As he opened the door, another opened in the distance.

Sean leapt up. Hissed words. "Ask him noo, Joe – ask him aboot the Apple-Mac."

Joe shut the fridge. "Ask him yersel'!"

Seconds later Billy's tired face appeared in the doorway. Grin to Joe, tight smile to Sean. "Fancy seeing you here!"

Grin. "Hi, Mr King." Eyes to Joe then Billy. Throat clearing. "Er . . . Mr King: see how ye've goat that Apple-Mac . . ."

Joe grinned and slung an arm around nervous shoulders.

CHAPTER SEVEN

Just another Saturday night.

Joe leant an elbow on the cloakroom's counter and lit a cigarette. He looked at Gina.

She was eating sweeties, trying to give up the fags again. Crunch. Frown. "The polis phoned me up, Tuesday." Crunch. Crunch.

Joe exhaled. "Whit did they waant?"

Cough. Hand wafting cigarette smoke away, then into paper bag. Another sweetie into red mouth. Crunching. "Said it wis tae see if ah'd remembered onythin' else – 'boot last Saturday." Crunch. Frown.

"They phoned me tae." He stared past Gina at the rows of coats and jackets.

Relief. "They did?" Laugh. "Ah wis gettin' worried!"

"They hud Malkie up there at the polis station, Wednesday."

Quizzical. Another crunch.

"Says the polis waanted tae ken whit kin' o' company Georgie kep' ootside work, friends an' that."

Another laugh. "Ah didney think he hud ony friends." Crunch. "Did ye ever meet his wife . . . " Thoughtful. " . . . Whit wis hur name?"

Joe shook his head.

"Nice wuman . . . " Sober crunch. " . . . Yissed tae work behind the bar before your time, Joe." Crunch, then swallow. "Ah feel affy soarry fur her." Hand into paper bag. Another sweetie. Further crunching.

Joe ground out the cigarette in Gina's clean ashtray. He didn't want to think about Georgie. "You workin' Christmas?"

"Aye . . . " Laugh. " . . . Ah need the money. You?"

Joe nodded. He didn't.

She held out the paper-bag.

Joe shook his head.

She shrugged, took another sweetie.

Joe watched as she sucked thoughtfully. Then:

76

"No sign o' him the night, then?"

"Who?"

"Angie's boay."

Joe smiled. "Sean's goat himsel' a joab baby-sittin' the night – an auld wuman up the stairs fae them, the daughter's away tae the Bingo."

She laughed. "That'll keep him oota trouble . . . "

Joe laughed and lit another cigarette. He watched Gina watch the ritual.

Longing. Glazing at the curling smoke. "Whit ah widney dae fur . . . "

"Come oan – ye canny gie in noo, Gina."

Sigh. Hand into paper-bag. "Ah suppose not." Crunching. Pause, then: "So . . . huv ye pit yer money in fur the wreath? Funeral's oan Friday, ah hear."

Joe nodded.

"Davie sez Mr King's makin' up the difference fur a guid wan – an' a wee somethin' fur . . . " Frown. " . . . Whit is that wuman's name?"

Sound of loud music behind. Joe turned.

Back view of bare back, topped by helmet-cut red hair as the door to the dance-floor reclosed.

Joe stared. The Ewan-kid. Actually was eighteen – he'd checked with Angie.

The door reopened. More noise.

A group of boys swayed towards him. Bobble hats, two bare-chested, one in leather jacket. Others in sweaty tee-shirts. They paused outside the toilets. Three went in. One waited by the door. The other swayed on up to the cloakroom.

Joe turned back to Gina.

Frown, words through crunching: "Wait for it, man – the first loast ticket o' the night."

"Er . . . look . . . er, I've canny find ma . . . " A deep resonance.

Something in the voice. Joe turned.

Behind, Gina. Practiced patience: "Sorry, pal – ah canny gie oot ony jaickets withoot tickets. Ye'll huv tae wait 'til the end." Crunch.

Joe stared. The smell of menthol rose from the figure in waves. Tears streamed down pink, shiny cheeks: the vapour-rub was doing its job. Eyes red and blinking under black bushy eyebrows. Bobble hat pulled tight over ears.

An almost-classical face peered back.

Joe continued to stare.

Older than the others. Hairless, sweat-soaked chest. A silver 'Ban-the-Bomb' sign dangled between remarkably well-developed pecs. The figure blinked, then grinned. Perfect teeth. "Hey, man? Gonny lend us ten pee?" Accent not quite right.

Toilet door opened. Voices: "C'moan, Andy – we're goin' back in."

Four boys waited.

Joe turned to walk away. PC Hunter was virtually un-recognisable out of uniform. But off-duty or not, he was still polis.

Behind: "Hold on – ah'll be in in a minute, Danny." Then hand on his arm. Loud. "Gie us ten pee . . . " Hiss. " . . . It's Joe, isn't it? A word . . . " The hand removed. Andy Hunter walked towards the public telephone.

Joe followed, hands into pockets. Finding ten pence piece.

Behind, the door opened. Sound poured into the foyer, then drained away.

By the telephone, Andy turned, wiping eyes with a muscly forearm. Low voice. "Christ! How can they stand this?"

Joe stared. Billy's words: 'Leave the police to me . . . ' He backed away.

Low voice: "Look: I thought you ought to know. That kid's in again tonight . . . "

Joe stared.

" . . . Your . . . nephew, isn't it? Blond kid in a 'Raiders' cap, nose stud?"

Joe stepped forward. "Sean's at hame . . . "

"No, he's down the front near the stage, with a group of girls. Get him outta here . . . " Eyes on wrist. " . . . You've got about fifteen minutes." Wiping face with bobble-hat. "I'll explain later." Bobble hat back on head. Loud voice.

78

"Ya mean bastard! Away an' fuck yersel'!" He ran off towards the dance-floor.

Joe waited until his heart had slowed a little, ground out cigarette under foot, then followed.

The dance-floor was shrouded in a thick fog of dry-ice and semi-condensed sweat. The noise no longer registered. Joe walked down to the front and peered over twelve hundred bobbing heads.

Fuckin' Sean.

His fists balled. Joe plunged into the dancing sea . . .

. . . eight base-ball caps later his Matrix tee-shirt was soaking. It stuck to his body, a wet jersey shadow.

A dark-haired couple collided with him, grinned, then backed away.

Joe began to look for red-hair. He scowled – should've known better: if Ewan was here . . .

He struggled through heaving bodies to just in front of the stage. His eyes stung as he scanned the crowd.

Nothing . . . then . . .

. . . something? Joe lowered his gaze.

In the corner, sitting on the floor . . .

Joe walked over, grabbed a skinny arm and hauled Sean to his feet.

Dancers would've scattered, had there been room to do so. Joe clenched his teeth and pushed the resisting figure through a wall of teenagers, off the dance-floor and out towards the staff entrance.

In the fire exit his ears popped as silence and low thumping throbbed in his head. Protests from in front became audible:

"Man, ah've left ma jaicket back there . . . "

Joe fumbled one-handed for a key, unlocked the door.

Sean was struggling like a puppy: "Haud oan, man . . . "

Joe pressed the push-bar. Anger filled his mind. He let go the arm and turned.

Sean rubbed bruised flesh, looked up.

Joe stared into a pink sweating face. "Get oot . . . " He moved away from the doorway.

Open mouth, then: "It's pourin', man . . . "

Joe stuck hand into pocket. He thrust keys towards the boy. "Go back tae the flat an' wait . . . me an' you need tae talk." He pushed a protesting Sean out into the rain then pulled and locked the door behind him.

As he turned to walk back to the dance-floor, twenty kilowatts of sound cut out.

Joe looked at his watch – 1.15am – and walked on. Through the door's safety-glass bright-lights became visible. Then an amplified voice. Low, resonant tones, English accent:

"Can I have your attention, please . . . ?"

Joe sighed and walked on past the door to the dance-floor, along the corridor leading to the foyer. A fuckin' raid . . .

Two hours later an army of uniformed officers were still searching the toilets.

The foyer was a shanty town of unkempt, shuffling kids. Joe patrolled the queue of pale, worried faces who waited to be questioned. As far as he knew, no drugs had been found . . . yet. He paused, looked across the foyer.

Gina was methodically handing coat after coat across the cloakroom counter to three of the men who had accompanied PC Hunter earlier. A cigarette dangled from a red bottom lip. Voice at his side:

"How lang we liable tae be here, man?"

Joe turned.

The red-head, arm round the shoulder of a panic-stricken blonde girl. She began to whine: "What dae they need ur names fur, mister? Ma maw disney ken ah'm here."

Joe shrugged. What were the police going to do with twelve hundred names and addresses? He lowered his voice. "Goat onythin oan ye, Ewan?"

"Naw . . . " A white cap bore the legend No Fear.

"Then ye've nothin' tae worry aboot." Joe turned to walk on.

Hand pulling his arm. Frightened. "Sean wis carrying man . . . ye see him onywhere?"

Joe scowled and walked on. In front, he could see Davie

the manager, ashen-faced, talking to Malkie. Joe walked over: "How lang is this gonny take? The natives ur gettin' restless."

Davie frowned. "Fuck knows! Ah'm tryin' tae reach Mr King, Joe – ken where he is the night?"

"Should be at the flat . . . or mebbe oan his way here – ye tried the car-phone?" Maybe he was running Sean home . . .

Frantic nod. "Christ! He's gonny go daft if he walks in oan this." Eyes flicking over Joe's shoulder: "Er, officer? Kin ah huv a wee word?" He walked with quick, small steps towards a group of uniforms.

Joe looked at Malkie. "They fun' onythin'?" Hands into pockets.

Scowl. "Wan o' the drug-squad goat offered a joint in the bogs. The kid's ootside in the van." Eyes scanning the crowded foyer. Head shaking. "Aw' this fur a wee bitta dope . . ."

Last Saturday it had been sulph and eccy. Maybe it was only dope tonight . . . Neither the police nor the licencing-board made fine distinctions. Joe found his cigarettes, extended them to Malkie.

He took one.

Joe lit both.

Angry voice behind: "Come oan, Hunter . . . oota the way!"

"Sir!" Resonant voice.

Then Malkie: "Oi, yous . . . "

Joe watched a group of kids begin to wander away from the orderly queue. Malkie moved forwards, herding.

Voice in his ear. "You got your nephew out, I take it?"

Joe turned. No bobble hat, eyes still red and sore-looking. Pecs semi-hidden by black leather bikers' jacket. He frowned. "Aye . . . thanks fur the tip-aff."

Andy Hunter patted pocketless sweat-pants, then hands into jacket pockets. He looked at Joe's cigarette.

Joe extended the packet.

"Thanks . . . " He took one.

Joe lit it for him. The Zippo flared in the handsome face. Andy Hunter inhaled gratefully. A flash of guilt

81

narrowed the brown eyes. The cigarette cupped, semi-hidden by long fingers.

Joe grinned. "Should you no' be takin' statements or somethin'?"

Large hand rubbing eyes. "Off duty, now . . . I've done my bit for tonight . . . " Frown. " . . . But it's the last time I volunteer for undercover work – and damn the promotion prospects." Drawing on cigarette. "How do you stand that level of noise, night after night?"

"Ye git yissed tae it."

Hand through spiked hair. "Look: is there anywhere quieter we can go?"

Joe tensed. Billy's words: 'Leave the police to me . . . '

Hand moved down, palm against ear. "How long before the ringing stops?"

Joe relaxed.

Off-duty.

He looked at Davie's office . . . then spotted Davie disappearing towards the upstairs bar. "C'moan . . . " He led the way to the door marked Manager.

"So . . . " Joe held out a glass of whisky. "Get much o' a haul, then?" He looked towards the half-open door. Raised voices.

Andy Hunter took the glass, sipped. "Waste of time, really . . . " He frowned. "Orders from above, though – you know how it is . "

Joe blinked. He knew. "Whit happens noo?"

Sigh. "We get all their names and check them, then continue with the search until Sergeant Anderson decides otherwise – the two with the dope'll probably get a caution." Laugh. "Possession's not what the big white chief's after . . ." Brown eyes began to water. Sniffing. "Shit!"

Joe smiled.

"That bloody Vick!" Large white handkerchief produced from pocket. Nose blown. "Thought it was meant to help colds, not bring one on."

Joe laughed. "Only if ye rub it oan yer chest – no' under yer eyes!" The aromatic balsam was employed to heighten lightshows.

Wide mouth laughing through tears.

Joe lit a cigarette.

Silence, then: "You're a hard man to get hold of, Joe."

Joe bit the filter.

"I phoned a couple of times, but you never seem to be in." Pause. Glass to lips, then: "Royal Engineers, wasn't it?" Casual, friendly.

Joe gazed at the whisky-glass. Billy had been right. It would all be there on the PNC . . . Hamburg, Colchester, the dishonourable discharge.

"See much action?"

"A bit." Joe stared the row of tiny indentations which circled the glass an inch below the rim. He waited.

"Any chance?" The glass moved out of sight.

Joe looked up.

A leather-clad arm outstretched, hand in tilting motion.

Joe lifted the bottle of whisky and poured.

"Thanks." Then quizzical: "You not havin' one?"

Joe put down the bottle. It would all be there in his record. "No."

Smile. "Thought you squaddies all drank like fish!" Glass to lips.

"No' these days." He drew on the cigarette and looked at the floor.

"Must've been a good life." Envy.

Joe shuffled his feet.

"The instructor up at Stewart Street's ex-army."

Sweat was prickling on his chest. Joe sighed.

Andy Hunter talked on. " . . . He's a hard bastard to please."

Joe raised his eyes.

Face flushed from the whisky. "There's an opening coming up after Christmas, in one of the ARV units."

Joe stared. Armed Response Vehicles.

Low voice. "Sideways promotion I know, but I'd really like to get it. My scores to date haven't been too bad, but I'll really need to impress them."

Joe removed a fragment of filter from bottom lip.

"You kept up your fire-arm skills?"

Joe sighed. He had been quite good, once. But since Hamburg . . . "Ah'm a bit rusty."

Laugh. "You must be better than me – you with a gun-club?"

Joe shook his head. If Andy Hunter had looked at his record, he'd know . . .

"Bishopriggs have a good one – fancy givin' me some tips sometime?"

No way.

Sounds of sipping, then silence gulfed between them.

No way. Joe sighed. Or . . . ?

Sean: now safely out of harm's way. Thanks to a cop.

One good turn? Joe blinked.

"They're a good crowd . . . " Laugh. " . . . Not all cops. Businessmen, and the like."

Joe stared at the almost-classical face.

"If you're interested, I'll sign you in." Casual.

Billy.

The polis.

Sean . . .

One good turn.

"How about it?"

Joe stubbed out cigarette. "Maybe . . . " What harm could it do?

Grin. "Great . . . how's this week suit you?"

A sound behind.

Joe looked up.

From the doorway, cold green eyes flickered behind steel-rims.

Joe smiled. "They found ye, then . . . "

Billy turned away, closing the door behind him.

Joe looked at Andy Hunter. "That's the boss arrived. Ah'll huv tae go."

The tall man stood up. "Me too . . . " Eyes to wrist. "Christ! I'm on early."

Joe laughed. "No rest fur the wicked, eh?"

Andy smiled. "Something like that." Zipping up jacket. "I'll give you a ring during the week."

Something made Joe hesitate. "Mornin's ur best. Mair chance ye'll catch me."

Nod. "Thanks for the drink." Walking to door. "Bye . . . "

Joe watched as the man strode from the office. He ran a hand over his face, then went to find Billy.

CHAPTER EIGHT

At four am Joe turned off Argyll Street and into Glassford Street.

Pre-Christmas shop-windows glinted in the rain.

Joe sighed. He'd eventually spotted Billy engrossed in conversation with a burly guy in a blouson jacket – another plain-clothed cop, presumably.

On the corner of Glassford and Ingram Street he paused at traffic-lights. The red man shone through a haze.

Then some kid had passed out, and by the time Joe and Malkie had got her into the office and brought her round, Billy had vanished again.

The red man changed to green.

He crossed Ingram Street and walked towards the Italina Centre.

The police had eventually left . . .

Joe glanced at his watch.

. . . About fifteen minutes ago. He'd seen Billy again, briefly, across the foyer. A swift glance, then no recognition.

Joe smiled, a hand into pocket for keys.

Billy was discreet. At work, it was boss and employee.

Joe grinned. Like always. Then scowled, hands deeper into pockets.

Where were his fuckin' keys?

Joe sighed.

Sean . . .

He walked up to the security-gate and pressed 3/1.

No answer. Rain dribbled over one ear.

Joe pressed again. Twice.

Nothing . . . then: "Yes?"

Mouth to the speaker: "It's me, Billy . . . "

Buzzing interrupted his explanation. The lock clicked.

Joe pushed open the gate and walked into the courtyard. As he passed the fountain, more buzzing ahead. The controlled-entry door swung open. He jogged up three flights of stairs. As he turned onto the top landing, he could see a triangle of light from an open doorway. He walked towards it.

In the kitchen Billy was sitting at the table, reading. He didn't look up.

Joe took off a soaking jacket. "Sean get hame okay?"

Billy didn't answer.

Joe began to undo shirt buttons, then walked into the bathroom. He grabbed a towel, rubbing hair.

Footsteps behind.

Joe stopped rubbing, looked up.

Billy stood in the doorway.

Joe grinned. "Where did you git tae?" Then sobered. "The raid'll no' affect yer Christmas licence, wull it? Ah mean, they didn't fun' whit they wur efter."

"Did your friend tell you that?" Billy stared.

Joe raised an eyebrow. "Who?"

Billy stared. "Angel-face."

Joe hung the wet towel over a rail and sat down on the side of the bath. He began to undo Docs. "Oh, Andy?"

Soft laugh. "That his name, is it?"

Joe fumbled with a lace. "Aye – Andy Hunter, 'member? He said he phoned here . . . " A smile twitched his mouth. " . . . Wis goin' oan aboot some posh gun-club . . . "

"Are you interested, Joe?"

Voice above him. Joe looked up. One good turn? He frowned. "Ah'm a bit oota practice masel', but ah kid eye-ways . . . "

"That's not what I mean."

Joe stared. Billy's expression was hard to read.

"Are you interested in Angel-face?"

Joe stood up. "Whit?"

Cool smile. "You heard, Joe . . . You certainly interest him."

"Ach, away!" Joe pulled off Docs. "He wis jist bein' friendly. He's an okay guy . . . " He looked up at Billy. " . . . Fur polis. Did me a favour."

Did you a favour.

One good turn?

Sean: Underage and in possession of E.

Definite grounds for licence review.

Cold laugh. "And what might that have been?"

Joe walked towards the doorway. Billy's voice behind him:
"Don't turn your back on me, soldier!"

Heat filled Joe's face. Inside Tangas his prick stirred.

Not now . . . He paused. "Drap it, Billy – okay?" He
walked from the bathroom.

Billy followed.

Back in the kitchen, Joe switched on the kettle. A soft
laugh behind:

"You'd look good together, you and Angel-face – I'll give
you that, Joe. Two hard bodies." Frozen smile. "Bet he
fucks like a . . . "

"Shut up, Billy!" Joe spun round. "Ah couldny gie a toss
aboot Andy Hunter." Rage flashed in his head. "Ah'll no'
go tae the fuckin' gun-club wi' him if ye dinney . . . "

"Oh? He's invited you out, then?"

Joe frowned. "Ah'll no' go, if it'll make ye happy . . . "

"Oh, it's what would make you happy that counts, Joe."
Amused smile.

Joe blinked. "Ah don't need onywan else Billy – ye ken
that . . . "

Hard voice: "Tell me more about this . . . favour."

Joe clenched his teeth. "Lea' it, Billy . . . it wis nothin' . . ."

Cold, angry voice. "Oh, but I think it was . . . " Knocking
sound, then key-sounds . . . then door opening. Billy
turned. "What the fuck . . . ?" Joe stared as a wet head
appeared at the end of the hall.

Unsure: "Er . . . hi . . . " Deferential. " . . . Mr King . . . "
Back to Joe. "Jist returnin' yer keys, man." Dripping hand
outstretched.

Billy looked at Joe. Glacial green eyes. "What's he talking
about?"

Joe sighed. "Ah'll tell ye later, Billy . . . "

Frosted anger. "You'll tell me now!" He walked towards
Sean. "Where did you get these?"

Joe watched as Billy grabbed the keys from Sean's hand.
"Ah gave them tae him."

"You did what?" Billy turned slowly.

Behind, Sean was shivering.

Flashing eyes pinned Joe to the spot. He stared.

Billy walked towards him, swinging the key-ring. "You never do that, okay? This is my home – my keys." Icicles for words. He stopped inches away. "Christ knows who might have got their hands on them."

"Ah widney gie them tae onywan, Mr King – oanest!" Earnest words from Sean.

"Shut it, you!" Cold, myopic eyes continued to stare at Joe.

Sean flinched.

"Hey, go easy oan him, Billy – it wis ma fault." Joe rubbed his face. "But there's nae harm done. Let me gie the boay a len' o' a jaicket an' he'll be aff . . . "

Snort. "Keys, jackets . . . what next, Joe?" Mirthless laugh. "Let's make up the spare bed and he can move in! Christ, he spends more time here than I do."

Joe flinched. "Ah thought ye didney mind . . . "

Explosion. "Well, I do fuckin' mind!" Green eyes shining. "Everywhere I turn, there he is."

Joe sighed. "Ye should've telt me . . . "

"Told you what – that I'm not running a home for every waif and stray in Glasgow?" Snort. "Just because I gave you a bed doesn't mean the offer is open to the rest of your family."

"Calm doon, Billy . . . "

"Ah'll jist be aff then . . . " Tentative words from behind.

"Wait in the other room, Sean!" Joe looked at Billy. "Kin we no' talk aboot this later?"

Acid. "Get out, Sean . . . and I don't want to see you here again, understand?"

Quiet voice. "Sure, Mr King . . . sorry aboot . . . er . . . " Words tailing off.

Joe walked past Billy towards the cowering figure. He lifted a denim and a leather jacket from the coat-stand, handed the denim to Sean. Then turned. "Mebbe ah should go too." He stared into emotionless eyes.

The stare returned.

Both men stood silently. Minutes passed.

Then a sigh. Joe watched as Billy's expression began to change. Something unreadable flitted across the once-angry face, something new. Then a half-smile.

Billy walked towards Joe. "I'm sorry . . . " He removed steel-rimmed glasses and rubbed eyes. "That fuckin' raid . . . it's the last thing I need." Head down.

"Ah ken . . . " Joe patted a thin shoulder, then turned to Sean: "Away an make some coffee . . . "

"Sure, man." Relieved.

Joe watched Sean slip past into the kitchen, then looked at Billy.

Ahead, the sound of a door closing.

Joe kneaded a hard shoulder, feeling taut sinew beneath the cotton. He continued to knead.

Eventually muscle began to relax. After a couple of minutes, Billy pulled away. Glasses back on. "Get Sean something dry to wear, then get him home – his mother'll be worried." Head raised.

Joe ran a hand through the fine blond hair, nodded.

"Oh, and tell him I didn't mean it . . . " Sigh. " . . . He's always welcome here – okay, Joe?"

Joe smiled. "Sure." Then frowned. "You get aff tae bed ye look done-in."

The half-smile again. "Yes, sir." A parody salute. Billy strolled off towards the bedroom.

Joe stared after him, then walked into the kitchen.

A warm body pushed against him. Hands over his stomach.

Joe blinked, immediately awake. He pushed back.

A prick nestled between his buttocks.

Joe sighed.

The hands moved to waist, tightening. Billy's erection dragged up and down arse-crack.

Joe bit bottom lip and closed his eyes. Then a hand on his prick. He opened his eyes, turned, disrupting the S shape. He pulled the warm body to him and kissed Billy's neck. "Whit's the occasion?"

The hand was stroking his arse. "Mmm?"

Joe licked an ear. "Ah kin count oan wan haun the number o' times ah've woken up wi' you still here!" He yawned, stretched.

90

Soft laugh. "A real treat for you, then."

The hand cupped one cheek. Joe moaned. He knew he should say something. "Look, Billy . . . aboot last night . . . "

Laugh. "You sound like Celia Johnson!"

Joe frowned. "Who?" Two hands cupped two cheeks. His prick twitched. "Look: ah ken ah wis oota line, giein' Sean the . . . "

"Forget it, Joe." Fingers moving down from arse.

Joe opened his legs.

A wrist rubbed thighs.

The fingers moved on, and up to his balls. Joe clasped hands around Billy's neck and leant back, allowing access.

Billy was stroking the ball-sac now, rubbing a tightening testicle between thumb and forefinger.

Joe sighed as the pressure increased, as the thumb and forefinger became a ring which began to move over the length of his twitching prick. His arse-hole contracted in a shiver of pleasure as Billy's forefinger broke the ring to stroke the head of his prick, rub the sensitive rim of flesh just beneath the head, teasing the foreskin. Joe arched his back, thrusting his prick forward into Billy's hand.

. . . Then a thumb, circling his anus.

Joe closed his eyes as another ring began to spasm uncontrollably . . .

. . . Four hours later he ran a warm sponge over pecs. Hand to the shower-control, he turned up the pressure. Hot jets of steaming water coursed over shoulders. Soothing . . . then stinging. Joe paused, fingers to neck. He pressed, winced.

Billy had broken the skin.

Joe traced two jagged marks and continued to wash.

When he could bear the temperature no longer he switched off the shower and grabbed a towel.

At the sink he wiped steam from the mirror, and stared.

Glowing skin stared back, matching the area around a thin, red scar.

Joe ran hand over chin, frowning. A shave . . . He reached up for a Bic, hand brushing a smoked-glass bottle. He paused.

91

Oddfellows.

He seized the cologne and peered at the label.

'88'.

Joe smiled. No wonder he could never remember the fuckin' name.

No name. Just a number.

Joe frowned. Like he had been . . .

Like Michael had been . . .

Joe removed the bottle's gold-coloured top and sniffed.

The familiar smell filled his nostrils. Memories beyond Billy seeped into his mind . . .

Childhood memories . . .

Bags of chalky sweets. Sitting on Michael's knee, his mother's half-reprimand:

'You'll ruin his teeth.'

Michael biting the sweet, giving half to Joe . . .

He replaced the lid on the cologne and sat the bottle back on the shelf.

Michael Macdonald. Eight years older. Always there for him.

– at six, when Joe had been beaten-up by three eight year-olds.

– at seven, when he had drunk half a bottle of whisky and his father had given him a leathering.

– at eight, when he'd run away from home.

– at nine, when their father died . . .

– at ten, when life hadn't seemed worth living.

Joe sat down on the edge of the bath. Sweat dripped from forehead onto face. He let it trickle down into eyes.

Sitting with Michael . . . talking . . . Michael understanding in a way no-one else did. Wrestling with Michael . . . sleeping with Michael when Joe was too scared to sleep alone . . . Michael's arms around him . . . Michael's strong arms holding him . . . strong hands brushing away the tears . . . then a warm mouth kissing them away, kissing everything away . . .

Joe sighed, drunk with memory.

Michael's hands exploring Joe's body, then Michael's hands on Joe's hands, showing him how to explore his and

92

Joe's own body . . . pleasure-giving hands, warm hands, reassuring hands . . . loving hands.

Joe smiled, remembering long months of sensation, of learning, of loving . . .

. . . Michael had packed-in the buses and signed up the following year. Royal Engineers.

Joe smiled. Different battalion, same uniform.

A sixteen-year man: good wages.

Michael and Angie married the same year. Angie already pregnant.

Two families to support now: a sixteen-year man.

After ten Michael was dead. Car-bomb. Cyprus. Off-duty at the time. An army technicality: no compensation due.

Joe sighed. At the time he had been nine-hundred miles away in Germany.

Michael had always been there for him.

He hadn't been there for Michael, when it mattered.

Angie wouldn't let him be there for her . . .

Joe clenched his fists.

. . . But he would be there for Sean. Joe stood up, dried himself briskly, then walked back to the bedroom and dressed.

Fifteen minutes later he was on a bus to Springburn.

Petershill Road was slick with rain. Joe peered out through smeary glass. Sunday afternoon. Quiet.

The bus slowed.

Joe got up and walked past the three other passengers.

The bus stopped.

Joe got off.

The bus drew away.

In a wake of spray, Joe looked across the road.

A group of women in slippers and headscarves queued at solitary ice-cream van parked at the pavement's edge. He smiled.

It never left – it didn't need to: the nearest shop was half a mile away, and closed early.

Joe glanced at a white, pebble-dashed cube which sat alone, a little from the road. On the pub's back wall, two grafittied words:

'Dirty Grasses.'

Joe raised his eyes.

Above, two fingers of twin towers poked up thirty-five floors into a grey sky. The Red Road flats had once been the highest in Europe. Three years ago, somewhere in Hungary had robbed them of the title.

Joe stared into the sky.

Built for families, in the sixties . . . some planner's idea of a joke. Ten years ago the families had moved out, the twin-blocks sold off to developers. Now . . . ?

Joe rubbed rain from his eyes.

One block housed the Glasgow YMCA, the other – Red Road Court – was privately rented to students, nurses, single people.

Joe sighed. His mother hadn't been pleased, when Angie had moved from the family home to here:

'No place tae bring up a kid . . . '

Michael had been dead a year. Sean had been ten.

His mother had been right.

But Angie had moved just the same. Joe knew why.

His mother's Shettleston flat had become a shrine to Michael – her firstborn – dead at thirty-four.

It had stayed that way until she herself had died, last year.

'No place tae bring up a kid . . . '

The ice-cream van's chimes ground into life.

Joe blinked and crossed the road.

An out-of-sync 'Greensleeves' tinkled drunkenly in his ears as he walked through the empty car-park towards the block's controlled entry. He smiled.

Two extremes: the inhabitants of both the Italina Centre and Red Road Court valued their privacy.

Joe pressed 31/3.

A crackle.

He pressed again, twice.

More crackling. Wind whistled down the intercom, then: "Aye?" Electronic-voice, sexless.

Joe frowned. "Sean?"

Suspicious: "Who wants tae ken?"

"It's me, Sean – buzz us up, eh?"

Relaxing: "Sure . . . " Crackling laugh. "The lift's still gettin' serviced, mind!"

Buzzing.

Joe sighed, pushed the door open and walked towards concrete stairs.

As he climbed, Glasgow shrank into toytown below him.

As he climbed, he counted.

On step four hundred and thirteen Joe pushed open the landing door and strode towards Flat Three. Knocked.

The door opened. Puffy face, rubbing sleep from red eyes. Baseball-cap the wrong way round. Twinkling nose-stud. Bare legs. Eternal sweatshirt, the embroidered 'l' semi-unravelled. "Hi, man." Sean stepped back, hugging the door. "Ye made it, then." Grin.

"Ever take that thing aff?" Joe gestured to the cap.

Sean laughed. "Ma hair's a mess."

Joe walked past him into the flat. "Yer mither in?"

Door closing behind him. "No' yet . . . " Yawn. "Whit time is it, onyway?"

Joe glanced at his watch. "Nearly two."

Sean breezed past. "Eight 'til four shift, the day." Opening door ahead. "Waant a coffee?"

"Aye." Joe followed the loping figure down the narrow hallway into the lounge.

CHAPTER NINE

The room was unnaturally cold, damp-feeling. A pair of still wet trainers sat in front of the one-bar electric fire.

Sounds of running water from the kitchen, then dish-clatter. Joe lifted three empty tape boxes from the sofa and sat down. He looked around.

Reasonably tidy . . . for once.

A personal stereo, Sellotape holding the back in place, lay on the floor beside a cheap ghetto-blaster. Over the back of the battered sofa a pile of clean, but unironed washing.

Joe turned to the inert one-bar fire and switched it on. Above, on the chipped tile mantle, two framed photographs. He picked up the larger.

Sean. Taken last year, before the nose-stud. Shirt and school tie. Uncomfortable-looking. Blond hair slightly shorter. Eyes defiant. Grinning.

Joe smiled and replaced it, picking up the smaller photograph. His heart swelled.

Family group. Taken six years ago. Michael in uniform, one arm around a beaming Angie, the other on the head of a nine year-old boy. The same grin.

Joe smiled, then scowled. Not a boy anymore. Into E and Christ knows what else . . .

From the kitchen sounds of a radio blared into life, then voice over noise: "It'll huv tae be black, Joe – nae milk!"

He stood up, still holding the photograph. "Ah'll nip doon tae the van." He placed it back with the other.

"Eh?"

Joe raise his voice. "Ah said ah'll go doon tae the . . . "

"Don't boather – they never huv ony oan a Sunday." Blond head in doorway. "Ma maw'll bring some in wi' her." The head disappeared. Then shout: "Waant some toast?"

"Naw." Joe walked into the small kitchen. He looked around, sighed. The mess was in here. Three black bin-bags of rubbish leant precariously against the balcony door. An empty milk carton lay amidst a sea of Kit-Kat wrappers.

The floor was wet. Joe sniffed . . . then scowled. He stared towards the ancient cooker.

Sean was pouring hot water into two mugs and turning three slices of blackening bread, all while twitching to deafening music.

Joe switched the radio off.

Sean stopped twitching.

Joe frowned, looked at the brimming sink and other debris.

"We'll huv tae clear aw' this up afore yer mither . . . "

"Ah'll dae it later, Joe." Wave of hand. Crouching to open fridge door. Low voice: "Fuck . . . ah hate dry toast." Bobbing up, turning. A smile.

Joe didn't smile back. "We need tae talk."

The smile wavered. Sean seized the mugs, handed one to Joe. He grabbed a piece of toast and began chewing. "Whit ye wanna talk aboot?" Crumbs wiped from mouth.

Joe sighed. "Don't act it, Sean – ye ken fine well."

Head down, walking towards the door.

Joe followed him into the lounge. "Where is it, then?"

Eyes raised. Blue pools stared, all innocence.

Joe returned the stare, added knowing. "Ah wis talkin' tae Ewan . . . "

Sean blinked, then frowned. "He's gonny kill me." Another bite of toast.

Joe drank from the mug, frowned. The coffee was bitter.

"Ye saved his skin, Sean, so ah don't see how . . . "

"This is how." Crouching, he picked up a soggy trainer. Hand inside. Then withdrawn. A wet paper package waved. "It's aw' dissolved, man . . . " Wide eyes. " . . . Thirty quid's worth." He raised the package to his nose, and sniffed. "Think ye kid lick it?"

Joe stared. "Where did you git thirty quid?"

Grin. "Ewan's money – no' mine. He privides the . . . capital, ah provide the contacts!" Pleased with himself.

A smile twitched Joe's lips. He suppressed it, staring at the soggy bundle. "Well, Ewan's capital's melted – that'll teach the pair o' ye. Yous'll huv tae suck it up through a straw . . . "

Insulted. "Ah widney touch it, man – oanest!" Baseball-cap removed, a hand through dirty hair. "That's stuff's shite . . . ainly mugs use it." Cap replaced.

Joe frowned. The truth?

Last bite of toast. "Ewan's still intae it though, but he's daft – ah telt him that . . . " Mouth wiped, mug to lips. Scowl of distaste. "Thinks he's that cool, wi' his Cats an' his poxy Gaultier jaicket an' his eccy . . . "

Trouble in paradise? "Why did ye agree tae carry it fur him, then?" Joe sat down.

Head lowered. Mumbling. "He's ma mate." Hand gripping mug.

Joe fumbled for cigarettes. "Did he git ye intae The Matrix, last night?"

Nod. "Parta the deal. Ah wis skint . . . Ewan opened wan o' the fire-doors fur me."

Joe lit a cigarette and scowled. The alarm-connection was dodgy on two of the fire-exits, one of which remained lockless. He'd told Davie about it three times already. He looked up.

Carefully unfolding the damp scrap of paper. "Ken how much they mugs'll pay fur this crap?"

Joe lit another cigarette.

Proud. "Two quid a tab – and ye take them five atta time fur a guid hit. Ah kin git them fur peanuts aff this guy ah ken. We . . . " Adding up in head. " . . . Kin make a hunner quid fur every thirty we spend . . . "

"It's illegal."

"No' this stuff, it's no' eccy . . . " Laugh.

"Well, whitever it is, it soon wull be!"

Snort. "So's the drink in Dubai."

Joe gripped the cigarette. "Eccy's bad fur ye, ye never kin whit it's cut wi' . . . "

Laugh. Eyes to glowing tip. "Think whit you dae's healthy?"

Joe tensed.

"Anyway . . . " Pointing to grey, semi-melted, vaguely-pill-shaped sludge. " . . . This is different, chemical-free . . . whit-dae-they-ca'-it? . . . herbal . . . "

98

Joe held out a hand.

Carefully, Sean raised the package and passed it to him.

Joe stared at the damp substance.

Sean talked on. "It's goat aw' soarts o' juices in it, fae South America an' . . . "

"It's still E . . . "

"Naw, man – Moon Dust – safer than eccy. Ewan's tried it."

Joe dragged eyes from the semi-congealed mess.

Sean was huddled in front of the fire, hugging himself. An empty coffee cup sat beside a pink foot.

Joe sighed. Ewan this . . . Ewan that. "Ye no' goat ony other mates, these days?"

Muffled words. "Ah like Ewan – he's a guid laugh."

He's three years older.

"Whit aboot yer pals fae school?"

Dismissive snort. "Kids!" He jumped up, switched off the fire and turned.

Joe raised an eyebrow. The lounge was still fridge-like.

Shrugged explanation. "Too expensive tae run." Sean rubbed at a scarlet-dimpled thigh.

Joe stared at the tall figure. A kid . . . and not a kid.

Sean threw himself down on the sofa. He laid the damp package carefully on the arm then picked up the head-set and began to fiddle. "Ah'm lea'ing the school onyway – efter Christmas."

Joe reached for an ashtray. "Ye're whit?"

"Waant tae help ma maw oot mair." Pulling at Sellotaped section. "Ah'm sick o' eyeways bein' skint." Eyes to Joe.

Joe stiffened. "Whit aboot yer exams?"

Shrug. "Waste o' time."

Joe stubbed out the cigarette, then seized the Moon-Dust and shoved it in a pocket.

"Oi, man . . . " Angry. "That's oor . . . organic investment!" He lunged sideways, throwing himself onto Joe.

"Organic or no', the polis kin still try an' dae ye fur it."

Laugh. "They've goat tae catch me first!" He grabbed Joe's head in a mock arm-lock and began to wrestle.

Joe disentangled himself easily. He held onto a skinny

arm, stared into the grinning face and scowled. "Ye're a fuckin' idiot, Sean – there wis a raid last night!"

Thoughtful frown. Then: "Ah . . . " The grin again. " . . . It's as well ye goat me oot early – eh? Now . . . gie's ma Moon-dust."

Joe stared into wide blue eyes. "Whit ye lea'ing the school fur?"

Sean twisted free and began to search Joe's pockets. "Ah'm gettin' oota this dump – ah'm goin' places."

Anger pulsed in his head. He glanced up at his brother's photograph, then frowned. "The ainly place you're goin's back tae Longriggend Borstal, if ye . . . "

From down the hall, the sound of keys, then: "Sean? You up yet?" Tired voice. Door closing. Footsteps.

Sean looked at Joe, then winked: "Ah'll no' tell if you'll no'." Then: "In here, ma . . . "

Joe turned.

Small, blond figure in doorway. Cheap-spiral-permed hair frizzed by rain. Pale, make-upless face. Thirty-four but looked a hundred. Padded-nylon arms weighted by two bags marked Capital.

Joe moved forward.

So did Sean.

Both reached for bags.

Angie smiled up at them. "Ma two boays ur affy helpful, all o' a sudden." Mock suspicion. "Whit yous bin up tae?" She dumped bags on floor.

The lie came easily . . . too easily. Joe draped an arm around a padded shoulder. "Jist came tae visit ma favourite wuman – nae law against that, is there?"

She laughed, sat down.

"Waant a coffee, ma?" Sean hovered.

Angie unpoppered, then unzipped coat. "Aye, son, on ye go . . . "

"Did ye bring in milk?"

"In wan o' the bags."

Joe watched as Sean lifted the two plastic carriers, pretending to stagger. He disappeared into the kitchen. Joe sat across from Angie, extending cigarettes.

"Thanks."

He took one himself, then lit both.

Grateful exhale, then: "Christ! It's freezin' in here . . . pit that fire oan, eh Joe?"

A courtesy gesture he knew she couldn't afford. Joe smiled, then complied.

Angie kicked off shoes. "That's better . . . " Legs stretched out towards the bar's weak glow.

Distant voice. "Waant me tae make ye some toast, ma?"

"No' thanks, son – just the coffee." Cigarette to lips, contented nod to the kitchen. " . . . He's a guid boay really, eh? Ah think aw' that . . . trouble's behind him, noo."

Joe drew on his cigarette and continued to lie.

It was almost six when he got home. Joe closed the door, locked it then walked through to the kitchen.

No Billy.

He took off his jacket, hung it over the back of a chair then walked though to the lounge. The PC's green screen glowed, but no sign of Billy.

Joe sighed and walked from the room.

The bedroom door was closed. Joe knocked softly, then opened. He looked in.

Billy was kneeling in front of the wardrobe, surrounded by a spreading stain of jackets and trousers. He turned.

Joe grinned. "Loast somethin'?"

Stare. A hand raised.

Joe walked into the room.

Fingers held . . . ?

Joe walked over to Billy, paused.

. . . A crumpled £50 note. It twitched. "Where did you get this?"

Casual.

Joe stared. "'Sno mine."

Cool smile. "It was in the pocket of your jacket."

"Must be yours." Joe sat down on the bed.

Billy stood up. "No way, it's . . . "

"Sean's dealin' E." Joe rubbed his face and stared at the floor.

Cool laugh. "Don't change the subject! I want to know where this came from."

"Whit?" Joe looked up. Sean . . . E. The banknote waved in his face. "Och, ah don't know."

Billy sniffed the note. Nose wrinkling. "Cologne . . . expensive – Armani, I'd say." Eyes glinting. "What've you been up to?"

Joe blinked. Sean . . . arrested.

"Well?" Impatient.

Joe stared, then blinked again. Last week. Ramblin' Rosie. He sighed. "Some wuman at The Matrix – ah telt ye aboot her . . . " He grinned at the memory. " . . . 'Member? Hen nights . . . she oaffered me a joab strippin'!"

"And did you?" Amused smile.

"Did ah whit?" Sean . . . police-record.

"Did you give her value for money?"

Joe stood up, foot catching in a tweed jacket. "Whit wur ye lookin' fur, onyway?"

Hard, green eyes. "My blue tie – thought maybe you'd borrowed it."

Joe laughed. "Since when did ah keep ties in ma pockets?" He walked to the stripped pine bureau and opened the top drawer. "Here!" He lifted a blue Versace and turned, holding it out.

Billy took the tie. "No, not that one . . . my uni one."

Joe frowned. Sean . . . borstal . . . longer sentence, this time. "Whit's this sudden interest in ties? Will that wan no' dae?"

Billy stared. "You talking about the Over Twenty-Fives night?"

Sean . . . Michael's son. Joe raised an eyebrow.

Billy smiled. "Last Sunday. Rose MacCauly . . . it's coming back to me . . . " Laugh. " . . . She still drinking like a fish?"

Sean . . . his responsibility now. Joe stared. "Whit?"

Smile. "Never mind." A hand on his shoulder. "Where've you been all day?"

Sean . . . Joe frowned. "Angie's: Sean's dealin'."

Hand resting on shoulder. "At least he's not using himself

– and as long as he doesn't do it in my club, I think it shows a . . . certain initiative – don't you? Now, you're not working tonight."

An order, not a question.

His prick twitched.

Hand patting shoulder. "Kit inspection, soldier."

Beneath jeans, Joe began to harden.

Where the fuck was it?

He rifled in the wardrobe a third time.

From the bed, tutting.

Joe rubbed his prick and threw a pile of jeans onto the floor.

From the bed: "I'm waiting, soldier."

Joe sighed. "It wis cleaned, sir. Ah did it last week, but . . . "

"Ah . . . "

Voice nearing, then above him. "Your brother's service revolver?"

Joe turned. "It wis here."

Green myopic eyes. "Don't you read the papers, Joe?"

He stood up. "Whit?"

Hands on his shoulders. "Never mind." Laugh. "It's okay, Joe. You don't need to clean the gun – not anymore, at least."

"Whit dae . . . ?"

"I got rid of it."

"Why did ye . . . ?"

Cool smile. "It is unregistered, and technically . . . illegal."

Joe stared. "That never worried ye before."

Cool fingers traced his collar-bone. "You worry me, Joe. According to the papers, Paxton was killed with a gun very similar to . . . "

"Ah hid nothin' tae dae wi' that, Billy."

"I know that, Joe . . . "

A cool palm on each side of his face. Joe blinked.

" . . . But do the police?

Palms pressing. Joe stared.

"You were with me that night, Joe. But if that gun was found . . . "

103

"Where is it now?"

Laugh. "At the bottom of the Clyde."

Joe wrapped arms around the slim waist and buried face in Billy's neck. A hand stroked his hair.

"Relax, Joe. Leave the police to me. Now . . . "

A hand under his chin.

" . . . Forget kit inspection for the moment. What about going out to eat? The Cul-de-Sac, maybe?"

Joe frowned. "Aye . . . ah need a shave, but."

Laugh. A hand over his chin. Don't bother – it suits you." £50 note crushed into pocket of olive fatigues.

"Naw, but . . . "

"Keep it – it's yours anyway." Then the sound of keys jangling. "Come on – we'll take the Merc."

Joe looked over at the mess of clothes.

Billy caught his eye. "You can clear that up later . . . "

Hand on his arse.

" . . . Come on – I'm hungry . . . "

Joe followed Billy into the hall and down to the car-park.

Joe looked at his watch: almost midnight. He stared across the restaurant and sighed. Waiters hovered around a few dawdling diners, eager to clear tables. Gentle hum of low conversation. In the corner, a raucous party of about eight men were ordering more drinks. Joe turned back to the bar and lifted his Caledonian Clear.

Sean drifted into his mind.

Joe sighed. Dogging school was one thing. Getting into clubs underage was one thing. The odd tab of E was one thing.

Dealing was something else.

Dealing was worse than joy-riding.

Joe lit a cigarette.

Behind, the group of men started to sing.

Joe sighed, rubbed his face. He needed to spend more time with Sean. He glanced over his shoulder to where Billy and two men – one of whom he recognised as Andrew, the accountant, were talking. Joe frowned. Business again.

Business . . . deals . . . dealing.
  Billy's words: ' . . . shows a certain . . . initiative, don't you think?'

Joe didn't think. He drew on the cigarette.
  Any initiative had probably been Ewan's.
  Sean: fifteen, stupid.
  Ewan: eighteen, should know better.
  From behind, the sound of fingers snapping over low buzz of conversation.
  Joe turned.
  Billy was beckoning.
  Joe eased himself off the bar-stool and walked towards the table. Reaching Billy's chair, he paused, expectant.
  Cool smile. "I think I've left some documentation in the car." Keys extended.
  Joe took them.
  "On the back seat."
  Joe turned, walked from the restaurant.
  Outside, it was raining again. Joe turned up the collar of his leather jacket and tried to remember where they'd parked the Merc. Staring across the car-park, he spotted it, then began to walk. He peered through the back window into the car.
  A leather document-case lay on the back-seat.
  Joe opened the door, removed the case, relocked the door and walked back to the Cul-de-Sac.
  When he reached the table, Andrew the accountant was talking. Joe held out the document-case.
  Billy laughed at something Andrew said.
  Joe cleared his throat.
  Billy turned, looked at him briefly, then took the case.
  Joe walked back to the bar, sat down. He lit another cigarette, stared at the Zippo.

Someone needed to keep Sean in line.

105

Joe closed his eyes. What would Michael have done?

Behind, the sound of laughing and more singing. Pressure at his side. Then:

"Could you make one of those an orange-juice, mate?" Slurring.

Whisky fumes in his nostrils. Joe lifted the Caledonian Clear bottle, drained, then sat it on the bar. He sighed.

Behind: "Great! Thanks." Resonant slurring.

Then pressure lessening, the sound of footsteps moving away.

Joe scowled.

What the fuck was he going to do with Sean?

He lifted the bottle of mineral-water. Empty. Joe raised his eyes.

The barman was at the other end of the bar.

He drew on the cigarette, looked at his watch: half-twelve. He yawned.

From behind, fingers snapping.

Joe got off the bar-stool and walked over to the table, pausing behind Billy's chair. He waited.

Billy turned. Cool smile. "Kenny needs cigarettes . . . " Hand extended. Three pound-coins lay on a soft palm. "Bensons, I think?" Eyes to a balding man opposite.

Hard smile, then nod.

Joe took the coins, turned, located the cigarette-machine and fed them into its slot. He pressed a red button, waited, then lifted the gold packet and walked back to the table. Joe placed the cigarettes before Baldy.

Baldy smiled, lifting the packet.

Joe walked back to the bar.

The barman had reappeared. Joe picked up the empty Caledonian Clear bottle. "Another wan o' these, pal."

Stare, then bending beneath bar. Then bottle placed before him. "Wan-fifty, please." Nasal suspicion.

Joe took it, twisted off the top and drank. "Pit it oan their tab." He nodded towards Billy's table.

Sceptical. "Nae tabs in here, sir." The title grudging.

"Wan-fifty, please."

Joe sighed, began to search pockets. Nothing . . . then fingers tightened around crumpled paper. Joe pulled the £50 note from his pocket and held it out.

The barman took it, stared at it, then Joe, held the note up to the light then turned to the cash-register.

Joe smiled, raising bottle to lips.

The sound of electronic beeps, then: "Yer change, sir." A pile of tens, a five and an assortment of coins placed on the bar.

Joe let them sit there and lit another cigarette. From behind he could hear Billy's soft tones.

Pressure at his side. Then voice over his head: "Do you have change for the . . . er . . . telephone?" Low, resonant slurring.

Joe looked up.

Black tee-shirt. 501s. Fashionably-cut brown hair. Flushed, handsome face. Fingers tapping pound coin on the bar.

He looked away, ground-out cigarette in over-flowing ashtray. Then:

"Joe?"

Hand on his shoulder. Finger pressure. Drunken camaraderie.

Joe lifted eyes.

Smile. "I thought it was you." Bushy eyebrows raised.

Joe stared.

Laugh. "Andy . . . Andy Hunter – 'member?"

Joe remembered.

Voice thick with whisky. "Haven't seen you here before."

Joe frowned.

Behind, faint clicking.

Arm resting on shoulder. Then:

"On your own?"

"Naw, wi' . . . friends." Not his friends: Billy's friends. He looked away.

Beep of cash-register, then small pile of silver coins placed on the bar. Joe watched as Andy Hunter fumbled with them.

Behind, louder clicking.

A ten-pence piece rolled towards his ashtray. Joe stopped it with a palm, slid it towards the man beside him.

"Thanks." Andy Hunter picked up the coin. "Can I get you a drink?" Arm withdrawn, hand into pocket.

"Thanks, ah've goat wan."

Smile. Fingers through hair, eyes to the mineral water. "Wise man."

Behind, fingers snapping, then: "Joe!"

Resonant laugh. "I think someone's trying to get your attention!"

Joe turned.

At the table, Andrew the accountant was fiddling with a pencil. Baldy grinned. Billy's face was a mask.

Joe sighed, edged off the bar-stool and walked towards the table. Inches away, he stopped.

Billy pushed back a chair and stood up, document-case under one arm. "What have you been up to?" Cool.

"Nothin', ah wis . . . "

"Didn't you hear me, Joe?" Cold.

"Aye, but . . . "

"Then why didn't you . . . " Colder.

"Ah wis talkin' tae . . . " Billy's hand across his face.

Joe seized a slim wrist, fingers tightening. The slap silenced the room. Something buzzed in his head.

The mask didn't slip. Billy pulled his hand free. "You come when I say, understand?" Icy.

Joe rubbed a smarting cheek.

"Understand?" Green eyes glinting.

Joe lowered his head. "Aye, Billy."

"Now, get my coat. We're going." Nod to the table. "Goodnight, gentlemen." Billy brushed past and strode quickly towards the door.

Joe stared at Billy's business associates. The accountant looked away. Baldy grinned, tutting. A flush spread over Joe's face. He lifted a beige coat from the back of a chair. As he turned to leave, he met brown liquid eyes from the bar. Joe tried to smile. A hand-print stung on his cheek.

Andy Hunter's expression was unreadable.

Joe shrugged and followed Billy.

CHAPTER TEN

In the car, Billy was quiet. Joe removed one hand from the wheel and switched on the radio.

Voice behind: "Turn left here."

A squawk of music. Joe indicated, then turned the wheel. "We no' goin' hame?"

"Just drive."

"Sure, Billy." He switched the radio off. "Waant a CD oan?" Joe glanced in the rear-view mirror.

Billy stared past him.

Joe sighed. "Dae ye waant a CD . . . ?"

"Shut up and drive."

Joe shut up and drove. At the intersection of St. Georges and Possil Road he stopped. Eyes in mirror.

Billy stared past him, then: "Left."

Joe indicated, then turned up towards Port Dundas.

Possil Road was quiet.

Joe glanced at his watch: almost one. He stared at the flood-lit road ahead. "Didney think you kent onywan up here."

A hand on the back of his neck. "Right, then right again." Fingers tightened.

Joe turned the large car away from yuppy warehouse developments and towards the old factory area. A side-street. Less light here. He flicked onto full-beam and peered, slowing.

Derelict buildings slouched past in shadow. At the end of the street, a turning. Joe took it. Then:

"Stop."

Joe cut down from second to first. Then neutral.

The powerful engine idled.

Neat nails pressed into flesh. Then:

"Out."

Joe peered through the windscreen, following the wipers with his eyes. He switched off headlights, then engine.

The wipers stopped mid-sweep. Then silence, broken only by staccato rain on metal roof.

109

In darkness, Joe unbuckled seat-belt.

"I said out!"

Joe opened the door and got out of the car. Beneath black Levis his prick was hardening.

Water coursed over head, running into eyes, ears, mouth. Joe gripped slick metal with hot fingers. Jeans hung loose over thighs, already soaking. The number-plate's sharp edge dug into shins.

Behind, Billy thrust again.

A wave of pain rose then broke over him. Joe pressed a stinging face to the Merc's shining bonnet as his prick ground against grilled chrome.

Billy withdrew.

The wave receded.

Mumbling behind.

His left ear filled with water then deadened again. Tidal sound came and went. Then another thrust, harder now. Joe clenched teeth and arched back, inverting the pressure. Something warm dripped onto his neck. Sweat mixed with sweat mixed with rain, cooling rapidly. Joe licked dry lips with drier tongue.

More mumbling behind. Hands seized wrists, exerting a parallel pressure, pinning him to the metal surface.

Joe raised head, ears popping, like underwater. Or flying.

The mumbling became words: "Disobedience, soldier . . ." Billy rammed harder.

Joe kissed the bonnet's surface, tasted turtle-wax. Balls spasmed against steel.

A laugh behind. "You come when I say, understand?"

Joe moaned, tried to think of something else.

The Cul-de-Sac.

Baldy's grin.

Andy Hunter . . . Sean . . .

His cheek stung. Joe frowned.

Billy's groin against buttocks, grinding, soaking pubic hair against wet flesh.

Pressure deep inside. He closed his eyes. Pain exploded on eye-lids.

110

"Don't ever disobey me again, Joe." A sigh. A final thrust . . .

. . . then heat . . . wet heat. Billy's body covered his, pressing him down onto the cold liquid surface. Quick breath in his ear. Then slowing. Then emptiness . . .

Billy withdrew.

Spunk began to dribble down a wet thigh. Joe tried to raise himself from the bonnet. Thighs refused to close . . . arse-hole refused to close. One knee brushed the Merc's silver star. He turned slowly. Legs were jelly: prick was iron. A few yards away, through the gloom, Billy was wiping himself off with a white handkerchief. Joe blinked, waiting for permission.

Handkerchief balled and thrown away.

Rain pattered on metal. Then:

"Get into the car. I want to go home." Footsteps in the rain.

Joe stared.

Billy was gone.

He peered into wet darkness. A small light appeared inside the car as Billy opened the passenger-door. Then:

"Get a move on! It's pouring." Billy got into the car and closed the door.

Joe sighed, pulled sodden jeans up over quivering thighs. Cramming his erection behind metal zip, he fastened belt, opened the car door and slowly got in.

Soft purring in the distance.

Joe pulled the duvet over his head.

The purring stopped.

Joe smiled. Wrong number.

Then a click. Then Billy's smooth voice filled the bedroom:

'You have reached 0141-852-5154 . . . '

Joe frowned. Billy didn't have an Ansa-phone, didn't need an Ansa-phone . . . not with the mobile.

' . . . Please leave your message after the tone . . . '

Joe sat up, scowled, moving onto side. His arse hurt.

Beep. Beep. Amplified throat clearing, then another

111

voice – deeper, more resonant:

"Joe? Andy Hunter here. It's one o'clock, Monday."
Pause. "Er . . . you left your change behind, last night . . . "
Pause. "Forty-odd quid. Thought you'd want it back. Give
me a ring on 634-6729 after eight. Speak to you later."
Click. Whir.

Joe rubbed his face, then looked at the alarm-clock: just
after one. He yawned, threw off the duvet and eased
himself out of bed. On the far side of the room, a white
rectangular object where the mobile usually sat. Joe walked
towards it, peered at the surface. Looked like a mobile,
with extras. He stared at a digital display which read '2',
plus a number of buttons. He pressed one.

Nothing happened.

He pressed another, yawned.

Still nothing.

Joe shrugged. He'd ask Billy to show him how it worked.
Turning, a heap in front of the wardrobe caught his eye.
Jackets, trousers . . . pockets protruding awkwardly. Joe
sighed, turned back and began to pick up his clothes from
the floor.

Monday was . . . quiet.

Tuesday. Office party at The Matrix. Drunken couples
groping each other under tables. In the foyer, Joe held open
the door as the last of the revellers departed. As he turned
back into the club:

"Successful function?" A hand pushed open the door.

Joe smiled. "Aye – nae trouble, at least. Whit you doin'
here?"

Billy patted a briefcase. "Andrew wants some figures . . .
deliveries for September, or something . . . " He walked
towards Davie's office.

Joe frowned. "Ah coulda brought them hame fur ye, ye
shoulda phoned . . . "

"Last minute thing . . . hold on and I'll give you a lift."

Joe watched as Billy disappeared into the office, closing
the door behind him. He shrugged, and lit a cigarette.

112

Wednesday night, Billy arrived at two on the dot. Same briefcase, different reason:

"The Apple-Mac's crashed. I need July's bank statements. Want a lift?"

Joe looked at Gina, who was waiting for her taxi, then back at Billy.

Cool laugh. "Calton, isn't it?"

Deferential red-slash smile.

Billy threw Joe the Merc's keys. "I'll just be a minute."

Thursday: not usually a takings-night. Billy brought the Jeep to a smooth halt beside the Datsun and the Merc.

Joe waited until the engine died. He stared at Billy. "Look, man ah've bin thinkin' . . . "

Billy removed keys from ignition.

" . . . Ah kid dae the late night-pick-ups fur ye – or The Matrix wan, at least."

Amused smile. "You know how I like to do things by now, Joe." Car door opened. Billy got out.

So did Joe. He placed the heavy leather wallet on the Jeep's bonnet. "But ye're oot aw' day, Billy. Ah work nights ah'm oan the spot, so tae speak. It wid be nae trouble tae . . . "

"Leave it, Joe." Door locked, keys in pocket.

Joe sighed and followed Billy out of the car-park.

In the bedroom he examined the new telephone. Its digital display read '3'. In the background, a series of beeps. Then a soft click. Rustling. The sound of notes placed between reinforced steel shelves. Tonight's take had been almost four thousand. Joe stared at the telephone.

Cool voice behind: "Expecting a call?"

"Naw." Joe prodded a button.

Whirring, then nothing.

He took off the bikers' jacket. "Gonny show me how this thing works?"

Voice at his shoulder: "Don't concern yourself with it, Joe – I'll let you know if Sean or Angie phone."

He rubbed the display with an index finger. Andy Hunter: five nights ago at the Cul-de-Sac. He never did return that call.

"Okay, Joe?"

Something in the voice, something . . . different. Not a question . . . not really. Joe continued to rub. "Sure, Billy . . . " He shrugged. It didn't matter – the fifty quid wasn't really his anyway.

Hands on his waist, hard fingers kneading.

Joe sighed, turned. He rested arms on Billy's shoulders, felt the tension.

Behind steel rims, green eyes glinted.

Joe pushed a strand of blond hair back from the pale face and stared into glacial eyes. "Onythin' wrang, Billy? Ye've bin . . . quiet."

No response.

Billy's eyes were mirrors. Joe gazed at his own reflection. "Are ye . . . worried 'boot somethin'?" Dark pupils bored into his.

No response.

Joe searched the smooth face for an answer, found none. He stroked fine, soft hair. "Tell me, Billy . . . tell me whit's wrang. Maybe ah kin help."

Billy's hands moved lower, onto arse. A sigh, then: "My problem, Joe – doesn't concern you."

It was still there – the something in Billy's voice. Joe flinched.

The hands stopped.

Joe lowered his head.

One hand moved down, fingers gently tracing his arse-crack. Then less gently.

Joe clenched his teeth. A shiver of pain. He sighed.

Billy's fingers moved to belt.

"Listen, Billy . . . can we . . . ?" Joe raised his head.

The fingers paused. Amused smile. "Can we . . . what, Joe?" Myopic pupils huge.

Joe stared. Heat was spreading over his face. Something was wrong.

Below, the fingers began to undo belt.

Joe stayed them. "Kin we talk?" He rubbed a smooth knuckle.

114

Cold laugh. "Got a headache, have we?"

Joe sighed. His head was the only part of him that didn't ache. But that wasn't the problem. He rubbed Billy's ear.

Billy pulled away, fingers undoing his own belt.

Joe frowned. The sound of a zip. Pressure on his shoulders. Joe draped arms around Billy, pulling the slim body against his own. Mouth searched for mouth, wanting to reassure, to be reassured.

Billy's head turned away.

Pressure on shoulders increased.

Joe bit his lip. Not now . . . He looked down.

Six inches held between well-manicured fingers.

Joe knelt. Billy's other hand on the back of his head, pushing. Joe closed eyes, formed lips into a silent 'o' and felt Billy's hard prick thrust towards the back of his mouth.

"Ye missed a guid do, yesterday, Joe . . . " Cigarette packet extended.

Joe stared at Gina. Another Saturday night . . .

Red-slash smile. "Georgie's funeral – ah wis surprised ye wurney there."

Joe took a cigarette, patting pockets for the Zippo. Georgie . . .

Gina struck a match, held it out.

Joe stared at the cigarette. Yesterday . . . Friday . . . Billy . . .

Laugh. "Ye waant lit or no'?"

He looked up. Flame licked at red-tipped fingers. Joe placed cigarette between lips and lowered his head. Then puffed.

She shook out the match, striking another for herself. Cigarette bucking: "Aye – Mr King laid oan a guid spread in The Albany efterwards – ye missed yersel', Joe . . ."

Tuesday . . . Billy.

Wednesday . . . Billy.

Thursday, Friday . . . Billy.

He sighed. The past five days blurred into one, blurred into Billy.

In the background: "Eh, Joe?"

He looked up. "Whit?"

115

Quizzical eyes. "Ye wur miles away – onythin' wrang?" Concern.

Joe shook his head. "Naw – jist tired, Gina."

Grin. "Sean?"

Joe smiled. For once, Sean was the least of his problems. "Angie's cut-doon her oors."

Understanding nod. "The boay needs keepin' an eye oan." Eyes scanning behind. "Still . . . no sign the night, so that's somethin'!"

Joe laughed. Sean knew he set foot again in The Matrix on pain of death. "Aye . . . ah doot we'll be seein' ony mair o' him."

Voices from the door. Raised voices.

Joe glanced at his watch: just before one. The council's midnight curfew prohibited entrance to any club after midnight. He looked over to where Malkie stood.

Another voice: "I don't want to come in – just get Joe Macdonald for me – okay?" Low, resonant.

Joe sighed.

Gina laughed. "Ye're in demand these days!"

He stubbed out cigarette and walked towards the door. Beyond Malkie's bulk he could see another outline. Denim-clad, fashionably-cut hair. Below bushy eyebrows brown eyes caught his:

"Can I have a word?"

Malkie turned, quizzical.

Joe nodded.

Malkie shrugged and walked away.

Joe stared at Andy Hunter.

Smile, then hand into jeans pocket. Folded notes produced, held out.

Joe stared.

The notes remained extended.

Joe blinked. The Cul-de-Sac. Last Sunday. Billy . . . He took the notes, crumpling them. Heat spread over his face.

Hand back into pocket. Loose change produced. Three pound coins and a fifty pence piece counted into palm. Then held out.

Joe lifted the change, half-smiled. Usually, the police

116

received the backhanders.

Andy caught his eye, smiled back.

A joke shared.

Then bushy eyebrows formed a V. "You should pick up your phone-messages more often." Face expressionless.

Joe scowled. He didn't know how.

Shrug. Turn. "Maybe see you sometime . . . "

"Haud oan . . . " Joe sighed. "Thanks fur . . . " He jiggled the change in his palm.

Andy turned back to face him. Waiting.

Joe gazed at his feet.

"Everything . . . okay?" Soft voice. Concern.

Joe flinched. The Ansa-phone was his problem. Billy was his problem. By proxy, Billy's problems were his problems. He rubbed cheek with rough fingers.

"Look: I know it's none of my business . . . "

"Ye're right – it isney . . . " Red spread to the roots of his hair. He looked up, stared at the handsome face.

Andy's expression was unreadable.

Joe sighed. His problem. He tried to smile. It froze, half-formed.

Behind, sound surged into the foyer as a door opened.

Andy joke-frowned. "The natives are getting restless!"

Joe stared at the handsome face. Maybe one native in particular. The Cul-de-Sac . . . Billy's slap . . . the unreturned phone-call – or calls. Did Andy Hunter understand? Joe stuffed notes and change into trouser pocket.

Did he even understand anymore? His mind buzzed with Billy.

Silence hung between them. Joe shuffled his feet. Go . . . just go.

Andy Hunter didn't go. He smiled.

Joe scowled.

Cigarettes produced, packet held out.

Joe shook his head and moved towards the door. The sound of lighter flicking, then:

"Didn't see you at the funeral, yesterday."

Joe stopped. "Naw, ah wis . . . " Naked . . . on the bedroom floor . . . alone . . . all afternoon. " . . . workin'."

Soft laugh. "You really didn't like George Paxton, did you?"

Joe turned, stared at the denim-clad figure. Andy Handsome Face became PC Hunter.

"Hey, don't worry – your alibi's sound." Cigarette to pink lips .

Georgie . . . Joe blinked.

"Just because you didn't get on with the guy, doesn't mean you killed him!" Laugh. "I mean, where's your motive?"

Georgie . . . Sean. Eccy. Another slap, two weeks ago. Joe traced the fading scar on his cheek.

"No . . . " Cigarette to lips. " . . . Paxton had bigger enemies than you, from what the DI says . . . "

Joe gazed at his feet.

" . . . In fact, seems like you were one of the few who really had Paxton's number. His family thought he was some kinda saint!"

Joe looked up.

Frown. Hushed low resonance. "It would've helped if you'd told us straight-off that Paxton was dealing drugs." Mildly admonishing.

Sean . . . Joe fumbled for cigarettes.

"We wasted a lot of time taking useless statements from Christ knows who, when we should've been looking elsewhere."

Joe lit a cigarette. "How did ye fun' oot aboot . . . ?"

Eyebrows V-ed. "Your . . . boss told us."

Joe stared.

Confusion. "Thought you'd know." Exhale. "Oh, Mr King's been very helpful – surprising, given it was his club Paxton was dealing in. Still . . . " Cigarette to lips. " . . . it's best to be honest." Laugh. Mock-policeman voice. "We always find out in the end, you know!"

Joe frowned. Had Billy left Sean out of the Georgie picture?

Strong denim-clad shoulders leant against a wall. "Seems Paxton had quite a little business going."

Joe cleared his throat. "So the polis think . . . ?"

Smile. "Yeah – two hundred MDMA tablets turned up in his sock drawer, so it looks like Paxton was killed either for, or because of, drugs." Frown. "The DI's considering an organised crime connection. That would explain the use of a gun."

Joe stared.

Cigarette ground out underfoot. "And while we're on the subject of guns . . . "

The guy was playing with him! Joe walked to the door, unlocked and held it open. Fingers tightened around the metal handle. "Thanks fur pickin' up ma change . . ." Go.

Surprised voice behind. "No problem . . . er . . . "

"Seeya aroon' . . . " Just go. Knuckles white on handle. Voice at his side:

"You've got my number, Joe."

Joe blinked. He had Andy Hunter's number, all right. "Guidnight." He stared at his feet. Just fuckin' go.

Sigh, then: "Sure . . . goodnight, Joe."

Denim brushed his bare arm. The musky scent of fresh sweat in his nostrils. Joe locked the door behind Andy Hunter and walked back towards the dance-floor.

Two hours later, he scanned Mitchel Street.

No red Jeep. No Merc. No Datsun.

No Billy.

Joe glanced at his watch: half-two. Three nights in a row he'd been given a lift he hadn't wanted. Now, when he'd appreciate the shelter of a warm vehicle . . . Joe turned up jacket collar against icy rain and began to walk.

Billy's business problems.

Sean . . . Georgie Paxton . . . drugs . . . police-attention . . . licensing boards.

Joe frowned. Billy would get brownie-points for co-operating with the police over Georgie's dealing. One good turn would see him alright when it came to extended licenses and all-dayers. Joe quickened his pace.

No PNC-check. No 'further questioning' . . . Andy Hunter's handsome face lingered . . . not official questioning, anyway.

119

Joe scowled. Why hadn't Billy told him the pressure was off?

Joe walked briskly along Argyll Street, turning up into Glassford Street.

The Ansa-phone . . .

The questions . . .

The slap . . .

The lifts . . .

Ahead, The Italina Centre rose from a smoggy mist. Joe looked up.

Three floors above, a single light burned in the bedroom.

Joe fumbled for keys, inserting one in the grilled-gate's lock. He turned, pushed then closed the gate behind. After jogging across the courtyard past the fountain he unlocked the main door and ran up three flights of carpeted stair. Outside 3/1 he paused, shaking rain from hair. Fingers trembled as he inserted three keys in three double-locks, then turned the door-handle.

The hall was in darkness.

"Billy?" Joe struggled out of leather jacket and threw it on the floor.

No response. A shaft of light jutted from beneath the bedroom door.

Joe smiled. The Apple-Mac must be back on-line. "Billy?" He knocked softly then pushed open the bedroom door.

CHAPTER ELEVEN

The smell hit him first. Alcohol . . . lager.

Billy didn't drink lager.

Behind the yeasty tang, another smell. Warm, more visceral, more man-made.

Men-made.

Sweat. Vomit . . . salty . . . shitty.

Joe stared across the bedroom at Billy's dressing-gowned back. A single spot-light illuminated loose strands of blond hair. Beyond, stray rays bounced off the red silk sheet which covered the bed. "Whit ye dain'?"

Billy turned. Myopic green eyes glinted. Naked beneath the open robe, skin shone slick with moisture. A semi-erect prick was slowy retreating down a lightly-muscled thigh. Husky voice. "Ah, Joe . . . just in time. I need a rest." He walked to a basket-chair and sat down.

Joe stared at the bed. "Whit the fuck . . . ?"

A pale body lay on the red silk sheet. Thin arms secured to bed-head by yellow nylon rope. Long dark hair further obscured pillow-buried face. Beside where the mouth would be, a dark spreading stain.

Buzzing in his ears. Joe stared at the figure.

White buttocks glistened under fierce light. A single trickle of blood leaked from between splayed thighs onto already red sheets.

Joe's eyes travelled down one hairless leg, its ankle tethered to metal bed-frame. The other limb pulled up awkwardly under body.

Sigh. "I'm off for a shower." Billy breezed past in a wash of Oddfellows.

Joe continued to stare at the inverted Y. He moved closer, eyes never leaving the prostrate body.

In the distance, the sound of running water.

Inexplicable rage throbbed in his brain. Joe walked to the side of the bed and seized a handful of dark hair, pulled.

No resistance. No sound.

Joe released the handful.

Head fell back onto pillow.

"Fuck!" Rage dissolved. Joe knelt at the side of the bed, smoothing hair back from a pale face. He stared.

A young face.

A bruised face.

The right eye beginning to swell. Long wet lashes rested on translucent cheeks.

Tear-tracked cheeks.

Vomit encrusted nostrils and lips.

Peaceful lips. Not-moving lips.

Not breathing?

Joe fumbled with the nylon cord, scowled. Billy tied a good knot.

Not good enough.

Joe freed bony wrists, then moved to the foot of the bed, undoing the remaining tether. He pushed the inert body over into the recovery position.

Head lolled. The smell of lager, stale sweat and sick drifted up.

Joe held the kid's face between trembling palms, placing an ear to nose.

Definitely not breathing.

He wiped vomit from lips, thrust a finger between white even teeth.

No obstructions.

Joe withdrew finger, pushed the boy further over and tilted the head back. Pinching pale nostrils he inhaled, then placed mouth over mouth and blew. He tasted lager, blood and ... spunk. He raised his head, waiting.

Nothing.

Mouth over mouth again.

Nothing ...

Joe's heart hammered.

... Then a cough. The head jerked between palms.

"Ye're okay, pal ... " Joe stared.

Eye-lids fluttered, then closed. A groan. Another cough. Then retching. Watery, yeasty vomit dribbled sideways from cracked lips. Then a sob.

Joe wiped the trembling mouth. Placing hands under

122

armpits he propped the kid up against the bedhead, then pushed a veil of dark hair out of eyes.

More sobbing.

Joe turned, scanning the room. His towelling dressing-gown hung behind the door. He got up, grabbed the robe from the hook and draped the heavy fabric around a limp body.

Nose wiped on the back of hand, then one eye gradually opened.

Joe sat on the side of the bed and stared.

A pin-pricked pupil stared back. Scared . . . then shrunk to terrified. "No . . . please don't . . . " Rounded vowels, educated.

Joe frowned, hand on a shaking shoulder. "It's okay, it's okay, ah . . . "

"Don't!" The word screamed. Knees drawn up under towelling robe. Skinny arms over face and head. The kid rolled onto side.

Joe removed hand, stood up and stared at the foetal ball.

Sobbing became deep gasping breaths.

A different rage throbbed in his ears. Joe stood up and walked towards the bedroom door. His foot kicked something. He paused, stared, watching as an empty San Miguel bottle skittered across the polished floor. Red flashed in his brain. He bent down, seized the bottle, smashing it against the door's edge.

Behind: "Oh Christ! Please, don't hit . . . "

Joe frowned and moved into the hall.

Darkness.

He clenched the bottle's jagged neck between fingers and walked towards the bathroom.

A wet towel lay on the floor. In the steamed mirror:

'Enjoy yourself. Back later.' Letters streaking.

Joe turned and strode back into the hall.

Kitchen: empty.

Lounge: empty. Joe paused in the middle of the room, blood pounding.

'Enjoy yourself . . . '

A kid . . .

A kid's body . . .

A fuckin' kid . . .

Joe turned and threw jagged glass at teal-coloured plaster.

A thud . . .

The kid's puffy eye, the bruises . . .

Joe stared, breathing heavily.

Eventually the pounding subsided.

He stared at the wall, at the bottle-neck now protruding from grey plaster. Then Joe walked back to the bedroom.

Beneath boots, glass crunched on polished wood. Yards from the bed he paused, staring.

The fetal ball remained curled.

Joe sighed, walked over to the bed and sat down.

The fetal ball flinched.

Joe frowned. "Listen tae me. He's gone. Ah'm no' gonny touch ye. Jist tell me if yer okay."

Silence.

Joe stared. On the towelling over the kid's arse, a red, spreading stain. He stood up. "Stay there." Joe walked over to the telephone.

Its green display mocked him. But at least he could dial out. Joe punched three nines, then waited. Then: "Ambulance and police."

"No!" Muffled protest.

Joe turned.

The fetal ball was uncurling. Arms removed from head. Long fingers wiping tears from cheek. "I'm okay . . ." Sniff. Fear streaked the bruised face. Fear . . .

Billy-induced fear. Joe stared.

On the other end of the phone a voice asked for the address.

Joe ignored it, continued to stare.

Pink skin. A dusting of freckles. Probably quite good-looking, under the bruises. "Really . . . I'm okay."

He frowned. "You sure?"

Braver now. One puffy eye still tightly shut. Nod. "Just let me go home." Towelling robe whipped off, legs swung over side of bed. Then crumpling back onto red silk. Pain

124

criss-crossed pale face. "Oh, Christ." Hand to white thigh.

"Take it easy." Joe replaced the receiver and walked towards the bed. "Lie still."

The kid flinched.

Joe scowled. "Let me huv a look."

The kid flinched again.

Joe sighed. "Let me git an ambulance, then."

"No!"

Joe watched as the kid pulled up long legs and peered over shoulder. "C'moan, pal . . . " Soothing. " . . . Ah'll try an' no' hurt ye. Let me see."

Sigh. "Okay . . . " Then panic. " . . . But promise you'll not call . . . " Long legs slowly uncurled.

"No' if ye don't waant me tae." Carefully, Joe eased rigid buttocks apart.

Hiss of breath. Clenched teeth: "Ah, ya . . . "

Joe scowled. "Sorry, pal." He stared.

Four Billy-finger-shaped indentations were already bruising on soft white thigh-flesh. The kid's buttocks shuddered in spasms under the ferocity of Joe's stare, and whatever had gone on earlier. He sighed. "Try an' relax."

Two mounds untensed a little.

Joe palmed the mounds and peered into the kid's arse-crack. Smeary, brown-streaked goo stuck to his fingertips.

A shriek.

"Easy, easy." Joe continued to peer. The hole was a shivering, swollen wound desperately trying to reseal itself.

The kid flinched.

The hole contracted then relaxed.

A trickle of messy, reddish slime began to leak from the shrinking orifice, slowly at first, then more vigorously.

Joe pulled a handkerchief from jeans' pocket.

Beneath the kid, the silk sheet was soaking.

He grabbed a small, shaking hand. "Haud this here!" Joe pushed clean white cotton into trembling fingers then pressed both against a jagged, inch-long tear in the left-hand side of the arsehole. Then he seized the dressing-gown, laying it over the quivering body. "Ah'm callin' an ambulance!" He stood up.

Panic. The bruised face crumpled. "Please don't . . . "
Sob. "My mum and dad . . . "

Joe stared at the thin figure. "How auld ur ye?"

Sniff. "Fourteen, but . . . " More sobs.

Joe sat down on the bed and gently pulled the kid towards him. Strong arms around skinny shoulders. Limp, heaving shoulders.

Scrawny arms thrown around his neck.

Warm tears seeped through the Matrix tee-shirt. Joe pressed the kid to his chest, stroking damp, matted hair.

The sound of a child's crying filled the bedroom . . .

Later, Joe raised his face from the kid's hair and stared down at pale limbs.

A stained handkerchief lay inches away. The bleeding seemed to have stopped.

He eased himself back, and examined the pink face. Both eyes puffy now. The injuries looked painful, but superficial.

"Okay?"

Closed-eye nod.

"Is there onywan ah kin phone fur ye, a pal or somethin'?"

Headshake.

Joe sighed. "Well, ye canny go hame luckin' like that!" He scowled. "Think ye can manage as fur as The Royal?"

Fear. Eyes shot open, blinking rapidly.

"'S'okay - they'll no' ask ony questions . . . " In his experience, they never did.

Uncertain. "I think I'm okay, I . . . " Blush spreading over face. " . . . just had too much to drink."

Joe scowled.

Feigned nonchalance. "I'll get off now, if you could . . . my clothes . . . " Finger pointing to a chair.

Joe stood up and walked to where jeans and a leather jacket lay in a heap. He picked them up. An unopened tube of KY, a sealed packet of Mates and a Crunchie fell from a pocket. Joe frowned, stared then bent down, lifting the objects.

Throat clearing. Hesitant. "I was hungry . . . he . . . "

"Ah bet he did!" Joe stared over at the bruised kid, then

back at the Crunchie. Like taking candy from a baby. He scowled.

Billy had got his money's worth.

Billy always did.

Joe stuffed chocolate-bar and the rest back into pocket then tossed jacket and jeans across the room.

"Thanks." Caught with a shaking hand.

"What's yer name?" He watched as the kid gingerly edged legs over the side of the bed and onto floor.

"Robin." Feet apart, knees bent. White, almost bleached skin glistened under fierce light. Sparse dusting of freckles on back and shoulders. Boyish, unmuscled. Barely masculine. Then a wobble. Thin body swaying.

Joe moved forward, placed a steadying hand on slender waist.

Robin turned, a hand on Joe's shoulder.

He watched as the kid eased pale limbs into faded denim, noting the tear had definitely stopped bleeding.

Fingers gripping shoulder, then removed. Zipping. Then: "My trainers . . . where's my trainers?"

Joe scanned the floor. An expensive white sports-shoe protruded from under the bed. He knelt. Inches from the trainer, an empty HT Special packet. Joe pushed it away. His hand settled on something moist. He raised a palm: three used condoms adhered. One streaked with red. Joe scowled, peeled them off. He reached for the shoe and its partner, then stood up and handed them to Robin.

"Thanks." Arm braced against bedroom wall, undoing laces.

"So . . . where'd he pick ye up?"

One red eye raised, curious at the curiosity.

Joe stared at the battered body.

Eyes lowered. Knee raised to tie laces. Pain-splattered face. "The arcade . . . Sauchiehall Street."

Joe frowned. He knew the place, had been there with Sean. It closed at ten. Joe glanced at his watch: at least four hours . . . for a Crunchie.

Billy had got his money's worth.

Billy always did.

Shy voice. "Do you . . . " Gesturing with long fingers.
" . . . live here too?"

Billy.

The slap.

The unnecessary lifts from work.

The pocket-searches.

Robin.

Joe scowled. "No' ony mair." He stared at the bruised
face.

Robin chewed on a pink bottom lip.

A kid . . . a fuckin' kid! Joe walked towards the door.
"Ah'm running you tae casualty . . . an' nae arguments!
You need checkin' ower."

"No, please, I . . . "

Joe paused, turned.

Blush. " . . . I don't think I could sit down." One blue eye
raised. Hesitant. "Will you . . . er, walk me up there,
though?"

"Sure, pal." Joe tried to smile. He strode to the door, then
paused.

Slow, laboured steps behind.

In the hall, he picked up his jacket from the floor then
paused.

Shuffling behind. Then: "Nice flat, isn't it?" Overawed,
impressed, despite the pain.

Joe clenched a fist. He knew the feeling. He stared down
the dark hall.

His home for almost a year.

His and Billy's.

Joe marched towards the front-door, opened it.

He had to leave . . . Joe clenched fist tighter . . . couldn't
be sure what he'd do if he stayed. Thrusting hand into
pocket, he removed a set of keys and placed them on the
hall table. Turning the safety-catch, Joe opened the door
and ushered Robin out into the night.

Petershill Road was deserted apart from a few figures
huddled in tenement doorways. Breath tight in his chest,
Joe paused and tried to push the last hour from his mind.

The Royal's casualty department. Disapproving frown from green-robed doctor as the limping kid was led away. Then giving details at Reception:

'Relative?" Smile.

" No . "

"Name?' Still smiling.

"Robin."

"Surname?"

"Dunno."

"Address?" Encouraging look.

"Dunno."

Green-robed doctor appeared behind counter. Whispered conversation with receptionist, then:

"Age?" Frown.

"Fourteen, ah think."

More looks. Deepening frown . . .

Then standing in a packed waiting-area, wanting to leave, wanting to stay. Feeling useless.

Then green-robed doctor walking towards him. Mouth a hard line. Low voice. "Superficial tearing . . . we've cleaned him up a bit . . . couple of stitches . . . he wants to see you . . ." Scowl.

A curtain drawn back. In the corner, a nurse. The sound of running water. Robin on side, on bed. Long dark hair secured in ponytail. Face looking better. Naked from waist down. Grateful smile.

Trying to smile back. Mouth frozen.

Cold voice from behind. "Let me call the police, Robin – you can press charges. Don't be afraid, this man'll not . . . "

Surprise on bruised face. "Oh it wasn't . . . " Shy smile. "I don't even know your name."

Then running from the cubicle.

Shouts behind.

Continuing to run. Heart hammered in chest.

Running across the M8, up Springburn Road, away from Robin, the police, Billy.

Running towards where no questions would be asked. Only pausing . . . ?

Joe glanced up at Red Road Court's thirty-three floors. A

couple of lights broke up the dark outline, but he couldn't tell from which floor. Joe scowled, walked past a shuttered ice-cream van towards the controlled entry. He pressed a button.

Nothing . . .

Joe sighed and pressed again, twice.

Nothing . . .

Tightening in his chest. Joe laid palm over the raised metal-panel, exerting pressure. Seconds passed . . .

Then irate crackling voices:

- "Whit the . . . ?"

- "Dae you ken whit time it . . . ?"

- "Forgoatten yer key again, ya . . . ?"

- "Ewan?"

Joe removed hand from panel, lowering head. "Sean? Buzz me in . . . "

Curious: "Whit you dain' here, Joe?" Then fear. "It's no' ma maw, is it? Huz somethin' happened tae ma . . . ?"

Angry crackling. Female voice. "Sean Macdonald! Kin ye no' gie yer pals a fuckin' key if they're gonny be . . . "

Buzz. The door swung open. Joe walked into the freshly-painted foyer and towards the lifts. One was coming down.

Joe pressed the UP button and waited.

Seconds later metal doors slid apart. A blond tornado flew out. Fingers seized leather jacket: "Whit is it, Joe? Whit's happened?" Eyes scanning face, then foyer.

Joe gripped a bare arm. "Nothin's happened, Sean." Nothing that concerns you. He looked at wide blue eyes. "Ah jist need a bed fur the night."

Fingers released jacket. Relaxing. Then grin. "Ye loacked yersel' oot?" Broader grin.

Joe scowled at the bare-chested figure. "Something like that."

Sean rubbed goose-fleshed arms and shivered. "Christ! Ah'm frozen!" Hopping from one bare foot to the other. Baseball-cap at odd angle. Around neck, headphones jiggled.

A smiled twitched at mouth, the first in about three hours. "Where's yer stud?"

Slapping arms with pink hands. "Fuckin' thing went green – ah took it oot." One finger to tiny hole in left nostril.

Joe laughed then turned, pressing the lift button.

Metal doors trundled open.

Sean darted into the lift. Impatient. "Well, c'moan if yer comin'!"

No explanation necessary, no questions asked. Joe stepped into the lift and pressed 31.

Doors trundled shut and the lift moved upwards.

CHAPTER TWELVE

The flat was cold. Joe watched as Sean switched on the one-bar electric fire. In a corner, black and white images flickered on a silent TV. Heat spread over his face. Joe shivered, looked away. The reassurance of the familiar was short-lived.

"Waant a coffee?" Hand grabbing sweatshirt from floor, struggling into faded blue fabric.

Joe stared at Sean, then back at the TV. "Ah didney wake ye up, then?" Voice echoed in ears.

"Me?" Laugh. "Naw . . . " Words fading.

A silent figure swept across the screen, fast-forwarded. Oriental features blurring. A subtitle appeared. He tried to read it.

"Eh, Joe?"

He turned.

Grin. "Coffee?"

Sean swayed slightly. Joe blinked. The memory of lager and shit churned in his stomach. He fumbled for cigarettes, tried to light one with a shaking hand. Holding the filter with sweating fingers he noticed a thin smear of blood on index-fingernail. Joe exhaled. Gorge rose in his throat. Sound fizzed in his ears as the cigarette slipped to the floor. He turned and walked unsteadily from lounge into toilet.

Kneeling, he vomited, closing eyes. Acid burned mouth. In Dettol-smelling darkness a film projected onto his eye-lids:

Billy . . . picking-up a fourteen year-old in the Sauchiehall Street arcade.

Billy . . . driving a fourteen year-old kid back to a £140,000 flat.

Billy . . . giving the kid drinks.

Billy . . . giving the kid attention.

Billy . . . beating up the kid . . . fucking . . . hurting . . .

Billy . . . betraying?

Joe vomited again.

Light, then a single voice:

"You okay, Joe?"

Arm round his shoulder. Joe opened eyes and spat into toilet-bowl. A towel thrust at him.

"Here."

Other knees beside his.

Joe looked up.

Concern in blue eyes. Forced cheerfulness. "Thoaght ah wis the wan that wis eye-ways throwin' up!"

A hard towel dabbed his mouth. Joe seized it, rubbed his face.

"Somethin' no' agree wi' ye?"

Joe stared. Robin's physical pain disagreed more than his own emotional hurt. "Aye . . . that's right, Sean." He flushed the toilet and stood up. "Look: ah'm really tired . . . "

Sean still on knees. "Sure, Joe . . . ye kin huv ma bed. Ah'll sleep oan the . . . "

Joe turned. "Jist gie me a blanket or somethin'. Ah'll take the couch."

"But . . . " Clambering to feet.

Joe walked slowly from the toilet and back to the lounge. He sat down.

On-screen, the images were strobing now.

Stomach empty, mind still full, Joe looked away.

Voice at his side. "Here's the spare duvet."

Soft fabric on his lap. Joe blinked. "Thanks." Strobing caught his eye. He looked at Sean, who was watching the screen. "Whit is that onyway?"

Grin. "*Tetsuo*".

Joe raised an eye-brow.

"It's Japanese. Goat it oot the video-shoap. It's aboot these two guys who turn into machines . . . "

"Pit it aff, eh?" Sweat trickled into eyes.

"Aye, sure Joe." Remote searched for, then seized, pointed.

The images died.

Joe sighed and stretched out on the sofa's rough fabric, pulling the duvet up over his head.

Distant voice. "Ye don't waant a coffee, then?"

A smile teased his mouth. "Naw thanks, Sean. Jist sleep . . . " A wave of welcome blackness broke over him . . .

133

Joe blinked.

The venetians had been raised. Light filled the small room.

So did sound . . .

Joe pushed back the duvet, eased his body from under its pleasant weight and walked over to a ghetto-blaster. "Ye'll wake yer mither!" He switched it off.

Laugh from another room. "She's no' back yet . . . "

Joe walked towards the laugh. In the kitchen, Sean was pouring water into two mugs. He turned:

" . . . She phoned, though . . . " Laugh. "Tae check-up oan me! Ah telt hur whit happened, how ye'd loacked yersel' oot, an' she said ah wis tae make ye yer breakfast afore ye went."

Joe sighed. Went where?

Sean was pouring milk into mugs. "So . . . we've goat toast, toast . . . or if ye feel like livin' dangerously, ye kin eye-ways huv toast!" Turning, one mug extended. Grin.

Joe took it, frowned. Why was Sean always so fuckin' happy! He walked back into the lounge, sat down, placing mug on floor.

Voice behind. "Well? Ur ye gonny risk the house-speciality?"

Joe looked up, blinked.

Feigned impatience. "The toast!" Grin.

Joe grinned back, in spite of himself. Sean was infectious. "Aye, go on, then."

"Total! Ah think there's a Kit-Kat somewhere . . . "

"Toast'll be fine." He scratched one armpit. Stale sweat prickled in his nostrils, mixed with the faintly medical aroma of A and E departments. "Ah'll swap ye the Kit-Kat fur a shower."

"Sure, but . . . " Frown. "Ah'll huv tae pit the immerser oan fur ye . . . takes aboot an oor tae heat . . . "

"Cauld'll be fine . . . " Joe stood up and peeled-off the Matrix tee-shirt. The odour of lager and tears rose in a wave. "You goat a top ah kid borrow, Sean?" Fingers undoing belt.

Thoughtful pause, then: "Ma maw's no' done a waashin' yet, but ah'll fun' ye something, Joe. Waant me tae bring it

134

through?"

"Aye." Joe sat on the sofa and began to unlace Docs.

"Whit size ur they?"

"Whit?" Joe looked up.

"Yer boots."

"Oh . . . eleven."

"Kin a try wan oan?"

Joe smiled. "You're no' size eleven . . . "

Hurt. "Ah'm a nine, but . . . jist tae see hoo they luck, kin ah, Joe? Go oan."

Joe tossed him a boot then unbuttoned flies.

On the floor, Sean was tearing off a battered trainer. He pushed it aside, then slid a bare foot into the Doc.

Joe pulled 501s over ankles then stood up.

"See? They're no' really that big oan . . . " Stare. Grin. Then: "Ah like yer knickers, man!"

Joe looked down at the tight, black Tangas. He frowned.

Sean laughed. "Naw, really . . . ah mean it! They luck guid." Back to tying laces. "Ma maw buys me wee boays' wans . . . " Face pulled. " . . . They're aw' baggy, gies ye a real riddy in the PE class . . . "

A warm shiver travelled up his spine. Joe grinned.

Sean stood up, feet in huge boots. "Aw, c'moan, man . . . they don't luck that bad."

Joe laughed. He had missed this, missed the closeness . . . the familiarity.

Sean fell back on the sofa, legs waving.

Joe seized a leather-clad ankle, tugging at a boot. "C'moan – get them aff! They're far too big fur ye."

Sean kicked with a free foot. "Ah'll tell ma maw aw' aboot yer wee skimpy knickers if ye don't let go . . . "

Joe avoid the kicks and pulled harder. "Ah'll tell Ewan ye still wear wee boays' knickers . . . "

Snort. Another kick. "He wears boxer shoarts."

Joe laughed. "Whit's wrang wi' boxer-shoarts?" He paused, still holding a leg.

Frown. "Whit? They're worse than wee boays' knickers, man!"

Joe grinned.

Sean took advantage, kicking himself free. He leapt from the sofa and ran across the room. Then paused in doorway, turning: "Ah'll bring ye a top an' a fresh towel . . . " Mock-frown. "The price o' them is ah get tae keep the boots oan!" Brushing blond hair from pale face.

Flash-back to another, paler face. A bruised face. Joe sobered.

Concern. "Hey! Ah'm ainly kiddin', man." Hair pushed from eyes. "Ah ken we agreed oan the Kit-Kat."

Joe manufactured a smile. "Ah'll git oan through then." He walked past a confused Sean and into the bathroom.

An hour later Sean was talking him through the sub-titled film.

Mouth full of toast, pointing to flickering images: "See? That guy knocked the other wan doon wi' his cor, killed him, but he didn't dee . . . came back an' turned the first guy into a machine." Munching. "Then they both turn into machines. This is a guid bit. Waatch . . . "

Door opening.

Joe looked up.

Angie. A wet Angie. Frowning. "Turn that racket doon, Sean!" A smile to Joe. "Didney think you'd still be here."

He stood up.

Laugh. Nod to Sean. "Ye must huv . . . whit dae they ca' it . . . high tolerance!" Shouting over video sound-track.

Joe smiled.

Angie leant over, seizing the remote from Sean.

The room silenced.

Then: "We wur watchin' that!" Mild annoyance.

Frown. Angie unfastened wet coat. "Huv ye gied Joe his breakfast?"

Mock-hurt. "Aye!"

Angie turned, then peered at Joe's chest. "Whit's that ye've goat oan?"

Joe looked down at the too-tight Rezerrection tee-shirt.

Laugh from Sean. "Ah gied him a top, tae . . . an' let him huv a shower!"

Joe stared at Angie. "Kin a huv a word?"

136

Sharp look. Then sigh. "Whit's he done?" Glare at Sean.

Indignant. "Me? Ah've no' . . . "

"It's nothin' tae dae wi' him, Angie." A look passed between them.

Understanding. Then: "Sean . . . " Hand into pocket. "Away doon tae the van an' get me twenty Club." Money produced.

Curious. Wide blue eyes from his mother to Joe.

Sharper. "Go on, son . . . "

"Ah've . . . " Searching for excuse. " . . . no' goat ma shoes oan!" Pleased at finding one.

Warning tone. "Sean . . . "

Blue eyes to Joe. Wanting to stay.

Joe sighed. "Get me twenty Bensons while ye're there?" Four pound coins extended.

Taken. Brightening. "Sure, Joe." Then snatching the tenner from his mother. Cheeky grin. "Whit dae ah get fur goin'?"

Angie scowled. "Ye get the backa ma haun if ye don't, that's whit!"

Joe smiled.

Wiry arms up in mock-fear. "Ah'll tell the social oan ye." Skipping out of reach of his mother's hand, Sean ran from the room.

Silence, then the sound of a door closing.

Angie peeled off wet coat, then produced cigarettes from pocket. She sat down. Packet extended.

Joe took one, lit Angie's then his own.

Exhale. "So . . . " Leaning forward. Sympathetic smile. " . . . Tell Angie all aboot it."

Joe frowned. "Can ah stay here fur a coupla days – jist 'til ah git masel' soarted oot?" Cigarette to lips.

"Whit happened? Did yous huv a fight?"

Joe shook his head. "It's finished."

Sigh. "Whit ye gonny dae?"

He leant back on the sofa. "Fuck knows . . . " He stared at the artexed ceiling.

"Ah though yous were gettin' oan okay." Surprise. "Mr King's a nice man, fae whit Gina sez . . . "

Nice men don't beat fourteen year-olds into unconsciousness. Joe closed his eyes. "Ah don't waant tae go intae the details, Angie."

"Sure, Joe, sure . . . " Patting his knee. " . . . It's yer ain business."

Understanding, or not really wanting to? Joe opened eyes and ground out cigarette. "Look: ah ken it's a loat tae ask, but . . . " He removed hands from face.

Angie was smiling. "Nae proablem . . . " Then embarrassed. "It'll no' be whit yer yissed tae, mind." Eyes scanning small room.

Joe frowned. You could get used to anything . . .

The slap.

The pocket searches.

Robin's tears.

. . . He had.

"It'll dae fine." He stood up. "Thanks, Angie." Joe looked at the family photographs on the cheap mantle. Three Macdonalds under one roof . . . again.

Laugh. "Ah'd keep ma thanks until ah've tried it, if ah wis you. "

Distant door opening, then slamming. Then Sean shot into the room. Blue cigarette-packet tossed to Angie, gold to Joe. "Well?" Panting. "Talked aboot yer wee secrets, huv yous?" Body thrown onto sofa. Personal stereo grabbed.

Angie sighed. "Git that pit o' a room o' yours tidied up, Sean – ye'll be sharin' it fur a while."

"The couch'll dae me." Joe pulled at the too-tight tee-shirt.

Disappointment from behind. "Ah don't mind . . . 'oanest! It'll be like the airmy."

Joe grinned. "You snore!" He turned. Sean punched his shoulder:

"Naw ah don't!"

Joe smiled. "Ye did the last time ah shared wi' ye!"

Shoulder pummelled. Snort. "That wis years ago . . . an' ah hud a cauld, ye cheeky . . . "

Angie's voice: "Cut it oot, you two!" Then laugh. "At least let me git ye somethin' decent tae wear, Joe." She stood up. "Ah think there's summa Michael's stuff some-

where." Not laughing now. Reddening. "Don't ken why ah
kept it . . . " A hand through damp, frizzy hair. Half smile.
" . . . But mebbe it'll come in handy, 'til ye pick up yer ain
claes." She walked from the room.

Behind, Sean grabbed an arm. "Huz Mr King chucked ye
oot?" Laugh. Other arm encircled Joe's neck.

Joe pulled free, stared at wide blue eyes.

Frown. "Oh, Christ, man! It wisney 'cause o' that thing
wi' his keys, wis it?"

Joe stared over a skinny shoulder. The keys. Over a week
ago.

Had it started then, or before?

Sean grabbed a cushion and began to pummel. "Ah
didney mean tae git ye intae trouble, Joe – oanest!" Fists
sinking into faded velour.

He looked at the pale, worried face, then grabbed a
handful of long blond hair. "Naw, Sean . . . nothin' tae dae
wi' you . . . " A smile twitched lips. " . . . No' this time!" He
yanked. Long fingers seized his:

"Ow, ya . . . " Laugh.

They began to wrestle.

Over Twenty-Fives' Night.

In the staff-room, Joe tucked the freshly-washed Matrix
tee-shirt into waistband and stared down at a heap on the
floor.

A blue sports-shirt stared up at him.

Michael's blue sports-shirt. Angie had a suitcase full of
his old stuff. Jeans, jackets, shirts . . .

A pair of Gola trainers . . .

Joe closed his eyes. Michael's other clothes fitted well
enough.

But he could never fill his brother's shoes.

Didn't know if he wanted to.

Angie's words: 'Stay as lang as ye waant, Joe – it'll be
nice huvin' a man aboot the place . . . '

Didn't know if he should.

' . . . An' ye kin keep an eye oan Sean fur me . . . '

Joe picked up his dead brother's sports-shirt and stuffed

it into locker, slamming door.

Sound ricocheted round the empty room, echoed in his head. Another door closing . . .

The door of 3/1.

The door of Billy's flat.

Another door closing on another life.

Joe sighed.

The sound of a door opening. Then: "Git a move oan – eh?" Malkie's voice from far side of the room.

Joe looked up. "Jist comin' . . . " He followed the bulky form back out into foyer.

Dripping red brush to already-shiny nails. "So . . . " Another coat of varnish stroked onto fingertip. " . . . How's the case goin'?"

Joe watched the delicate operation. "Whit ye oan aboot?"

Pink tongue-tip between red-slash lips, concentrating. Gina stroked again. Eyes on task in hand. "Yer polisman-pal. Thoaght he wid be keepin' ye up-tae-date wi' thur . . . whit dae they ca' it? . . . inquiries!" More stroking.

Joe stared. "Ah've no idea whit yer talkin' . . . "

Frustration. "Fuck!" Brush slipping. Tutting. Eyes raised. "See whit ye've made me dae!" Eyes lowered again. Right index finger carefully blotting unintended red smear. "The cop ah seen ye talkin' tae last night – whit wis his name?"

Joe blinked.

More frustration. "Him being polis, ah thoaght he'd gied ye . . . inside infurmation!"

Joe sighed. Georgie Paxton: a week, a lifetime away. Literally.

Andy Hunter: last night. Slightly less distant.

He produced cigarettes, extended packet.

Gina was blowing on one hand, shaking the other.

He grinned, extracted a cigarette from packet and placed it between red-slash lips.

Mumbled "Ta!"

Joe took one for himself, then lit both.

Gina puffed. "Good-lookin' guy . . . " Cigarette moving to words. "Whit's his name, again?" Feigned nonchalance.

Joe smiled. "Hunter . . . Andy Hunter."

"Aye – that's right." Cigarette bobbing on bottom lip. "Is he . . . ?"

Joe tensed.

Both hands shaking now. " . . . married?"

Joe relaxed. "No idea."

Thoughtful. "Ah didney see a ring . . . mind ye, a loatta guys don't go in fur them, these days." Cigarette grasped between knuckles.

He frowned. Georgie had liked his rings. Joe fingered the healing cut then pushed old feelings away and laughed. "Ye no' a bit auld fur Andy?"

Laugh. "Ach, away, ye cheeky bastard! Ye never hearda toay boays?"

Joe blinked. Toys . . . to be used, then thrown away.

A bruised, fourteen-year old face.

Robin: Billy's toy.

Joe drew on the cigarette.

Curious. "How auld is he, onyway?"

Joe scowled. "Who?"

Impatient. "Andy Hunter, Joe – ah mean, he canny be as young as he lucks . . . " Thoughtful. " . . . Probably aboot your age."

Joe stared.

"Eh, Joe?"

He focused on the red-slash mouth.

"Onythin' wrang, Joe?" Laugh. "Ye're no' wi us, the night!"

He shook his head. "Nothin', Gina." Joe tried a smile. It failed.

Eyes examining nails. Frown. "There's bin nothin' in the papers aboot Georgie fur days, noo. Ask Andy if onywan's . . . " Laugh. " . . . helpin' them wi' thur inquiries."

"Ah hardly ken the guy, Gina!" Filter gripped between hard fingers. Georgie Paxton. Andy Hunter. Billy. All part of the past. All associated with here, now.

Offended. "Sorry!"

Joe sighed. "Naw – ah'm sorry." He ground out cigarette in overflowing ashtray, then glanced at his watch: nearly

141

one. He looked at Gina. "Listen: kid ye cover fur me if ah nip aff early?" He needed peace, quiet. He needed Angie and Sean.

Red-slash smile. "Sure, Joe – nae problem. Away hame tae Mr King!" Shooing motion with red-tipped fingers.

CHAPTER THIRTEEN

An hour later he was walking up Barnhill Road. Joe patted the new set of keys in his pocket: new keys for a new life. Turning into Red Road, a stocky figure ahead. Whistling.

Joe peered into dimly-lit gloom.

Whistling grew louder. The figure neared, red helmet-cut hair and tattooed-sleeve jacket shining under sodium.

Joe smiled. "Oot late, Ewan!"

Whistling stopped. Returned smile. "Hope yer wearin' yer boady-armour, man!" Turning to stare up thirty-one floors.

"Whit dae ye mean?"

Laugh, then turn. "Sean an' his mither . . . she's gonny kill him!"

Joe stared. "She's no' fun oot aboot the organic eecy?"

Surprise. "You ken aboot that?"

"Ah wis the wan threw it away!" Joe laughed.

Frown. "Aye, well it's no' that . . . it's the band."

Joe raised an eyebrow.

Mock-surprise. "He's no' telt ye?" Zipping up leather against frost. "We're stertin' a band, soarta Primal-Scream-meets-Praga-Khan."

Joe stared, none the wiser.

Ewan stared back, shrugged, then: "Sean's on lead, but he's no goata guitar – bin practising oan ma brither's. Jim's sellin' it, Sean waants tae buy . . . "

"How much dis yer brither waant fur this guitar?"

"Oh, it's a guid deal, man. Strat coapy – four hunnerd new. Jim ainly waants a hunnerd an' fifty fur it. It's a bargain!" Footstamps against the cold.

Joe frowned. Sean didn't have that kind of money . . . neither did Angie. "Seeya, Ewan." He walked towards the flats.

"Seeya, man . . . " Laugh. " . . . An' mind yer riot-shield!"

On the thirty-first floor Joe pulled keys from pocket.

A thud. Then shrieking words.

He scowled, hoping Angie had tolerant neighbours. Joe inserted a Yale into cheap lock and pushed.

Louder shouting. Words audible now:

"Ah'm sicka this fuckin' rat-trap . . . "

"Don't use that language wi' me, ya wee bastard . . . "

"An' ah'm fuckin' sicka you, ya fuckin' . . . "

Joe slammed the door and strode towards the lounge.

The sound of a slap, then silence. Then:

"Oh Christ, son! Ah didney mean tae . . . "

Door wrenched open.

Joe stared at an angry face, its eyes heavy with undischarged tears. He grabbed an arm. "Sean!"

Arm pulled free. "Lea' me alain!" Tall figure rushing towards bedroom. "Ah'm oota here!" Door slamming.

Joe sighed. From the lounge, a sniff. He turned and walked towards Angie.

She stared at him. "Oh, Christ, Joe . . . " Features crumpling.

He draped an arm around heaving shoulders and led Angie to the couch.

Mumbling. "Ah'm soarry, but he jist pushes me too far."

Joe produced cigarettes. "Ah ken, Angie . . . ah met Ewan."

Sigh. Cigarette placed between quivering lips. "Thanks."

He lit it.

She inhaled, began to talk.

Joe listened . . .

. . . Twenty minutes and five cigarettes later he was still listening:

"Hyperactive, the doactor ca's it." Sniff. "His teachers say he's the same in the school . . . " Sniff.

Joe held out a handkerchief.

Angie took it. " . . . Canny sit still, eyewis talkin', disruptin' everywan else . . . " Nose blown. "Bin suspended three times this year aw' ready." Sniff. "Ah thought he wis ower all that kinda stuff – ah try tae talk tae him, Joe, but he jist sits there wi' that stupit grin oan his face. Ah canny git through tae him." Sniff. Change in voice. Regret into anger. "Never thinks aboot onywan but himsel' . . . goes

144

oan an' oan aboot claes, tapes o' this, tapes o' that, they damn boots he's eyewis whinin' fur . . . ah'm sicka the sound o' his fuckin' voice!" Red eyes raised. Softening. "Ah usually gie in, an' the wee bugger kens that, but . . . " Sniff. " . . . ah've no' goat the money fur ony guitars. He kens that tae, but . . . " Nose wiped. Angie stood up. Hurt, anger, remorse and frustration struggled on tear-stained face. She walked to the window. "Ah gie up, Joe . . . ah really dae." Turning. "Mebbe Longriggend wid be the best place fur him – ah canny dae a thing wi' him."

Joe joined her at the window, staring out through venetian slats.

She didn't know the half of it.

He frowned, looked down. A distant Glasgow twinkled below.

A Glasgow where Billy would be picking up the night's takings, as usual.

A Glasgow where £150 was chicken-feed.

Joe scowled.

A hand on his arm.

He turned.

Angie wiping eyes. Half-smile. "Sorry ye hud tae walk in on aw' this . . . it's ma proablem."

Joe sighed. Billy: these days he was always walking in on other people's problems.

But Sean was his problem.

Michael's shoes . . .

He patted Angie's arm. "Pit the kettle oan, eh?"

Hands twisting wet handkerchief. "Ah've never hit him before, but . . . " Red, pleading eyes, not wanting to ask. " . . . Don't think ah kin face the wee . . . "

Joe tried a smile.

Michael's shoes . . .

She shouldn't need to ask.

He ruffled the frizzy hair and went in search of Sean.

On the door, a yellow rectangle, black lettering:

Danger of Contamination. Keep Out.

Joe knocked.

Nothing.

He knocked again.

"Lea' me alain!" Frustrated and angry.

Joe turned the door handle and pushed.

The room was dark.

Joe brushed the wall for a light-switch, found one. Then stared.

A five-foot poster of Schwarzenneger in full combat gear leered down onto an unmade single bed. A wardrobe door hung open, as did the four drawers of a white, build-it-yourself chest of drawers. A smell drifted into nostrils. Joe sniffed: sweat, trainers and cheap fabric-conditioner. Also . . . strawberries? He blinked, eyes scanning mess for . . .

Half-hidden by a floral-covered duvet, Sean and one of Michael's old kit-bags. An assortment of jumpers and jeans protruded from the khaki. Socks, magazines and empty cassette boxes covered the floor. Muffled voice from the duvet: "Git oota ma . . . "

"Who's Ghengis Khan?" Joe leant against the door-jamb.

"Eh?" Blond head appearing.

"Ewan said yer band wis . . . "

Grin. "Praga Khan. Dutch techno . . . " Sitting up. " . . . They played The Tunnel coupla months ago. Totalled the place!"

Joe frowned.

Laugh. "Ah didney see them – Ewan telt me, gied me a lenna the tape."

"Ye still goat it?"

Nod. "Sure, Joe . . . " Scrambling off bed and onto floor. " . . . it's here, somewhere." Tape boxes into air.

He watched as Sean reached under bed.

"Ah . . . goat it!" Arm emerging, fingers holding cassette.

Joe stared at the pink face.

No sign of the slap.

No sign of the behaviour which had provoked it.

Anger on and off like a light switch. The Macdonald temper.

Sean grinned. "Ma Walkman's through in the other room. Waant tae hear it noo?"

Joe took the cassette, turned it over in his hands. The object of the exercise achieved: all thoughts of leaving home vanished. "Tomorra. It's late – an' we're aw' tired. You goat school in the mornin'?"

Frown. Then: "Aye . . . you workin'?"

Joe shook his head. "Two days aff."

Two days to find another flat . . . another life . . .

"Total, man!" Grin. Then frown. "Ah took *Tetsuo* back tae the vid-shoap . . . widda kept it oot fur ye, if ah'd kent ye were aff . . . "

"Nae time – things tae dae, Sean."

One eyebrow raised, then understanding. Solemn. "Sure, Joe." Pause. Appealing smile. "Ye've no' goat a spare hunnerd an' fifty, ah suppose?"

Joe frowned. His wage from the Matrix was two-fifty a week. Billy had always paid him . . . personally. Now?

Frown. Trying to look hurt. "It disney matter."

Joe laughed, picked up a sock and threw it at the kneeling boy. Then scowled. "Lea' aff the guitar stuff – okay?" Nod towards lounge. The meaning clear.

"Sure, Joe." The meaning taken.

"We'll soart somethin' oot . . . maybe Ewan's brother'll let ye pay it up . . . " Maybe a band would keep him away from eccy and The Matrix.

Hoot from the floor.

A sock sailed past Joe's ear. He smiled. "An' keep the noise doon – yer mither's beat." Hand on light switch. "Is it no' time ye wur in bed, tae?"

"Sure, Joe." Tee-shirt whipped over head, blond hair tangling. Long fingers undoing belt.

He stared at the skinny chest. "Guidnight, Sean."

"'Night, Joe . . . " Fingers unzipping jeans.

Joe smiled, switched off the light and walked back to the lounge.

Empty. Noises from the kitchen.

He walked to the doorway and stared through.

Cold air. The kitchen was empty. But the balcony door stood ajar. Joe joined Angie outside.

She was drinking coffee. A thin trail of cigarette smoke

147

joined steam from a mug.

Joe stood beside the slight figure.

A sigh condensed in sub-zero air. Then: "He okay?"

"Aye . . . he's away tae bed."

In the distance, a police-siren screamed.

Angie rested mug on wrought-iron railings. Cigarette to mouth, then: "Christ kens whit Michael wid think if he kid see the mess ah've . . . "

"Michael wid be proud o' ye, Angie." Joe stroked a thin arm, knowing it was true.

Snort. "Whit's there tae be prouda?" Exhaling a cloud.

Joe sighed. Michael had understood him: he would understand his own son. "Sean's tryin' it oan – ah wis jist the same at his age . . . a loata boays ur." He looked at the tired, strained face, the puffy eyes then fiddled with a frizzy curl. "Ye've done an okay joab. Thur's a loata kids worse than Sean . . . "

"But . . . "

"Nae buts, Angie. Ye brought him up fine . . . "

"But wid Michael huv . . . ?"

Joe closed his eyes: the years ebbed away. "Michael wid unnerstaun', Angie. Ye did whit ye hud tae, goat oan wi' yer life."

Michael had been there for Joe . . . was he still there for Angie?

The suitcase of his brother's clothes. Joe frowned. "Why did ye no' . . . remarry, Angie? It's bin six years . . . an' Sean kid dae wi' somewan tae keep him in line." Michael had been there for him . . .

Choking sound, becoming cough, then laugh. "Where wid ah fun' the time, Joe?"

He frowned.

She turned. Nose pink, matching eyes. "Oh, ah've no' bin a complete nun, but! Ah've hud ma moments . . . " Genuine laugh.

Joe smiled.

Frown. " . . . Ah don't ken how Sean wid take tae another guy aboot the place, but."

Joe looked away, staring out into yellow-dotted night.

Angie and Sean: a family. A family's problems. Not his family.

Laugh. "Oh, you're . . . different, Joe – mair like his big brither. He disney see you as – whit is it they say? – a threat."

Joe smiled. Big brother . . . brothers . . . ?

Hand on his shoulder. "You're good wi' him, Joe – you're whit he needs . . . "

Michael.

" . . . He respects you . . . ."

Michael.

Fingers tightening. "Ah'm jist some wuman naggin' him the whole time."

Joe took the tiny hand, squeezed it. "You're his mither, Angie. You're too . . . close tae him, right noo." The closeness of brothers . . . a different closeness?

Sigh. "Aye . . . mebbe." Low laugh. "Ah think he's a bit frightened o' you, Joe!"

He smiled, an arm around thin shoulders. "Me?" Michael had scared the shit out of him on several occasions.

Laugh. "Aye, you!" Sobering. "Ye're some sight when ye git angry, Joe. Ah'll never forget whit ye did tae that guy in the pub."

He closed his eyes. Years ago. His first leave home. Out for a drink with Angie and Michael . . . feeling like a spare prick. Too many drinks. Some comment about the uniform, from someone who knew nothing . . . until Joe had taught him a lesson. "That wis a lang time ago, Angie." Hammering in his chest.

Low voice. "Sorry, Joe, ah didney mean tae . . . "

"'S okay." He opened his eyes, looked at watch: nearly four. "It's late . . . c'moan in."

Cigarette ground out under slippered foot. "Aye . . . " Smile. "Ah need ma sleep – it's the ainly time ah git ony peace!"

They both laughed. As he followed her back into the flat:

"By the way . . . how wis work?" Balcony door locked.

Joe frowned. "Fine."

"Did ye see Mr King?" Tentative.

149

He scowled, walking through the kitchen and into the lounge. He paused by the sofa.

Sigh. "Ah'm sorry yous fell oot, Joe."

He sat down on the sofa and unlaced boots.

"Mr King wis guid tae ye, Joe." Apologetic. "Ah widda taken ye in, when ye came oota the airmy, but the Social widda bin funny aboot it, ye ken that."

Joe sighed, dragging foot from boot. He knew. He owed Billy.

Hand holding out two cushions. "Noo that ah'm working there's nae problem, acourse."

Joe took the cushions.

"But ur ye no' bein' a wee bit rash, Joe? That wis a nice flat, fae whit Sean sez . . . "

He took off another boot and began to undo belt.

" . . . No' waant tae think aboot it, Joe? Ah mean, ye wur oantae a guid thing, there . . . "

"Nothin' tae think aboot . . . " He dragged Matrix tee-shirt over head. "Noo . . . " He managed a smile. " . . . away tae yer bed, wuman!"

Smile returned. Nod. "Guidnight, then."

Light switched off.

Darkness enveloped.

150

CHAPTER FOURTEEN

A week passed.

A week like any other.

Seven days . . .

The last seven days had been . . . different.

Joe peeled back a rubber glove and glanced at his watch: almost three-thirty. He smiled.

A week of Sean and Angie had been . . . different . . .

He frowned. Totally different. Joe surveyed the spotless kitchen.

. . . the same, but . . . different.

Here, he was . . . in charge? He made decisions, took control.

No-one told him what to do and when to do it.

Joe leant back against the ancient gas cooker and sighed.

One-hundred-and-sixty-eight Billy-free hours.

He frowned, spotting a smear of grease. Different . . .

Different-better?

Joe rubbed the stain with a cloth.

No . . . just different.

A door slammed. Then: "You ready, man?" Running footsteps. Panting.

Joe smiled and snapped-off rubber gloves.

Blond, baseball-capped head round kitchen door. Grin, then stare. "Christ, man! Ah never kent it wis that colour underneath!" Walking to cooker. Blue eyes to Joe.

He laughed.

Frown. "Ye make me feel guilty, man." Nose wiped with back of hand.

"An' so ye should!" Joe bent down and tossed Marigolds into cupboard under sink.

Silence, then: "Ah tidied ma room, but."

Joe stood up.

Blue eyes stared. "Waant tae see?" Eager to please.

Joe frowned.

Different . . . the same, but different.

He yanked peak of baseball-cap, pulling it down over

151

the blue eyes. "Ah'll trust ye, Sean."

Laugh. Baseball-cap re-righted. "So . . . ur we goin', then?" Hopping from foot to foot.

Joe smiled. Ewan's brother had sold the guitar to someone else. Plan B was necessary. "Aye . . . when dis yer mither git in?"

Thoughtful. "Wednesdays . . . " Chewing pink bottom lip. " . . . Half fiveish, usually."

Joe walked into the lounge and grabbed his jacket.

Sean followed, still hopping.

"We'll get chips – eh?"

"Total, man!" Laugh. "Onythin' but your cookin' again!"

"'Least ah kin dae mair than toast!" Joe aimed a punch at the bobbing head.

Sean hopped away, grinning. "No much mair, though." He mock-slapped Joe's shoulder.

"You criticisin' ma fried eggs?" He zipped up bikers' jacket.

"No way, man – ah like yer fried eggs . . . " Laugh. " . . . But fur every meal?"

Joe smiled. The banter, the jokes . . .

Billy never joked . . . A stray slap caught the side of his face. Light stinging.

Laugh. "Goat ye . . . " Then not laughing. Concern. " . . . Christ! That's yer sore cheek – ah forgoat!" Long fingers traced the fading imprint of Georgie Paxton's ring.

Joe pulled away from the stroke. Something stirred in the pit of his stomach, something . . . different. He walked towards the door. "C'moan if yer comin'! Where is this place, again?"

Laugh. "McCormacks' – Bath Street. We kin git a number twelve straight there."

"Goat yer keys?"

"Aye." Laugh. "Ye goat yer money?" Sean pushed past him into the hall.

Joe patted his cash-line card. "Ah thoaght we wur jist lookin', the day?"

Ahead, Sean was holding the door open. Grin. "Ainly kiddin', man." Mock impatient. "Kin we go?"

Joe pushed him out onto the landing and locked the front door. Then turned.

Sean was prodding the lift's Call button.

Joe smiled. Nothing happened soon enough, or fast enough.

A ping. The lift doors parted. Sean rushed in.

Joe walked slowly towards the grinning boy.

" . . . An' that's a Fender Strat." Awed voice. Pointing.

"Like the wan Ewan's brither . . . ?"

"Naw!" Scornful. "Jimmy's wis a coapy." Sigh. "That's the real thing . . . " Fingering price-tag. " . . . Six-fifty's worth o' the real thing!"

Joe frowned. "Thoaght you said they did second-haun in here?"

Fingers stroked the guitar's scratch-plate. "Aye, they dae . . . " Turning. Huge blue eyes. " . . . Ah waanted ye tae see the . . . genuine article, but." Turning back to display. "See that wan at the back?" Pointing.

Joe scanned.

"The white wan."

Joe's eyes focused on an oddly-shaped instrument. He nodded.

"PRS . . . that's whit Boabby Gillespie huz." Turn, then explanatory smile. "Paul Reed Smith . . . the best, man!"

"An' how much did 'the best' set Boabby Whitshisname back?"

Sigh. "Well, he didney git much change oota a grand, let's pit it that way . . . "

Voice behind. "Can ah help ye, boays?"

Joe turned.

Older guy. McCormacks tee-shirt. Salesman's smile.

He frowned. "Whur's yer second-haun stuff?"

Salesman's smile fading. Eyes from Joe to Sean and back again. "Through the back . . . " Arm extended. " . . . We've no' much in stock, at the moment, what wi' the Christmas rush an' . . . "

"Let's see it onyway." Joe strode in the direction indicated.

Behind. "Wonder how lang it wid take us tae pay up the

PRS."

Joe laughed. "Forget it!" Reluctant footsteps followed him through to the back.

An hour later, they were eating chips at the Cathedral Street bus-stop. Joe wiped his mouth and looked at Sean. "The guy said there wis mair comin' in next week."

Disappointment painted the pale face. "Ah need it noo."

Joe balled wrapping and tossed it into a bin. "Whit wis wrang wi' the wans the guy showed us? The sunburst wan wis ... "

Scornful. "Coapy o' a coapy o' a crap guitar, Joe – kid ye no' hear that?"

"Kidda bin the amp."

Head shake. "AC30s ur the best, man – if onythin', the amp made it sound better than it wis." Licking greasy fingers.

Joe leant against the bus-stop. "When's yer next practice?"

Sean nibbled a cuticle. "Friday."

Friday ... wages day. Fifty left in the bank. Joe sighed, remembering. Not anymore: he'd given that to Angie yesterday.

A bus appeared. Joe peered at the number: thirty-eight. Not Barnhill. He looked at Sean. "Waant tae walk?"

Sulky headshake, staring at the ground.

Joe sighed, produced cigarettes then Zippo.

Head raised, disapproving blue eyes. "They'll kill ye, they things."

Joe flicked the Zippo, inhaled then blew smoke into air.

Theatrical hand-wave, then cough.

Joe grinned. "'Gie it a rest, eh?" A shoulder slumped beside him.

Sigh. "Ma maw's jist the same." Scowl. "The flat stinksa fags."

Joe frowned. Angie's one pleasure, from what he saw. "Since when did you git so ... health-conscious?"

Playful bump against him. "Aw' the teachers ur eyewis goin' oan aboot drugs, an' how bad they ur fur ye."

Joe sighed. Back to this again.

154

"They git drunk whenever they waant, smoke thur fags . . ."

"That's aw' legal, Sean!" He exhaled in the other direction.

"Lethal, mair like!"

"An' eccy's guid fur ye?" Joe frowned.

"Mebbe no', but at least it disney ruin' yer lungs an' fuck up yer liver."

"It dis Christ knows whit tae yer brain, though!" He ground-out cigarette underfoot.

Snort. "That's no' bin proved . . . "

"It's no' bin disproved either." A warm body lunged against him. "Where's that bus goat tae?"

Joe smiled. "C'moan – let's walk." He watched as a reluctant Sean levered himself off the bus-stop and grinned:

"We kid git a taxi." Hopeful.

Joe turned and began to stroll away. "Git a move oan, ya lazy . . . "

Car honking.

Joe tensed. Voice at his side:

"Christ, Joe – it's the polis!"

He turned, following Sean's eyes to where a white-and-pink striped squad-car had pulled in at the kerb. He frowned.

The driver leant across passenger-seat. Window wound down. "Thought it was you . . . " Liquid brown eyes over Joe's shoulder. " . . . And . . . Sean, isn't it?" Andy Hunter draped a blue-serge arm through the open window.

Joe frowned. Billy: Robin. Nearly ten days since the Royal. He'd debated . . . doing what? Phoning the police, reporting an assault? Joe rubbed his face. Robin's injuries were superficial; the kid didn't want his parents to know; he was probably getting on with his life, putting Billy behind him.

Like Joe should. It was over, in the past.

Behind, tugging at his jacket:

"Jist walk oan, man."

Joe stared at the almost-classical face.

It smiled, then: "Can I give you two a lift?"

Joe continued to stare.

Behind. "C'moan, man." More tugging.

Understanding flashed over the smiling face. To Sean.

155

"Don't want your pals to see you in a police-car, is that it?"

Movement behind. Then Sean was at his side. "Joe's no' done onythin. Lea' him alain!" Protective bravado.

Resonant laugh.

A smile twitched Joe's lips.

Andy Hunter grinned. Large brown eyes twinkled.

Joe turned to Sean. "You go on – ah'll catch ye up."

Concerned blue eyes.

Joe laughed. "Oan ye go, Sean – ah'll be fine!"

Blue eyes scanned face, then a shrug. "Okay . . . " Wary. " . . . But don't be lang." Hard look to Andy Hunter.

Sean walked away.

Joe turned back to the car, smiled.

The smile returned. "So . . . how are you?"

Joe lit a cigarette. "Ah'm fine."

Smile fading. "And . . . Mr King?"

Joe scowled. "He's fine . . . as far as ah ken."

Curious brown eyes.

Joe exhaled. "It's a lang story." Arm on the squad-car's wet roof.

Encouraging smile. "Does it have a happy ending?"

Joe laughed. "Mebbe – ah've no' decided yet!" He stared into liquid brown eyes . . .

. . . which stared back. Then glanced at wrist. "Look: I'm knocking off at eight. What about a drink?" Eyes raised.

Joe smiled. "Aye, sure."

Low resonant laugh. "Great – Delmonica's? About nine?"

Joe sighed. It was one thing to agree, in theory. But Delmonica's? Virginia Street. Just round the corner from . . .

Understanding. "Oh, right . . . I see. Well, what about . . . ?"

"Delmonica's is fine." Joe smiled. Billy was no longer a consideration.

Behind, the sound of heavy air-brakes.

Joe turned. A number twelve . . . "That's oor bus noo . . . " He looked towards a baseball-capped figure yards away and shouted over traffic. " . . . Sean!"

From the car. "I'd better move." Mock salute. "See you at nine."

A breathless Sean seized his arm:

156

"C'moan, Joe."

He turned back to the police-car, smiled then followed Sean onto the bus.

Low voice. "Whit did he waant?" Sean's body was warm beside him.

Joe stared through a misty window. "Nothin'."

Whisper: "Dis he ken aboot . . . the eccy?"

Joe sighed. "Huv ye done ony since . . . oor talk?" He turned.

Vociferous handshake. Blond hair whipped across earnest face.

"Huv ye sold ony?"

Another headshake, then blond strands peeled from pink lips .

Joe scowled. "Then thur's nothin' tae ken, is thur?" A hand punched his shoulder:

"Right, Joe." Wink.

A smile twitched at his mouth. He tried to suppress it. "Ah mean it, Sean." Joe fixed blue eyes with his own.

They widened, pupils dilating.

The bus lurched to a halt.

Joe broke eye-contact and stood up.

Laugh. "Nae time fur aw' that, these days, man – an' onyway, ah've goat ma guitar tae save up fur!"

Joe walked towards the front of the bus.

Behind. "It disney huv tae be an expensive wan, Joe – jist a guid wan. Ah mean, ah canny show the band up, can ah?"

Pneumatic doors hissed apart. Joe got off the bus.

Behind. "Ewan's goat a sequencer – ye should see it, man, it's brand new!"

Joe sighed and walked towards the flats.

As he reached the door of 31/3 Sean was in front, walking backwards.

Still talking:

"See, Joe? First we make a demo – Ewan kens somewan wi' a fourtrack, so we don't huv tae waste money oan studio-time."

157

Andy Hunter: was this a good idea? Joe walked into the dark hallway, frowning.

Sean continued to reverse, and talk: "Then we send coapies o' the demo tae people who'll like it . . . " Pause. Slightly irritated. " . . . Ur you listenin'?"

Joe pushed past him into the lounge.

Angie was watching television.

He took off jacket and sat down on the sofa.

TV volume reduced with remote. Head turned, smile.

He smiled back, then stared at the whispering news-reader. Andy Hunter. Delmonica's. Why not? Sweat trickled from an armpit. "Aw' right if ah huv a shower?"

Smile. "Sure, the immerser's oan. Gie it anoather coupla minutes." Frown. "There wis nae need fur that fifty quid, Joe – it's as cheap tae feed three as two."

"Ah like tae pay ma way, Angie." He began to unlace boots.

Purring from the hall, then a hoot:

"That'll be fur me . . . " Lounge-door kicked shut.

Joe took off boots and began to undo belt.

Minutes later, door banged open. Breathless voice. "Ewan met Mr King!"

Joe looked up.

A strand of dirty hair pushed out of eyes. "He wis in the red Landrover-thing – a Jeep, isn't it?" Excited face.

Joe stared at the bobbing figure.

Sean walked across the room and threw himself onto the sofa. Grin. "Mr King's goat three cors, ma – Joe showed me." Long legs sprawling. "Ah liked the big Merc best." Cushion seized. "Ah'm gonny huv wan like that when the band makes it big." Pummelling cushion. "Ah'll huv three, in fact! A white wan, a rid wan . . . an' a . . . "

Laugh from Angie. "An' whit aboot yer mither?"

A cushion hurled across the room. "Oh, don't worry – ah'll git you a wee runaroon' – a Fiesta, oar somethin' – tae dae yer shoappin' in." Expansive gesture.

Cushion caught and hurled back. "Ah, ye're affy generous, Sean."

Cushion pressed to skinny chest. "Aye – that's me."

Wiry arms embracing furry fabric.

Joe smiled. It was good to see them getting on.

Volume of TV increased.

Joe pulled off socks and tee-shirt. "Ah'll away an' huv that shower, then."

Sean was placing ear-phones in ears. He grinned, then winked.

Angie waved a hand. "Oan ye go, Joe – there's a clean towel over the bath, an' ah've washed yer Matrix tee-shirt."

"Thanks . . . " He ruffled her hair and walked towards the door.

In the bathroom he peeled-off jeans and Tangas then pulled back the green nylon curtain. A cheap shower-head was affixed to badly-discoloured wallpaper. Joe stepped into the bath and reached up.

Lukewarm water trickled over his head.

Joe turned up the pressure.

Slightly more lukewarm water.

He frowned and grabbed an oddly-shaped bar of soap from the side of the bath. Must have something to do with water travelling uphill – either that, or being shared with a hundred other flats. Joe lathered the bar between large hands and began to wash.

Sean's talk of cars . . .

. . . The Cherokee Jeep. The Merc.

Specifically, the Merc's bonnet. A wet night in Port Dundas.

Joe sighed, soaped face, hair, then shoulders.

An odour of . . . strawberries? Underneath, the scent of fresh sweat persisted.

He continued to wash. As hands travelled over pecs and onto stomach, he thought of other hands . . . softer hands.

Billy's tiled bathroom.

Billy's gentle fingers washing away pain.

Something stirred in the pit of his stomach . . .

Joe gasped and closed eyes.

Other images swam before him. Polished wooden floor, his body slick with sweat and spunk. Billy's spunk.

159

Hand drifted down. Fingers brushed groin. Surprise flushed his face.

Then the door burst open.

Joe glanced up.

"Okay if ah wash ma hair . . . ?" Wide blue eyes on Joe's hardening prick. Grin. "Don't mind me, man . . . "

The army. All boys together. Erections meant nothing.

Joe watched as Sean pulled off Rezerrection tee-shirt and walked to the sink. Tap turned on. Then:

"Fuck!" Spinning round. "Gie's summa yer water." Sean walked over to the bath and thrust a blond head under the trickle.

Strands of hair brushed thighs. Joe moved back.

Sean was rubbing head with dirty fingers. "Ye goin' oot, the night tae?"

"Aye." He pushed the oddly-shaped soap deep into an arm-pit.

"Where ye goin?" Hair thoroughly soaked, now.

Joe frowned. "Jist oot."

Laugh. "Aw', c'moan, man – tell me!" Pause, sniff, then: "You bin usin' ma guid soap, man?" Face raised, accusing eyes blinking through the wet.

Joe grinned. "That the strawberry stuff?" He lathered the bar one-handed.

Wiping eye-lids. "Aye . . . the Boady Shoap. It's expensive." Eyes opening. "Ma maw gets it cheap fae the factory – ah keep it fur special occasions. Ye kin wash yer hair wi' it, ken." Head back into shower.

Joe ran soapy hands over crew cut, lathered again then reached down and began to rub Sean's wet scalp. "Whit's special aboot the night?" Fingers into long, water-darkened hair.

Sean braced pale arms against the side of the bath. "We're auditioning a new drum-machine." Cough, then spitting.

Joe laughed. "Must be an affy special drum-machine fur ye tae git the expensive soap treatment!"

Snort. Head half-raised.

"Keep still!" Joe continued to rub pink soap into tangled hair, massaging the scalp with rough fingers..

Head lowered again. Laugh. "It's no' the machine we're auditionin' . . . "

"Must be an affy special drum-machine . . . operator!" He dropped the bar of soap, ran fingers through the length of blond wetness then angled the shower directly onto Sean's head and began to rinse. Long fingers joined his, two sets of fingers jointly rinsing, cleansing . . . working together.

Then Sean pulled away. Wet grin. "It might be." Enigmatic. Flipping back hair. Then dog-shake.

Joe stepped back, avoiding stray Sean-spray, then directed the shower-head back to his stomach. "No' gonny tell me, then?" He smiled at the bare-chested boy.

Laugh. "You've goat yer secrets . . . an' ah've goat mine!" Sean grabbed the towel and skipped from the bathroom.

"Oi! Bring that back!" Joe switched off shower and stepped out of the bath. He grinned, then looked down.

Amongst dark curls his prick was now completely hard.

Angie was alone when he returned to the lounge. The one-bar fire glowed weakly.

The sound of low music seeped through from Sean's bedroom.

He shivered. Thighs still wet beneath jeans, Joe walked past Angie's slippered feet and sat on the floor. "Did ye get me a *Times*? Tuesdays ur the flat days, ye said."

"Aye, Joe . . . " Rustling, then a folded newspaper produced from under cushion. Extended.

He took, unfolded it and began to flick. Near the back, Accommodation to Let. Gripping filter between lips Joe spread the *Glasgow Evening Times* over the floor and began to scan.

"Waant a coffee?"

"No' the noo." He ran index-finger down smudgy print.

Contented sigh. Then voice at his side: "It's . . . nice, huvin' ye here, Joe."

Eyes back-tracked up column to a bedsit in Shettleston: £60 a week, sorry no DSS. He grabbed a pen from the mantle and circled it.

"Ye're really helpful aboot the hoose. Must be the airmy

161

trainin' . . . " Laugh. " . . . Michael wis the same – eyewis tidyin' up efter himsel'."

Joe traced a second column, then paused: 'Room to let in West-End flat. £75 per week, plus share of bills. Professional person only . . . ' He frowned. Did an ex-army bouncer count?

" . . . It's guid tae huv somewan sensible tae talk tae . . . "

He circled the phone-number then ran pen further down.

Laugh. " . . . an' whitever yer dain' wi' Sean, it's workin'!"

Joe looked up.

Happy face. "Ten days in a row – ah canny believe it!"

He raised an eyebrow.

"The school . . . " Cigarette ground out in ashtray. " . . . Ah even gied them a ring fae work, tae check." Leaning back on sofa. "Quarter tae nine 'till quarter tae four aw' week – an' nae bunkin' aff in between eether!"

Joe smiled.

A hand on his shoulder. Laugh. "Aye . . . it's nice huvin' ye here, Joe . . . " More serious. " . . . But it canny be much fun fur you, sharin' a damp flat wi' a woman an' a wee boay!"

Joe frowned. Angie was wrong . . .

Stirring in his stomach. The shower, the closeness.

. . . Sean wasn't a wee boy anymore.

Concern. "Whit's wrang Joe – no' find ony flats?"

He stood up. "There's a couple. Ah'll phone them the noo' . . . " Joe lifted the newspaper and walked into the hall.

He replaced the receiver and frowned.

West-End and Shettleston: both gone.

Two others: gone.

Shared, non-smoking flat in Glasgow Green: no answer.

Voice by his side: "Nae joy?"

He shook his head. "Need tae git them earlier in the day."

"Never mind – if ye can staun' the sofa, we kin pit up wi' ye fur a wee while longer!"

He glanced at his watch: seven-thirty.

Andy at nine.

He looked at Angie. "Ony mair auld shirtsa Michael's ah kin borra?

162

CHAPTER FIFTEEN

In the heart of Glasgow's Merchant City Joe stood in front of the red sandstone building that was Sixty-Two Virginia Street.

Two centuries ago? Probably the headquarters of some tobacco merchant.

A century ago? Offices, maybe even a house.

A decade ago? Willy's Bar. Trendy, fashionable. Over-generous with their definition of over-eighteen. He had drunk here, while still at school.

Now? Joe stared through smoked glass. Café Delmonica – one of Glasgow's newer gay pubs.

Hands fumbled for cigarettes, found them, lit one.

The Zippo's huge flame flared, illuminating the narrow street.

Joe inhaled, then glanced at his watch: just on nine. He sighed.

This was a bad idea . . .

Behind, voices.

Joe moved to the side of the doorway and leant against a wet wall.

Behind, talking, laughing.

Joe zipped up bikers-jacket and lowered his head.

Three denim-clad figures passed in a cloud of aftershave.

Joe inhaled.

A door opened, then closed.

Aftershave . . . proper sharp-smelling, slightly harsh-smelling aftershave.

Not Oddfellows, not . . . what was the fuckin' number?

Joe sighed. This was a bad idea: too soon, too many associations with . . . He turned, and collided with someone. "Sorry, pal." Joe moved on past. Another smell. Lemons?

Laugh. "Where you off to?"

Hand on his arm. Joe paused, raising eyes.

Blue met liquid brown.

"Not late, am I ?" Worried. Hand removed. Broad fingers pulling back cuff to reveal luminous watch-face.

Joe sighed. "Naw, ah wis jist . . . "

"Waiting for me?" Smile.

Joe frowned. "Aye."

Andy walked towards the doorway. "C'mon, then."

Joe ground out cigarette under Doc and followed the tall figure into Delmonica's.

Even this early, the bar was busy. Joe stared into the back of countless heads.

"Get a table." Broad finger pointing to far corner. Then: "What do you want?"

Joe surveyed the crowded bar. Not to be here.

"Lager?"

He shrugged, peered at the handsome face. "Caledonian Clear. The blackberry wan, if they've goat it."

Smile. "Oh, I forgot you don't drink."

Voice behind. "Andrew! Where you bin hidin' yourself?"

Joe walked towards an empty table and sat down.

At the bar, Andy was talking to a smaller guy in a white Levi jacket. Joe watched as they were joined by two other men, both in leather, and a dark-haired girl. He sighed, stretched over and lifted a matchbook from the unused ashtray. Opening the safety cover, he tore off a red-tipped match and struck.

It flared.

Joe shook it out, then struck another.

It flared.

He stared at the flame.

In the background, a low rumble of music, but mainly voices. Joe looked across, scanning the alien collection of people.

Most were young . . . ish. Trendy-looking. Straight-looking. Joe smiled. If it wasn't for the few women and the leather . . .

"Ye'll burn yersel'!" Voice above him.

Joe looked up.

Guy in a tight, black tee-shirt.

Joe squeezed matchhead between thumb and index-finger. He scowled.

164

Growling laugh. "Yer mither no' tell ye aboot playin' wi' matches?" Sound of chair legs scraping. The guy sat down. "Kin ah git ye a drink?"

"Ah'm wi' somewan." Automatic response.

Persistent. "Ah'll buy him wan tae, then."

Joe stared at singed finger-flesh.

"Ah've no' seen you here afore." A hairy forearm pressed down on polished wood.

Joe continued to stare. This was a bad idea . . .

"Oan leave?"

Joe glanced up, eyes narrowing. Brown receding hair cropped close to skull. Sandy moustache above thin lips. Heavily tanned skin. Well-muscled chest beneath tight lycra. Older.

Heavy eye-contact. "Ah kin eyewis tell." Smile. Too-white teeth. "Whit regiment?" Whisky-breath.

Joe sighed. "Fuck aff!" He lifted the matchbook and struck another match.

"Temper!" Sound of chair-legs scraping. Then standing. Then:

"You making a nuisance of yourself Jimmy?" Low, resonant voice. Slightly mocking.

Joe shook out the match and glanced up.

Andy Hunter. Pint glass in one hand, blue-topped bottle in the other.

Surprise. "Oh, it's yersel', Mr Hunter!" Growling laugh. "Ah've jist bin tryin' tae talk tae yer pal here but he's no' very friendly."

Drinks placed on table. Joe seized mineral water and twisted off cap.

"Larry's in, Jimmy." Low, conspiratorial.

Anxious. "Where? Did ye . . . "

"At the bar. John said he . . . " Voices whispering.

Joe tipped bottle to lips and drank. Not blackberry.

Growling laugh. "Thanks, Mr Hunter. Mebbe seeya later . . . "

Whisky-breath singed Joe's face:

" . . . Bye-bye, soldier!"

A broad hand slapped leather jacket.

Joe tensed and lit a cigarette, then watched as the muscular figure weaved back through the crowd.

Chair-legs scraping. Then: "I got you peach – that okay?" Joe nodded, continued to drink.

Muted conversation behind, then: "Been in here before?"

"Aye, ages ago. It's . . . " He scanned the spartan decor. ". . . no' changed much."

"Where do you usually drink, Joe?"

"Ah telt ye – ah don't drink."

Sigh. "Okay then, where do you usually . . . socialise?"

Joe frowned. DiMaggios, Roganos, One Devonshire Gardens, the Buttery, the Cul-de-Sac . . .

Billy's hand across his face.

" . . . Ah don't dae aloata . . . socialisin'" He drained the bottle and glanced at the handsome face.

It smiled. "I sort of got that impression." Glass lifted, lager sipped. Then: "Life in civvies must take some getting used to – when did you say you left the army?"

He hadn't. "A year ago."

Hand propping-up interested face. "Did it have anything to do with . . . " Glass to mouth. Swallow.

Joe tensed.

" . . . your being gay?" Glass sat on table. "I mean, I know the US is trying, but our armed forces . . . " Bushy eye-brows V-ing for words.

Joe mirrored the frown, lit a cigarette. "Naw . . . no' really."

Broad finger tracing wet circles where lager-glass had stood. "Want to talk about it?"

Joe stared through a haze of cigarette smoke. "Ah . . . don't ken."

Laugh. "I'm curious – that's all." Glass to lips. "We've a lot in common, Joe." Hand wiping mouth.

He raised an eyebrow.

Frown. "Oh, come on!" Sigh. "The Force is as bad – if not worse – than the army. In theory, there's nothing to stop us joining the police." Glass raised. "Practice is a little different."

Joe stared. "Ye're no' . . . " He fumbled for the unfamiliar word. " . . . oot, then?"

166

Broad grin. "Of course I'm not – not as far as the job's concerned, anyway! Think anyone would work with me if I was?"

Joe lit a cigarette, glanced around. "But . . . aw' this?"

Smile. "The guy who was trying to chat you up – Jimmy? He knows what I do for a living." Laugh. "Mainly because I had to arrest him for importuning two years ago." Bushy eyebrows V-ed. "We came to an understanding. Jimmy knows to keep his mouth shut, but no-one else in here . . . " Surprise. "You must know what I mean, Joe, what the scene's like. Everyone's got something to . . . protect."

His face must've said otherwise. Joe gazed at the cigarette's glowing end.

Laugh. "You're a real innocent, aren't you?"

Joe tensed. "Ah ken enough tae get by." Now, at least.

Bushy V deepened. "Taught to you by Glasgow's very own Ronnie Kray, I take it?"

Joe stared. "Whit dae ye . . . ?"

"Joke! Joke!" Palms raised in defence. "I only mean, well . . . you've obviously not been around much, and William King is . . . a bit older than you."

Joe clenched sweating palms. "So?"

"Hey, take it easy . . . "

The words came before he could stop them. "Billy took me in when no-wan else waanted me, gied me a joab, somewhere tae live. The airmy fucked me up then waashed its hauns o' me. Ah hid nothin' – nae life, nae future – 'til ah met Billy . . . " Tightening in his chest. Joe paused. Shouting echoed in his head.

The bar was silent.

Joe stared past Andy Hunter's concerned face to several others, and scowled. "Ah owe him."

People began talking again.

A hand on his arm. Low words:

"Easy, Joe . . . take it easy."

Joe pulled away, stubbed out cigarette then immediately lit another.

Sigh. Glass raised, drained. "We can leave if . . . "

Words faded away. Joe closed his eyes, concentrating.

Slowly, breathing returned to normal, heart to a dull hammer. Pulsing red drained away from behind eyes. He frowned. Something else was draining away with the anger. Something he couldn't identify.

Something that had always been there.

Until now.

"Joe?"

A hand on leathered arm.

Joe opened his eyes.

The almost-classical face sombre. "Want to go?"

Joe peered into liquid brown. "Naw . . . ah waant tae talk."

Andy stood up. "Okay – but let's do it somewhere else, eh?"

Joe nodded, pushed back chair and followed a denimed back out of the bar.

The lounge of Andy Hunter's West-End flat was small, tastefully decorated. Joe kept his jacket on and sat down on a beige sofa.

Words buzzed in his head. He had to get them out.

Andy produced a bottle of whisky and two glasses from somewhere, poured liquid into both then handed one to Joe.

Joe took, drained it. "Ah didney lea' the airmy – they kicked me oot. Dishonourable discharge an' nine months in Colchester Military Prison – the Glasshoose?"

"I've heard of it." Smile. "What did you do – not polish your boots properly?"

Joe stared at the empty glass. "Ah struck an oafficer."

The smiled faded. "Still want to talk about it?"

Joe nodded. Words paced like prisoners in his head. He opened his mouth and set them free. "Two years ago. We were in Hamburg." He looked up at an encouraging face. "Ever bin there?"

Headshake. "Hear it's better than Amsterdam, though." Smile.

Joe scowled. "'S like Ardrossan, a fuckin' dump. Fulla auld tarts an' stupit young kids. Me an' summa the boays ended up in a bar doon by the docks. They jist wanted tae

168

drink an' git thur rocks aff. Ah'd hid enough. Went fur a walk."

Andy refilled his glass, then sat on the sofa's arm.

Joe closed his eyes. He could almost smell the oil from the freighters, the harsh German tobacco, the schnapps' fumes . . . the adrenalin. "Ah wanted leave . . . compassionate leave. It wis . . . " He swallowed hard. " . . . Michael hid bin dead four years an' ah'd never seen his grave. Sean wis runnin' wild, joyridin', gettin' himsel' intae trouble, messin' up. Ah wanted compassionate leave an' the bastards widney gie me ony!" Joe opened his eyes. The glass had been refilled. He drained it. "Ah wis luckin' fur trouble, man . . . an' ah found it. Ye ken aboot beastin'?"

Quizzical stare. Glass paused inches from lips. "Like an . . . initiation rite, isn't it?" Smile. "Organised bullying, from what I've heard."

Joe stared at the whisky.

Andy lifting the bottle, refilled.

Joe sighed. "There wis a British-base jist ootside Hamburg – Oesto somethin'. Met a coupla squaddies aff-duty. Said their Naffi wis guid fur a laugh. Ah went wi' them . . . "

Even after two years Joe shivered. He sipped the whisky. It soured in his mouth, like the army had.

" . . . We hid a coupla drinks – prices wur cheaper than ootside. Then wan o' the guys nodded tae another, then me. Said thur wis a beastin' tae be done, did ah want tae gie a haun'."

Andy extended cigarettes. "Is that usual? I mean, is beasting not a regiment-specific ritual?"

Joe stared at the handsome face. "Beastin's a waya life: we wur aw' squaddies, aw' British. Ah wis jist helpin' oot."

One preemptory-eyebrow raised. "And you went too far?"

Joe scowled. "Ah didney go far enough!" Whisky began to churn in his stomach. "It started aff fair enough – the usual slaps, punches, taunts. Then wan o' the guys really goat intae it. The squaddie oan the flair was well away – the beastin' shidda stoaped there. But this wan guy kept oan at him, poured a bucketa hoat water ower the poor fucker tae bring him roon' . . . "

169

"What was everyone else doing?"

Joe stared. "They watched." He reached for the whisky and filled glass. "When ah tried tae go git an oafficer, the other guys made it clear that wisney oan . . . " Joe closed his eyes. " . . . Wisney necessary. Ah hid tae stoap it – the squaddie gettin' the beastin' wis screamin'." The words brought it all back. He paused, heart pounding.

"And?"

Joe opened his eyes. "That wis when ah hit him." Joe blinked. "When the MPs pult me aff, the guy oan the flair wis deed an' ah'd hauf-kilt some . . . captain." Vomit rose in his throat. He swallowed it down, then buried face in hands. Silence filled the room. Buzzing filled Joe's head.

After a while, the buzzing stopped. He leant back on the comfortable couch and sighed. "So . . . that's me . . . "

A hand refilled his glass.

" . . . That's Joe Macdonald. Court-martial, nine months in the Glasshoose, dishonourable discharge for strikin' an oafficer." He raised whisky-glass to lips, downing contents in one.

"What . . . damage did you do?"

"Three cracked ribs, a broken arm and . . . " The words from his courtmartial burned in his head. " . . . multiple contusions to the face."

"What action was taken against the officer?"

"For whit?" Joe stared at the glass. It trembled.

Surprise. "For taking a beasting too far."

"None."

Shocked voice. "What?"

"Nothin' wis every proved against him – nae-one wid say whit happened. Oh, he goat a slap oan the wrist fur fightin', an' a month's compassionate when he came oota hoaspital. Then back oan duty." The trembling increased.

"But the authorities, the dead guy's family, I mean, surely . . . ?"

Joe scowled. "Accidental death. The airmy takes care o' its ain, Andy – like the polis dae." He laughed, a shudder growing in his chest.

The army . . .

The army . . .
The army . . .
Michael.
"A man was killed."

"Ma brither wis killed aff duty, blown away by a terrorist's bomb. The airmy wriggled oota giein' Angie the pension she wis owed, wriggled oota their responsibility tae Sean, by sayin' Michael'd knicked the cor . . . that it wis his ain fault." Joe stood up, hurled the glass across the small room. "Bastards the loatta them. Ah wis a six-year man, so ah kidney quit . . . but ah fuckin' made sure ah did some damage afore they finally threw me oot." He stared at a dripping damp patch where the glass impacted. "The airmy trained me well . . . too fuckin' well. But they didney figure oan me usin' whit they'd taught me against their ain kind." He sighed, turning. "Soarry aboot yer wall. Gie's a cloth an' ah'll clean it up."

Sympathetic brown eyes. "I had no idea."

Joe lit a cigarette with shaking fingers. "Took me years tae . . . git ower what happened tae Michael. An' when Sean goat . . . " He frowned, looked up. "Michael wis everythin' tae me, Andy . . . Ah signed-up 'causa him, wanted tae dae whit he did, be whit he wis . . . " He exhaled.

Michael . . .

Sean . . .

. . . heat in his stomach.

Silence, then a hand on his arm. "You must've been close." Angry. "I still can't believe an officer in the British army beat an enlisted man to death and nothing was done about it."

Joe rubbed broad fingers. "Believe it, man."

An arm round his shoulders.

He let it rest there. "At least ah hud the satisfaction o' gein' that bastard the kickin' he deserved . . . the kickin' ah shidda gied the whole fuckin' system."

"So . . . why were you only charged with . . . striking an officer?"

Joe smiled. "Technically, that wis aw' they hud. Nae witnesses, unnerstaun'? 'Least, none that wur sayin' onythin'.

171

Ah wis lucky they didney dae me fur the deid guy tae." He frowned.

Sigh. "But it wasn't fair – you were only trying to help. There must be some . . . impartial body you could've consulted."

Joe laughed. "Ye're missing' the point, Andy – ah wanted them tae chuck me oot!" He closed his eyes. "But the airmy wis ma life . . . ah didney realise jist how much ah needed it 'til the gates o' the Glasshoose closed behind me." Memories filled his mind, memories of Michael, of . . . of white ribbons and warm hands. "Ah wis luckin' fur something tae . . . replace it wi'. Thoaght ah'd fun it . . . "

"Billy?"

Broad fingers rubbed his shoulder. Joe nodded.

Arm removed. Andy sighed and lifted whisky bottle. "Another?"

"Aye . . . " He glanced at his watch: 3am. "Christ!" Joe stood up .

"What's the hurry?" Frown. "You're not back with . . . ?"

"Naw – that's aw' finished. Ah'm up in Springburn wi' ma sister-in-law." Joe sighed. "Goat tae fun somewhere else, though . . . somewhere o' ma ain." Eyes scanning the small room. "This rented?"

Laugh. "No – I've saddled myself with a £40,000 mortgage for this . . . " Smile. " . . . bijou residence."

Joe frowned.

Laugh. "You looking for somewhere in this area?"

Joe stared. West-End. Not his first choice. "Aye, mebbe."

"I'll keep my eyes open for you." Silence, then: "Thanks for telling me about . . . "

Joe frowned. "Ah wis surprised ye didney ken – ah mean, you're the wan wi' the big computer."

Confusion, then: "Oh, the PNC, you mean?" Smile. "I'm not in the habit of running a check on everyone I meet . . . " Laugh. " . . . Interesting though it might be." Stare. "What made you think I had?"

Joe picked up bikers' jacket and shrugged it on. "We . . . ah thoaght, what wi' me an' Georgie Paxton no' gettin oan, an' me threatenin' him an' that . . . "

"You were never a suspect, Joe. Anyway, even the mighty PNC can't venture into military territory." Laugh. A hand slapping back. "You could've done Christ knows what, but unless it was in civilian life, the police would never know!"

Joe frowned.

Billy:

'Let me handle them, Joe . . . one glance at the PNC and they'll know it all . . . '

"Want me to phone a taxi?"

Joe blinked. "Whit?"

Apologetic. "I'd give you a lift, but . . . " Eyes to almost-empty whisky-bottle.

Joe smiled. "Ye're okay, pal – ah kid dae wi' the walk!"

Smiled returned.

Joe walked towards the door.

Hesitant. "You busy Saturday?"

"Workin'."

Sigh. "I'm nights, Sunday onwards." Bushy eyebrows V-ing.

Joe seized a brass handle. "Whit aboot Monday?"

"Afternoon?"

Joe opened the door. "Aye – gie's a ring. Ye goat Angie's number?"

"No, I . . . "

"567-6893."

Pen grabbed from small bureau, brown eyes scanning for paper. Sigh. "Say that again?"

Joe repeated the number.

Andy wrote on the back of a pale, broad hand. Then smile: "Speak to you soon." Door held open.

"Aye, Andy – seeya." Joe walked from the flat, down two flights of stone stairs out onto Byres Road. He was light-headed, light-hearted . . .

Whisky . . . or talking?

"Christ, man! Ye're soakin'!" Surprised voice from darkened hallway.

Joe brushed a hand down wall.

Dull light illuminated a crouching figure, telephone

173

receiver to ear. "Seeya the morra, man." Disconnecting, then standing.

Joe closed the door and walked towards Sean. Water dripped into eyes. He blinked it away.

Laugh. "No' hearda taxis, man?"

He peeled off slick leather and hung bikers' jacket on coat-hook. Wet denim clung to thighs. Joe plucked at the heavy fabric. Then frowned. "You're up late."

Grin. "Oh, ah've bin in fur ages."

Joe stared the the baseball-cap and jacket. "Aye, sure." He walked past Sean into the lounge.

Darkness.

Joe switched on a light.

Voice behind. "That wis Ewan."

Joe sat down on the sofa and began to unlace boots. "How wis yer . . . audition?" He pulled. "Wis yer strawberry soap appreciated?"

Sean threw himself on the sofa. Sigh. "Ewan liked hur." Cushion seized, pummelled.

Joe looked up.

The pale face was grim. "Aye – some wee lassie wi' a drum-machine she'd goat fur hur birthday!" Scornful.

Joe laughed, pulling off another Doc. "Wis she ony guid?"

Snort. "Hudney even hearda Primal Scream."

"Kid she play, but?"

Laugh. "Ye don't . . . play drum-machines . . . "

Cushion battered off wet head.

" . . . Ye program them!"

Joe grabbed a skinny arm.

Sean wriggled away, still holding cushion.

"Well, kid she program it?"

Scathing. "Two-Unlimited's greatest hits!" Punching cushion with balled fist.

Joe stared. "Ah take it that's no' whit yous wur lookin' fur?" He began to unbutton fly. Then paused. "Away an' ᴉke a coffee!"

ᴉuest ignored. "She kent nothin'." Cushion punched

174

Joe stood up. "So? Audition somewan else." He walked into kitchen, switched on light then filled kettle.

Low voice at his back. "Ewan likes hur." A hand rubbed his neck. "Yer shirt's soaking, tae."

Joe flinched, moved away. "So? Ah still don't see whit the problem is." The kettle came to the boil, but failed to switch itself off.

"Ah mean, he . . . really likes hur." Sigh. Sean leant against a cupboard in a cloud of steam.

Joe switched off kettle, unscrewed lid of coffee jar and grabbed a spoon. His hand shook.

Scorn outweighing the hurt. "A fuckin' lassie, man – an' hur drum-machine's shite tae!"

Joe laughed in spite of himself. He looked at Sean.

A strand of blond hair between pink, pouting lips. Nose-stud back in place, flaring. Disapproving eyes. "Ah don't waant hur in the band, Joe."

He poured boiling water over granules. "Take a vote oan it at yer next practice. That's fair." He stirred. "Ye canny just write the lassie aff 'cause she's a girl." Joe stared at the sulky face. Or because Ewan's got the hots for her and you're feeling left out.

"Ye think that'd be best?" Eyes on the floor.

Joe bent down and opened fridge. He sighed. No milk. He closed door and lifted mug. "Aye. If she's as bad as ye say, Ewan'll be oot-voted."

Sulky eyes raised, brightening. Understanding. "Ye're right, Joe! Ah'll gie Gavin a ring . . . " Moving towards door.

"The morra, eh?" He glanced at wall-clock: 4.45am. "He'll no' be up at this time."

"But . . . ?"

"The morra, Sean!" Joe strolled past the tall boy and into the lounge. "Now, away tae yer bed and gie's peace."

Warm arms around his neck. "Aw', Joe." Disappointed.

He wrenched himself free. "Bed – okay?" He stared into wide blue pools.

Sean met his gaze, stared back. "Ye still like the swimmin'?"

Stirring in his stomach. Joe broke the gaze. "Aye . . . "

Swimming with Michael . . . Billy didn't like swimming.

"Mebbe we can go oan Sunday – yeah? Ah've no' been fur ages an' . . . "

"Aye, mebbe. Now, go on, Sean – ah'm tired." He walked to the sofa and sat down.

Happy voice. "Sure, Joe – seeya in the mornin'."

"'Night, Sean . . . " He waited for retreating footsteps.

Silence, then: "So that's a definate fur . . . "

"Guidnight, Sean!" He tried to think of something else.

Laugh. "'Night, Joe."

Footsteps, then darkness.

Joe sighed and began to undress.

CHAPTER SIXTEEN

His mouth was dry. His head thumped. Spunk crystalised on a hard thigh. Somewhere in the distance, buzzing. Joe tried to remember the dream which flitted on the edges of his mind. The Merc . . . rain . . . water coursing into his mouth. Something to do with . . . Sean? He turned over and tried to go back to sleep.

The buzzing stopped.

Joe sighed.

Then ringing.

He scowled and buried his face in a cushion. It smelled of strawberries.

Then door opening.

Then a sweet, sickly odour.

Then a cold voice: "You: home!"

The dream was taking another route. Sean was still there, whispering. Joe pulled the duvet over his head.

Someone pulled it away.

Joe groaned: "If this is meant tae be funny, ya wee . . ." He opened his eyes.

Semi-darkness. The door had closed again. Joe peered, blinked, peered harder.

"You: home!"

Joe slowly moved out from under the duvet and stood up.

Hard green eyes scanned his naked body.

He grabbed jeans from the floor.

Hard green eyes watched him dress. Then: "The car's outside."

Joe signed. "Ah'm no' comin', Billy." He walked to to the window and raised venitians. Watery light flooded the cold room. He turned.

Pale face topped smooth neck. Crisp shirt and tie. Sombre, Hugo-Boss business suit.

Joe frowned. Always business.

Billy stared.

Joe looked for cigarettes.

"What do you mean?"

Joe found cigarettes, lit one. His hand shook. "Whit ah said. It's finished, Billy."

Mirthless laugh. "Joe, Joe . . . you've made your point. Let's go home."

He avoided the green eyes. "This is ma hame noo." He drew on the cigarette.

Tentative knock on door. Then Sean's head appeared. Eyes past Billy: "Sorry fur interruptin', Mr King. Ah'm goin' tae the van, Joe. Want . . . ?"

"Git oot, Sean!" Eyes closed.

The door did likewise.

Low laugh. "This place is a slum. How can you . . . ?"

"Ah like it fine."

Disbelieving. "You also like your home comforts."

Joe opened his eyes.

Behind steel-rims, green eyes stared.

His stomach was churning. Whisky soured his breath.

"You need me, Joe."

"Ah don't need . . . onywan." The cigarette trembled.

Sigh. "You'll never find anyone who understands you the way I do." Billy's mouth was a hard line.

Joe walked back to the sofa and began to tidy away the duvet. Last night: Andy Hunter's sympathetic face, Andy's . . . understanding? The lightness he had felt walking home? "Well, ah huv."

Hard laugh. "Very funny!"

His throat tightened. Lungs refused to function. Voice in his ear:

"I'll see you downstairs, in the car." Measured footsteps walking away. Lounge door opening. Distant keys scraping in lock. Then from the hall:

"Oh . . . hi, Mr King!"

Joe tried to breathe.

Cool voice. "Hello again, Sean – you been behaving yourself?"

Laugh. "Sure, Mr King . . . ah kept an eye oan yer cor." Confidential. "Some boays wur hangin' roon' it, but ah goat ridda them."

"'Thank you."

Joe turned and smashed fist into wall. Air rushed from lungs. "Sean! Git in here!"

"Comin', Joe – seeya, Mr King." Baseball-capped head round door. Grinning. Skipping to window. Worried. "Hope the Merc's okay, doon there . . . "

Joe unclenched fist, rubbed knuckles then fumbled for cigarettes.

Thursday night at The Matrix: under-eighteens Rave. Early finish.

Distant, rhythmic thumps. Joe glanced at his watch: only an hour or so to go. He leant forward, staring into the empty cloakroom.

Behind, on the other side of the foyer, door opening. Sounds of laughing, then: "Aye, Davie – thanks . . . ah'll send him in."

Joe turned.

Red-slash smile. Matching fingernails waving brown envelope. "Santa's come early, this year!" Tottering on heels towards him.

Joe smiled, reached for cigarettes.

Gina edged past, ducking under counter. Heavy thighs stretched tight, black lycra ever tighter. Red-slash mouth appearing inside cloakroom.

Joe extended cigarette packet.

Dismissive wave of hand, then two inches of nail slitting brown envelope.

Joe stared.

Gina waved a fan of £20 notes. "Christmas bonus!" Flicking with red-tipped fingers. Laugh. "This'll come in handy."

Joe lit a cigarette.

Gina continued to flick the notes. "Your turn noo, Joe." Nod towards the manager's office. Eyes never leaving the money.

Joe grinned. Ready cash. It was welcome. He levered himself from the cloakroom's counter and strolled across the foyer.

The office door opened as he approached, revealing Davie's worried face.

Joe smiled. Davie always looked worried. He stuck out a hand. "Where's ma ill-goaten gains then?"

Sigh. Davie moved back into the office.

Joe followed. On the desk lay a column of small, brown envelopes, identical to Gina's. Behind the desk, Davie was opening a drawer. Joe perched on a corner of the desk.

Drawer closed. Davie held out a longer envelope. Worried smile. "Here ye go, Joe. Compliments o' the season." Sigh. "Christ knows, ye've proabably earned it."

Joe raised an eyebrow, took the package. It felt . . . heavy. He turned away, stuffing the envelope into inside pocket. "Thanks, Davie."

Sounds of glass clinking behind. Then liquid pouring.

Joe turned.

Davie raised whisky glass, then sipped. "Aw' the best, Joe."

He watched as Davie drained then refilled the glass. Joe frowned. "You okay?"

Question ignored. "Bit quiet the night. Maist o' the unner-eighteens wid raither be wi' the over-eighteens – eh?" Eyes raised.

Joe tried to make contact.

Davie's pupils swam like fish.

He smiled. "Aye, Davie – ah think yer right . . . "

Drunken laugh. "Oh, ah'm right aboot a loata things, Joe . . . " Sobering. Goldfish-eyes focusing. Goldfish-mouth opening, wanting to say something, then changing mind. "Oan ye go, pal – back to yer crowd control." Head lowered. Mumbling.

Joe stared. "You okay, Davie – seriously?"

Head slowly raised. "Me?" Drunken smile. "Me?" Dissolving into drunken laughter.

Joe walked from the office, across the foyer and towards thumping music.

Two hours later he opened the lounge door, scanning. "Where's yer mither?" He walked into the cold room.

Before the one-bar electric fire, Sean. Towel around waist. Damp hair straggling down damper back.

No response.

Joe leant over and disconnected headphones from personal hi-fi.

"Oi! Whit . . . ?" Head whipped round. Grin. " . . . Jeez, man!" Sean removed the towel and rubbed face.

Joe stared at the thin, naked boy, then turned away. "Where's yer mither?" He took off the bikers' jacket.

"Goat the chance o' an extra shift – she'll no' be back 'til three. We still oan fur Sunday?"

Sunday . . . Sunday. He rubbed a wet face. The Christmas bonus was fat in his inside pocket. The more-than-a Christmas bonus. He stared across the icy lounge.

"Eh, Joe?"

"Oh . . . aye . . . aye . . . " He walked across the room to a build-it-yourself display cabinet and opened a drawer. "Ye ken if yer mither's goat ony envelopes?" Joe rifled through red-printed documents. Voice above him.

"Dunno, man . . . " Knees cracking as pale legs bent. "Ah'll huv a luck."

Strawberry scent. That fuckin' smell. Joe tensed, stood up. "Pit some claes oan – eh, Sean?" He stared down at a skinny back. Vertebrae nobbles bisected pale skin, ending . . . Something stirred in the pit of his stomach. "It's freezin' in here!"

Snort. "Ah'm no' cauld!" Tossing documents into air. "She must huv some somewhere."

Heat in his stomach. Joe blinked, watching as Sean sat on the floor, long legs spread out in a V. A smile twitched his lips, then died. "Lea' it, Sean – ah'll get them later." He walked over to the sofa and sat down.

The more-than-a christmas bonus.

A lot of money.

Billy thought he could buy anything, everything . . .

"It's okay, Joe . . . " Voice from floor. "Ah ken there's some somewhere . . . the club gies them tae hur free – for invoices an' things . . . " Hoot. "Here ye go!"

A package of A4 envelopes sailed through air, landing a

foot away. Joe picked it up.

Voice at his side. "Writin' tae somewan?"

Joe glanced up. "Aye, that's right."

Sean sat down beside him, draping long legs over the sofa's arm. He fiddled with the headphone-connection, twisting the wire from side to side. The personal stereo nestled between thighs amidst a bush of wiry blond hair.

Joe sighed. He extracted an envelope from the pile.

The more-than-a-Christmas bonus.

A lot of money . . .

Throat clearing above. "Kin ah ask ye something Joe?"

"Ye're eyewis askin' somethin'!" He fingered the envelope.

Awkward. "Ah mean . . . ask ye somethin' serious."

Joe straightened, then turned. The band? Ewan and the lassie? He walked to an untidy coffee-table and began to search. "Ye goat a pen?"

"Ower there somewhere." An arm waved vaguely. Sean was sucking a strand of frizzing hair. He looked . . . young and old at the same time. Long lashes lowered. "Joe. Ken whit day it is?"

Another reminder. Joe sighed. "Aye, it's Friday an' ah ken we're goin' swimming oan Sunday . . . "

Impatient. "That's no' whit ah . . . "

Joe's stomach turned over. "No' the noo, Sean – eh?" He scanned the cluttered mantle. Everything but pens.

Hoarse voice. "Ah thoaght you widda . . . "

"In the mornin' Sean." Joe rifled behind old birthday cards and '10p-off' coupons. He frowned.

The £10,000 he'd received as a 'Christmas bonus' could do some people a lot of good.

Tightening in his chest. Not this ten thousand. Not anything that came from Billy King.

His eyes brushed a cheaply-framed photograph. Michael . . .

A cool body pressed against his. Damp arms around his neck.

. . . had been there for him. He needed him again. Now. Hot breath in his ear:

"Ye've forgoatten, Joe." Disappointed.

His stomach turned over. He seized the arms and turned. "Away tae yer bed an' gie me peace, Sean!" The words more harsh than he'd intended.

Sean wobbled, then regained balance. A hand through damp hair. Suddenly self-conscious. Towel back around waist.

Joe stared into deep blue pools.

Pale skin turning scarlet. Sean broke his gaze, broke free from strong hands and rushed from the room.

Joe sighed and turned back to the mantel. Behind Michael's photograph, a pen caught his eye. He picked it up, walked over to the sofa and sat down. Placing pen and envelope on top of yesterday's *Evening Times*, Joe sighed and searched for cigarettes.

The money was going back. No debate, no other way. Billy was the past, over and done with. Sean and Angie were the present. And the future?

Joe lit a cigarette and stared at his dead brother's photograph. Smoke drifted over, yellowing an already jaundiced mock-silver frame.

Joe continued to stare. Was Michael in the past? He gazed at his brother's strong body, remembered the feel of those strong arms around him, the feel of Michael's . . . Joe stood up and walked to the window, pressing a hot face against cool glass .

The past . . .

The past . . .

The past . . .

Eventually, the heat in his stomach cooled. Shards of ash dropped onto jeans. The future?

Michael had been there for him. . . he should be there for Sean.

Joe folded the envelope into quarters. He stuffed it and the pen into back pocket, stubbed out cigarette and turned. Billy's money was definitely the past.

The future could wait.

Only the present mattered . . .

In the distance, a door opened then slammed.

Angie? Joe glanced at his watch: barely two. He walked through to Sean's bedroom and stared into emptiness . . .

. . . Back in the lounge Joe picked up jacket and keys then left the flat.

Fifteen minutes later as he passed a lifeless Barnhill station, Joe spotted the moving outline of a baseball cap three hundred yards or so ahead. "Sean!"

The word echoed in the derelict darkness of Petershill Road. Ahead, the capped figure continued to run.

Unhearing . . . or unheeding.

Joe began to jog. Where the fuck was Sean off to – Ewan's? Wrong direction for Possil.

One hundred yards ahead, the figure slowed, paused, then crossed Springburn Road.

Joe frowned and broke into a sprint. The night was dry and cold, his body soon hot and wet. Something suddenly made sense:

'Ken whit day it is?'

Joe sprinted faster, pounding across Springburn Road. A taxi honked and swerved to avoid him.

Ahead, a spike-topped stone wall. Sean was nowhere in sight. Blood pounded in his head. Joe hoped the bent paling round the far side was still bent, and that he would still manage to squeeze through the gap it allowed.

He was breathing heavily now, but at least the mystery was solved. Joe slowed to a trot, turned left and began to circle. After a few minutes he located the paling.

Someone had fixed it.

Frowning, Joe reached up and gripped two cast-iron spikes. One foot braced against the stone wall, the other half way up a paling, he inhaled then hoisted himself over the railings, landing awkwardly on the soft grass beneath. He stood for a few moments, eyes adjusting to the darkness, then began to walk again.

He'd come here years ago, at about Sean's age, to drink cider and try to catch rabbits.

He'd been here only once in daylight, just over a year

184

ago. A cold, grey day.

Joe hoped he could remember the way.

He heard Sean before he saw him. Soft, breathless fragments of speech shattered the silent, dead world:

" . . . Aye . . . ah ken that . . . ah'll no' be goin' back tae the borstal . . . "

He turned towards the words, stared.

Sean was kneeling on wet grass, baseball-cap bobbing. Then head cocked, listening.

Joe continued to stare. Something burned in his chest, threatening to explode.

Low laugh. "Aye . . . ah remember. Five-aside. You, me, Joe . . . . " Head, voice lowered.

His eyes stung.

Sean talked on, the words inaudible.

Joe swallowed hard, then walked forward.

Sean fell silent, raised a capped head. Then long white fingers reached forward and traced the engraved lettering:

l6th December, 1990. Aged thirty-four.
'Michael Edward Macdonald.
Faithful husband of Angela, loving father to Sean.'

He bit back a sob.

What about Joe?

What about . . . 'caring, nurturing, faithful, loving brother to Joseph?'

No acknowledgement of what Michael had been to him.

No acknowledgement of what he had been to Michael.

Nothing . . .

Nothing . . .

Nothing . . . Perhaps it was better that way.

Perhaps words were . . . inappropriate.

Perhaps words were inadequate and that was the reason Michael and he had never . . . said them.

Joe stared down at the kneeling Sean, then crouched behind the silent figure and pressed hot palm to shaking shoulder.

It flinched beneath his touch, then relaxed. "Ye didney forget then?" Said without turning.

Joe rubbed through cheap fabric and lied. "Ah'll never forget, Sean." He had forgotten all too easily. Billy, Andy . . . the present was crowding in to obliterate the past.

Silence. Beneath his palm thin shoulders rose and fell. Then stumbling words. "Ah needed somewan tae talk tae, somewan who widney talk at me."

Joe flinched. Selfish – too many of his own problems, past problems. Too tied up to remember Sean's needs. Present needs.

Needs Michael had seen in Joe?

The words wouldn't come.

Apparently, they didn't need to. Sean's hoarse whisper filled the stillness. "Ah'm aw' mixed up, man. Tell me whit tae dae."

Joe swallowed hard. Was the request directed at him, or beyond? He rubbed the edge of Sean's baseball cap.

"Aye . . . ah ken. Joe's here, dad – no' see him? He's stayin' wi' us." Pause. Head cocked again. Then a soft laugh. "Aye, dad – he still snores."

Joe smiled. Michael. Years ago, sharing a room, sharing . . . so much more. Now? Taking responsibility for Sean, a responsibility which shouldn't be left to an over-worked woman and a dead man.

Silence.

He stared. Sean had stopped talking. Joe squeezed a thin shoulder. "Finished?"

Nod, then: "They widney let me go tae the funeral, Joe . . . said ah wis too young. But ah wanted tae see . . . "

Joe gripped Sean's arms, stood up and turned the boy towards him.

Blue, red-rimmed eyes.

Then arms around waist.

Joe sighed and pulled Sean to him. "There wis nothin' tae see, Sean. Remember yer dad like he wis, not . . . "

The hard body shattered by a bomb.

The strong face ripped into bloody shreds by two pounds of nails.

186

The lifeless corpse which rested feet below in the best coffin Angie could afford.

" . . . like this. He widney want ye comin' here, Sean. He'd want ye tae git oan wi' yer life." He'd want me to get on with my life.

Snuffling against his chest.

Joe ran a shaking hand over Sean's back. "Ye come here . . . often?" He smiled at the ambiguous words.

Headshake. "No' before the night . . . took me ages tae fun' . . . " Pause, then: "Bin thinkin' aboot ma dad a lot, though . . . "

Joe frowned. You and me both.

" . . . Thoaght it might help tae talk aboot . . . "

"Whit?"

Sigh. "People ur eyeswis buggin' me – teachers, ma maw . . . ah needed tae talk tae somewan . . . " More snuffling.

Joe pulled Sean more tightly against his chest. "If ye want tae talk tae onywan, talk tae me – okay?"

Blond head raised. The baseball cap fell off. "You're busy, Joe – ye've goat yer ain . . . problems."

His stomach melted. His problems were nothing compared to this. Joe pulled away, manufactured a grin. "Ah've eyewis goat room fur mair."

"Sure?"

Joe stared into the ashen face. "If it's bugging ye that much, ah want tae ken!"

Blue eyes narrowing. Long pause. Then hoarse voice. "How . . . " Throat clearing. " . . . How dae ye ken if ye're . . . er . . . bent?"

Joe stared.

Sean fiddled with a strand of hair. "Eh?"

Instinctively, Joe dropped arms and moved away.

Sean stooped to retrieve baseball-cap. "Aw, Christ! This is a fuckin' mess." Angry, confused, upset . . .

Joe blinked. "Hey! Come oan – it's no big deal." The lie echoed in darkness.

Sean kicked at a clump of grass. Scarlet face illuminated by distant street-lights. Mumbling. "Whit's the best word fur it? Ah mean, bent's whit Ewan ca's it."

187

Joe frowned. "Ye've asked Ewan?"

Horror. "No way, man! Ah mean, bent's whit Ewan sez, when he's wanting tae . . . insult somewan." Wan smile. "Gay sounds . . . stupit."

Joe ran a hand through hair, then stared at the flushed face. "Don't gie it a name, then. It's jist . . . " He groped for words. " . . . how some guys feel." It was so much more.

Wiping nose on back of hand. "Don't think ah ken how ah . . . feel." Uncomfortable.

Michael's words came reeling back to him. "That's no' . . . unusual. Ye're growin' up, Sean – that's aw'." Joe sighed. "Whit brought aw' this oan anyway?"

"Ah wis thinkin' aboot . . . Longriggend."

Joe stared. "Whit's that goat tae . . . ?" Realisation. "Wis there somewan there ye . . . liked?"

"No . . . ." Then silence.

"His somewan bin' . . . boatherin' you, Sean?"

Muffled: "Naw . . . nothin' like that."

Joe frowned. "Then whit's upsetting ye?"

More silence.

Joe sighed. For someone who wanted to talk Sean was very quiet. "Look: the borstal wis years ago. Ye wur . . . whit: thirteen?"

"Aye, but . . . "

"That's young . . . ye're ainly fifteen noo . . . "

"Nearly sixteen!"

"That's still young . . . "

Annoyed. "That's whit the guy oan the bent switchboard-thing said!" Embarrassed. "We yissed tae dae it aw' the time – me an' Ewan – fur a laugh! Phone up . . . " More embarrassed. " . . . Talk dirty tae the guy an' that." Pause, throat clearing, then: "Ah wis curious, that's aw'. The boays in Longriggend yissed tae . . . " Throat clearing. " . . . They tell ye nothin' aboot being . . . bent at school . . . It's jist aw' makin' babies an' that . . . " Words tailing off.

Joe stared. Curiosity . . . healthy curiosity.

Sigh. "Ah phoned the switch-board guy oan ma ain, tae ask him." Scowl. "He wis fuckin' useless! Telt me tae phone back in three years' time!"

188

Joe frowned. Acts were technically illegal. Information should be above the law.

Sean perched on the edge of his father's headstone. "Ah jist wanted tae know how ye ken if ye're bent, that's aw'." Frustrated.

Joe rubbed his face. He was worse than useless. Something Michael had once told him. Joe looked across at the tear-streaked face. "It's whit ye feel comfortable wi', Sean. Some guys ken early oan, others . . . " It had taken him years to come to terms with his own situation. " . . . take langer." He smiled. "It'll work itsel' oot."

Sean glanced down between splayed legs at gilt lettering. "Did ma dad ken you wur bent . . . er, gay?" Eyes flicking between inscription and grass.

Joe stared at a slab of inert, grey granite. Yes . . . "Ah never telt him . . . " Never had the chance. He looked at Sean. " . . . but that disney mean he didney ken."

"He wis . . . awright aboot it?" Curious.

"If you feel . . . comfortable wi' yersel', other people'll dae the same, Sean. If they don't, they're no' worth boathering aboot." He walked over and pushed frizzing hair back from the pale face. "Is this helpin'?"

Furious blush. "Ah think so . . . " Thoughtful. "No, no' really."

"Ah don't ken whit else tae say, Sean – ainly you ken how ye feel."

Deeper blush.

Joe sighed and lit a cigarette.

Blue pools looking up. "So how dae ye ken if ye're bent?"

Joe smiled. "Ye jist . . . ken."

Snort. "Dis it coont if ye don't like lassies?"

Joe laughed. "Ah like lassies fine . . . "

Sean jumped up. "But ye dinney want tae fuck them?"

Joe sighed. He didn't want to fuck anyone . . . His eyes scanned Sean's slim outline . . . or hadn't. Heat in his stomach. He shivered. "No, ah don't want tae fuck them . . . but it's no jist aboot fuckin', it's mair aboot . . . "

"Love?" The word supplied scornfully.

189

Joe flinched. "No . . . it's aboot being comfortable wi' yersel', wi' yer ain boady afore gettin' involved wi' other people's . . ."

"Other guys?"

Joe nodded. The other body inches away. "An' it's aboot trust, Sean." Joe turned away from his brother's grave and his brother's son, heart racing. "It's aboot respect an' trust an' . . ." The words stuck in his throat.

A voice from behind. "Ah don't unnerstaun . . ." Disappointment badly hidden.

Joe sighed. Ewan . . . this was about Ewan. "People huv . . . crushes oan other people. It disney mean they . . . fancy them, see? It's jist . . . somethin' everywan goes through . . ."

Years ago.

A well-built PE teacher.

Joe sighed. "Is this helpin'?" A hand clutched his shoulder.

Hoarse voice. "A bit."

Joe closed his eyes. Trust . . . responsibility.

Michael's trust.

Joe's responsibility. He turned, sought refuge in humour, like Michael had when talking was . . . difficult. He manufactured a smile then mock-punched Sean's head. "Onyway – yer dad's probably tryin' tae organise a five-aside wi' the Big Man up there. He'll huv better things tae dae than listen tae your rubbish!"

A shadow of a grin returned. Mock-punch returned. "Away, man – ah ken there's nae heaven. Ah'm no' a wee boay ony . . ."

"Then don't act like wan." Joe ducked away from another, less-mock punch. "Think aboot whit ye're feelin' fur . . ." Ewan? Some kid at school? Joe pushed an unfamiliar emotion to the back of his mind. "Onythin' else bothers ye, ye tell me – okay? Lea' yer dad alain – Christ! Is it no' enough ye pester the life oota the livin'?"

Sean grinned.

Joe tried to grin, failed. "C'moan – let's go hame." An arm around his shoulders.

Joe flinched, pushed it away.

190

Sean grinned again, pushed back, like it was a game.

They both fell onto frosting grass.

Sean tried to pin Joe's arms to the ground.

Joe struggled, flipping the tall boy over, then straddling slim, sweatshirt-clad hips. Beneath iron thighs Sean's body heaved in bucking movements.

A light, then voices: "Oi! Whit's goin' on there?"

Joe tensed.

A breathy laugh. "Fuck! The polis. C'moan, before they dae us fur . . . daein' whitever guys dae in cemeteries at night!" Sean wriggled out from under him and shot towards the railings.

Joe stood up then followed.

Two hours later, Sean was asleep.

Joe walked through the kitchen out onto the balcony.

Thirty-one floors below a pre-dawn Glasgow still glittered. He pressed the envelope to the wrought-iron railings, surface and began to write. Then he withdrew a large brown envelope from back pocket, emptied Billy's money into the newer, then licked, sealed. Joe sighed.

Ten thousand pounds.

A lot of money . . .

But not his money.

Joe stood for a while, watching as the sky lightened over Easterhouse. Then he turned and went back into the flat.

In the empty lounge, he found some stamps under a cracked ornament.

On the floor, in front of the inert electric fire, a still-damp towel.

CHAPTER SEVENTEEN

"Late finish the night?" Angie from the kitchen.

Joe continued to lace up Docs. "Aye – Setturdays ur eyewis late. You workin'?"

Laugh. "When wis ah no'?"

He stood up, lifting a personal hi-fi from the sofa. "Where's Sean?" He fingered the ear-phones.

"Oot wi' Ewan, ah think – said somethin' aboot another rehearsal."

Joe frowned. Sean, Ewan and the lassie with the drum-machine.

From the kitchen: "By the way, Joe . . . " Head appearing around door. " . . . Hope ye dinney mind, but ah checked yer cashline card this mornin'." Smile. "Yer wages went in okay."

Joe grinned. His money. Money he had earned. Not like the ten thousand at present on its way back to sender. He frowned, remembering Davie the manager's words . . . Maybe he had earned that, too. "'Course ah don't mind, Angie – hauf o' it's yours, onyway!"

Head back into kitchen. "Telt ye afore, Joe – it's as cheap tae feed three as two."

Joe walked towards the voice. In the kitchen, Angie was washing dishes. He watched, frowning. Sean . . . Thursday. Sighthill cemetery. Responsibility.

Trust.

A warm feeling spread in his stomach.

Laugh from Angie. "Ye're no' lookin' very happy, Joe!"

He tried a smile. "Ah'm fine – jist tired. Sean say when he'd be back?"

She dried hands on a dish-rag. "Sometime the night – he's huvin' his tea at Ewan's. Said he'd mebbe see ye later, an' no' tae forget aboot the morra."

Joe picked up jacket from the back of a chair. The morra? "Aye . . . mebbe."

Surprise. "Aff already?"

Joe nodded. "Aye – late finish, early start." He ruffled

the frizzy hair. "Don't work too hard!"

She grinned. "Tell Gina ah wis askin' fur her."

"Ah wull." He lifted keys and walked towards the door.

Joe glanced at his watch: eight thirty. Davie was late. He'd had to use his keys to let Gina and an assortment of bar-staff into The Matrix half an hour earlier. Joe gazed through relocked doors at the gathering queue.

"Did yer pal gie ye ony . . . inside information, then?"

Joe turned, raised an eyebrow.

Gina grinned, winked. "The polis-guy."

Joe smiled. Wednesday seemed a lifetime away. "Andy's no' married, if that's whit ye mean!"

She mock-clipped his ear. "Cheeky bastard – ye ken ah wis ainly kiddin' 'boot that!"

Joe walked back to the cashier's desk.

Gina followed, heels flicking. "Did he tell ye onythin' about Georgie?"

Joe sighed. "We didney talk shoap."

Irritated. "He musta said somethin'."

Joe stared through the cashier's grill. Andy Hunter hadn't said much, but what he did say had made a difference. Joe produced cigarettes.

Lighter flaring beside him.

Joe bent his head to the flame, inhaled.

Gina clicked the Zippo shut and tossed it to him. "Ye left it here, last night – lucky for you ah fun' it."

Joe caught the Zippo, rubbing the shiny surface between hard fingers. Another present from Billy: should it be returned?

Gina was talking again. "Well, mebbe ah'll no' need you tae keep me up-tae-date, ony mair."

Joe looked up.

Mock-smug red-slash. Red-tipped finger tapping side of nose. "Ah've heard the polis huv goat a hot lead!"

Joe smiled at the TV-cop language.

"Ah'm no' jokin'. A wuman up the stairs fae me kens wan o' the guys works oan the *Record*, an' he telt her the polis're luckin' intae a coupla other . . . incidents."

Joe laughed. A friend of a friend of a . . .

"He sez it wisney the drugs Georgie wis kilt fur – ah mean, they fun aw' they eccy tabs at his hoose, didn't they?"

Joe stared.

"Naw, fae whit the wuman upstairs' pal sez, somewan jist walked intae Georgie's hoose, shoat him, then left." Conspiratorial. "Thur wis nae sign o' forced entry, either."

Joe drew on the cigarette.

"Noo, if ye wur Georgie, an' ye wur dealin', wid ye answer the door at three in the mornin'?"

"If ah wis expectin' a punter . . . "

"Ah, but Georgie wis meant tae be workin'! It wis ainly 'causa . . . " Smile. " . . . that wee disagreement you an' him hid, that he wis at hame at aw', at that time."

Joe watched the cigarette's glowing tip. "He mighta phoned somewan, arranged tae . . . "

"The polis huv goat a print-oot fae BT. Nae phone-calls fae or tae Georgie's hoose that night."

"Mebbe he didney phone fae hame."

"The polis huv goat the taxi-driver that took Georgie hame. Picked him up ootside here an' drapped him at his door."

"Disney mean he didney go back oot tae phone . . . "

"Why wid he dae that, when there's a perfectly guid wan where he is?"

Joe smiled. "Yer pal's pal's bin workin' hard, but whit makes him think whoever shot Georgie didney dae it tae git drugs? Mebbe they thought the place'd be empty . . . "

Red-slash smile. "If you wur efter Georgie's drugs, wid you shoot him, then lea' the drugs behind?" Triumphant.

Joe frowned. "Aye, Gina – mebbe ye've goat a point. But if Georgie wisney shoat fur the drugs, why . . . ?"

"The wuman up the stairs' pal disney ken that yet, but he's workin' oan it."

Thumps on glass door.

Joe turned. Outside, the punters were getting impatient. He looked at his watch, then across to where Malkie and two other bouncers stood, smoking. Joe ground out cigarette under boot, then caught Malkie's eye.

194

The large man raised an eyebrow.

Joe nodded, produced keys and walked towards the waiting crowd.

It was near to ten by the time Davie appeared. The last of the punters were being processed.

Joe looked up from deep in a girl's shoulder-bag.

Worried eyes under thinning, windswept hair. "A word." Walking towards the office.

Joe re-zipped the shoulder-bag, returned it to its owner then followed.

Davie was staring into his office through the open door, hand on handle.

Joe grinned. "Hud tae git in tae git the bar-float, man. Wondered whit hid happened tae ye."

Davie walked into the office, took off a damp jacket then turned.

Joe smiled.

Davie looked away.

"Whit word did ye want?"

"Shut the door, eh?"

Joe obliged, then perched on the edge of Davie's desk. "Well?"

Davie sat down, began to fiddle with a paper-clip. "Ah'm soary, pal." Head lowered. Drawer opened. Rifling, then a cream sheet of paper pushed towards him.

Joe stared at the P45. "Whit ye oan aboot?"

Sigh. "Yer services ur no longer required, Joe."

"Whit dae ye mean?"

Davie opened another drawer, produced a bottle of whisky and two glasses. "Whit ah said. We don't need ye ony mair, Joe." Top unscrewed, liquid slopping onto desk, then into glasses.

Joe blinked.

"Ye'll be paid up 'til the end o' the month, but there's nae need tae work yer notice."

"Huv ah done somethin' wrang, Davie?"

Headshake. "No' as far as ah'm concerned, Joe. Ye're a guid bouncer. If it wis ma decision . . . " One glass pushed across the desk. The other lifted, drained then refilled.

Joe knew whose decision it would be. He scowled.

"Ah'm soary, Joe."

He lifted the glass, drained it. "Want me tae stay 'til the end o' the shift – ah mean, ye'll be shoart-staffed the night an' . . . ?"

Headshake. "Jist go." Head lowered, glass drained.

Joe picked up his P45 and walked from the office.

In the staff-room, he opened his locker.

. . . don't need ye ony mair.

. . . don't need ye ony mair.

. . . don't need ye ony mair.

Joe began to stuff stuff into a duffle-bag.

Behind, door opening. Then: "Whit ye dain', Joe?"

He ignored Gina and continued to fill the bag.

"Joe?"

He turned. "Ah'm no' needed ony mair." He slammed the locker door and made to walk past her.

Gina caught his arm. "Haud oan, Joe. Whit's happened?"

Anger flared in his brain. "Ah've annoayed fuckin' King Billy an' he's sacked me!"

Shock. "Kin he dae that, ah mean . . . ?"

"King Billy kin dae onythin' he waants, it wid seem!" Joe clenched his fists.

"Naw . . . that's no' right, Joe. Ye canny be laid-aff jist like that. There's . . . they tribunal things. Ye kid tell them."

Joe closed his eyes. Tell them what: that he'd not really been needed in the first place? That Billy had created the job for him? That he was the only non-agency bouncer in The Matrix? That he'd stopped sleeping with the owner and had subsequently been fired? Joe sighed. "Naw ah couldny, Gina. 'Sno worth it."

Hand rubbing his arm. "Whit'll ye dae, Joe?"

"Fun another joab, ah suppose." He opened his eyes and stared at red-slash mouth.

It frowned. "No' so easy, Joe."

"Christmas is comin' up. Ah'll fun somethin'." Would he?

Thoughtful. "Aye – that's an idea. Ye kid try The Metro – ah ken a lassie collects glasses there. They're eyewis losin' bouncers."

Maybe there was a lot of it about. Joe sighed.

"Aye, an' there's yon new place opened up doon Custom House Quay . . . "

"Ah'm no' agency, Gina."

Snort. "They dinny care, fae whit ah hear."

"Georgie yissed tae be doon there, did he no'?"

Laugh. "Aye – shows ye the kinda guy they'd take oan." Sobering. "Ah didney mean . . . " Confusion.

He smiled. "Ah ken, Gina – thanks fur the tip. Ah'll gie them a ring."

"That's it, Joe – an' remember: onythin' ah kin dae . . . " Reassuring red-slash smile finishing sentence.

He smiled back. "Thanks, Gina. Ah'll manage." Last month's wages safely in the bank. A month's lying time would join them.

Joe pulled away and opened the staff-room door.

Maybe it was for the best. The last tie with Billy well-and-truly cut.

"Gie's a ring, sometime, Joe – let me ken how yer dain', eh?"

"Sure Gina – be guid." Joe walked from the staff-room. In the foyer, a group of five boys were singing loudly, blocking a fire-exit. Joe smiled: not his problem anymore. He shifted kit bag onto shoulder and walked away.

Rain soaked his hair as he walked up Petershill Road. Joe glanced at his watch: barely eleven. He walked on.

The first Saturday night in almost a year he hadn't been working.

Joe swerved to avoid two kids on bikes, then stared up at the glistening Red Road flats. Somewhere above the thirtieth floor, a light burned. He smiled. At least he had a home to go to. Then frowned.

Home.

He waited on the pavement's edge as a silent police-car swept past, then crossed the road.

Home. Where the heart is.

Fumbling for keys he unlocked and pushed open the entrance-door. As he walked towards the lift the sound of slamming echoed in the lurid yellow foyer. Joe pressed the call button, waited.

Home. He frowned. Trust. Responsibility.

Not his home. Not really.

He pressed the call button again.

No home.

No job.

Trundling sounds, then lift doors parted.

Joe stepped in, pressed 31.

No home.

No job.

Lift doors closed. Movement upwards. Angie and Sean. Family. Their home was his home.

No job . . .

Joe smiled. He had a year's experience under his belt. Good bouncers were always in demand.

Minutes later the lift stopped. Joe stepped out and walked towards Flat Three. Outside it was still raining. He brushed water from hair and inserted key in lock.

From the lounge, a low bass rumble.

Joe closed the front door, removed jacket and walked towards the noise.

In the lounge, Sean and Ewan were eating burgers out of polystyrene cartons. The TV blinked silently. Sound from a ghetto-blaster filled the room.

Ewan raised his head. "Hi, man." Then continued to munch.

Sean leapt up, yellow-container extended. "Whit you dain' hame? Waant a chip?"

Joe shook his head and walked through to the kitchen.

Sean followed. "Wis thur another raid?"

Joe filled the kettle. "Naw . . . " He plugged it in, then turned. "Whit yous two bin up tae?"

Burger bitten. Mouth full. "Audition."

Joe smiled. "Ewan oot-voted oan the lassie?"

Grin. Chewing. "Naw – she changed her mind aboot him!" Laugh.

Joe rinsed a mug. "So: ye goat somewan else?"

Vigorous nod. "Big guy fae Milton: Keith somethin'. Ah think he's okay, but Ewan . . . "

Voice from doorway. "He's an auld hippy, man!"

Sean grinned. "Naw he's no', man! Jist 'cos he . . . "

Ewan broke in, eyes rolling. "Thinks Primal Scream sound like The Stones!"

"'Well, they dae!" Sean threw the burger container at him. " . . . A bit."

"No' noo they dain't!" Ewan caught the container, crushing it.

"Thur early stuff dis, though!" Eyes to Joe. "Keith's gonny lend me his auld Stones albums, so ah kin . . . "

"Ah'm aff hame, man!" Ewan shrugged. "It's a band decision – 'member?" Laugh. To Joe: "Jist 'cos some auld hippy said he kid sing . . . "

Sean grabbed Ewan, face scarlet. "It wisney that!"

Laugh. Still to Joe: "Telt him he lucked like John Bon Jovi, an' Sean wis aw' pleased . . . "

Mock-pummelling the red head. "Jist 'cos ah wis talkin' tae the guy . . . "

Ewan grabbed Sean's hair. "Talkin'? When yous gettin' married, eh?"

Sean pulled away. Parody of grin. "Yer jist jealous!"

Ewan laughed. "O' some auld hippy?" He zipped up tattooed sleeve jacket. Face was in danger of matching hair.

The kettle switched itself off. Joe dragged his eyes from the Sean/Ewan spectacle. Without an audience, it moved back into the lounge.

Joe spooned coffee into mug.

From the other room, further exchanges. Then the sound of a door closing.

Joe poured water, added milk.

Voice at his shoulder: "Make me wan, eh?"

Joe turned.

Sean was grinning. "We still oan fur the morra?"

Joe rinsed another cup. "Aye . . . sure. What wis that aw'

aboot?" He turned.

Sean frowned. "Ewan's bein' . . . difficult! Keith's okay, he's bin in bands before . . . "

Joe smiled. Ewan and the lassie. Tit for tat. He filled Sean's mug and handed it to him.

"Thanks, man." Sean wandered away.

Joe followed.

In the lounge, Sean switched TV off and turned music down. Then frowned. "Whit are ye dain' hame so early?" Flopping onto floor.

Joe sat on the sofa. "Ah've loast ma joab." He lit a cigarette.

Wide eyes. "Whit happened?"

Joe sighed. "Ah wis never agency, Sean – nae proper contract. They jist don't need me ony mair."

Blue eyes stared, then narrowed. "Whit ye gonny dae?"

Joe frowned. He'd been through all this with Gina. "Ah'm gonny get another joab."

Sean held out an ashtray.

Joe took, used it.

Worried. "Ye'll no' be . . . " He glanced away. " . . . movin' oan, wull ye?"

Joe smiled. "No' yet, Sean." Stirring in his stomach. Sean was sprawling in front of the fire. Joe stared.

The stirring spread lower.

Sean flipped onto back, long fingers clasped behind head. "That's guid."

Joe stared.

Blond head propped up on one hand. Blue eyes pooling. "It's better wi' you here."

Joe broke the gaze, stood up. "Ah'm tired, Sean."

Quizzical eyes. "It's early, man – want another coffee? Mebbe somethin' tae eat?" Scrambling to feet. Eager eyes. "Ah kin dae ye some toast."

Joe sighed. "Naw Sean – jist gimme a bitta peace."

Grin. Grabbing headset from floor. "Sure, Joe – we kin talk the morra." Mock-punching chest.

Joe moved away and began to unpack duvet.

"Oh . . . somewan phoned fur ye."

Joe paused.

"Some guy – Andy, ah think he said. Wants ye to phone him back."

"The night?"

"Didney say." Ear-phones into ears, hi-fi clipped to waistband. "Didney sound very urgent."

Joe sighed. He'd phone in the morning.

"Want a haun makin' up yer bed?" Sean grasped a duvet-edge.

Joe shook his head. "Ah'll manage."

Grin. "Suit yersel'."

Long fingers ruffled short hair.

"Seeya in the mornin', then."

Joe watched as long, loose limbs loped towards the door and tried to think of something else.

CHAPTER EIGHTEEN

"Thanks onyway, pal." Joe replaced telephone receiver and drew a pencil line through the fourth number.

The Metro: nothing doing.

The Tunnel: nothing doing.

Cleopatra's: nothing doing.

Even Circa . . .

Joe sighed, lifted the receiver and dialled. One last try.

Ringing at the other end, then a gruff voice: "Yes?" Vaguely familiar.

Joe parroted his request.

Silence, then: "Whit agencies ye worked fur, son?"

Joe explained.

"Ye goat ony experience?"

Joe elaborated.

"The Matrix?" Surprise. "Billy King's club?"

Joe clarified.

"You Billy's boay?"

Joe bit his lip.

Gruff laugh. "Joe, isn't it?"

Joe chewed.

Tutting. "Ye've been a bad boay, Joe, fae whit ah've heard." Gruff laugh.

Dimaggios. Baldy. The leer. "Forget it . . . "

"Haud oan, Joe. Ah'd like tae help ye oot – really. Mebbe we kid come tae some soarta . . . " Leering laugh. " . . . arrangement?"

Joe sighed. "Dae ye huv any joabs goin' or dain't ye?"

Gruff laugh. "At the club? Naw – Billy widney like it. But if ye'd consider . . . ?"

Joe replaced the receiver.

'Billy widney like it'.

He frowned. The run-up to Christmas and, miraculously, no-one needed any bouncers.

Correction . . .

He leant against an artexed wall.

. . . No-one needed this bouncer.

Yawning sound.

Joe turned.

Angie rubbing sleep-stained face, then pulling housecoat round a thin body.

He smiled. "Did ah wake ye?"

Another yawn. Frizzy headshake. "Whit time . . . ?"

"Two-ish. Waant a coffee?"

"Aye." Walking past him towards lounge. "Sean up?"

Joe followed. "Huvney seen him." Didn't want to.

She continued on into the kitchen.

He sat down on the sofa. The room was its usual ice-box.

From the kitchen: "Guid night?"

Joe rubbed his face. "Aye. You?"

Laugh. "No' bad. Ah . . . "

A blond explosion from the hall. Sean, swinging sports-bag, baseball cap the wrong way round. "Ye ready, man?" Grin.

Joe stared.

The grin faded. "Ye've no' changed yer mind, huv ye?" Wide blue eyes.

Angie appeared from kitchen holding two mugs. She handed one to Joe then sat down. Frown to Sean. "Let Joe drink his coffee afore yous go, son."

Joe stared.

Sean sat on the floor. "Ye huv." Disappointed.

Angie laughed. "We've aw' goat other things tae think aboot, 'part fae you, son."

Joe sighed: it was all he thought about. He looked down at long sweatshirt-clad legs.

Rummaging in pocket. Stifled yawn. "Want wan, Joe?" Jiggling sound.

He looked up, took a cigarette from the extended packet.

Further rummaging, then sigh. To Sean: "Away doon an' get me matches, eh?"

The Zippo bulged in Joe's pocket.

Sean stood up, foot-dragging.

Laugh. "Joe'll be ready by the time ye git back."

Blue eyes bored into his skull. He didn't meet them.

Money produced, then the sound of a door closing.

Joe sighed and looked up.

Angie was sipping coffee.

He opened his mouth.

She beat him to it. "Ah'm glad ye made the offer, Joe. He yissed tae swim a lot when he wis younger, but these days . . ." Frown. "Only his mooth gits ony exercise."

Joe knew when he was beaten. "Ah'll need tae git some trunks fae somewhere."

Laugh. "Borra a pair o' his – they might be a wee bit wee, but." Mug placed on fireplace, she stood up and walked from the room.

Joe stared past the half-empty mug at his brother's photograph.

Michael had been there for him . . .

Angie and Sean re-entered the room at the same time. He held matches. She gripped a shiny purple fragment, tossed it towards him.

Joe caught the trunks.

Sean laughed. "Ye'll never git intae them, man." Sports-bag unzipped. Baggy shorts produced. Sean walked towards Joe and held the garment out at waist height. "You take these – ah'll wear the Speedos."

Joe stared.

Angie lit a cigarette. "Ye goat two towels?"

Nod, carefully repacking swimming-trunks.

"Presentable wans?"

Faded blue and greying white edges exposed in bag. Sean looked up for approval.

Angie sighed. "They'll huv tae dae, ah suppose. Whit pool yous aff tae – Springburn?"

Scathing. "It's fulla kids." Grin to Joe. "Whitehill's better – an' their sauna's eyewis deid oan a Sunday."

Joe watched Angie's pleased face.

No way out.

Responsibility, trust . . .

He lifted bikers' jacket, tried to smile.

Sean grinned. "Ye kin share ma strawberry soap, if ye want." Sportsbag rezipped, hoisted onto thin shoulder.

"Huv a guid time, boays!" Angie followed them to the

front door. "Ah'll see yis later."

Joe followed Sean towards the lift.

He blinked, spat then hoisted himself onto the side of the pool.

Three lanes away, a white-and-purple outline was elegantly turning for a twentieth lap.

Joe wiped chlorine from eyes and looked across to where a well-built figure in shorts and tee-shirt was remonstrating with a group of pre-teen kids. Shouts, splashes, then two irritated whistle blasts. His eyes swept away, brushing the mothers-and-toddlers at the shallow end. Echoing, good-natured shrieks rose up to fill the swimming area. Joe tightened a drawstring waistband. He'd forgotten how much he liked water. Lowering himself back in, he supported weight on elbows. Lukewarm waves lapped at nipples. A shiver followed. Joe smiled.

From the other side of the pool, the attendant met his eyes, smiled back.

Then someone grabbed his foot.

Joe braced arms against poolside and kicked.

The hand remained tight. Then pulled.

Joe frowned, then gasped as water coursed up to envelop his head.

A soft, wet blanket blurred his vision. Joe blinked. Blood sang in his ears, deadening another sense. Then an arm around his neck. Strong legs wrapped themselves around waist.

Joe reached behind, seized a handful of purple lycra and threw Sean forward, over right shoulder. Sound fizzed, ebbing in and out.

Hands on his waist again.

Joe grabbed two thin wrists, kicking down hard on the pool-bottom. Together, they shot towards the surface, two heads appearing just to the right of an old guy in cap and goggles, who scowled.

Sean grinned, dragging Joe poolside.

He watched the white body slide upwards onto the edge.Then a hand extended.

Joe took it.

With some effort, Sean pulled him onto the edge, then grinned.

Joe grinned back. "Stronger than ye look, eh?"

Wider grin. Water-darkened ponytail flicked over shoulder.

Joe stared at the wiry arms. Thin blue veins spidered long muscles.

Hands wringing water from hair. "Ye huvin' a guid time?"

Joe pulled in feet as the elderly walrus snorted past on his return journey. "Aye." He was: other distractions, other bodies.

"Feel this."

A hand seized his wrist. Joe laid a broad palm on Sean's upper arm.

The boy made a fist.

Nothing happened. Flushed face.

Joe smiled, squeezed. "Swimmers' muscles ur different." Sean's arm was warm beneath his grip. "Less tae see." A splash took his attention. Joe watched as a brown, over-developed torso appeared from beneath artificially-created waves and began a showy butterfly. Weighty biceps soon slowed the swimmer to a less impressive crawl. "Ye don't waant tae look like that, dae ye?"

Chlorine-reddened eyes followed laboured progress. Then moved back to Joe. "Naw – ah want tae luck like you." He scrambled to his feet. "C'moan – race ye!" A white and purple flash dived in, barely breaking the surface.

Joe smiled, followed.

Seconds later they surfaced together at the shallow end, amidst a gaggle of giggling girls.

One whistled, nudging her friend.

Joe grinned as Sean blushed, then watched as the purple-clad arse waded through three feet of water, accompanied by more whistles.

A girl in polka-dot bikini patted his arm. "Whit's yer pal's name?"

Irate voice from poolside. "Comin' tae the sauna, Joe?"

He looked up at the pale, dripping figure. "Aye, Sean."

Giggles from the girls.

Joe smiled, winked at Polka-dot then hoisted himself out of the water.

Sean had been right. The sauna was quiet. It was also surprisingly large. In the far corner, an overweight man dozed contentedly under *The Sunday Post*. Muffled snores punctuated a warm, comfortable silence.

Joe picked up a ladle, dousing already steaming coals. From above, a yawn. Then:

"Ah kid lie here aw' day."

Joe looked up at the shelf parallel with his shoulder.

Sean pressed face to pine slats. Drying strands of blond hair curled over pink cheeks. Joe smiled as tiny pools of moisture evaporated frown the boy's sweating back. "Ye're jist a lazy bugger at heart – admit it. Aw' that swimming's jist an excuse tae lie aboot in here."

A limp hand batted his head, then flopped away. "Ah've earned it."

Joe watched as one of the tiny pools overflowed and began to trickle down the spine length. Droplets gathered at the base, swelling in number, then spilled into the crack of Sean's arse.

Pink buttocks twitched.

Joe laughed, picked up his towel and dabbed the sweat-dappled skin.

Sean groaned. "That's nice . . . " Head buried in arms, mumbling.

Joe pushed the ponytail to one side and patted again. Beneath the heat-flush, Sean's skin was flawless alabaster. His eyes travelled down the long lean back, pausing at the last vertebra. Fine blond hair dusted two lightly-muscled mounds, becoming thicker over thighs.

Stirring in groin. Joe flinched, ceased patting.

"Don't stop." A different groan, protesting. Then Sean turned over.

Joe stared, prick hardening . . .

. . . at the small pinky-purple snail which lay amidst a

wiry blond crotch.

He blinked, then switched his gaze to Sean's face.

Eyes closed. Thick lashes resting on sweating cheeks. Lips parted in a sigh. Hands clasped behind head, revealing blond, bushy armpits.

And a birthmark, in the left.

Joe stared. He had an identical mole in his right.

As had Michael.

Joe touched the birthmark, eyes skimming down a skinny, hairless chest, past large nipples.

Sean sighed softly. The snail twitched.

Heat in his stomach. Joe stood up. "Get ye ootside, Sean!" He lifted towel and walked towards the door.

Behind, a faint, protesting moan and a stifled snore from the guy in the corner.

It had stopped raining. Outside the swimming-pool Joe leant against railings and lit another cigarette. Beneath bikers' jacket his body glowed. Beneath jeans another remnant of the sauna was stubbornly refusing to fade, despite three cold plunges.

Behind, the door opened.

Joe turned.

A woman and three small children emerged.

Joe stared past them. Still no Sean. He ran a hand over his hair and gazed back at the road.

Reality seeped in.

Work. A job. A way of making a living.

He sighed. Maybe it was time to move on, out of Glasgow. For a number of reasons.

Behind, the door opened: "No kept ye, huv ah?" Laughing voice.

Heat in his stomach. Joe ground out cigarette under Doc.

Maybe it was time to move on.

A hand on his shoulder:

"Too hot for ye, eh?"

Smell of strawberry soap filled his head. Joe turned, avoiding the clear blue eyes. "Aye, Sean. Too hot." They began to walk home.

He heard the activity before he saw it.

Sean was talking about the Keith guy as a screaming squad-car sped up Petershill Road ahead of them. "You'd like him, Joe – he's bin aboot a bit." Laugh. "He's saved whales, an' that kinda thing."

Joe stared across to where two stationary squad-cars were joined by the speeding one. Queuing customers at the ice-cream van leered towards a crowd of navy serge uniforms, not wanting to lose their place, but not wanting to miss anything either.

Sean danced on ahead. "Bet it's Mr McGhee an' his cor, again. Fuckin' alarm's eyewis goin' aff."

Joe walked more quickly, catching up with Sean just as the boy pressed the intercom. He scowled. "Ah've goat ma keys . . ."

Sean pressed again. "This is quicker."

Cracking voice: "Yes?" Not Angie.

Sean leapt back.

Joe moved forward, producing keys. "Ya stupit . . . !"

Crackling 'Yes?' again.

Joe lowered mouth to grill. "Sorry, pal – pressed the wrang button."

Cracking ceased.

Two uniforms moved forward and pushed open the main door.

Sean nipped in behind them, swinging sportsbag.

One of the uniforms grabbed an arm. "Where you aff tae, son?"

Miffed. "Ah live here!" Wrestling arm free.

Joe tensed. "Thirty-wan/three. Macdonald."

Another uniform appeared. "You Joe Macdonald?"

Sean elbowed past. "Whit if he is?" Prodding lift call-button.

Joe stared at the bulky police officer. "Aye. Whit's happened?"

The lift appeared, doors parting. Sean got in. Joe followed. So did three uniforms. The bulky one lowered head to radio:

"Sir? He's here. We're oan oor way up."

209

The lift doors slid shut.

Pounding in his ears. Joe closed his eyes.

Georgie . . .

At his side, Sean was surly:

"Whit dae yous waant?"

"Nothin' tae dae wi' you, son."

"Whit dae ye want wi' Joe?"

Joe opened his eyes. "Aye, whit dae ye want?"

A flabby expressionless face told him little. "Upstairs wid be better, pal." The words told him less.

Pulling at his arm. Joe turned.

Flushed pink face, quizzical eyes.

Joe tried to smile. "Some sorta mistake, Sean. Don't worry."

Unconvinced. "Ah want tae ken whit's goin' oan."

The lift stopped. Doors parted. Joe could see more uniforms outside the door of Number Three. Pounding in his ears.

Georgie.

An alibi provided by Billy.

An alibi that could be withdrawn.

Like the job had been withdrawn.

"Come on, pal." A strong arm seized his elbow.

Sean was running on ahead. "Ma? Whit's goin' oan?"

Angie appeared in the doorway, frizzy hair framing a confused face. "Joe, whit's . . . ?"

"In ye come, pal."

The strong arm propelled him forward, past Angie, into the dark hallway. There was a smell.

A familiar smell.

Joe inhaled.

Ahead, the lounge door opened.

Wet sheepskin.

Joe moved towards a pewter-headed figure, then stopped. "Inspector . . . ?" He couldn't remember the guy's name.

Sheepskin-coat spun round. Pewter features matched the hair. "Ah, Mr Macdonald. Sit doon. Ah need a wee word."

In the hallway, he could hear Sean and Angie whispering. Joe sighed.

210

Georgie.

Billy.

He stared at the grey face, then sat down. "Okay, let's hear this word."

Sheepskin coat scowled. "Where wur you last night?"

Joe stared. Last night? Not twelve nights ago?

"Well?"

"Ah wis workin'"

'Where?"

"Ye ken where ah work – The Matrix."

Hard smile. "Where ye yissed tae work, ah think ye mean."

Joe stared.

"Well?"

"Well whit?" Joe rubbed his face.

Sheepskin-coat sighed. "Where wur you between four and seven am this morning?"

"Here."

"Can onywan confirm that?"

"Aye. Sean wis here too."

Hard smile. "Joined at the hip, ur yis?"

Behind, someone laughed.

Joe frowned. "Look: whit's this aw' aboot?"

Sigh. "Early this morning a sum of money wis stolen fae a safe in The Matrix's office. It wis there at four, when the club closed, an' no' there at seven."

Joe stared. Weekends, Billy usually kept the takings at home. "How did they git in? Wis it that dodgy fire-exit?"

Hard smiled. "They used keys, Mr Macdonald." Hand to mantelpiece. "Keys like these, possibly."

Joe stared at his Matrix key-ring.

"You no longer work there, Mr Macdonald – is that right?"

"Aye."

"Why didn't ye return yer keys?"

"Ah furgoat, ah suppose. Ah widda . . . "

"Acrimonious, wis it?"

Joe raised an eyebrow.

"Did ye leave of yer ain accord, or wur ye sacked?"

211

Joe scowled. "Ah wis sacked."

Tutting. "Surplus tae requirements?"

"Davie said he didney need me ony mair, if that's whit ye mean."

Sheepskin-coat stared.

"Davie – the manager?"

Nod. "Right. Ah've hid a word wi' him. Sez ye took it well."

Joe shrugged. "Whit else kin ye dae?"

Hard laugh. "Some people, if they felt they'd bin . . . unfairly dismissed . . . an' if they hid a set o' keys they'd furgotten tae haun' back, might decide they wur due some sorta . . . redundancy money."

Joe stared. "Loats a people huv keys fur . . . "

Headshake. "Ainly you, the manager an', of course, the owner." Frown. "Davie wis at hame wi' his wife at the time concerned . . . " Tight smile. " . . . And ah don't think Mr King wid rob his ain club – dae you?"

Joe scowled. "Ah wis here last night."

Sheepskin-coat sighed, then turned to a uniform. "Huv a word wi' the boay, an' see if the woman kens onythin'." Whispered conversation.

Joe rubbed his face. "How much did they git?"

Sheepskin-coat turned. "Ten thoosand quid."

CHAPTER NINETEEN

"Sit down, Macdonald."

Joe stared. The 'Mr' had disappeared seven hours ago, somewhere on the journey from Red Road Court to Stewart Street police-station. He sighed, and sat.

Opposite, Sheepskin-coat was removing the garment. At his side a thin girl in white blouse and black skirt fiddled with a twin-cassette machine. Abruptly, it emitted a shrill tone from tiny speakers, then cut out.

Sheepskin-coatless pulled out a chair and sat down. Throat clearing. "Preliminary interview with Joseph Macdonald. Present are DI Monroe and WPC MacIntyre. Time . . . " Eyes to watch. " . . . six thirty five, am."

Joe stared. "Ah want a solicitor."

Hard smile. "Think ye need wan, eh?"

"Naw, but . . . "

"The duty-guy's tied up wi' somewan else, at the moment." Grin. "We kid take ye back tae the cells tae wait, if ye like."

Two hours questioning at the flat. Thirty minutes in the car. Three hours alone in a cell. Another three hours in another room, with another man, without a tape-machine. Joe rubbed his face. "Jist git oan wi' it."

"That's better." Nod to the tape-machine. "This is as much tae protect you as us." Laugh.

Joe stared .

"Now . . . " Opening folder, rifling. " . . . Let's go over this again."

Joe sighed. What else did they need to know?

"Ye arrived last night fur work – when?"

"Jist before eight. Davie wisney there. Ah used ma keys tae let everywan in . . . "

"These keys: where did ye get them?"

Joe sighed. "Emergency wans – Davie'll tell ye. Bi . . . the boss gave them tae me."

"Ah, yes, Mr King. How lang huv ye hud them?"

"'Boot six months. Ah wis tae take over if Davie wisney

213

there, fur ony reason."

"Used them before?"

Joe shook his head.

"Fur the benefit o' the tape, Mr Macdonald shakes his heid. These keys . . . " Rifling in pocket. " . . . Ah'm showin' Mr Macdonald a setta four keys. Tell me whit they open."

Joe picked up the key-ring, counted. "This wan's the roller-shutter. This wan's the main door. This's Davie's oaffice." He stared at a third, smaller, stubbier key. "Ah don't ken whit this wan dis."

"Fur the benefit o' the tape, Mr Macdonald indicates the key tae the office safe."

Joe stared. "Ah didney ken that wis whit it wis fur."

Hard smile. "Ye sure aboot that?"

Joe stared.

"Fur the benefit o' the tape, Mr Macdonald fails tae answer."

Joe switched his eyes to the tape machine, in which two sets of tiny wheels spun slowly.

"Noo, Macdonald. Ye worked at The Matrix club . . . ?"

"Ten months."

"An' before?"

Joe sighed. "The airmy. Ye ken aw' this – ah telt Andy – PC Hunter, the night efter Georgie . . ." He stopped.

Tiny wheels continued to spin.

"Aye, Macdonald – ah remember. Ye hid nae alibi that time, either, 'til yer boss came forward." Smile. "He'll no' be dain' that this time, son – ye're oan yer ain, noo."

Now: different from before.

Before? Billy sorted things out.

Now?

Joe scowled and stared at tiny, twin wheels.

Somewhere in the background, a voice droned on.

Joe continued to stare.

Twin wheels continued to spin.

Hard laugh, then:"Earth tae Macdonald, come in Macdonald!"

Joe blinked, turning to stare at pewter hair.

A strong hand tapped pen on table. Sigh. "Where is it?"

"Where's whit?"

"The money?"

"Whit money?"

"The ten thousand quid."

Back in Billy's bank account, or the bedroom safe. "Ah don't ken . . . " Joe frowned. " . . . Ah've no' goat ony ten thousand quid." That much was true.

Laugh. "Hidden it, huv ye?"

Joe stared.

More drumming. "Save yer sister-in-law an' her boay a loata trouble if ye jist tell us where, son."

Angie . . .

Sean: taken away in a different squad-car. Released, or still here? Joe watched nicotined-stained digits hit Formica table in sequence.

"Hope she's no' hoose-proud, son." Grin to the WPC. "They boays kin leave a bit o' a mess sometimes."

Angie. She didn't need this. Joe stood up. "Ah've telt ye, ah've no' goat ony ten thousand. Ah left The Matrix aboot ten last night an' went hame. Ah didney go back oot. Sean wis there – he'll tell ye." The small room became even smaller.

Commanding voice. "Sit doon, Macdonald!"

Joe sat, arms by sides.

"Listen, son. The boay sez ye wur there aw' right, but ah'm afraid his word's no' enough." Laugh. "Ah kinda get the impression if ye wur Jack the Ripper he'd swear otherwise!"

Joe stared.

Gentler words. "Joe, Joe . . . .ye wur sacked – let's say it wis unfair dismissal. Ye're no' wi' an agency, it's comin' up tae Christmas, ye're hard-up, ye hud a setta keys . . . " Grey eyes piercing his.

Joe met the gaze.

Sheepskin-coatless bored deeper. "Ah wisney gonny tell ye this, but it seems Mr King disney want tae press chairges. Jist wants his money back." Pen laid on table. "Come oan, son – yer ex-boss is giein' ye a chance. Don't throw it back in his face. Tell us where the money is an' save yersel' a loata trouble."

Joe broke the gaze. He didn't care anymore. "Ah wis nowhere near The Matrix yesterday morning an' you canny prove ah wis . . . "

Knock at the door. It opened.

"Fur the benefit o' the tape, PC Michaels enters the room."

Joe watched as the bulky uniform ignored him, made eye-contact with Sheepskin-coatless, then shook his head. He left.

Sigh. "Ye goat a bank-account, Macdonald?"

"Aye."

"Gonny gie's yer permission tae luck at it?"

Joe stretched back in his seat. The flat-search had evidently turned-up zero. "Be ma guest. Ah've nothin' tae hide." That much was true.

Sheepskin-coatless looked disappointed. He sighed. "We'll see, Macdonald." Hard stare. Silence, then: "Interview terminated at . . . " Eyes to wrist. " . . . seven-oh-five, am."

Joe watched the thin girl switch the tape-machine off, remove two tapes then push them towards him. He stared.

She smiled. "Choose wan an' sign it, sir." Pen lifted.

Joe took it, signed.

Sheepskin-coatless was putting the coat back on. "Pick up yer stuff at the desk, Macdonald, when ye' lea' yer bank details wi' the sergeant – an' stay where we kin fun' ye." He strode from the room.

Joe stared at the WPC.

She smiled. "That's it – ye kin go." Sealing signed tape in cellopohane bag.

Joe stood up. Nearly eight hours, then nothing. He patted pockets: no cigarettes either. He sighed and walked from the room.

Outside, it was still dark. Joe stood in the police-station's doorway and watched the rain. He reached for cigarettes, lit one. The Zippo's petrol fumes filled his nostrils.

Billy.

' . . . you need me, Joe . . . '

He squeezed the cigarette's dampening filter.

216

Billy's money.
Billy's flat.
Billy's job.
Billy's . . .
Joe frowned. He needed none of it.
He needed . . . Joe walked back into the reception area.
The desk sergeant stared at him.
Joe scowled. "Ye owe me a phone-call, pal."
Hand pointing behind him.
Joe followed the fingers to a public call-box. "Thanks fur nothin'!" He fumbled for change, then walked towards the telephone . . .

. . . .Angie answered almost immediately: "Joe! Ur you okay?" Tearful-sounding.
"Aye, ah'm fine. Did the polis make much o' a mess?"
Sniff. "Christ! Don't worry aboot that. Ur ye sure ye're okay? Sean waited aroon' fur ye, but they telt him tae go hame."
Joe frowned. "He okay? Did they keep him lang?"
"'Boot an oor." Sniff, then laugh. "He's in his bed noo. Wanted tae wait up fur ye, but ah made him go." Pause. "Whit's it aw' aboot, Joe? The polis widney tell me onythin' an' ah kid get fuck-all oota Sean."
He scowled. "A mistake, Angie. The polis'll soart it oot."
"Come oan hame, Joe – ye must be beat."
He sighed. "Too wound-up. Ah'm goin' fur a walk."
"But . . . ?"
"Away tae yer bed, Angie. Ah'll tell ye aw' about it later."
"Sure ye're okay?" Worried-sounding.
He manufactured a laugh. "Aye – guidnight." He replaced the the receiver and collected an unused ten pence piece from the machine.
Noise behind. Talking, joking. Then a closer voice. "Can't keep away, eh?"
Joe turned.
Andy Hunter zipped up nylon windbreaker. "What you doing here?" Casual, then peering at him. "You look awful."

Joe sighed. "Fancy somethin' tae eat?"

The handsome face grinned. "Best offer I've had all shift." He moved forward towards the door.

Joe followed.

The café bulged with a variety of uniforms – police, postmen, traffic-wardens, the luminous yellow waterproofs of road-sweepers.

Joe pushed his plate away.

Andy Hunter continued to eat, then eyed Joe's untouched breakfast. Smile. Bushy eyebrows raised. "I know it's not the Cul-de-Sac, but . . ."

Joe scowled. "Ah'm no' as hungry as ah thought." He lifted a mug of tea.

"Do you mind?" Andy gestured towards his plate.

"Be ma guest."

Andy exchanged his own empty plate for Joe's full one.

"So . . ." Munching. "I take it you didn't just come to Stewart Street at seven in the morning for my sparkling conversation!"

Joe lit a cigarette and began to talk . . .

. . . Half an hour later, the café was still busy. Andy Hunter's bushy eyebrows V-ed:

"You sent the money back?"

"Sure ah did – whit wid ah dae wi' ten thoosand quid?"

Smile. "I could think of a few things." Then frown. "And you're sure it wasn't intended as some sort of informal redundancy pay-off?"

"Ah goat it afore ah wis sacked – fae Davie, the same time everywan else goat thur Christmas bonus. Ah thought it wis a . . . present . . ." He stared at the salt and pepper containers.

Quizzical stare.

Joe parted the condiments with a blunt forefinger. " . . . fae Billy."

"But that's all over, isn't it?"

"Aye." He widened the space between salt and pepper.

Sigh. "Could've been a mix-up. Maybe Davie gave you

218

the wrong envelope . . . or the right one at the wrong time."

Joe pushed the salt container to the far side of the table. "Aye . . . mebbe. But that disney dae me ony guid, noo."

"Why didn't you tell the DI about all this?"

Joe stared at the salt, then the pepper container. "Ah tried tellin' him in ma heid, but it didn't sound . . . right."

Andy Hunter reunited condiments. "Mmm . . . I suppose it is a bit . . . far-fetched."

"Listen, it's true! Ah goat it, ah sent it back, ah wis sacked, an' then . . . aw' this happened."

"I believe you, Joe – no-one could make something like that up." He lifted a mug and drank. "Do you know who reported the break-in?"

Joe shook his head. "Mebbe no-wan – the alarm's connected tae the polis-station. They'd ken the moment it went aff."

"Who's the key-holder?"

"Ah widda thought that wis Davie: the polis goat him at hame."

Frowning pause, then: "Any idea why you were sacked?"

Joe shook his head.

"I mean, you didn't . . . hit anyone, or anything like that?"

Joe sighed. "Ah liked the joab – ah wis guid at it, tae. Everythin' in ma life wis fine, until . . . " A kid's bruised and battered face filled his mind.

"Why did you and Billy King split up – if you don't mind me asking?"

Joe closed his eyes. "Whit is it they ca' it . . . irreconcilable differences?"

Sigh. "I saw what happened, that night at the Cul-de-Sac." Tentative .

Joe laughed and opened his eyes. "That? That wis nothing! Billy an' me hud . . . an understandin'."

Andy wasn't laughing. "It's my understanding that . . . those sort of 'understandings' are best kept in the bedroom."

Joe smiled. The bedroom.

Billy's bedroom.

On the floor.

His prick began to harden . . .

"Anyway, that's your business." Hand over fashionably-cut hair. Thoughtful. "Who else has keys to The Matrix?"

Joe scowled. "Me, Davie . . . an' Billy."

"Let's say the alarm was de-activated: who knows the code?"

"Me, Davie . . . an' Billy."

Laugh. "Think someone's trying to set you up?"

Joe shrugged. "Don't ken whit tae think." He stubbed out cigarette and immediately lit another.

"You know *Roadhouse*?"

Joe rubbed his crotch. "Is it a new club?"

Laugh. "It's a film. Richard Widmark, Ida Lupino and some other guy . . . Joseph Cotton, I think."

Joe shook his head. "Disney mean onythin' tae me."

"Shame! This all sounds a bit like the plot!"

Joe frowned. "Ah don't watch a loata films."

"Forget it, then."

Silence, broken by shards of conversation and dish-clatter. Then:

"Found another job yet?"

Joe frowned, shook his head. "Ah need somewhere else tae live, as well."

Smile. "Things not working-out with you and your sister-in-law?"

Heat in his stomach. Joe closed his eyes. "She disney need aw' this hassle."

"Sure." Pause. "I could put you up for a coupla days, if you don't mind the sofa."

Joe opened his eyes. "Thanks, pal – ah'll mebbe take ye up oan that if ah canny fun' onywhere else."

Mock-insulted. "Suit yourself!"

"Ah didney mean . . . "

Low, resonant laugh. "I was joking, Joe – lighten up! Look: as far as the missing money goes I'm sure you've nothing to worry about. If the DI had anything at all to link you with the break-in, you wouldn't be sitting here now. He's probably giving the manager exactly the same routine as we speak!"

Joe stared.

'Mr King . . . doesn't want to press charges . . . just wants his money back . . . '

"Hey! What am I thinking about!"

Joe looked up.

The handsome face smiled. "If you're serious about finding somewhere else to stay a . . . friend of mine's got a flat in Dennistoun."

"Ah widney want tae pit onywan oot . . . "

"It's okay – he's abroad. I'm meant to be keeping an eye on the flat for him, but I never seem to get the time." Brown pupils twinkling. "You'd be doing me a favour – and you could stay as long as you want."

Joe sighed. No Billy.

No Angie.

No Sean. His stomach flipped over.

"At least have a look at it – eh?"

Joe smiled. "Disney matter whit it looks like – ah'll take it!"

Laugh. "Great." Eyes to watch. "You go pick up your stuff. I'll nip home and get the keys." He stood up. "Eighteen Craigpark, flat 1/1 – meet you there."

"Ah don't ken Dennistoun that well."

Laugh. "The number's 564-5128 if you get lost."

Joe sighed, stood up. They walked from the crowded café. Outside, Andy paused. "Maybe your sister-in-law will be glad to see the back of you, but I know someone who won't." Teasing.

Joe scowled and tried to think of something else. "Ah'll see ye there, then." He strode off towards Cathedral Street.

''Here's the address and phone-number, so ye'll ken where ah'll be." Joe scribbled on a pad, then turned to stare at what remained of Angie's lounge. "Ah'm soarry aboot aw' this." He watched as she replaced the last floorboard then stood up:

"Whit wur they luckin' fur, Joe?" Confused eyes.

"Nothin' fur you tae worry aboot." He re-righted an armchair and sat down.

Angie crouched on the floor beside a shattered photograph frame. "Is it somethin' tae dae wi' Sean?"

Joe tensed.

Angry. "If that wee bugger's bin up tae onythin . . . "

"Nothin' tae dae wi' Sean, Angie – it's ma fault."

Quizzical stare. "Ye've eyewis bin straight wi' me, Joe. Why wull ye no' . . . ?"

"It wid take too long." He sighed. "It's better fur every-wan if ah jist leave noo."

Disappointed smile. "Ah'll miss huvin' ye aroon', Joe an' so wull . . ."

"Ah'll be up fur the resta ma stuff the morra, Angie." He stood up, fumbled in pocket. "Here's yer keys." Joe picked his way over debris and into the hall.

From a half-open bedroom door: "Joe?" Sleepy voice. "They let ye oot . . . ?"

He walked swiftly down the dark hallway and out into morning gloom.

222

CHAPTER TWENTY

The door slammed.

Joe stared at the immaculately-decorated room. Mottled grey/blue walls – 'teal', Andy had called it – a darker grey carpet and a large, lead-coloured leather sofa. He walked past a smart wooden coffee-table to the oriel window and looked out. Opposite, ten o'clock mass was getting underway at Our Lady of Good Counsel. Joe watched a red Mercedes pull in to allow Andy's small, silver Clio to manoeuvre around three chapel-bound middle-aged women, then up Craigpark towards the Parade. He yawned.

His brain was tired, his body still warm from yesterday's sauna. A knot of tension pulsed in his stomach, adding to the heat. The smell of cigarettes, his own sweat and the faint odour of Sheepskin-coat's wet coat caught in his throat. Joe peeled off biker's jacket and tee-shirt, then sat down on the lead-coloured sofa and began to unlace boots.

The flat was quiet.

After 31/3 Red Road Court, very quiet.

He kicked off Docs, got up and wandered through to the bathroom, undoing belt as he walked. Underfoot, springy carpet became polished wood. The knot in his stomach clenched, then unclenched . . . and re-clenched.

The bathroom was clean, green, tiled, and slightly damp-smelling. Joe examined a shelf below a small shaving-mirror.

A bottle of Listerine and an old Bic.

He turned and scanned the small room. Andy had said the flat's owner – a doctor, at present in Rwanda – wouldn't mind if he made himself at home. Joe rubbed a sweaty shoulder, placed plug in plug-hole and turned on both taps.

A chugging sound, then water flooded over white enamel.

Joe watched as the bath began to fill, then wriggled out of jeans and walked into the bedroom. In bright, December light he stared at the futon with its sand-coloured cover

223

and smiled.

After two weeks on Angie's lumpy sofa, it looked good.

After eight hours in a police-station, it looked even better. Beside the bed, on what looked like an old wooden trunk, a lamp and three – one open, two closed – books. He walked to the window, lowering a bamboo roller-blind.

The room turned sepia.

In the lounge, the telephone purred.

Joe walked towards it.

The lead-coloured sofa sighed as he sat down and picked up the handset.

Buzzing at the other end.

Joe replaced the receiver and stared at the answering-machine. Another closed book.

The sound of deepening water filtered through the silence.

Stomach still pulsing, Joe eased Tangas out of his arse-crack and walked into the bathroom.

The telephone rang twice when he was in the bath, a further three times when he was in bed.

Joe answered all the calls.

The caller remained silent.

Easing his body back under the sand-coloured duvet, he debated taking the phone off the hook, then decided against it. He glanced at his watch: nearly mid-day. Eight hours should do it. His body was relaxing, the tension ebbing away from his stomach . . . ebbing lower.

On the edge of sleep, a faint purring. Joe pulled the duvet over his head and blanked out the sound.

A vague stirring in his groin.

He smiled, yawned, a hand reaching down towards a half-hard prick, which hardened further at his touch.

Joe closed his eyes, fingers grasping the length of pulsating meat. A panoply of images danced on his eyelids as he caressed himself.

Billy . . .

Michael . . .

Billy's prick . . .

224

Michael's prick. . .

He paused, playing with the ball-sac.

Shivers coursed the length of him. Joe sighed and moved hand back, tugging the foreskin up towards the head.

Billy . . .

Michael . . .

Blond . . . blond . . .

On the periphery of spidering darkness, another blond. . .

Joe squeezed eyelids and moved his hand more quickly.

Blond . . . blond . . . darker hair . . . darker eyes . . .

His prick twitched violently against sweating fingers as his mind's eye zeroed in on . . .

Andy Hunter.

Joe smiled, pausing to rub the head of his prick with a rough thumb.

The image was unfocused, unspecific. Joe concentrated, honing the thought . . .

He gasped, thought centring around Andy's naked body . . . and a low, resonant voice.

He came quickly and efficiently, shooting warm spunk onto stomach and lower chest as tension dissolved.

When he woke up, sepia still filled the bedroom. Joe blinked, stretched. Then listened.

No music.

No voices.

No Angie.

No . . .

Joe groaned, tried to think of something else. He looked at his watch: just before ten. He shook his wrist, then raised it to one ear: faint ticking. He peered at the bamboo blind.

Definitely light.

He had slept almost twenty-four hours.

Sitting up, he spotted a dressing-gown on a hook behind the door. Joe levered legs over the side of the low bed, stood up and strolled across the room. The robe's soft fabric brushed five flaccid inches as he tied the belt loosely. He sighed, turned and rolled up the bamboo blind.

Brighter light rushed into the sand-coloured room.

Soft purring from the lounge.

Joe walked towards it. As he picked up the receiver:

"Settling-in okay?"

The last voice he heard before sleeping . . . the first when he awoke. Joe smiled. "Aye." Then frowned. "You try tae phone last . . . yesterday?"

"Not me. Barely in myself. I hate the change-over from nights to days – gives you jet-lag."

Joe laughed.

"Just wanted to make sure you'd found everything all right. Anything you need to borrow, I'm sure Phillip won't mind." Resonant laugh. "He'll probably dine out for months on the 'I shared my flat with a soldier' story."

Joe scowled, ignored his twitching prick and stared at yesterday's debris of clothes which scarred the orderly room. "Ah tidy-up efter masel' – he'll no' ken ah've been here."

''Oh, he'll know." Chuckle. "Anyway, you okay for money? I mean . . . ?"

"Ah'm fine." Two months' wages would last a while. "How dae ah work the answerin'-machine, by the way?" He stared at the off-white rectangle.

Laugh. "It's a bit of an antique! What's it read at the moment?"

"There's a rid 'H' showin'."

"Press the extreme right button once."

Joe did so. A beep. The red 'H' changed to '0'.

"That should do it. To play back any messages, press the middle button lightly. The machine'll reset itself afterwards, okay?"

"Aye. Thanks." Joe ran a hand over his hair. "Is it okay if ah huv another bath?"

Resonant laugh. "The place is yours while you need it, Joe – you don't have to keep asking!"

Joe smiled. "Thanks man – ah owe ye."

"Nothing to owe – you're doing me the favour. Phillip would never forgive me if I let his precious flat get burgled."

"Ah'll luck efter it fur him."

"Great. Now off you go for your bath – maybe see you later?" Tentative.

Joe grinned as an awakening prick began to edge up his inner thigh. Then frowned: other thoughts, other . . . responsibilities. "Make it the morra, eh?"

"Sure, Joe. I'll ring first, make sure you're in. Be good!"

"Seeya, man." He replaced the receiver, then looked down. Under the heavy dressing-gown his erection was throbbing. Joe smiled, stood up and went to run another bath.

By six o'clock, he had been to the bank, the supermarket, bought a couple of new tee-shirts, eaten, cleaned the bathroom, found the hoover and picked up his messages.

Five silences.

Joe lit a cigarette and stretched out on the lead-coloured sofa.

The telephone purred.

Joe picked it up. "Aye?"

A voice, this time. A grinning voice. "Hi, man – kin ah come an' see ye?"

Joe gripped the cigarette. "Hi, Sean."

"Kin ah come doon?"

Heat in his stomach. "It's no' ma flat, Sean . . . "

"Meet me, then."

Joe closed his eyes. "That's no' a guid idea."

"Why no'?"

Joe fumbled for a lie. "The polis still think ah nicked that money fae the club. Ah don't want you involved."

"Did ye?"

"Did ah whit ?"

"Did ye nick the money? Is that why ye moved oot?"

Joe sighed. "Ah didney nick onythin', Sean, but ah don't want you or yer mither gettin' ony hassle fae the polis."

Snort. "Ah kin handle them, man!"

Despite himself, Joe smiled.

"An' onyway: you wur there fur me, wi' the eccy an' the raid an aw' . . . "

Joe opened his eyes. "Jist lea' it, Sean! " Heat burned in his stomach.

"But . . . ?"

Heat spread over his groin. "Fuck aff, Sean!" Joe put the phone down. His hand trembled.

Immediate purring.

He snatched the receiver. "Ah said fuck aff, Sean."

Silence, then the familiar buzz of a dialling tone.

Joe sighed, replaced the receiver. He stood up . . .

Michael.

. . . . stared around the neat room. . .

Michael.

. . . . and tried to think of something else. After a while, he walked into the kitchen and began to open cupboards. The cleaning materials were under the sink. Joe filled a bucket with hot water, pulled on Marigolds and began to scrub the floor.

Andy Hunter came round the following afternoon. In uniform. He sat on the lead-coloured sofa and listened as Joe played back another six silences. Bushy eyebrows V-ed.

"Probably some sort of line-fault. . ."

Joe stared at the serge-clad figure.

" . . . Or one of Philliph's old boyfriends, trying to make a point!" Resonant laugh. "Talking of old boyfriends . . . I've some good news for you."

Joe stared.

"Told you it would sort itself out. Apparently, the ten thousand quid has turned up." Hat removed. "Hadn't been at the club in the first place – Billy King phoned the station this morning, all apologies for wasting police time – he found it at home."

In an envelope, postmarked Springburn. Joe frowned. He could still smell wet sheepskin.

Resonant laugh. "Okay then – don't rush to thank me for telling you you're off the hook!"

Joe tried to smile. "Sorry, man – other things oan ma mind."

The handsome face grinned. "The thought of being young, single and fancy-free that depressing?"

Jobless, homeless, rootless . . . Joe stood up. "Naw . . . no' really. Can ah git ye a coffee or somethin'?"

Headshake. Deep brown eyes looked away. "Sit down, Joe."

Joe sat. His prick twitched unexpectedly. He smiled at the response.

Andy was staring towards the oriel window. "So . . . "

Joe stared at the back of a serge collar. The smile widened. Reaching over, he ran a finger over a slightly bristly neck.

Andy flinched, turned.

Joe stared, heart pounding.

Expression hard to read, then: "Look, I don't want you to think I . . . "

"'S okay, Andy . . . " Joe stood up, whipping tee-shirt over head, eyes never leaving the figure on the sofa. Prick was hardening against the waistband of his jeans.

Release . . .

Release they both wanted.

Andy Hunter grinned, stood up and began to undress.

An hour later, the phone purred.

Andy disentangled an arm from around Joe's neck and seized the receiver: Breathless "Hello?" Then held it out.

Dialling tone.

Andy replaced the receiver, raised a bushy eyebrow. "Get onto BT, tell them to intercept all calls . . . if it bothers you."

"It disney . . . bother me." Joe draped sweating arms around well-muscled shoulders and pulled Andy back down onto the floor. His body was glowing . . . two bodies were glowing. Joe absently wiped Andy's spunk from chest-hair then leant over and kissed a bushy eyebrow. "So this is whit Strathclyde's finest git up tae when they should be oan duty!"

A dry mouth brushed his neck, then Andy pulled away. "C'mon . . . let's have a shower." He stood up, extended a hand.

Joe grabbed slick fingers and led the way.

"I wanted you the first night we met." Head lowered, barely-dry fingers fumbling with shirt-buttons.

229

Joe grinned, watching as Andy dressed. "Ah ken."

Head raised, grin returned, then fading. Throat clearing. "This has nothing to do with . . . what we just did – right?"

Joe cocked an eyebrow. "Whit has?"

Eyes averted. "Look: how well do you know Billy King?"

Joe frowned. "This yer idea of pillow-talk?" He tried to smile.

"Sorry . . . " Turning to look for boots. Half-laugh. " . . . Do you mind talking about him?" Turning back. Bushy eyebrows raised.

Did he? Billy was past . . . over. Joe leant back on the lead-coloured sofa and reached for cigarettes. "No' really . . . ah know him well enough. Why?"

"You lived with him . . . how long?"

"Nearly a year. Whit . . . ?"

"Tell me about Billy, Joe."

Joe stared. "Tell you whit?"

Andy straightened up and wandered over to the window. "What he was like, your impression of the man."

Joe laughed. "Whit he wis like in bed?"

Andy turned. Handsome-face solemn. "No Joe. What he was like as a person."

Joe stared, then looked away. "Billy's okay." Automatic.

"Why did you break-up with him?"

Joe lit a cigarette, inhaled . . .

Robin's bruised and battered face.

. . . then exhaled. "Things wur gettin' a bit . . . " He gazed at the cigarette. " . . . heavy."

"Was he . . . abusing you?"

Joe stood up and joined Andy at the window. "Dae ah luck abused?"

Soft brown eyes brushed his naked chest. "It doesn't always show, Joe." Lifting jacket from chair.

Joe reached for an ashtray. "Billy was guid tae me, Andy. Ah owe him."

"You seen him since . . . er, you left?"

Joe sighed. Angie's. Three days ago. Another hassle. "Wance."

"And?"

Joe sat the ashtray on the window-sill. "Ah'll no' be seein' him again." He stared at the serge-clad figure. "Ye gonny tell me whit this is aw' aboot?"

Andy ignored him. "What do you know about his . . . business-practices?"

Joe stared at the grey carpet. "Billy's business is his ain. Ah kept ma nose oot."

"He gave you a set of keys to his club, Joe – and the alarm combination. Sounds like he trusted you . . . "

"Ah worked fur him – that's aw'."

Laugh. "Oh, come on, Joe. You lived with the guy for a year. Surely he told you something about what he did during the day?"

Joe watched a fragment of ash drop onto the springy grey carpet. "Ah worked at The Matrix, an' sometimes did the banking fur the bookies. That's aw' ah ken aboot his . . . business practices."

"Ever meet any of his friends?"

Andrew the accountant. Baldy. The Cul-de-Sac. "Ah drove him tae meetin's and the like. Ken faces, but no' names." He drew on the cigarette. "'Whit's this aw' about?" Joe looked at the handsome mouth.

It frowned. "I'm not really sure. Bits and pieces I've picked up over the past weeks. Just talk, probably."

"Whit soarta talk?"

The brown eyes became evasive.

Joe seized a serge-clad arm. "Whit soarta talk?" He stared into Andy's face.

It clouded. "About bookie's cashiers with their hands in the till, about . . . friendly takeovers, councillors suddenly eager to dispense licences for clubs that shouldn't really be open at all, about beatings . . . "

"Whit's that got tae dae wi' Billy?"

Andy talked on. " . . . About employing dodgy characters like George Paxton . . . "

"Georgie wis dealin' – Billy hates drugs, but he canny be expected tae vouch fur aw' his . . . "

"Drugs wasn't why Paxton was killed, Joe – not directly, anyway. There's . . . something else."

Joe frowned. "Ye've bin listenin' tae the woman upstairs fae Gina's mate!"

Quizzical stare.

Joe explained.

Andy smiled. "The press love an unsolved murder."

Joe stared. "You're sayin' Billy wis involved in Georgie's death?"

"No, no – and anyway, he was with you and your nephew at the time Paxton was shot. No, I'm more interested in exactly how he runs his little empire, obtains the licenses for his tatty clubs."

Joe stared past the figure in serge.

Police interest . . .

Billy's tired green eyes.

Business-dinners with men he hated.

Licking the boots of grubby councillors.

Joe frowned. "Billy works hard tae keep whit he huz – ah ken that."

"Very much a one-man operation, isn't he?"

"That's Billy's way – he didney trust onywan . . . "

"He trusted you with keys and alarm-combinations."

"He trusted Davie wi' the same – go talk tae him."

Laugh. "He wasn't sleeping with Davie, though, was he?" Thoughtful. "It was a monogamous relationship, I take it?"

Joe raised an eyebrow.

Smile. "I know you weren't playing around – Christ! I gave you the come-on often enough, and got knocked back – but Billy King . . . " The words tailed off.

Joe lit another cigarette.

Robin's bruised and battered face.

He opened his mouth, then closed it again.

Andy grabbed a tie. "I wonder."

"Whit?"

Smile. "Nothing – just idle curiosity, I suppose."

Joe stared. Curiosity: there was a lot of it about.

"I know he was good to you Joe, but there's a lot more to Mr Billy King than benevolent business-man." Pause. "Does he own a gun?"

232

Joe blinked. "Why dae ye want tae ken?"

Shrug. "Just curious."

His own/Michael's gun, now at the bottom of the Clyde. "Naw, he disney need wan!" He stubbed out cigarette and lit another.

Laugh. "That's what I thought. Your Mr King has other ways of getting . . . what he wants."

Heat spread over Joe's face. He walked back to the sofa and sat down.

Andy continued to stare out into darkening sky.

Joe rubbed his face.

Then: "Sean still using E?" Casual.

Joe frowned. "How did ye . . . ?" Billy?

"That night we raided The Matrix he was high as a kite. Christ! Joe – think I don't know a kid on E when I see one?"

Thumping in his chest.

"I can see how close the two of you are – when I picked him up to confirm your alibi for the time of Paxton's death the kid was really worried about you." Soft voice. "It's good, what you do for Sean, Joe . . . "

Thumping increasing. "He's no' usin' eccy ony mair."

"Glad to hear it. I . . ."

Joe stood up. "Look! Kin we drap this? Ah don't ken onythin' aboot Billy's business-practices . . . "

Robin's bruised and battered face.

Robin crying in his arms.

" . . . an' ah don't want tae!"

Hands raised in mock-defence. "Okay, okay . . . " Radio-squawk. Andy bent the handsome face forward to answer it.

Joe walked into the kitchen and filled kettle. From the lounge, muttered conversation. Then arms around his waist:

"Got to go, now . . . " Mouth brushing ear. "Seeya later?"

Joe placed kettle on draining-board, turned and pulled Andy to him. "Gie me a ring . . . " He buried head in a serge-clad shoulder. Strong hands lowered from waist down to arse. Joe smiled, felt his body start to respond.

233

Andy pulled away. "Have a think about what I've said. If there's anything you want to tell me about Billy King, it'll be off-the-record – you know that ."

Joe turned away and switched the kettle on.

Sigh. "I'll give you a ring later . . . " Warm mouth on the back of his neck. " . . . 'Bye, Joe." Footsteps.

Joe waited until the front door slammed then walked back into the lounge. From the window, he watched Andy get into a pink-and-white squad car and drive away.

Two women walked a small dog around a large puddle.

A red Mercedes slipped smoothly from Our Lady of Good Counsel's carpark.

The kettle switched itself off.

As he walked into the kitchen Joe heard soft purring, then the sound of an answering-machine recording silence.

Later, the phone rang again. Joe picked it up.

"Thought ye'd be up tae collect the resta yer stuff, Joe."

"Hi, Angie. " He frowned. "Whit stuff – there's no' that much o' it, is there?"

"Couple pairs o' jeans an' a jaicket – an' yer nice watch."

Joe looked at the Tag Heuer on his wrist. "They're no' mine, Angie."

"Well, they're no' mine either, an' . . . " Silence.

"Angie?"

Hard voice. "He's at it again, the wee bastard. Ah thought aw' that wis ower wi'!"

Joe lit a cigarette. "Whit ye oan aboot?"

Tension vibrated down the phone-line, then: "That wee bastard's back at the shoapliftin'. Ah caught him before – 'boot a year ago – an' ah thought we'd thrashed it aw' oot. He's bin as guid as gold fur weeks, an' noo . . . "

"Take it easy, Angie!"

"Ah'm searchin' that tip o' a room o' his!" Furious. "Christ kens whit else he's goat hidden away!"

"The polis widda seen onythin' valuable, Angie – mebbe it's stuff he's borrowed aff Ewan – ye ken whit the paira them ur like."

Slightly calmer, but still unconvinced. "Aye . . . maybe."

Hesitation, then: "Kid you huv a word wi' him, Joe – tae pit ma mind at rest? He'll talk tae you."

Joe tensed. "Ah . . . "

"Please, Joe. Ye ken whit ah'm like – it'll end in another fight."

Joe sighed. "Okay, but don't search his room. Let me talk tae him first."

Eager. "Sure, sure. He'll be in the night."

Joe stubbed out cigarette. "Ah'll be there." He replaced receiver and moved to the window.

Outside, red sodium had yet to turn amber. Joe rubbed his face. Other, more pressing problems seeped into his mind.

Billy . . .

Billy's . . . business practices.

Billy the businessman . . .

. . . versus Billy the man.

A year ago. Nearly midnight. Huddled in a doorway, having managed to sell only five copies of *The Big Issue*. Tired, wet. Nowhere to go.

Billy . . .

A Jeep pulling up. Electrically-lowered passenger window. Inside, a pale face. Green eyes behind silver-framed glasses. Smooth voice. 'How many have you left?'

Standing, extending soggy bundle with shivering hand. Looking into green, concerned eyes.

'You feeling okay?'

Nodding. Pulling biker's' jacket up to ears. Shivering and sweating at the same time.

'What's your name?'

Husky words.

Car door opening. Two word command.

Obeying. Sinking back against the Jeep's leather upholstery.

'I'm taking you home.'

Joe stared down at Craigpark.

The women with the dog were back.

A car glided past in semi-darkness.

Billy King had taken him in, given him a bed, a job . . . so

235

much more.

He owed Billy.

Joe looked around at the darkening room and frowned.

Robin's bruised and tear-stained face . . .

Joe shivered then walked to the telephone and punched in digits.

An answering-machine answered.

He cleared his throat. "Andy? Ah thought aboot whit ye wur sayin' . . . we need tae talk."

CHAPTER TWENTY ONE

Petershill Road was a dark, wet blur. Joe zipped up bikers' jacket and walked past a deserted ice-cream van towards the Red Road flats. He looked up.

Thirty-one floors above, a dotted band of light.

Joe sighed and pressed a button.

Electronic squawk: "Joe?"

"Aye, Angie. It's . . . "

Buzzing. He walked through the opening door and made for the lift.

As the doors closed, so did his eyes.

Sean was a magnet. Joe couldn't stay away.

Using, dealing. Shoplifting?

Jumped emotions churned in his stomach.

The lift moved upwards.

Problems. More problems . . .

He smiled. At least Billy had 'found' the ten thousand. Then frowned.

Robin's tear-streaked face loomed before him.

Joe opened eyes in sync with lift doors.

As he walked towards 31/3, the front door opened. Worried face beneath frizzy blonde mop:

"Thanks fur comin', Joe."

He nodded, walked past her into the cold flat.

A hand on his arm. Whispering. "He's goat a guitar tae, noo. Wullney say whur it came fae neither."

Joe paused. "Gie me a coupla minutes wi' him."

"Sure, Joe."

He walked on into the lounge.

Over the side of sofa, shiny black Docs on the end of long legs. A blond head raised. Nose-stud twinkling. No grin. Head lowered.

Joe smiled. "Hi, Sean."

"No tellin' me tae fuck aff this time, then!" Fiddling with personal hi-fi.

Joe looked for the Sellotaped back-section. There wasn't one. He sat down opposite Sean. "Ah didney mean it – ah

237

wis tired an' . . . "

"Makes nae difference tae me, man." Low voice. Long fingers continued to fiddle.

Joe sighed, glancing around the untidy room. Angie had made a good job of righting Strathclyde Police's wrongs. In a far corner, balanced between a rebuild-it-yourself bookcase and standard lamp, an oddly-shaped instrument. Joe stared at the white guitar, then Sean. "It's a guid coapy . . ."

Blond hair flipped from face. "'Sno' a copy!" Pink lips sneering. Sean swung legs from the sofa and loped towards the Paul Reed Smith.

Joe sighed. "So ye goat it, then."

Sean stroked the guitar's neck. "Aye, man – it's totally brand new!" He fingered strings, then picked up the instrument and walked back to the sofa.

"Borrowed it, huv ye?"

Sean picked out a brief melody, then began to strum unamplified strings.

Snort. "Bought an' paid fur, this is."

Joe stared.

The strumming continued.

"Sean?"

"Whit?" The strumming stopped.

"Luck at me, Sean." Joe stared at a blond crown.

Sean stared at the PRS.

"Where did it come fae?"

Sneer. "Telt ye – it's mine."

"Where did ye get it?"

Strumming.

Joe stood up. "Quit that, wull ye?" He gazed down at the long-limbed boy.

Sean gazed up, blinked, then scowled. "'Sma hoose – ah kin dae whit ah want." The strumming continued.

Joe fumbled for cigarettes. The Zippo flared in a cloud of petrol-fumes. He nudged a shiny, size nine boot. "Like the Docs."

Sean tucked his foot under himself.

Joe stared. This was all wrong. From the mantle, a cracked family photograph glared.

238

Michael had been there for him . . . in all sorts of ways.

Joe seized a skinny arm. "Come on, then – let's hear it!" He pulled Sean to his feet. "Where did aw' this come fae?"

Skinny arm wrestled free. "Aw' whit?" One hand still holding the guitar.

Joe regripped a slim wrist, fingers tightening around a metal strap. He wrenched Sean's arm up. "This . . . " Eyes on the Tag Heuer. " . . . The boots, the guitar." He scowled. "Yer mither says there's other stuff, tae . . . "

"Ma stuff – ma business." Snort. Arm pulled free.

Joe stared. "Ur you dealin' that crap again?"

Laugh. "Widney waste ma time." Head raised, defiant blue eyes. "An' it's no' causa onythin' you said!" Laugh sliding into sneer.

"Tell me where ye goat them fae, then." Last week in Sighthill cemetery. Joe softened. "C'moan, Sean, we kin soart it oot . . . "

Low voice. "Ye're no' ma faither, Joe. Ah don't huv tae tell ye onythin'." Scornful eyes to the cracked photograph.

Anger balled in his chest. "Ye'll fuckin' tell me, ye wee . . . " Joe pulled an arm back, fist clenched.

Sean looked up. Fear in the blue pools, then . . . something else.

Joe lowered his arm, eyes locked with Sean's.

The something else narrowed into scorn. Then Sean broke eye-contact.

Joe's arm was lead as it dropped down to side.

Sean picked up the guitar and sat down on the sofa. The strumming recommenced.

Joe stared. This was all wrong. Eyes travelled down the slender tee-shirt-clad back. Heat in his stomach.

This was a fuckin' mess.

He stood up and turned. From the mantle, Michael's disappointed eyes followed him into the hall.

Beside the telephone Angie was chewing a nail. "Well?"

Joe sighed, avoiding her gaze.

Tearful-sounding. "He's gettin' too auld fur me tae spank, Joe – an' when ah shout at him, he just laughs." Pause. Hesitant. "Ye widney consider . . . ?"

Joe shuffled. "Ah canny move back in, Angie. Ah'm too much hassle . . . "

Pleading. "He wis much better when you wur here, Joe – mair manageable. Yous goat oan great – we aw' did. Why . . . ?"

"Ah jist canny, Angie – okay?" Words filled the dark hall.

"As ye like, Joe."

More disappointment. He tried to think. "Ye goat Ewan's number?"

"Aye, but . . . "

Joe lifted the telephone. "Geez it."

Angie recited.

Joe dialled.

Ewan's phone rang four times, then: "Aye?" Older, male voice.

Joe leant against the wall. "Kin ah speak tae Ewan?"

"Haud oan . . . " Crackling, shouting in the background, then:

"Aye?" Wary.

"It's Joe, Ewan, Sean's . . . "

"Oh, hi, man!" More relaxed. "How ye dain'?"

Joe scowled. "It's whit ye've been dain' that ah'm interest in."

"Whit dae ye mean?"

"You an' Sean bin oan a shoapping-spree?"

Laugh. "Whit ye oan aboot?" Comprehension. Then anger. "Ah've never nicked onythin' in ma life, man! Who telt ye ah did?"

Joe sighed. "Where did Sean git his guitar?"

Curious. "Whit guitar?"

Joe tensed. "Ah've no' goat time fur aw' this, Ewan. The white guitar – the Paul Whatshisface wan."

Laugh. "So he goat wan at last."

"Ye've seen it, then?" Pressure on his shoulder: Angie, trying to hear.

Faint hurt. "Huvney seen him fur days, never mind ony guitar!"

"Whit's happened tae the band? It split up?"

"Naw . . . but Sean hisney bin tae the last coupla practices."

Joe frowned. "Yous huv a fallin' oot?"

Snort. "He said he's no' goat ony time fur bands, noo' . . . " Laugh. " . . . says he's goat better things tae dae!"

Joe scowled. The drum-machine operator? "Did yous fa' oot ower the . . . " He fumbled for the name. " . . . Keith guy?"

Surprised. "Naw – he turned oot tae be okay, goat some guid ideas aboot . . . "

"These better things – whit did Sean say, exactly?"

Snort. "Jist that." Laugh. "Ah think he's goat himsel' a new friend!"

Joe tensed. "Whit's that supposed tae mean?"

Laugh. "Ask him, no' me."

Angie was whispering something he couldn't hear.

Impatient. "Look, man – ah'm gettin' ready tae go oot, an' . . . "

"Sure – thanks, Ewan."

Buzzing. Joe continued to hold the receiver.

At his side: "Well? Huv they bin shoapliftin'?"

Joe replaced the receiver. "No' accordin' tae Ewan." He turned. "Gie it a coupla days, Angie – eh? If mair stuff appears . . . " He closed his eyes, felt her disappointment grow. Joe sighed. Andy Hunter. "Look: ah ken this guy. He's wi' the polis."

Fear replaced disappointment.

"It's okay – he's a . . . mate. Mebbe if he his a word wi' Sean, casual-like." He ruffled the frizzy hair.

Brightening. "Think that wid help?"

Joe tried to smile. "Couldny dae ony hairm. Ah'll ring him when ah git in – okay?"

Grassing-up Billy to help Sean . . .

One good turn?

"Thanks, Joe." Sigh. "Ah ken we're a lotta boather tae ye."

He walked past the small figure towards the front door. "It's the least ah kin dae, Angie. Ah'll gie ye a ring later – okay?"

"Sure, Joe . . . " She brushed past to open the door for him. "Speak tae ye soon."

He walked out onto the silent landing.

Back in the doctor's flat, the answering-machine read '4'.

Joe pressed the play button, and took off wet leather.

Three silences, then a woman's voice. Noise in background, then: "I'm trying to reach Joe Macdonald. If this is the correct number, could he please phone 564-9876, extension 45 as soon as possible. Thank you."

Joe waited as the machine re-wound and re-set itself, then dialled.

It was nearly ten when he reached the Royal's Accident and Emergency Department. A police-car pulled away on rain-slicked tarmac as automatic doors opened to embrace him. Joe walked past two teenagers holding up a third, towards a perspex Reception window.

A woman with short red hair glanced up.

Joe stared. Not the same woman to whom he had given Robin's details three weeks earlier. But the same encouraging smile.

He cleared his throat. "Joe Macdonald. Somewan phoned me aboot . . ."

"Ah, yes." Frown. Glance at folder. "You'll be Mr Hunter's . . . friend?"

"Aye. Andy Hunter. Whit's happened?"

"Take a seat, Mr Macdonald. I'll tell the doctor you're here." Pointing to crowded waiting area.

Joe caught sight of a No-Smoking sign. "Ah'll be at the door." He walked back to the entrance, lit a cigarette and thought of Andy Hunter's strong body and handsome face.

Half-an-hour later, he was staring at a not-so-handsome one.

Above a purpling cheek, one liquid brown eye was almost shut. Wheezing breath escaped from blood-encrusted nostrils. To the side, a line of twelve

242

stitches pinched puffy pink flesh. Andy's mouth moved towards a smile, which immediately became a scowl. "Looks worse than it is." Husky whisper.

Joe stared. "Whit happened?"

Barely audible. "Got mugged." Cough. "Wallet and watch."

"When . . . who . . . ?"

Andy closed his one good eye. "Don't you start!" Words slow and hoarse. "I've had half C division in here already!" Another smile attempted. Another frown produced.

"Where'd it happen?"

"Outside my flat, after I'd left you . . . and before you ask again, I was jumped from behind." Hand to skull. "Tyre-iron, from the feel of it. Some scum I booked getting their own back, no doubt!"

Joe looked to where a squashy, bluish section of scalp winked through a shaved area in the fashionably-cut brown hair. Helplessness filled his head.

Hoarse, non-resonant laugh. "Well, don't just stand there!" Arms extended.

Joe seized one hand, kissed it then sat on the bed's edge. "Want me tae take ye hame?"

Bushy eyebrows V-ed dramatically. "Now he offers!"

Joe feigned a smile. He knew the routine. "C'moan – it's yer big chance!" Still holding the broad hand, he winked.

Andy laughed, winced, then tried to change position. Pain shadowed the injured face.

Joe released the hand, then gently gripped the well-muscled torso and eased Andy upright.

"Thanks."

Joe let one hand rest on a hard waist, the same hard waist he had held only hours before.

"I'm a little disappointed it took you so long to get here."

Joe removed the hand. "Ah wis up at Angie's . . . " He paused. Was now a good time?

Intact bushy eyebrows V-ed. The rest of the face creased with pain.

Now wasn't a good time. " . . . Get yer stuff an' ah'll take ye hame – nae arguments."

One brown eye suddenly focusing. Faint smile. "They're keeping me in."

Joe looked away. "Thought ye said it looked worse than it wis?"

Hoarse laugh. "You know doctors . . . one look at my gorgeous body and it was internal examinations all round!"

Joe stared at a green curtain. Useless . . . helpless. "Is there onythin' ah kin dae, onythin' ah kin . . . bring ye?" He turned.

Faint smile. "Could you feed my cat?" One liquid brown eye blinked.

Joe laughed. "Nae problem!"

The whisk of curtain-rings. "Keep it down in here." Joking. "This is a hospital!" Deep, bass voice. Another whisk as fabric redraped around the cubicle.

Andy smiled weakly at the green-pyjama-ed figure.

The doctor picked up then thumbed through a chart. To Andy: "We've found a bed for you, Mr Hunter." To Joe: "A word?"

Joe stared.

The doctor raised an eyebrow, then flicked the curtain aside.

Joe smiled at Andy, then followed. Outside the cubicle he peered at the wide black face.

It sobered. "Probably nothing. We'd like to keep him in for a few days, take some X-rays, maybe a CAT-scan." Eyes narrowing. "The slashing looks dramatic, but the wounds are superficial. However, he took quite a beating." Pause. "Are you . . . a relative?"

Joe rubbed his face. He was always turning up at hospitals with battered and bruised men. A large palm patted his arm.

No response expected. "Don't worry. Like I said, it's probably nothing. Just a precaution. We don't like to take any chances with head injuries."

A nurse squeezed past, twitching back the curtain with a latexed hand.

The doctor was talking again. "Have you spoken to the police, Mr . . . ?"

Joe stared at the again-closed green curtain. "Macdonald. Naw . . . ah ainly fun' oot Andy hid been jumped aboot an oor ago. There's nothin' ah kin tell them."

Sigh. Then: "Want to see him again before he goes up to the ward?"

Joe nodded.

The doctor pulled back the green curtain.

Andy was flirting with the nurse. "What time do you get off, then?"

Joe watched as the nurse removed a needle from Andy's left buttock and shook his head.

"This one needs more than light sedation!" Smiling at Joe, he left.

Joe sat on the edge of the bed.

Andy's visible pupil was huge as the sedative began to kick-in. "The flat keys are in my pocket. For some reason they didn't want them."

Joe followed the eye to a damp-looking bundle in a polythene bag. He crouched, pulled open the neck and fumbled. Andy's blood smeared shaking fingers.

"Thanks, pal – I owe you one." Words beginning to slur.

Joe pocketed the keys. "Nae need." He smiled. "Ah'm noo baby-sitting two posh flats!"

Andy's eyelid fluttered. Whisper. "You will come back, tomorrow?"

Joe leant over and pushed a lock of chestnut hair from the sweating forehead. "Aye . . . an' ah'll bring yer cat tae visit ye!" He paused. "Whit yer address, again?" Lips lowered to brush sweating skin.

Faint words. "Twelve Huntly Gardens. Two up. The little key's for the alarm . . . it's behind the . . . in the hall . . . " One eye closing and the sentence disintegrated.

Joe watched for a second, then turned and left the cubicle.

The alarm was behind the coat-rack in the hall of Twelve Huntly Gardens.

The cat was asleep on Andy's bed.

Joe reset the first, fed the second, then got a taxi back to Craigpark.

As he entered the warm flat, the phone was ringing. Joe looked at the machine: no messages. He picked up the receiver.

"Not much of an Angel-Face now, is it?" Cold laugh.

Joe tensed. "Billy?"

"You'll need to close your eyes next time he fucks you . . . or have him take you from behind!"

Joe opened his mouth. Words wouldn't form.

A mirthless laugh echoed in the ear-piece. "Permission to speak granted, soldier."

"Why did ye dae it, Billy?"

Cool words. "I'm surprised you need to ask, Joe."

"Why, Billy?"

Icy words. "Is he good, Joe? Is he better than me?"

"Whit we hud's . . . finished, Billy – ye ken that. Andy an' me ur just . . . "

"First-name terms, I see!" Mocking. ''Andy: how sweet! You once said he understood you. Wonder if he'll still . . . " Pause. " . . . understand when he sees the state of that angel face of his."

Joe's fingers tightened around the receiver.

"Your cosy little love-nest's been overturned, Joe. I shouldn't be surprised if PC Angel-Face Hunter never wants to see you again, let alone allow you to stay in his flat."

Two bruised and battered faces merged into one. A shiver ran down his spine. "Ah'm goin' tae the polis!"

Laugh. "And tell them what? That I slashed your pretty boyfriend? Don't fancy his chances when his colleagues get wind of his . . . off-duty activities. And what can you prove, anyway? You're an ex-squaddie, ex-bouncer . . . " More laughing. "Just one big X, without me, soldier."

Joe closed his eyes.

The laughing stopped. "We were good together, Joe . . . " Almost gentle. " . . . I understand you more than PC Scarface ever could." Almost a whisper. "Back to barracks, soldier. You've been AWOL quite long enough."

Joe replaced the receiver, crouched and unplugged the telephone.

It made a satisfying sound as it smashed off a mottled grey wall.

CHAPTER TWENTY TWO

Greying, semi-darkness seeped through the lounge window.

On the lead-coloured sofa, Joe glanced at his watch: almost eight. He rubbed sore eyes and ran a hand over bristly chin, then stood up. Calf muscles cramped. He flexed each leg in turn then walked up and down springy grey carpet. Cramp slowly subsided into a dull ache.

Andy.

He stared across the lounge at the remains of a telephone. He walked towards it, crouched, then picked up the receiver, pressing it to his ear.

No buzzing.

Joe stared at the dangling flex, then bent down and plugged wire into answering-machine.

Miraculously, buzzing.

He dialled, listened, then spoke. Then listened again as a voice informed him that Mr Hunter had had a comfortable night, and could be visited that evening between seven and nine. Joe replaced receiver, then walked to the window.

Below, dark shadows were amassing for early mass. A lone woman walked a small dog. In the chapel car-park, a three-pointed star twinkled on a chrome grill.

Joe stared.

As he watched, headlights flicked on and the car moved off. He couldn't see the driver.

Joe walked back to the sofa and lit a cigarette.

Billy: Andy Hunter.

Billy: Robin Without-a-Surname.

Billy . . . Georgie Paxton?

Joe frowned. Billy had been in the flat, with him and Sean, at the time of Georgie's death. He tried to think.

Ages ago. The Duke Street branch of William King: Turf Accountants. Picking-up takings. A skinny girl, Matrix face, talking about . . . some guy, from the Shawlands' shop?

Joe picked up the telephone and dialled 192.

248

The operator gave him Duke Street's number.

Joe dialled.

Cheryl was in early. After pleasantries, she was eager to gossip.

An hour later, his body felt better.

Something inside felt worse.

He took a bath, cleaned the bathroom, the kitchen, then the bathroom again.

The something inside was still there.

Joe peeled off rubber gloves and fumbled for cigarettes.

The packet was empty.

He sighed, picked up jacket and went out.

Outside the garage-shop, on the forecourt – a red Merc. Joe strode towards it. Inside, a blonde woman was playing with a small child. Joe turned away and headed back down Craigpark.

In the lounge, the doctor's answering-machine read '3'. Joe took off jacket and replayed. A cold voice echoed round the silent flat.

"Back to barracks, soldier . . . back to barracks . . . back to . . ."

He lit a cigarette, then unplugged the machine from the phone.

It rang almost immediately.

Joe stared at it for seven rings, then picked up the receiver.

Out-of-breath. "Is he wi' you, Joe?"

He sat down. "Angie?"

"Is he wi' you?"

"Naw . . ." He stared at the cigarette.

"Oh, Christ! Where the fuck is he?"

"Take it easy, Angie. Maybe he's oan his way here. When did he go oot?"

"'Boot ninish – just efter you left an' . . ."

"He's bin oot aw' night?"

"Ah've phoned Ewan, some o' his auld pals, but

249

naewan's seen him. Ah don't kin where else tae try." Sniff. "Whit's the name o' that arcade he yissed tae like?"

Joe closed his eyes. The threat to leave home finally executed. Michael had been there for him . . .

"Should ah phone the polis, Joe?" Frantic. Starting to cry. "He's ainly fifteen. Anythin' kid . . ."

"Calm doon, Angie." His heart hammered. "He'll turn up. His he taken ony claes, or onythin'?"

"Naw, his guitar's still here . . . an' the resta his stuff."

Relief flooded into his brain. "He's jist walkin' off temper, Angie – ah yissed tae dae that. Gied ma mither at least three near-heart attacks!"

Out-of-patience. "Ah took time off work tae be here fur him, an' he goes an' dis this!" Tears of frustration replaced worry.

Joe sighed. As far as he'd been aware, Sean was out more than he was in, nights. Ewan . . . the band . . . The Matrix. Sighthill cemetery?

Talking to the one man who was always there for him.

Talking to the one man who always would be there for him.

He lit a cigarette.

"Ah canny take any mair time aff. Where is he?"

He suddenly felt very tired. "Don't worry. Ah think ah ken where he'll be . . . an' he'll be back when he's hungry. Git off tae yer work. He's goat his keys, hasn't he?"

"Aye, but where . . . ?"

"He's probably jist dain' it tae annoay ye, Angie. Don't let him get tae ye. Ah'll keep ringing the flat – gie me yer work number."

She recited.

He wrote it down.

"If ye ken where he is, Joe, wull ye no' go an' get him?" Sounding better, but curious.

Joe blinked. Not his place . . . not now. "Gie him some time, eh Angie. He's wi' . . . he'll no' come tae ony hairm."

"But . . ."

"Don't worry – yer wee boay's growin' up, that's aw'. Needs time away fae his mammy!"

Semi-laugh. "Ye're probably right, Joe. It wis jist . . . weird tae wake up withoot him there."

Heat in his stomach. He knew the feeling. "I'll ring ye later – okay?"

Almost calm. "Aye, Joe. Thanks." Dialling tone buzzed.

He replaced the receiver and looked at his watch. Almost half-nine. Joe grabbed jacket, keys and left the flat.

In daylight, Sighthill's towerblocks dwarfed the tallest monument in the sprawling cemetery. Michael's headstone was easier to find this time. Sean was going to prove more difficult. Joe crouched down in the wet grass and stared at his brother's grave.

Talking had worked for Sean . . .

Joe swallowed and opened his mouth. To say . . . what? He stuck a cigarette between trembling lips.

That he still loved Michael, and always would?

That Michael had been there for Joe in a way few other brothers ever knew?

That he still missed Michael's strong, warm arms around him?

Heat in his stomach . . .

Fifteen minutes later Joe caught a bus to St Georges Cross.

The Sauchiehall Street arcade was still closed. Joe walked down to Nobles' Amusement Centre on Argyle Street.

Open, but Seanless.

Passing Mitchel Street he glanced up towards The Matrix – more out of habit than anything else.

In MacCormacks, the guy in the tee-shirt remembered him, but not Sean.

Joe scanned every MacDonalds for a specific Macdonald, every Dunkin Donuts, every record shop, every blond head in an early-morning city-centre.

Nothing. He headed east.

In Nobles' Duke Street branch, he asked a bored-looking girl behind a mesh window if she had seen a blond boy with a baseball-cap.

She shrugged, nodding towards a bank of computer-games.

Joe stared at a row of baseball-caps.

None belonged to Sean.

Outside, on Duke Street, two greying men pushed open the door to William King: Turf Accountants.

Joe sighed and walked up Hillfoot Street.

Back in the flat, he dialled.

The phone was answered almost immediately. Invisible grin. "Hi – that's me hame. Wull ah see ye later?"

Joe disconnected, then redialled. It took the soap factory a while to track Angie down. She sounded relieved when he told her the news, than despairing:

"Will ye no' huv another word wi' him, Joe – ah canny be dain' wi' this."

"He's a big boay noo – he kens whit he's dain'." Heat in his stomach.

Snort. "As lang as he's under ma roof, he'll tell me whit he's dain' an who he's dain' it wi'!"

Joe sighed. "Ah'll try an' git up the night – okay?"

Happier. "Thanks, Joe. Better go . . . " The line buzzed.

Joe replaced the receiver, yawned then began to undo Docs.

Seconds later he crawled under the sand-coloured duvet.

Second after that, he was asleep.

There was a smell.

Joe inhaled.

A warm, bed smell of skin and sweat. And underneath? Something sweet and . . .

Joe inhaled again.

. . . fruity.

He sighed and turned over, burying his face in salty-tasting skin.

An arm encircled his waist.

Joe enfolded the slim body.

Warm, loose limbs flattened themselves against him. A

252

wet mouth brushed his ear, then slid across stubble. A hot tongue probing at lips.

Joe groaned, pressed a hand behind the blond head.

Two mouths met. A tentative tongue traced teeth. Then soft lips moved against his.

Joe pressed harder.

Pressure reciprocated.

Beneath the sand-coloured duvet his prick was iron. A hairy thigh ground against his groin.

The kiss went on for hours. Joe breathed through other lungs, drowning in a saliva sea.

Then long fingers were travelling over his body, rubbing spine, moving downwards.

Joe sucked a last mouthful then broke away. He stared at red, swollen lips, pulling a stray hair from his mouth.

Tentative fingers back-tracked over stomach then downwards, lingered between his legs before moving upwards again, tracing the length of his prick.

Joe groaned and lowered his head for another kiss.

Joined at the mouth, two sets of hands explored two very different bodies.

Heat in his stomach. Joe closed his eyes and tried to think of something else. In a deep armpit rough fingers traced soft, bushy hair, then something raised and hard.

Pressure in his groin.

Mouths separated.

Hot breath in his ear. "Joe, Joe . . . " Then licking.

A hard prick teased his own.

Joe stroked it with shaking hands.

A groan, then long fingers clasped behind his neck.

One shaking hand probed lower, brushing tight, hair-dusted balls.

Another groan. More licking.

The sound of low breathing ebbed in and out. Saliva chilled and became sticky on his ear-lobe. Joe exhaled, seized a thigh and pushed it aside. Fingers travelling past tight balls, the skin became slicker, more damp. He pressed the length of a forefinger to the length of an arse-crack and pushed.

"Joe, Joe . . . " Long legs wrapped themselves around his waist, thrusts wincing with his name.

He withdrew his hand, licked forefinger, then returned to the already moist opening. A nail's length edged in. Joe buried his face in damp hair, inhaling a mixture of smells.

A gasp.

Joe withdrew the finger. A restraining hand on his. Then:

"Naw . . . don't stoap."

He edged forefinger back into the opening, which widened to admit him. Warm, quivering muscle closed around the second knuckle . . . then beyond. Joe slid back to nail, then thrust again.

Moans accompanied the quickening movement as more urgent thrusts pressed a hard prick against his stomach.

One hand caressing a smooth back, Joe continued the finger-fuck. Everything in sync: hands, tongues, hips, fingers. Two bodies merging into one. Then a voice in his head:

"Wull ah see ye later?"

Joe paused, heart hammering. Finger still massaged by tight sphincter muscle, he propped himself up on one elbow. "Where wur ye?"

Blue pools stared. "Luckin' fur you, Joe." Pink lip chewed. "Whur were you?"

"Dain' the same." Beneath the sand-coloured duvet his prick exploded . . .

He woke up, choking back a name as warm spunk splattered lips, neck and upper chest. His body convulsed violently, sending shivers from groin to brain. Joe raised quivering hands to his face and pressed hard.

Slowly, the convulsions lessened. He hugged the sand-coloured duvet around an aching body. In his head, someone screamed.

Ward Three was busy.

Joe pushed past an elderly couple bearing grapes, pulled up a chair and sat down. "How ye feelin'?" He kissed a pale forehead.

254

Weak smile. "Better than you look! Heavy night?"

Joe frowned. "Somethin' like that." He looked down at the muscular arm from which a thin, rubber tube protruded. "Whit dae the doactors say?"

Parody of a smile. "X-Ray clear, CAT-scan was a bit fuzzy." Hollow laugh. "They think they've found my brain, and want to explore, see what else is in there!"

Joe looked up. "Whit dae ye mean?"

"Routine, my dishy doctor says." Andy was fingering stitches. "Never liked the 'pretty policeman' image, anyway!" Weaker smile.

Joe sighed, leant over the bed. "Billy did this."

Bushy eyebrows V-ed. "What?"

Joe lowered his voice. "He eyewis thoaght thur wis somethin' goin' on, wi' you an' me. Ah guess me movin' intae yer pal's flat clinched it fur him . . . that, an' . . . " A memory of two hard bodies moving as one flashed into his mind. ". . . the other afternoon."

One brown eye stared. "You serious?"

Joe rubbed his face . . . "Ah left a message oan yer machine, the night ye wur jumped." . . . and began to talk . . .

. . . about the phone-calls.

. . . then about Robin.

His voice sounded strange. Joe stopped talking when he had said it all and stared.

Andy was holding his hand. "I should've told you the whole thing."

Joe stared. "Whit whole thing?"

Andy sighed. "There's been speculation about Billy King for years. Oh, nothing definite, nothing we could get to grips with. The odd beating, when the take in one of his bookies' was short. A cashier, jumped on his way back from the match – coincidentally, just after he'd been caught with his fingers in Billy King's till. Par for the course, most of it . . . or at least it was, until recently."

Joe blinked.

"Billy ever talk about . . . your predecessor?"

Joe shook his head. Andy's fingers were twining with his own.

"I never met him, myself. Jimmy – the guy from Delmonicas?"

Joe stared, then nodded.

"He knew him vaguely. Bit like you, in fact. He'd done time – that's where he and Jimmy met – his wife divorced him when he was inside, wouldn't let him see the kids . . ."

"He wisney . . . he wis straight, then?"

"I don't think Billy King cares, to be honest. With him, as far as I can make out, it's not really about sex at all." Frown, then hand-squeeze. 'It's a power-trip. He likes to control people . . ."

'You owe me, Joe.' Something ripped down his spine.

". . . I didn't tell you before, because I thought you could handle it, that it was what you . . . got off on."

He could. It was . . .

. . . or had been.

Joe stared at the stitched-together face. "It is jist sex. Robin was jist sex." He closed his eyes and saw a terrified, fourteen-year-old face, and knew he was wrong.

Low voice. "Robin Connolly. Fourteen. Gay, and very confused. Pride and joy of Frank Connolly, convenor of Glasgow District Council's Licensing Board." Angry. "Ring any bells?"

Joe scowled. "At least the polis kin dae somethin' aboot that."

The battered head shook slowly. "Frank resigned, after granting Billy King a special licence for his Christmas Eve all-dayer, and renewing those on the other five clubs – despite police advice. The family are moving south. Robin's off to boarding-school."

"How dae ye ken . . .?"

"A concerned nurse phoned Gay Switchboard, after Robin refused to have anything to do with the police." Smile. "I do a shift, every now and again – my contribution to community relations. I've kept in touch with Robin . . . worked out the rest from what you've just told me." Bushy eyebrows V-ed. "He got off lightly."

"Whit dae ye mean?"

Memorised words. "Four months ago, the body of a

fifteen-year-old male surfaced in the Clyde. Every bone in his body was broken, but he died from strangulation."

"So?"

"The kid was Archie Summers' nephew, Colin."

Joe stared. Summers . . . Summers . . . a slim watch in a brown leather box . . .

"Mr Summers owns – owned – a chain of cafés recently acquired by one William King in a . . . friendly takeover." Eyebrows V-ing. "Nothing like a family bereavement to speed up. . . . negotiations." Rubbing dry lips. "You really know nothing about Billy's business-interests, do you?"

Joe stared. "Ah cleaned his cors, worked at his club. He gave me a bed, fucked me. End of story." He blinked. "Robin . . . is he okay?"

Soft voice. "He was very scared at the time, but you saved his life, Joe – there's no doubt about that."

Joe watched as Andy raised their entwined fingers to lips, kissed them gently.

"Robin told me all about you." Sigh. "Wish you'd told me about him."

Joe released the hand, stood up. "So whit dae we dae noo?"

"Nothing. There's nothing we can do. Billy King always covers his tracks." Sigh. "I'm sure now he had something to do with Georgie Paxton's death but – as always – he's got his alibi. And there's nothing I can get a handle on."

Joe gazed at the white bed-sheet and sat down.

Alibi.

False alibi.

The night of Georgie's death, Sean and Joe had been alone in the flat.

False alibis cut both ways: Joe couldn't break Billy's without re-focusing attention on himself and Sean.

He looked from white sheet to white face.

Grimace. "If this was his handiwork . . . " Fingers stroking stitches. " . . . He does his homework, your Mr King – I'll give him that. Knows where I live, knows where you're living – even the phone number, and Phillip's ex-directory."

A bell rang. Angie and a phone-number given for emergencies only. Joe scowled. Around, the sound of chairs scraping on lino. Joe looked up.

Serious face. "Get out of Phillip's flat, Joe. Move into a hotel . . . " Frustration. "I can't do anything here, not yet . . . " Lopsided smile. " . . . And I'm probably reasonably safe. But you . . ."

"Billy's never laid a finger on me." The Cul-de-Sac slap.

Eyes lowered. "You've a selective memory. . . "

Joe stood up. "Ma . . . predecessor: whit happened tae him?"

One brown eye looked up and blinked. "Jimmy's no idea. Never saw him again." Low voice. "Promise me you'll find somewhere else to stay." Scowl. "Fuck! I'm stuck in here until they . . . "

"Ah'll . . . " Rage rose in his chest. The words wouldn't come.

Angry voice. "There's nothing you can do, Joe. Leave it." A strong hand seized his wrist. "Stay away from Billy King." Fingers dug in. "I mean it."

Joe stared. There was nothing he could do.

Again.

He frowned. "Ah'll come back an' see ye the morra – eh?"

"I'd still rather you got as far away from Billy King as . . . "

Sean. He'd promised Angie a word. "Ah canny lea' – no' yet onyway." He rubbed pale fingers.

Andy frowned. "Have it your own way." Then a half-smile. "You fed Big Boy, yet?"

Joe raised an eyebrow.

"He gets half a tin of Whiskas twice a day – and remember to change his litter-tray."

Joe grinned. The fuckin' cat. "Ah wull." He mock-punched a bare shoulder. "Seeya the morra then."

Grin. "Sure." Sobering. "And remember . . . "

"Nae problem." With a mock-salute Joe walked from the ward.

In Twelve Huntly Gardens, Big Boy had come when called.

Joe stroked the orange cat's thick fur, watching, while it ate.

Billy . . . business.

Joe leant against a beige work-surface.

It was always business.

Andy wasn't business.

Joe wasn't business.

Had Georgie been business?

Big Boy weaved between his legs, rubbing a warm body against Docs.

Joe looked at his watch: nearly eleven. He walked through to the bedroom.

Big Boy followed.

Andy's bed was red-and-black striped.

Joe stared at the duvet, remembering its sand-coloured, now-spunk-splattered cousin in Craigpark.

He couldn't go back.

Not tonight.

Not because of Andy.

Not because of Billy.

Big-Boy leapt smoothly onto the red-and-black striped duvet, marring the cover's pattern.

Joe smiled, sat down on the bed and began to unlace Docs. He watched as the large orange cat kneaded the fabric into a comfortable shape, then stretched out.

Joe laughed, peeling off jacket, tee-shirt. He tickled the cat's stomach. "Neither o' us should be in here, eh boay?"

The cat purred contentedly, then yowled briefly as Joe moved it to one side and stretched out on the bed.

CHAPTER TWENTY THREE

He awoke with hair in his face.

Joe pushed the cat away and sat up.

Not . . . the doctor's flat.

He blinked.

Andy's flat.

He levered himself from the black-and-red-covered bed and went into the kitchen.

Big Boy followed, mewing softly.

Joe fed the cat, changed the litter-tray, made a coffee then washed.

In the mirror above the sink he stared at a shadow-face. The mark left by Georgie's ring was faint, but still there, would remain so for a while, maybe for ever.

Like Billy's marks on Andy.

He dried the shadow-face, hung the towel back on its rail and walked through to the lounge.

Big Boy was sitting on the small sofa.

Joe sat beside him, stroking with a rough hand. Helplessness coursed through pulsing veins, diluting into uselessness.

After a while, he reached for cigarettes.

After three cigarettes, he reached for the telephone, dialled, listened, spoke. Then listened again.

Mr Hunter would be transferred to the Male Surgical Ward later today, following the procedure.

Joe tensed.

A reassuring voice assured him there was nothing to worry about. Minor, exploratory surgery. Routine.

Joe disconnected, then redialled.

Angie took a while to answer. "Sean? Where . . . ?"

"It's me, Angie. Sorry ah couldny make it last night . . . "

"He didney come hame again, Joe." Quiet resignation.

Joe sighed. "Did ye see him at aw', yesterday?"

"He wis here when ah goat back fae work – aw' dressed up in his new gear. Where's it aw' coming fae, Joe? Whit's he up tae?"

260

Joe stroked Big Boy. "Ah don't ken, Angie . . . "

"If he's no' shoapliftin', it's somethin' worse, Joe, somethin' he dis at night." Pause. "If it's no' the joy-ridin' again, whit . . . oh, Christ!"

Breath burned in his lungs.

"He's dealin' drugs, Joe – it's goat tae be. Oh Christ!"

"Ah asked him 'boot that – he said naw, an' ah believe him."

Angry. "'Well, he's gettin' money fae somewhere. Whit the fuck's he up tae?"

Under his hand, Big Boy languidly arched an orange back.

"Yer pal – the polisman: kid he huv that word wi' him, Joe . . . ?"

"Andy's . . . busy." He glanced at wristwatch: nearly midday. "Look: ah'll be up in aboot an oor."

Michael had been there for him . . .

Relief. "Thanks, Joe – ah 'preciate it." Tired laugh. "How're you dain' yersel'? Ah've bin that . . . "

"Ah'm okay, Angie." Rough fingers clenched automatically. Big Boy yowled then leapt onto the floor. Joe stared at a handful of orange fur. "Seeya in an oor." He replaced the handset, and looked around.

An orange blob cowered behind an armchair.

Joe sighed then went into the bedroom to find his Docs.

Half an hour later he was stuffing sand-coloured duvet cover and sheets into the doctor's washing-machine. On the way back from Andy's flat he'd scanned the streets for blond boys in baseball caps.

He had spotted six: none were Sean.

Joe programmed the washing-machine, then rummaged through cupboards until he found one filled with sand-coloured duvet covers and sheets. Seizing a pile, he re-made the doctor's bed, tidied up the lounge, then grabbed a jacket and keys.

It was twenty to one.

Early afternoon sunshine glinted on thirty five floors of

261

window as he crossed the road towards Red Road Court.

Beneath leather he could smell his own sweat, and a slightly catty odour. He pressed the buzzer for 31/3.

Angie buzzed him up.

In the foyer, a hand-painted sign secured to dull steel doors told him the lift was under service. The same scrawly writing apologised for any inconvenience.

Joe turned towards the stairs.

By the tenth floor, he had thought of three approaches to Sean.

By the twentieth, three became two.

At the thirtieth he paused, staring down at a sunny Glasgow. His heart pounded. He wasn't out of breath. Joe leant against the stair rail and blinked.

Robin and Andy's faces flashed onto eyelids.

Joe ran a hand through hair: Sean should be the least of his problems.

Robin . . . Andy . . .

He could go to the police, tell them what he knew.

Joe sighed. What did he know?

His ex-lover had picked up, fucked and roughed-up a fourteen-year-old boy, who would probably deny the whole thing anyway?

His ex-lover had beaten up – or had had beaten up – a member of Strathclyde Police with whom Joe had had a one-night stand?

Joe sat down on the stairs.

During last night's conversation, Andy had not mentioned doing anything about his own injuries.

Billy knew he wouldn't, had said as much.

Andy had been more concerned about Georgie's death.

Georgie.

Georgie.

Joe kicked at the stair-rail.

His ex-lover had shot – or had had shot – Georgie Paxton, because . . . what?

George had been dealing, in his club?

It sounded . . . flimsy, unconvincing.

The whole thing sounded flimsy and unconvincing.
Joe stood up.
No proof, no nothing.
He could do nothing about Billy.
Michael had been there for him . . .
But he could do something about Sean. Joe ran up the last flight of stairs and pounded on the door of Flat Three.
It opened slowly, an inch or two.
A tear-streaked face beneath frizzed-out hair. "He's back." Should sound relieved, but didn't.
The door opened gradually, like it weighed a ton.
Joe stared, heart hammering.
Michael had been there for him . . .
Amidst the tenderness, the gentleness, Michael had often taken a hard line, slapped him. Hard.
It had worked then.
It would work now.
Joe pushed past Angie and strode into the flat. After two centrally-heated environments and mild weather the cold, damp atmosphere prickled his skin as he walked down the dark hallway and opened the lounge door.
Another closed softly behind him.

A blond figure in a bright pink jacket lounged on the sofa.
Joe stared.
Studiedly casual glance. Snort. "Whit dae you want?"
The scorn wrenched at his stomach. Joe turned, closing the lounge door, then turned back and walked towards Sean.
A pale face beneath freshly-washed hair.
Newly-combed hair.
Sean . . . didn't look like Sean. He looked . . . different . . .
Joe inhaled.
. . . Smelled different.
Not strawberries.
But still sweet. Oddly-sweet.
"Well?" The pale face contorted in a sneer.
Joe's stomach flipped over. He could do a lot of things to that face.

263

Slapping it wasn't one of them.

He sat down opposite and took in the rest of Sean.

Black tee-shirt under pink jacket. Denims. Black Docs. All new-looking.

No baseball-cap.

The all-new Sean.

Even the eyes were different. Joe tried to catch one of the blue pools, but they floated away. He cleared his throat. "How ye dain'?"

Snort. "Whit's it tae you?"

Joe manufactured a shrug. "Nothin' . . . but yer mither's worried."

Laugh. "Fuck her! Nothin' tae worry aboot – ah'm no' botherin' onywan!"

Joe fumbled for a cigarette he didn't want. "Huv a guid time last night?"

His own shrug mirrored. "Aye, fine."

"An' the night before?" Joe flicked the Zippo.

Sean looked up. "Still no' kicked the habit, ah see."

Joe caught a blue pool, glimpsing the old Sean. He smiled.

Sean scowled, looked away.

"Clubbin', wur ye?" Joe drew on the cigarette.

Snort. "Kid's stuff." Long, denim-clad legs stretched, then crossed at ankles.

"Ye didney yist tae think that."

A hand rubbing nose-ring. "Ah didney yist tae think a loata things."

Joe sighed. This was going nowhere. "Whit ur ye nickin' tae pay fur the gear – cors, cor radios?"

Laugh. "Ah dinny need tae nick onythin'." Jumping to feet. "Thur . . . presents." Boastful.

"Who fae?"

"Jist . . . somewan." Smug. Swaggering walk to mantel.

"Yer . . . friend?"

Pause, mid-swagger. "How dae you . . . ?" Blue pools narrowed to slits.

"Ewan says ye've chucked the band, Sean, chucked him an' Keith. Who's yer new . . . friend?"

Snort. Long fingers smoothing denim-clad thighs. "Ewan: whit dis he ken? Him an' that Keith-prick ur a buncha losers!" Dismissive laugh.

Joe lied. "Whit ye dae is yer ain business, as far as ah'm concerned . . ."

"That's bigga ye!"

" . . . But yer mither's worried, Sean. If ye'll no' tell her, tell me." He forced a smile. "Come oan – whit's the big secret?"

Hard stare. "Whit dae you care?"

Heat in his stomach. Sean looked older, and younger at the same time. Joe stood up and walked towards him. Words burbled at the back of his throat. He swallowed them down. "Yer – ainly fifteen, Sean."

Stare. "Ye dinney unnerstaun'." Long fingers jammed into pockets.

"Try me." Joe laid hot palm on a pink shoulder. Muscle bunched beneath expensive fabric. "If ye've goat intae . . . trouble, Sean, ah kin . . . "

"Away back tae yer polis-pal!" Sean pulled away.

Joe stared. Was this what it was all about? He watched as Sean walked to the window. "Luck: ah'll no' tell onywan . . . " Definitely not Andy: he had enough problems. ". . . if ye dinney want me tae." Joe blinked. It was like talking to a stranger, only worse.

Mumbling. "Ah don't care whit ye dae." Silence.

Joe walked around the sofa and joined Sean at the window. Two rough hands on two pink shoulders. "C'moan, man . . . " He breathed in the sweet smell.

"Lea' me alain!" Slim body whipping round. Hard stare. Behind the twisted mouth, the flicker of an old grin. "Loser!"

Joe stepped back as Sean pushed past him and left the room. The sound of a door slamming. Then a low voice.

"Widney tell you eether, eh?"

Joe turned.

Angie slumped in the doorway, eyes on Sean's wake.

Joe sighed. "Let's huv a look at his room . . ."

An hour later, Angie had left for work, reluctantly. She was looking older. Both she and Sean seemed to have aged years in the space of a few days.

Joe stood in Sean's room. An invader, an intruder.

But Angie needed to know.

He wanted to, needed to know.

Sean's territory.

Space was important when you were fifteen.

Joe sighed: space was always important.

Sean shared his space with Angie. She had a right to know what was going on.

He didn't. Joe stared at three heaps on Sean's narrow single bed, looking for clues.

'New . . . friend.'

The clothes-heap: two pairs of Versus jeans, three Emporio tee-shirts, a leather waistcoat, a leather baseball-cap with *No Fear* on the front.

The CD-heap: Oasis, two Primal Screams, Blur, TechnoDance Ten, Supergrass, all still cellophane-wrapped. Sean didn't own a CD player. Joe frowned. It was only a matter of time . . .

The assorted-heap: fancy guitar-strap, a handful of leads, some sort of effects-pedal, a heavy chrome chain – belt?

Joe sat down and sighed.

That fuckin' smell. Everything stank of it. His head buzzed with cat-smells, hospital-smells, damp-smells . . . He glanced across the messy room to a fourth heap of plastic and paper carrier-bags, retrieved by Angie from under the bed. They had evidently contained the fruits of Sean's new *friendship*. Joe reached across and grabbed a handful. He opened the first.

Nothing. He tossed it aside.

The second: nothing. He tossed it aside.

Then he stopped.

Sean had a new friend: so what?

The new friend was generous: so what?

Sean and the new *friend* stayed out all night: so what? Sean and Ewan had often done the same.

266

Heat in his stomach. Sean was big enough and ugly enough to look after himself. Heat spread up his body, flushing face.

It was none of his business.

Joe hurled the remaining carriers across the room.

A white slip of paper fluttered from one, landing on a pile of unwashed socks.

Joe watched it flutter, then stood up. Fingers plucked at the *Access* receipt. Eyes scanned:

'Jacket . . . . . £365.'

Retailer's imprint: Versace.

The receipt stank of the same sweet, familiar smell.

Eyes scanned the card-holder's imprint.

W. King.

Joe stared.

Billy . . .

Billy . . .

Billy . . .

Billy . . .

Joe crumpled the receipt into a tight ball.

The familiar sweet, childhood odour rose from the thin paper in waves.

Oddfellows.

Billy's smell . . .

. . . and Michael's smell.

Blood pounded in his head. Joe turned and walked back to the lounge.

CHAPTER TWENTY FOUR

He was still there three hours later when a door banged. Joe tensed. "Angie?"

Silence, then the sound of another opening.

He stood up and strode into the hall. The door to Sean's bedroom was ajar. He walked towards it, nudged the bottom with a Doc.

The door swung back, revealing a bright pink jacket. Joe watched as Sean rifled through the piles of CDs and clothes. He sighed. Oddfellows billowed in clouds.

Sean paused, turned. Face matching jacket. "Ye've bin goin' through ma stuff!" Hurt? Anger? Expression hard to read.

"Why did ye no' tell me?" Joe tried to sound casual. He'd fucked-up every other conversation. He'd get this one right.

Something – relief? – flashed across the flushed face. Sean turned back to the CDs. "S'none o' yer business."

"True, but yer mither wis worried ye . . ."

"Well, ah'll be gettin' oota this rat-trap soon, so she disney need tae worry ony mair." Two CDs into pocket, then reaching under bed.

"Kin we talk aboot it, Sean?"

"Ah've nothin' tae say tae you."

"C'moan, Sean." Joe stared past a blond head at Schwarzenneger's manufactured expression. "There's things . . . ye don't ken aboot . . . Billy."

Snort. "Aboot you an' him?" Hard laugh. "Ah ken aw' ah need tae!" Stuffing tapes into other pocket. "Ye're a loser, Joe."

Joe tensed. "Billy . . . uses people."

Mock-baby-talk. "Awww . . . did the nasty man hurt Joe's feelin's? Did . . . ?"

"That's no' whit ah'm meanin'!"

Baby-talk dropped. "Billy disney want ye, so you grassed him up tae yer polis-pal."

"Whit?"

Laugh. "At least be oanest aboot it, man! He chucked ye oot, 'cause you wur gettin' . . . heavy wi' him. You couldny stand the thoughta losin' that flat, an' aw the perks o' the job, so ye're tellin' people lies aboot him . . ."

"Shut up an' listen, Sean!"

Blond head whipped round. Sneer. "Ye've nothin' tae say, man!"

Joe stared at a stranger's face. "Ye've bin wi' . . . Billy, the last two nights?"

Mock-evasive. "Ah mighta bin." Bottom lip licked.

Heat in his stomach. Angry heat.

Robin . . .

Andy . . .

Colin Summers . . .

Sean turned round and sat on the bed. "Billy kens people in the . . . music-business. Says he's gonny get me free studio-time, says ah don't need losers like Ewan . . ." Pointed stare. " . . . or you."

Joe swallowed back rage.

Sean burbled on. "He's guid tae talk tae, is Billy. Ah kin . . . tell him things ah canny tell onywan else . . ."

Joe blinked. Michael had been there for him.

Was Billy there for Sean?

" . . . an' he's a guid laugh!"

Joe scowled.

Andy wasn't laughing.

Robin wasn't laughing.

Colin Summers wasn't laughing.

Sean laughed. "Ye're jist jealous. Billy disney want you ony mair an' . . . "

Joe's hand whipped across the sneering face.

Laughter cut short. Sean stared, then raised long fingers to a palm-imprinted cheek. Blue pools blazed. "That's right – hit me. Hit me like ye hit those army guys. That's how they threw ye oot, isn't it? Couldney control yer fuckin' fists!" Standing unsteadily. Fingers still pressed to cheek. The other hand gesturing. "C'moan then. Beat me up. Gie me a guid kickin'. That'll solve everythin' – eh?"

Joe stared. His palm stung. Heat drained away from face.

Snort. Sean lowered hands then picked up the remaining CDs from the bed and brushed past him.

Joe continued to stare into empty Sean-space.

Michael had been there for him . . .

He levered himself off the door frame and followed Sean into the lounge.

A pink back faced him. "Billy's gonny introduce me tae . . . people."

"An' whit dis Billy get faes you, fur his trouble?"

Sean spun round from bagging the PRS guitar. "Billy an' me huv . . ." Smug smile. ". . . an understandin'."

Joe's heart died.

"Says ah kin help him wi' the clubs – tell him whit soarta music's goin' doon well wi' the punters. We're tryin' a jungle night next month . . . an' he's gonny teach me tae drive." Stuffing guitar into fabric-case.

Joe blinked. "Look, Sean: don't rush intae things – eh? Gie it some time."

Low voice. "Ah'm no' a wee boay ony mair. Ah ken whit ah'm dain'. Billy's helpin' me work things through."

Joe scowled. Sean smelled like Billy, was starting to sound like Billy.

Billy could be very helpful, very gentle . . .

. . . when it suited.

Robin's bruised and battered face.

Zipping, then: "Well, that's me."

Joe stared.

Guitar hugged to chest. "Ah'm away tae rehearse."

Joe scanned the face for a trace of the old Sean. "Where?"

"A mate's hoose."

He sighed. "Need a haun wi' yer gear?"

Headshake. Blond hairs adhering to pink lips. Long fingers pulled them away. "Don't need onythin' fae you, ony mair."

Joe's legs were lead as Sean stalked past him.

"Tell ma mither ah'll see her later."

Joe let him go.

Useless.

Helpless.

In the distance, a door slammed.

On part of his life.

On maybe all of Sean's life.

Joe sighed and walked into the hall to the telephone.

Thirty minutes later, after ten fruitless calls, it was answered.

Joe tensed. "Billy?"

Soft laugh. "Well, well! To what do I owe this honour?"

Joe gripped the receiver.

"How's your policeman?"

"Ah never hid onythin' tae dae wi' Andy when ah wis wi' you, Billy – ah telt ye that. Why did ye . . . .?"

"I've no time for this, Joe. I'm . . ." Soft laugh. " . . . busy."

Joe closed his eyes. "Don't hurt him, Billy."

Feigned-innocence. "Who, Joe?"

His heart hammered.

Laugh. "Oh, you mean young Sean?"

Blood pounded in his ears.

"I always wished I'd met you at fifteen, Joe. So malleable, so fresh, like ripe fruit."

Strawberries.

"Ever fucked a virgin, Joe?" Soft laugh. "Oh, of course not. That's not your thing – is it?"

Sean's slim body under Billy's flashed into his mind. Joe blinked. "Kin ah . . . come back tae barracks, sir?"

Hard laugh. "Last post has sounded, soldier!"

"Please, Billy?"

Cold laugh. "You disobeyed an order, soldier."

His prick stirred. "Yes, sir. Sorry, sir."

"Missing it, are you, soldier?"

Buzzing in his head. "Please, Billy . . . "

"Your . . . position's been filled, soldier. Dismissed!" The line buzzed.

Joe replaced the receiver, then lifted it and redialled.

Hard voice. "I said dismissed, soldier!" Buzzing.

Joe continued to hold the receiver.

271

Andy . . .
Robin . . .
The Summers' kid . . .
Nothing mattered any more.
Only Sean.
Joe dropped the receiver.
It clanged off a cheap, metal table.
Nothing mattered.
Only Sean . . .
Joe zipped up his jacket and left the flat.

It was lighting-up time when he reached Martha Street. Joe cupped hands round cigarette and lit up.

In the gloom beyond, through the arches of Glasow City Chambers, he could see the outline of the Italina Centre.

Somewhere, in another part of Glasgow, Andy Hunter was undergoing exploratory surgery.

Under another part of Glasgow, the bodies of Colin Summers and Georgie Paxton were mouldering away.

Somewhere, in another part of Britain, Robin and his family were getting on with their lives.

Joe bit the cigarette's filter.

Billy: business, always business.

Sean wasn't business . . .

Joe walked on down Martha Street, through the archway past a window-display in which a pink, much-admired jacket was no longer displayed.

Outside the Italina Centre he paused, looked up at the second floor.

A single light burned.

He'd stood here on so many other evenings.

Home.

Coming home.

Home . . . where the heart was.

Joe walked towards security gates and pressed a buzzer.

Home wasn't here.

His heart wasn't here.

Crackling, then: "Yes?"

Joe lowered his head to the grill. "Billy? It's . . . "

Buzzing. The gate swung open.

Joe walked through as he'd done every night for almost a year, crossed the same courtyard he'd crossed every night for almost a year.

A year.

A year.

Ahead, the second security door swung ajar.

Joe walked through.

How could he not have known about Billy's . . . business practices?

A year.

He knew nothing.

Joe ran up three flights of stairs.

Home. Once.

It would be home again.

If that's what it took . . .

The door to 3/1 was open. From inside, faint music.

His heart hammered. Beneath jeans, five flaccid inches were stirring.

Home.

Joe inhaled.

Oddfellows.

It was like he'd never been away.

He pushed open the door, closed it behind himself, then walked down the hall towards the lounge.

Faint music became less faint.

He pushed open the lounge door.

Loud music hit him like a blow.

He stared.

Same room. Same Apple-Mac blinking. Same back of same silver-blond head. Same smell. Joe sighed. "Billy." The name was obliterated by pounding drums. He walked into the room.

From the CD player, a surprised voice, raised over the noise. "Whit's he dain' here?"

Joe turned, stared. A pink jacket lay on the polished wooden floor. Inches away, a black tee-shirt. Propped up against one wall, an oddly-shaped case.

Bare-chested, Sean stopped dancing.

273

Joe stared.

From the Apple-Mac: "Get Joe some of that mineral water you both like so much, Sean." Sharp words cutting through the music.

Compliant. "Sure, Billy." Scornful eyes on Joe, Sean breezed out of the room.

Joe turned towards the Apple-Mac. "Whit's he dain' here?"

Soft laugh. "It's like an echo. You two are so alike." Billy got up from the screen and walked towards the CD player. He picked up the remote, pointing.

The volume lowered.

Billy walked back to the Apple-Mac.

Joe stared. Like a rat to a trap, baited with Sean. "You kent ah'd come."

A well-manicured finger pressed the keyboard.

The green screen blinked out.

Cool laugh. "You know me well, Joe . . . better than I know you, it would seem."

"Here!" Grumbling voice from behind.

Joe turned.

Scowl. A bottle of Caledonian Clear thrust at him.

Joe took it, noticed it was Wild Blackberry. He stared at the pale figure. The music cut out.

Sean stared back, still scowling.

Cool laugh from behind. "Change the CD Sean, would you?"

Grin. "Sure, Billy."

Joe watched as a tight, denim-clad arse made its way across the room. "He's comin' hame wi' me!"

Sean whipped round. "Naw, ah'm no'."

Joe frowned. "Aye, ye ur . . ."

"Boys, boys!" Soft laugh. Billy got up from the Apple-Mac. Cold green eyes to Joe. "We need to talk." Smile to Sean. "Primal Scream, I think."

Compliant. "Sure, Billy." Sean knelt before the CD-player.

Joe stared at almost-translucent skin.

A voice by his side. "Sit down, Joe." Soft fingers on

leathered shoulder.

Oddfellows, then rage in his head. Joe seized a slim wrist. A splash of loud music broke over the silent room. "He's comin' hame wi' me!" Joe grabbed thin shoulders, staring into cold, myopic eyes. He balled one fist, pulling it back to shoulder height.

Music pounded.

Joe locked eyes with cold, green pupils.

Under his grip, Billy didn't flinch, but continued to stare.

Joe tried to see behind the gaze.

Nothing.

He gripped harder, closing eyes to get away from cold green.

Another time, another place.

Hamburg . . . wanting to get home for Sean . . . be there for Sean.

Biceps throbbed. Every muscle in his body tensed.

Pain.

Even words beneath pounding music. "Hit an officer, would you, soldier?"

This officer had trained him well. Joe's arms fell away, thumbs aligning with jeans seams. He turned, opening eyes.

Sean was dancing, slim pale wrists raised over head. Oblivious.

Voice in his ear. "That's better. Now, sit down."

Joe's knees buckled. He sat on the beige sofa.

On the other side of the room, Sean swayed, strumming an imaginary guitar.

Joe stared at the lithe, surprisingly graceful figure.

Low laugh in his ear.

Joe turned. "Ye don't want Sean, Billy." He stared into cold eyes.

They blinked. "No . . . I don't want Sean. I never did."

Joe looked away, focusing on a slim, sweating chest.

Billy talked on. "What would I do with a dirty, slummy little toe-rag like that?"

Joe continued to stare.

"He's served his purpose, brought you to me." Hard

laugh. "I knew you'd come back, Joe. We're good together. I understand you . . ."

Relief thundered through his veins. "Send Sean hame tae his mither." Joe tried to drag his eyes from the slim figure. He failed.

"With pleasure. But later."

Hard fingers gripped his shoulder.

"You owe me, Joe."

He shivered. "Ah ken that, Billy. But ah'm back noo."

Tutting under guitar riffs. "AWOL, disobeying an order, attempting to strike an officer . . ."

Sean whipped round to face them. Eyes closed. Grinning.

Joe's stomach flipped over. He tried to concentrate on Billy's words. "Ah ken that. Ah'm sorry."

More tutting. "Sorry's not enough. You hurt me, Joe. You left with no explanation, I didn't know where you'd gone."

Heat in his stomach, spreading down into groin. "Send Sean hame, Billy. Then we kin . . ."

Sean opened his eyes. Blue pools bored into Joe's brain.

Joe sighed. ". . . dae whit we yissed tae, Billy. But let Sean go hame first, eh?"

A hand squeezed his shoulder. "The charges are serious, Joe. It's not just a dirty kit this time."

Joe locked eyes with Sean. Go . . . go . . . go . . .

Sean grinned and danced on.

Words in his ear. "The punishment must be more . . . severe, this time, Joe – you understand that."

"Aye, Billy . . . onythin' ye like." Eyes travelled down Sean's body.

"Let's list the charges, then. Firstly: sleeping with the enemy, to quote a trite film."

Andy's stitched-together face flashed onto his eyelids, joined by a memory of quick, hard, enjoyable sex . . . but didn't stay long. Sean's blond hair filled Joe's vision.

"Secondly: absent without leave."

Sean was mouthing along with pounding music.

"Thirdly . . ." Pause. "You sent the money back."

Joe blinked. "You telt the polis ah'd nicked it."

Soft laugh. "You hurt me when you returned my

present, Joe. It's only fair that I . . . hurt you."

Joe followed Sean's body as a pale arm stretched to grab the remote. Volume soared. A fake US accent filled the room:

'. . . Get your rocks, get your rocks off honey . . .'

The word echoed in Joe's head.

Sean was swaying again, grinning at him, then to his left.

Joe followed Sean's eyes to Billy's pale face. He watched a pair of myopic green eyes sync with two blue pools.

Sean grinned.

Joe turned and looked up at Billy.

A faint smile twitched thin lips. The silver blond head turned towards him.

The track ended.

Billy's words broke the silence. "I think I've found a punishment to fit the crime."

CHAPTER TWENTY FIVE

Sean lifted a Caledonian Clear bottle from the floor and poured droplets over a sweaty face.

Joe stared.

Music pumped on.

At his side, a soft laugh:

"He means a lot to you, doesn't he?"

Glass bottle pressed against a pink cheek.

"Very . . . laudable, the way you raced down here to protect his . . . virtue."

The dancing stopped. "Okay if ah use yer bog? This stuff goes straight through ye!" Breathless words.

One nod. "Bring me a grapefruit juice on your way back." Eyebrow raised to Joe.

Sean waited.

Joe glanced at a still-full Caledonian Clear bottle and shook his head.

Sean scampered from the room.

Joe stared at a thin mouth, then drank.

The thin mouth smiled. "I never guessed for a moment, you know – until now."

Joe wiped burning lips and continued to stare.

Billy stood up.

Joe followed the movement with his eyes.

"It would appear I went to all that trouble with PC Angel-Face for nothing."

Joe watched as Billy strolled towards the CD player and lifted the remote. "Ah telt ye there wis nothing tae that. Andy's jist . . . a mate." He knew it wasn't true.

Billy talked on. "All the time I was thinking about you and him when I should've seen what was staring me in the face." Aiming the remote. Volume decreased.

Joe blinked at Billy's back.

"Very cosy. Just the two of you . . . and Angela, of course."

"Whit you oan aboot?"

Turning. Myopic green eyes flashed across the room.

"Sean."

Joe tensed. "Whit?"

Sigh. Smile, then: "Thought I knew you, your body, inside out, Joe . . . seems I really don't know your tastes . . . or all of them at least."

The CD cut out.

Joe inhaled silence.

Billy stood up. "I'm sure he's gay, you know." Measured steps across the polished floor.

Joe frowned. The questions, the confusion, the conversation at Michael's grave. "Sean disney ken whit he is – no wan dis at that age."

Soft laugh. "Oh, come on! I knew much earlier, lots of guys do. I'm aware you were a . . . late developer." Walking around the sofa. Stopping behind. Gentle fingers on hard shoulders. "Poor Joe . . ." Fingers kneading. ". . . All that violence, all those repressed emotions finding expression in anger . . ." Fingers stroking hard shoulders. ". . . merely because you couldn't understand what your brain was telling your body." Fingers pausing. "Sean knows his own mind – aside from that, you're so alike, you two . . . I think it's the eyes. He has that same look you get sometimes: hard, bruised, but sort of vulnerable at the same time." Soft hands again kneading hard muscle. "Brings out the . . . paternal in me." Low laugh.

The door flipped open.

Sean flopped in, holding a glass of beige liquid and another bottle of Caledonian Clear. He held the glass out to Billy.

One soft hand from hard shoulder. "Thank you, Sean."

Almost-demure nod.

Joe watched as Sean swayed across the polished floor to no music. Finger flicking CD from case.

Then music again.

Then more swaying.

A voice in his ear. "Tight little arse – eh, Joe? To be the first . . . a great privilege." Citrus fumes and Oddfellows.

Joe stared at the dancing figure.

No . . .

279

No . . .
No . . .
No . . .
Sean and Billy.
Billy and Sean.
Ex-lover and . . .?
Laughing in his ear. "Very apt, I think."
No . . .
No . . .
No . . .
". . . You betrayed me, soldier, forced me to teach PC Angel-Face a lesson – something I didn't really want to do . . ."
No . . .
No . . .
". . . so it's only right the punishment fits the crime."
No . . .
Sean swayed over to the sofa.
Joe followed with his eyes.
Breathy words in his ear. "Go on, then. Fuck him."
Joe stood up. "Whit?"
The music cut out.
Sharp voice scything through silence. "Fuck him the way I fuck you."
Sean stopped dancing.
The music started again.
Something cold filled his stomach. Joe shook his head. "We kin go oot in the car, Billy, up Port Dundas way . . ."
Hard laugh. "I think my idea's much better – don't you, Sean?" Voice directed across the room.
Sean stared.
Harder laugh. "He's told me all about you, Joe – how you ran off and left him, just when things were . . . working-out between the two of you. Now's your chance to make it up to him – eh Joe? Keep it in the family, so to speak."
Joe stared at Sean.
Blue pools twitching behind dark lashes. Grin fading. Eyes to Joe, then Billy. Long fingers grabbing a stray strand of blond hair, twisting it around.

280

Joe tried to smile. "C'moan, Sean. We're goin' hame."

Half-grin. Words over pounding music. "It's a joke – right?" Blue pools flashing between green eyes and blue dots.

Joe stood up, seized a sweating arm. Heat in his groin. "C'moan: we're leavin'!"

Something cold poked the back of his neck.

He turned.

Colder smile. "You're not going anywhere."

Joe stared at the gun's dull sheen. "Ah thoaght that wis at the bottom o' the Clyde." A sweating arm pulled free from sweating fingers.

Awe-struck. "Man, is that a . . .?"

Billy smiled. "Your father's, I believe." Smile broadening into grin. "How appropriate!"

Joe stared down the barrel of Michael's service revolver. "Get yer jaicket, Sean. . ."

"You're not leaving – and that's an order, soldier."

Joe's eyes flicked from Billy to the gun and back again. "Ah don't take . . . oarders fae you ony mair." He turned away.

Pressure on the side of his head. Then tingling spread down his spine.

Then darkness.

Singing . . .

'There's a rainbow inside your mind . . . there's a . . .'

Strange voice. Female voice. CD-ed voice.

Then other voices in the distance. Fizzing, warped.

One angry, guttural.

The other vaguely amused.

Joe concentrated.

Words blurred into senselessness.

'. . . I'm your fantasy . . .'

He opened eyes and dragged himself upright. "Git oot, Sean." His mouth wouldn't work: the words were a formless moan. Something warm trickled over one ear. Joe stared.

Billy and Sean swam.

281

Joe blinked, refocused.

Sound and vision re-formed. On the sofa, Billy nursed the gun, smiling. Over by the window Sean was shouting:

"You're no' real, man – whit did you dae that fur?"

Joe swallowed down vomit. "Lea' it, Sean."

Huge blue pools rippled towards him. "Oh man – you okay?"

Joe nodded. The head movement was a bad idea. Blood pounded behind his eyes. He watched as Sean grabbed a crumpled pink jacket and ran across the room towards him. A shaking hand on his arm:

"C'moan . . ." Blazing eyes to Billy. ". . . Let's gie him a doin', Joe. He's aw' talk." Pulling.

Hard laugh. "I don't think so."

Joe's feet wouldn't move.

Sean tugged. "C'moan, Joe . . ."

Billy stood up. "Tell him, Joe."

Quizzical blue pools. "Tell me whit?"

His mouth was dry. Joe stared as Billy raised the gun, levelling the dull metal at Sean's head-height.

Cold smile. Green eye-lock. "Tell him you don't strike an officer."

Billy's eyes bored into the deepest part of him.

"Tell him, soldier." Small, measured steps across the polished floor. The gun held steady.

Half-scared, half bravado. "Fuck aff, ya . . ."

"Shut up, Sean!" Icy words. Billy smiled at Joe.

Sean froze.

Obedience: another Macdonald family trait. Joe flinched.

Inches from the bare-chested figure, Billy flicked a blond curl from the pale face. "One squeeze – that's all it takes." Barrel pressed against a sweating forehead, then removed.

Sean was motionless.

Joe stared at the floor. "Ye never strike an oafficer, Sean."

Harsh laugh. "That's better. Now . . ."

The CD cut out.

". . . fuck him, or watch him die: it's up to you, Joe."

Billy's words hung in the air.

Sean's grip was tight on his arm. Joe looked up, stared

into confused blue pools.

Billy talked on. "You've caused me a lot of trouble, Joe, forced me to do . . . things I hadn't planned to do . . ."

Joe searched Sean's eyes.

". . . I saw the mark left by Paxton's ring after that night, can still see it, if I look very closely."

For a glint of the old Sean.

"He damaged my property. I couldn't have that, now – could I?"

Swimming-pool Sean.

"He died screaming like a baby." Cold laugh. "Thought it was over his little drugs-scam."

Guitar-shop Sean.

"He never knew the real reason. Maybe I should have told him, eh Joe? Maybe I should've made sure Paxton realised what he'd done."

Laughing Sean.

"PC Angel-Face . . . that was only a warning. You're vulnerable, Joe, easy prey. I knew his game, even if you didn't. He had to be taught a lesson . . ."

Shower-Sean.

" . . . Like Frank Connolly had to be taught a lesson." Sigh. "Ah, little Robin Red-breast and his virtual-reality games. Spent hours up in that arcade, feeding money to those machines, in between trying to pick up anything that floated past."

Sean, drying his hair in front of a one-bar electric fire.

"I showed him reality, showed Mr Licensing-Board Connolly the reality of his precious son." Hard laugh. "Did him a favour, really. Robin's a disaster waiting to happen. If it hadn't been me it would've been someone else . . . someone who didn't know when to stop."

Heat in his stomach. Joe sighed.

"It had to be done. Almost twenty years I've worked to make William King a name in this grubby city. I couldn't afford to lose my licences – not now, not when The Matrix was just taking-off." Pause.

Joe stared at Sean.

Sean stared back. Deep in bottomless blue, something

stirred.

"Did I tell you about Scott, Joe? I like to look after what's mine . . ."

Heat in his groin. "Ah'm yours, Billy – but Sean's no'." Joe dragged eyes from rippling pools and focused on myopic green slits.

They shone. The click of a safety-catch. "Want me to kill him – want me to do it, Joe? I've done so much for you already." An arm around Sean's stiff shoulders. The gun pressed millimetres into soft flesh. "This would be such a little thing."

Joe shook his head. His prick was hard.

No . . .

No . . .

No . . .

Not like this.

Billy released Sean, who wobbled.

Joe grabbed a slim waist, steadying the blond figure.

Billy smiled. "That's it, soldier. Face up to the consequences of your actions. Take your punishment like a man."

Joe stared at the small grey circle on Sean's forehead, then lowered his eyes.

Sean met the gaze.

Joe flinched as long, warm fingers moved to trace the deep cut on the side of his head. He shook them away, saw his blood on Sean's fingertips.

Angry words came in a rush. Sean stared at Billy. "Ah thought ye liked me, man, really liked me, ah thought you an' me wur . . ." Eyes flicked to Joe and back to green dots. Scowl. "Aw' the time this wis aboot . . ." Eyes to the floor ". . . you an' him!" Anger fading into injured pride.

Joe frowned. This was no time for hurt feelings.

Billy's low laugh seeped into his mind. Then a hard voice. "Get on with it, boys!"

Joe stared at Sean.

Sean stared back, unblinkingly.

Hoping he saw understanding in the blue eyes, Joe wiped blood from his neck and began to undo Sean's fly.

284

No music.

Three types of breathing.

Billy. Crouching. Feet away. Slow, even breaths. Like nothing was happening. Expensive fabric of expensive trousers pulled loose over thighs, tight over groin. One nearly-manicured hand fumbling with belt buckle. The other holding the gun, trained on Sean.

Joe was naked. Breath caught in dry throat as he followed the gun-barrel with his eyes. Adrenaline flowed through veins. His arcing prick twitched.

Panting. Sean sitting on polished wood. Reluctant to undress fully, expensive jeans bagged around white knees, whiter Calvins bisecting pale torso. Lightly muscled arms hugging bare chest. Pink jacket in a heap yards away, beside leather bikers', newish socks and shiny Docs, size nine.

Joe kicked his own boots aside, walked towards Sean and gazed down.

Dark lashes fluttering on flushed cheeks. Eyes closed. Swollen lips parted.

Joe shivered.

Cold or anticipation?

A parallel shiver rippled over the pale body.

Cold, anticipation or fear?

Joe dropped to his knees, stretching out a hand towards the beautiful body. He stroked Sean's shoulder. Rough fingers stumbled over smooth skin.

Dark-lashed lids sprang open.

Pounding in his head. Prick twitched again, as a droplet of precum seeped from within. Joe knelt beside the slim boy, stared at hairless chest and stomach.

Sean shivered.

Joe frowned.

Only one thing mattered.

He looked over to Billy.

Hard smile. "Very touching, soldier. Now fuck him." Tugging at belt buckle with neatly-manicured fingers. The gun held steady.

Joe looked down. The curve of smooth white flesh hurt

285

his eyes. He stared back up at Billy. "He's . . . young. Huv ye goat ony . . .?"

Harsh laugh. "Saliva and shit were good enough for you, soldier!"

Joe scowled then seized two handfuls of new denim and pulled off Sean's jeans. The movement was swift and efficient. He applied it to the Calvins.

In the background, slow applause.

Joe's head flipped up.

One-handed applause. The gun was steady in an iron grip.

At his side, movement. Joe turned.

Sean was on his feet. A blush spread over the non-grinning face, seeping down onto chest. Amidst a thicket of tight blond curls, an unconscious prick. Throat clearing. "Whit dae . . ." Not Sean's voice. Throat cleared again. "Whit dae ye . . . want me tae dae?" Chewing bottom lip. "Ah mean, where dae ye . . . want me?"

An echo of countless nights with Billy ripped through his soul. Joe swallowed hard, stood up and scanned the room.

The sofa.

The back of the sofa.

Over the back of the sofa.

Soft laugh. "Take him on the floor, Joe. I want you to see his face."

Joe's eyes flipped back to Sean.

Weight shifting from foot to foot. Aware this was different – not the shower, not the swimming pool, not the sauna. Aware of the two sets of male eyes sweeping over his body. Blue pools to Joe's prick.

Aware this was something more?

Joe tried to smile. It only made things worse.

Sean smiled back, the smile of a trusting fifteen-year-old . . . or an understanding near-adult?

Joe frowned, searched inside for anger, found only . . . heat.

Sean sucked at a stray strand of hair, then pushed it away.

Hard laugh. "Get on with it, soldier!"

Joe looked up at Billy.

The gun still trained on Sean.

Joe frowned. Andy's slashed face . . .

Robin's bruised and beaten body . . .

The anger came easily now. He stepped forward, gripped two smooth biceps and pushed Sean backwards, knocking the legs from him with a bare right foot.

"Hey! Whit . . .?" Sean toppled, landing heavily on the polished floor. A shadow of pain criss-crossed the pale face.

Joe frowned with concern, then pushed the emotion away. "Shut it!" Kneeling, he raised two pale legs to his shoulders and rested shaking fingers on two hard mounds. He eased one, then two thumbs into Sean. Prick brushed top of thigh.

Sean flinched.

Emotion came rushing back. Joe removed one hand and seized a rigid shoulder. "Easy, easy . . ." Like talking to an injured animal, a beast.

A beast about to be beasted.

The shoulder relaxed slightly.

Joe sighed, ran one damp finger down the moist crevice of Sean's arse-crack . . .

More flinching.

Joe spread Sean with one hand, licked a finger of the other and began to probe.

Tight, resisting.

Prick twitched higher.

Stroking the warm tunnel, Joe leant down and brushed straggling blond hair away from a pink face.

Less tight, less resisting.

Sean threw arms across face, mumbling.

Joe probed further, opening, stretching. Preparing. His prick trembled against stomach.

Sean whimpered.

Joe withdrew the finger and lowered Sean's shaking legs.

Hard voice from the far side of the room. "Enough foreplay, soldier!"

Only feet away, Billy was in another world. Joe stared down at Sean's pale body.

Blond head raised, mouth open. A single tear tracked an ashen cheek.

Joe eye-locked with swimming blue pools. "Relax, Sean. C'moan . . ."

Watery blink. "It feels . . ."

"Ah ken. Jist relax." His heart forced his mouth to lie. "Ah'll make it quick." His prick wanted hours of this, hours of touching, stroking, licking, knowing.

What his prick wanted didn't matter.

What he wanted didn't matter.

Nothing mattered anymore.

Only Sean.

The word fizzed in his ear.

Then a hard voice through the fizz: "I'm losing my erection, Joe."

The words pulled him into now. He unglued eyes from Sean's then glanced up.

Huge green pupils. Belt buckle hanging loose. Billy's hand tug-tugging at six hard inches. Cold smile. The gun barely moved.

Movement at his side. "Joe?"

He looked down.

Arms hugging a skinny chest. Bare feet sliding on slick, polished wood. "Jist do it, man!"

Joe scowled.

Not like this.

Not like this.

He edged forward and pushed Sean's legs up towards the blond head. As knees touched hairless chest Joe pressed a hairy forearm against the back of Sean's calfs, holding them there.

A gasp of panic.

Joe stretched his body to cover Sean's, one hand holding the struggling boy steady, the other fumbling for the arse-hole. He looked down at a pink, sweating face, at blue, confused eyes, then up.

In front, Billy's left hand tug-tugged on. On his right,

288

inches from Sean's blond head, the gun remained almost motionless. Green eyes fixed on Joe. Soft words. "Need any help?"

Joe lowered himself back onto knees, focusing on Sean's white arse.

Soft laugh. "Feels right, doesn't it?"

Joe stared down at Sean. It didn't . . . feel anything. It just . . . was. He spat into a palm, coated his prick then roughly moistened the already damp orifice.

Instinctive clenching.

With one hand Joe pinned Sean to the floor, seizing prick with the other, guiding himself into the tight, dusky-pink opening.

Sean's scream filled the room, echoing in Joe's head. Warm muscle grudgingly enveloped the first three hard inches. He leant forward, subduing struggles with his weight and tried to think of something else.

There was nothing else.

Only Sean.

Joe withdrew a little then thrust forward. Balls slapped lightly off white arse.

Sean was moaning now, hands grabbing at Joe's shoulders, finding a grip, holding on.

Joe smoothed soaking hair from a crumpled face. "Oh, Christ!"

Sweating fingers slid off sweatier flesh, scrabbling at the floor behind.

Joe covered one of Sean's hands with his own and thrust again.

Heaven and Hell melted into one, melted into fucking Sean.

Above the slap of flesh on flesh, another sound.

Harsh, laboured breathing.

Joe raised unfocused eyes.

Billy's contorted face. Left hand tugging more quickly. The smile grim with excitement. Gun quivering, the barrel drooping. Fingers loosening as everything else tightened.

Sean was panting, starting to thrust back . . . or struggle.

Joe seized shoulders, thrusting deeper into a warm vice.

Home.

Where the heart was.

Pants turned to sobs.

Joe eased a crimson-streaked prick three-quarters-out of Sean. His heart stopped.

Sobs turned to words. "No . . . no . . . Joe . . . no, don't . . ."

Billy was mumbling.

Joe tried to look up, couldn't. Prick slid in more easily this time. Pressure built in balls.

Billy's words were louder now: "Joe, Joe . . ."

Sean gulped in air, nails screeching on polished wood beneath the wilting revolver.

Joe buried his face in Sean's hair, arms around the smooth neck. Against stomach and chest, the young body tensed.

Joe closed his eyes.

Billy's breathing filled the room.

Under him, Sean became rigid and lurched upwards, hands flapping on smooth floor. Joe tried to think of something else. He couldn't.

A low, animal sound filled the room.

Inches ahead something clattered from spasming fingers.

Then the sound of a single gun-shot.

Against Joe's stomach, Sean's thighs buckled, dissolving under impact as spunk pumped out into a limp body.

A smell.

Joe's head filled with a smell.

Oddfellows, strawberries, spunk, blood . . .

. . . and the smell of target practice.

Strands of blond hair stuck to his cheek as he peeled his face from Sean's neck.

Silence sang in his ears. The choking smell caught in his throat. He forced it back out, opening his eyes.

He was still on top of Sean.

Joe looked up.

On the wall behind where Billy had been crouching, a red and grey stain spread over blue paper.

290

CHAPTER TWENTY SIX

Joe withdrew from Sean's hot body.

A whimper. White thighs splayed.

Legs trembling, he reached over and removed his service-revolver from white-knuckled, powder-burned fingers.

Cordite veiled in the air, dividing the room.

Three feet away, Billy's neatly-manicured hand clutched a still-hard prick. Spunk speckled linen trousers.

Joe's eyes travelled up a red-splattered shirt, ending where the head should have been, then stared.

Steel-rimmed glasses still perched amidst a mess of shattered bone and mushy cartilage.

"Oh fuck, oh fuck, oh fuck, oh . . ."

Joe looked down.

Sean raised his head. Blue pools overflowed onto scarlet cheeks.

Joe gently pulled Sean to him.

"Oh fuck, oh fuck, oh fuck, oh . . ."

Heat from a burning face prickled his neck. Joe stroked soaking hair. "S'okay . . ." He stared at Billy's softening prick . . .

. . . By the time Sean had calmed down, Billy was completely flaccid.

Joe brushed blond hair aside and tilted the pink face upwards.

The eyes were closed, the breathing easier.

He grabbed a crumpled pink jacket from a few feet away, draping it around thin shoulders.

They shivered.

Joe stood up and carried the limp body to the sofa.

Snuffling.

He laid the now-foetal bundle on soft fabric, re-adjusting the pink jacket. Then stared.

Eyes moving beneath eyelids. Then dark lashes raised.

Pupils pin-pricked his heart. Joe tried to smile.

Pink lips twitched, but refused to grin. Dark lashes lowered.

Silence.

The sound of sleep-breathing.

Kneeling, Joe continued to stare.

Sometime later he got up and reached for his clothes.

Dressing quickly, he then searched for Versus jeans and an almost-new black tee-shirt.

Smeary palm-prints were fading on the highly-polished floor. Tiny red dots freckled a shiny surface.

Joe blinked.

Get out.

Get out.

Get out.

He turned back to the sofa and gently shook a pink-clad shoulder. "C'moan, Sean. We're goin' hame. It's over." The boy's crumpled clothes trembled in his left hand. With his right, Joe picked up Michael's service revolver and tucked it into a back pocket.

Instinct took him back to Springburn.

Instinct made him check that Angie was still at work.

Instinct made him put a mumbling Sean to bed.

A different instinct let him give in, when long, still-shaking fingers refused to let go of his.

Joe cradled a blond head in huge arms. He sighed, staring up at the large poster which dominated the bedroom wall.

Sean snuggled in closer, breath shallow in lungs . . .

After a while, instinct took over again. Joe edged the duvet aside and began to undress the sleeping boy.

Outside the Royal Infirmary, he dumped Sean's clothes into a skip labelled: 'For Incineration.'

Half-an-hour later, he was sitting at Andy Hunter's bedside. A white curtain segregated this bed from the rest of the sleeping ward.

Not visiting-time, a nurse had frowned, glancing suspiciously at the still-bleeding wound on the side of Joe's head.

Family emergency, Joe had half-truthed: Andy deserved an explanation.

The too-white face smiled up from a too-white pillow. "Amazing what they can do, these days. Exploratory brain-surgery and not even a general anaesthetic – I was awake the whole time . . . ."

"He's deid."

Bushy eyebrows V-ing. "Who's dead?"

Joe sighed. "Billy's deid. Ah shoat him." He stared into liquid brown eyes. "Ah'm goin' tae the polis. Whit shid ah tell them aboot . . . the rest?"

Wriggling white-clad shoulders on whiter pillows. A bandaged head dragged itself upright. "Keep your voice down!" Peering through bleary eyes. "What happened to your head?"

Joe frowned. "Ah want them tae ken whit Billy . . . wis. Tell me whit tae say."

Sigh. "Tell me what happened."

Joe re-told a version of events . . .

. . . a version which didn't include Sean.

A nurse poked her head through the curtain split. "It's getting late, Andy . . . ."

A large hand shooed her away.

Joe focused on the IV drip. "So? Whit shid ah tell them?"

A sigh, then: "Fucked if I know!"

Joe looked at the pale, battered face. "Billy hid it comin', Andy – you ken that. Georgie, Robin, the other kid, whit he did tae you. He mentioned some Scott guy . . . ."

"Your predecessor, Joe. Jimmy – the guy from Delmonicas? – popped in earlier. Scott Morton. He had the audacity to go back to his wife. Billy King . . . ."

"Ah don't want tae hear whit he did, Andy . . . ."

Sean.

". . . but he'll no' dae it again!"

Liquid brown eyes met his. "Hmmm." Silence, then:

293

"Self-defence'll be hard to prove. The evidence against Billy is as shaky as ever. It'll be your word against a dead man's that any of this happened at all – the word of a would-be respectable business-man . . ."

"It wisney business, Andy – no' aw' o' it. Georgie wis causa me. You wur causa me . . ."

Sean.

Silence, then: "Where's the weapon?"

Joe blinked. "In ma poacket, wi' . . ."

Sean's keys to Billy's flat.

" . . . the keys."

"What?"

Joe stared. "It's ma gun – ma brither's gun, onyway . . ."

Michael had been there for him . . .

Michael's gun had been there for Sean . . .

Angry. "It's probably also the gun that killed George Paxton, Joe. No alibi, motive . . . means . . ." Frown. "They'll do you for two murders."

Joe blinked. None of this made any sense.

Sigh, then: "You'll need to go back."

"Whit?"

"Go back to Billy's flat, take your brother's gun and . . ."

Joe bent head and listened.

Midnight.

Joe inserted a key in the controlled entry and stared up.

Above, a glow from the third floor.

Lights on, no-one home.

He turned key in lock, pushed open gate and jogged across courtyard towards the heavy main door.

Leaden legs ran up two flights of carpeted stairs.

Home . . . where the heart wasn't.

Sweat-slicked fingers stroked another key into another lock, then pushed.

The door swung open.

A smell blossomed out.

Oddfellows and . . .

He closed the door softly and walked down the dark hallway.

Oddfellows and cordite and . . .

He turned into the lounge.

A single shell-light blinked above the sofa.

Oddfellows and cordite and strawberries and . . .

He plucked the gun from his pocket.

Oddfellows and cordite and strawberries and blood.

Not fuck-blood.

Joe stared across yards of polished wood, then wiped the gun carefully with the edge of his tee-shirt. Vomit rose in his throat.

Six years in the army, and he'd never seen a gun-shot wound like this one.

Holding the weapon through jersey, he blinked, then walked to where Billy's body lolled against the wall. With shaking fingers, he removed the limp prick from right hand, replacing with the gun.

The flesh was still warm.

Joe shivered, then walked into the kitchen. From beneath the sink he removed a handful of large, black bin liners, a pair of Marigolds and three cleaning-cloths before walking back through to the lounge.

When he'd finished, the flat was spotless. The PRS guitar and the CDs sat in a black bin-liner, in the hall. Another held three Caledonian Clear bottles and a selection of cleaning rags.

Joe stared at the smearless floor.

He had never been here. It had never happened.

More importantly, Sean had never been here.

Joe blinked. Sean . . . Angie. He walked through to the bedroom and lifted the telephone receiver.

Seven digits, five-rings-and-an-irate-night-supervisor later, a breathless voice hissed down the line.

Joe sighed. "Angie? It's me. Look, Sean's at hame, sleepin' aff too much cider. We've hid a talk, it's aw' soarted oot. Nothin' fur you tae worry aboot. Gie him a bitta time tae himsel' – eh? Ah'll seeya soon." He disconnected, removed Marigolds then seized two bin-liners.

Michael had been there for him . . .

He was there for Sean . . .

. . . really there.

As he left the flat clutching the bin-bags, Joe dropped Sean's keys onto the hall table.

Weak, winter sun filtered in through Venetians. Joe turned from the bay window and sat down on the lead-coloured sofa.

On the doctor's coffee table, today's *Record.*

Joe glanced at his watch: the taxi was booked for ten. He picked up the newspaper.

'Suicide of Glasgow business-man.'

Joe stared at the byline: the friend of the woman upstairs from Gina? Eyes flicked back to the start of the story.

'Early Monday morning . . . '

Monday . . . Monday. Three days ago.

A lifetime ago.

' . . . the body of Glasgow business-man William 'King Billy' King was discovered in the lounge of his expensive, Merchant-City flat . . . '

Home . . . where the heart wasn't. Where the body was.

' . . . Owner of the infamous Matrix, several other clubs and the William King chain of Turf Accountants . . . '

Joe lit a cigarette.

' . . . Mr King, thirty-nine, was unmarried and lived alone.'

Joe rubbed the Zippo between rough fingers.

' . . . Sources say police are treating the death as suicide, stating there was no sign of forced entry, and that robbery was not a motive . . . '

Low purring.

Joe glanced at the telephone, shrugged, then re-scanned newsprint.

' . . . Mr King died from a single gun-shot wound to the head . . . '

More insistent purring.

Joe scowled and read on.

'It is thought pressures of business, plus concern over his possible involvment in the death two weeks ago of Mr

George Paxton . . . '

The telephone bored into his brain.

Joe lifted the received. "Aye?"

Low resonance. "Seen the papers, Joe?"

"Hi, Andy. How you feelin'?" He stubbed out cigarette.

"Better. Hope you've been feeding Big Boy regularly."

Joe sighed. It was something to do. "He's like a fuckin' tank!"

Laugh. "A little weight'll suit him." Sobering. "You have seen the papers, I take it?"

Joe scowled. He'd hardly given Billy's death a thought. "Aye, but . . . "

"It's gone like clockwork, Joe. Billy King's death points everywhere but you . . . "

"But suicide . . . ?"

"That's the official line, Joe. Unofficially, word is that Billy was involved in some sort of auto-erotic game that went wrong – you know the sort of thing." Pause, then quizzical. "How did you manage to shoot him just as he was coming?"

"Disney matter, Andy."

Phlegmatic sigh. "You did a good job on the flat, by the way. Just enough of your fingerprints to prove you did at one time live there, not so many that they start to wonder."

"How dae you ken aw' this if yer still in hoaspital?"

Laugh. "I've talked to more cops since the . . . mugging than I ever did before. Take a kicking and earn the respect of your colleagues!"

Joe scowled. "Billy wis paid back fur whit he did tae . . . "

Angry. "That's not why you . . . ?"

"No' really, Andy. It wisney planned – ye ken?"

Sigh. Then: "Have the police contacted you?"

"Aye . . . Monday. Ah telt them ah wis at the hoaspital wi' you . . . "

"Good. That's been confirmed."

Joe closed his eyes. "Thanks fur . . . yer help, pal. Ah owe ye." Sean owes you.

Husky resonance. "You owe me nothing, Joe. Forget it." Pause, then: "You still want to . . . give us a go?"

Joe glanced at his watch: just after nine. The taxi was due at ten. "Told ye last night . . . yeah!"

Low resonant laugh. "No strings, right? Just a place to sleep until you find your feet."

Joe smiled. "Bet that's whit ye say tae aw' the boays!" He sobered. "Me livin' there'll no' . . . interfere wi' yer joab?"

"That might not be . . . relevant much longer – indefinite paid leave, courtesy of my consultant neurologist." Less bright. "I've been doing a bit of thinking – maybe the Force isn't really for me."

"You're a guid cop, Andy . . . "

"Good cops don't help cover-up deaths – accidental or otherwise!"

Joe sighed.

"But that's only the thin edge of the wedge. I've been thinking for a while I could do more . . . good elsewhere – counselling, victim-support, that sort of thing."

Joe smiled. "Whitever makes ye happy, pal."

Doorbell sounds.

Joe frowned. One last loose end to tie up. "Seeya in aboot an hour, Andy . . . "

"Yeah, Joe . . . I'll be waiting." Receiver buzzing.

Hammering on door. Then a voice:"Joe?"

Stomach flipped over. He stuffed the newspaper down the side of the lead-coloured sofa and walked into the hall.

More hammering.

Joe opened the door, turned and walked back into the lounge.

Sean followed.

Joe stared out of the window. Below, on Craigpark, two women were exercising a dog. It sniffed the wheels of a red Merc. Joe followed its progress with narrow eyes.

Andy Hunter wasn't the only one to have done some thinking.

Voice behind. "Ma maw says ye're goin' away, Joe. Don't."

The dog lifted its leg and peed against one of the Merc's

back wheels. The lie was for Angie . . . for both of them. "Ah've goat tae, Sean." Joe watched one of the women reprimand the dog.

Sigh, then:"Is it 'causa me, whit ah . . . ?"

"It's causa a loatta things, Sean."

"Oh . . . "

Joe exhaled on cold glass. He etched a four-letter name in the condensation, rubbed it out then pressed hot face to icy glass. "Look, Sean . . . aboot whit happened the ither night . . . " He closed his eyes. The memory of Sean's warm body beneath his . . . the memory of Billy's shattered face . . .

A hand on his arm. "Did ye want tae dae it?"

Joe blinked. He wished he had, wished it had been his finger on the trigger . . . "Aye, Sean. If ye hudney goat tae the gun first ah widda . . . "

"Naw, ah mean did ye want tae fuck me?" Low voice.

Joe closed his eyes. Fingers tightening on arm.

Sean talked on. " . . . 'Cause ah wanted ye tae."

Joe opened his eyes. Voice at his side.

Sigh. "No' like that, but – no' wi' a gun oan us an' fuckin' Billy King gettin' aff oan it!" The hand withdrawn.

He patted pockets for cigarettes, found none.

"Joe?"

He turned and looked at Sean.

Old sweatpants, battered trainers, the Daniel Poole copy, Raiders baseball cap. Nose-ring. Long fingers thrust into pockets. Not grinning.

Joe scowled.

Sean studiously watched the dog-walkers. "When ye wur stayin' wi' us ah yissed tae wish ye'd come intae ma room at night . . . " Low laugh. " . . . Yissed tae lie there wi' this fuckin' big hard-oan, tossin' masel' aff an' thinkin' aboot whit it wid be like wi' you." Sigh. "In Longriggend, when ither boays fucked each other at night ah'd watch . . . but that wis different: they aw' hid lassies oan the ootside, wur ainly . . . making do 'cause there wis nothin' else tae fuck."

"Sean . . . " Joe stared at the skinny boy. Memories of nights years ago, of lying in bed with Michael, his mother in

299

the next room, of touching the untouchable, stroking the unstrokable, of warmth and holding and tenderness and . . . love? "You an' me . . . "

"Let me finish, eh?" Taut words.

Joe sighed and watched as Sean scribbled on steamed glass.

"Ah wanted ye tae like me like ye liked that bastard Billy King. Ah thoaght when ye fell oot wi' him, things wid jist . . . happen wi' us . . . " Voice cracking." . . . but they didney." Slow, measured words, like something committed to memory. Sad laugh. "Christ! Ah really like ye, Joe – ye gie me a hard-oan like no-wan else dis – but when ye left the flat ah fuckin' hated ye, ya bastard!"

Joe stared into angry blue slits. "Dae ye still hate me?" Understand . . . understand what Michael instinctively knew, what took me years to understand.

The pale face wore a new expression. "Fuck, ye ken ah don't, ah . . . "

Unuttered words hung between them. Something needed to be said . . . Michael had never explained . . . maybe hadn't known how.

Joe turned away. Sean's speech deserved something in return. Staring at the lead-coloured sofa his brain wouldn't function.

"Ah'm soarry, Joe." A hand on his shoulder. "It wis the wan thing ah kidney tell ye – ah don't ken why. Mebbe 'cause ah hidney done it wi' a guy, ah felt . . . "

Joe walked to the coffee-table and picked up cigarettes. The Zippo shook in his hand.

"Don't go 'causa me, Joe – that's aw' ah'm sayin'. Ah ken ye ainly did whit ye hud tae oan Sunday . . . "

"Oh, Sean." Joe stared at the pale, guilty-looking face. Not a kid's face . . . not any more . . .

. . . a kid growing up.

. . . a kid who was all the things he'd been, feeling all the things he'd felt.

Joe smiled. Billy had been wrong about a lot of things.

Billy had been right about one.

Eyes on the pale face, Joe stubbed out cigarette.

Sean deserved an answer.

Sean deserved the truth.

Joe clenched his fists and locked eyes with his dead brother's son. "Ah like ye in a way ah don't huv tae think aboot, Sean. It's jist there, but ah canny dae onythin' aboot it." He exhaled and spilled his heart . . .

Thirty minutes later Sean was sitting at his feet, place face flushed. "Ah don't understaun', Joe . . . " Chewing bottom lip. "If ye feel the same aboot me as ah feel aboot you why . . . ?"

Heat in his stomach. Joe sighed. "We're too . . . close, Sean – ye need tae fun' oot things fur yersel' . . . by yersel'. Ah wasted years tryin' tae fun the sorta thing me an' Mi . . . yer dad hud . . . " The words made it real, made Joe face the truth. Michael Macdonald: a brother, a father, a lover . . . all rolled into one. An ideal, a fantasy . . . not made for the real world, a world in which Sean had to learn to function. "Dae ye understand, Sean?"

Unconvincing nod.

Joe ran the back of an index finger over a pink cheek. "Ah love ye, Sean . . . an' ah ainly ever said that tae wan other guy."

Blue eyes raised."Billy?"

Joe shook his head. "Yer dad, Sean . . . ah said it tae yer dad an' it's . . . stoapped me sayin' it tae onywan else."

Grin. "Ah love you too, Joe . . . ah've loved ye ever since . . . "

He removed his hand and stood up. "There's aw' kindsa love, Sean – different loves fur different people. Don't git them confused . . . don't try tae git them aw' fae the wan person. It disney work . . . " Something in his heart was about to burst. Joe blinked through blurred vision and watched as a single tear made its way down Sean's pale face. He continued to talk, speak the words Michael should have spoken to him. "Ye ken Andy – the polis-guy? Ah'm gonna stay wi' him fur a while. Ah like him, Sean – we git oan well, he's . . . " Joe paused as the words caught in his throat.

Not Michael.

301

Not Billy.

Not . . . you.

" . . . a mate, Sean. Mates ur great . . . maybe mates ur the maist important thing. Maybe ah'll love him as a mate, maybe as somewan ah want tae spend the resta ma life wi'. Ah don't ken – nowan really kens until they try it."

More tears joined the single track, overflowing from wide blue swimming pools.

Joe felt his own eyes stinging. "Ah'll eyewis love you, Sean . . . nothin' can change that. It's a . . . special love, a love that will eyewis be there . . . "

Sean's sobs filled the room.

Joe ignored the sounds of a breaking heart. " . . . but we canny . . . act oan it, Sean – ken whit ah mean?" He stared down at the top of a quivering baseball-cap. His stomach melted. "You need tae fun other people . . . other loves. Ah'd be haudin' ye back, Sean . . . an' ah wullney dae that . . . "

Mumbled words. "Ah don't anywan else, Joe . . . ainly you."

From somewhere deep inside Joe found the strength to say what he knew he had to. "Forget whit we did the other night . . . ah huv. Ye're jist a kid, Sean . . . ye need another kid tae explore yersel' wi'. Ah'll be here fur ye, but ah'll no' be part o' yer life . . . ah don't want tae be." Amongst all the lies he'd ever told himself, that was the hardest. Roughly, Joe seized heaving shoulders and dragged Sean to his feet.

A flushed face peered at him through sodden lashes.

"You still a wee boay wi' a crush oan his uncle, or ur ye man enough tae agree wi' me, Sean?" He stared deep into the blue eyes, searching for the answer he needed . . . the extension of pretence . . . and not pretence . . .

Sean blinked, tried to look away.

Held the slim shoulders firm, feeling Sean's warm skin for the last time. "Yeah?" The word echoed round the silent room. Molten emotions trickled down his spine.

As one pair of blue eyes stared deep into another, silent agreement passed between two men.

Men.

Not a kid and a man.

Two men who knew the score, knew the way things worked.

Sean knew Joe was right. He smiled – not a grin, not an expression Joe had ever seen before.

An adult smile, with all the confusion and ambiguity of an adult emotion.

Joe found himself grinning. Life was confusing . . . love was ambiguous.

Michael had been there for him . . .

He would be there with Sean . . . in his mind, in his heart.

Nowhere else.

In the distance, doorbell sounds, then:"Taxi fur Macdonald!"

Reality leaked into the still room. Joe released Sean's shoulders and glanced over at a hold-all. Soft voice at his side:

"Want a haun, man?"

Joe watched as Sean lifted the hold-all and walked past him towards the door. For a few seconds he stood motionless in the middle of the lounge, reluctant to let the old life go, suddenly apprehensive . . . even frightened.

Then Sean turned, the pink face mock-admonishing. "C'moan, man . . . ye don't want tae keep Andy waiting!" The new smile.

Joe laughed, picked up cigarettes and joined Sean at the door.

Also available

Jackal in the Dark

David Patrick Beavers

Set in Los Angeles as the 1970s draw to a close, *Jackal in the Dark* is the story of a nineteen-year-old student whose life revolves around discos and parties, beach and campus, drugs and casual and virtually meaningless sex. But a chance encounter with the beautiful but distant Rex causes the nihilistic hero to find himself yearning for love and possession. Meanwhile, into his chaotic life comes Taylor, a seventeen-year-old hustler abused and brutalised by his pimp . . .

ISBN 1-873741-16-2

£7.99

The Jackal Awakens

David Patrick Beavers

In this self-contained sequel to *Jackal in the Dark*, Beavers has written a gritty contemporary love story, the action of which is set in the early 1980s. The anonymous hero has moved from Los Angeles to New York, kicked his drug habit and joined Alcoholics Anonymous. Yet although the externals of his life have been smoothed into almost conformity, he is deeply dissatisfied. When he meets and invites home a straight model called Jeremy, his life changes once again – not necessarily for the better.

ISBN 1-873741-22-7

£7.99

The Heart in Exile

Rodney Garland

First published in 1953, *The Heart in Exile* is perhaps the most famous pre-Wolfened British gay novel. 'This is a strange novel, perhaps because it is about strange people, in that they differ from the rest of us who call ourselves normal,' Frank G Slaughter wrote in *The New York Times,* reviewing the American edition. 'And yet' (as the reader will quickly learn from this sensitive and deeply perceptive novel of the homosexual and his underworld) the 'queer' makes up a substantial segment of the population . . . ' A classic, *The Heart in Exile* takes the form of a thriller and a quest. Why did Julian Leclerc commit suicide on the eve of his marriage to a rich young woman? Will Dr Anthony Page discover the answer - and what more will he discover before he is fully satisfied he has resolved the mystery? Unavailable for many years, this timely new edition includes an Introduction by Neil Bartlett.

ISBN 1-873741-23-5

£8.50

The Biker below the Downs

Graeme Woolaston

In *The Biker Below the Downs,* Graeme Woolaston has written a thought-provoking novel about aspects of gay life not usually explored in fiction. When John – a middle-aged and well-heeled Scot on holiday in a small Sussex village – first sees his leather-clad biker neighbour he feels an immediate attraction. And both are aware of it. After an encounter with a naked youth in an adjoining garden, John realises the two boys are lovers and that he is attracted to both. But a chance remark made by the biker leads John to make a set of discoveries which shock and move him. The story of a man discovering the son he didn't know he had and a boy discovering the father he'd never known, *The Biker Below the Downs* is compelling, richly comic and strongly erotic.

ISBN 1-873741-25-1

£8.50

Disorder and Chaos

Simon Lovat

When Keith, a civil servant in his late thirties, encounters Nick, teenaged, beautiful, down-and-out, utterly dishonest and amoral, a sequence of events is set in train which move inexorably towards tragedy. And what is the connection between obsessive Monica and her eating disorders and the lesbian couple to whom Keith supplied sperm? Why do Monica's glamourous mother Zoe and her dentist father Lenny barely communicate? Why is Lenny's business partner intent upon blackmail? In this compelling first novel – which bears comparison with early Ruth Rendell – Simon Lovat explores the darker reaches of human experience and the consequences of secrets, repression and obsession in a way which leaves the reader breathless with suspense.

ISBN 1-873741-26-X

£8.50

Brutal

Aiden Shaw

Brutal is a raw and powerful debut novel which explores the life of a young man who makes his living as a prostitute. Paul, with the help of therapy is trying to challenge what he has become – a person out of control on drugs and alcohol, desiring abusive and degrading sex, estranged from people he once loved. Moreover, he is facing his own mortality while living with HIV. Increasingly disappointed by the way men relate to each other, he discovers that there are women around him to whom he can turn.

Set mainly in London's underground club scene – where drug use is commonplace and casual sex something of an inevitablity – *Brutal* offers an extraordinary, sometimes bleak portrait of a lost generation for whom death is as much a companion as lovers, friends and family. Yet this is far from being a dispiriting novel, and although the subject matter may shock, the shining honesty of the writing will prove life-affirming and an inspiration.

ISBN 1-873741-24-4

£8.50

Millivres Books can be ordered from any bookshop in the UK and from specialist bookshops overseas. If you prefer to order by mail, please sent the full retail price and £1 (UK) or £2 (overseas) per title for postage and packing to:

Dept MBKS
Millivres Ltd
Ground Floor, Worldwide House
116-134 Bayham Street
London NW1 0BA